Swiss Family Robinson

~

Swiss Family Robinson

~

M. Wiss

Illustrated by
Bob Ellis

SMITHMARK

This edition published in 1996 by
SMITHMARK Publishers,
a division of U.S. Media Holdings, Inc.,
16 East 32nd Street
New York, NY 10016.

© Anness Publishing Limited 1996

SMITHMARK books are available for bulk
purchase for sales promotion and premium
use. For details write or call the
manager of special sales,
SMITHMARK Publishers Inc.
16 East 32nd Street
New York, NY 10016
(212) 532-6600

ISBN 0 7651 9984 X

Produced by
Anness Publishing Limited
1 Boundary Row
London SE1 8HP

Publisher: Joanna Lorenz
Project Editor: Fiona Eaton
Picture Researcher: Vanessa Fletcher

CONTENTS

Colour Illustrations

"We held the two paddles longways, and thus we passed without accident through the breach in the ship." (Chapter 2)

"The young monkey, on perceiving Fritz, sprang nimbly onto his shoulders." (Chapter 4)

"We returned to finish our aerial palace, which now began to make an imposing appearance." (Chapter 11)

"I have caught him! – I touched him!" cried Fritz . . . "The tortoise is ours!" (Chapter 18)

"We glided with the rapidity of a bird along the mirror of the waters." (Chapter 21)

"I counselled them . . . to add the exercises of running, jumping, getting up trees." (Chapter 22)

". . . the training of the wild ass, which we named lightfoot." (Chapter 30)

"What say you, now, Father?" said Jack. "A single fish of this troop would fill a tub!" (Chapter 34)

CHAPTER ONE

A SHIPWRECK, AND PREPARATIONS FOR DELIVERANCE

~

Already the tempest had continued six terrible days, and far from subsiding on the seventh, its fury seemed to increase. We had wandered so materially from the right track that not a creature on board knew where we were. The ship's company were exhausted and the courage which had hitherto sustained them now began to fail. The masts had been shivered and cast into the sea; several leaks appeared, and the ship began to fill. "My children," said I to my four boys, who clung to me in terrible alarm, "God can save us; but if He sees fit that we should not be saved, we must but rely that what He does is most for our good."

My excellent wife wiped her tears and became more tranquil and encouraged the youngest children, who were leaning on her knees.

At this moment a cry of "Land! land!" was heard through the roaring of the waves, and instantly the vessel struck; a tremendous cracking succeeded, as if the ship was going to pieces; the sea rushed in; we perceived that the vessel had grounded and could not long hold together. The captain bade the men lose not a moment in putting out the boats. The sounds fell on my heart like a blow from a dagger. "We are lost!" I exclaimed, and the children broke out into piercing cries. I then recollected myself; and addressing them again I exhorted them to courage, by observing that the water had not yet reached us, that the ship was near land, and that

9

Providence would assist the brave. "Keep where you are," added I, "while I go and examine what is best to be done."

I left my family and went on the deck. A wave instantly threw me down and wetted me to the skin; another followed, and then another. I steadied myself as well as I could, and when I could look around a scene of terrific and complete disaster met my eyes: the ship was split in two. The ship's company crowded into the boats till they could contain not one man more, and the last who entered were now cutting the ropes to move off. I called to them to stop and receive us also, but in vain; for the roaring of the sea prevented my being heard, and the waves would have made it impossible for a boat to return. My best consolation now was to observe that the sea could not enter the ship above a certain height. The stern, under which was the cabin that enclosed all that was dear to me on earth, had been driven to a considerable height between two rocks, where it appeared fixed; at the same time, in the distance southward, I descried, through clouds and rain, several nooks of land.

Sunk and desolate from the loss of every chance for human aid, it was yet my duty to appear serene before my family. "Courage, dear ones," cried I on entering their cabin, "all is not yet lost! I will not conceal from you that the ship is aground, but we are at least in greater safety than we should be if she were beating upon the rocks: our cabin is above water, and we may yet find means to reach the land in safety."

What I had just said appeased the fears of all, for they had the habit of confiding in my assurances. My wife, however, more accustomed than the children to read my inmost thoughts, perceived the anxiety which devoured me. I made her a sign which conveyed an idea of the hopelessness of our situation, and I had the consolation to see that she was resolved to support the trial with resignation.

"Let us take some nourishment," said she, "our courage will strengthen with our bodies."

Soon after the evening set in: the tempest and the waves continued their fury; the planks and beams of the vessel separated in many parts with a horrible crash. It seemed impossible for the boats to escape the raging of the storm.

In the meanwhile my dear wife had prepared our meal, and the four boys partook of it with an appetite to which their parents were strangers. They afterwards went to bed, and in a short time, were snoring soundly. Fritz, the eldest, sat up with us.

"I have been thinking" said he after a long silence, "how it may be possible to save ourselves. If we had only some bladders or cork-jackets for my mother and my brothers, you and I, Father, would soon contrive to swim to land."

"That is a good thought," said I; "we will see if we can bring it to bear this very night, for fear of the worst."

Fritz and I immediately looked about for some small empty tubs or casks, or tin canisters, large enough to float one of our children. These we fastened two and two together with handkerchiefs or towels, leaving about a foot distance between them, attaching this sort of swimming-jacket under the arms of each child, my wife at the same time preparing one for herself. We all provided ourselves with knives, some string, and other necessaries which could be put into the pocket.

Fritz, who had been up the whole of the preceding night, and was fatigued with laborious occupation, now lay down near his brothers and was soon asleep; but their mother and I, too full of anxiety to close our eyes, kept watch, listening to every sound that seemed to threaten a further change in our situation. We passed this terrible night in prayer, in agonizing apprehensions, and in forming various resolutions as to what we should next attempt. We hailed with joy the first gleam of light which shot through a small opening of the window. The raging of the winds had begun to abate, the sky was serene, and with hope swelling in my bosom I beheld the sun already tinging the horizon. Thus revived in spirit, I hastily summoned my wife and the boys to the deck.

"Now let us consider," said I, "what we had best do."

Fritz advised that we should all throw ourselves into the sea while it was calm, and swim to land. "Ah! that may be well enough for you," said Ernest, "for you can swim; but we others should soon be drowned. Would it not be better to make a float of rafts, and get to land all together upon it?"

"Very good," answered I, "if we had the means for contriving such a float, and if, after all, it were not a dangerous sort of conveyance. Come along, my boys, let each go a different way about the ship, and see what he can do to be useful, and what he can find to enable us to get away."

They now all sprang from me with eager looks to do what I had desired. I, on my part, lost no time in examining what we had to depend upon in regard to provisions and fresh water, the principles of life. My wife and the youngest boy visited all the animals, whom they found in a pitiable condition, and nearly perishing with hunger and thirst. Fritz repaired to the ammunition chamber, Ernest to the carpenter's cabin, and Jack to the apartment of the captain. Scarcely had Jack opened the door, when two large dogs sprang joyfully upon him, and nearly suffocated the boy with their affectionate licking of his face and hands in their delight at seeing a human being once more.

By and by my little company were again assembled round me, each proud of what he had to contribute. Fritz had two fowling-pieces, some powder, and some small shot contained in horn flasks, and balls in bags. Ernest produced his hat filled with nails, and held in his hands a hatchet and a hammer; in addition, a pair of pincers, a pair of large scissors, and an auger peeped out of his pocket. Even the little six-year-old Francis carried under his arm a large box of fish-hooks.

"I, for my part," said my wife, "have brought nothing; but I have some tidings to communicate which I hope will secure my welcome. What I have to tell is, that I have found on board the ship a cow and an ass, two goats, six sheep, and a sow, all of whom I have just supplied with food and water, and I reckon on being able to preserve their lives."

"All this is admirable," said I to my little labourers, "and there is only Master

Jack, who, instead of thinking of something that might be useful, has done us the favour to present us two personages, who no doubt will be principally distinguished by being willing to eat more than we shall have to give them."

"Ah!" replied Jack, "but I know that if we get to land, you will see that they will assist us in hunting and shooting."

"True enough," said I, "but be so good as to tell us how we are to get to land, and whether you have contrived the means."

"I am sure it cannot be very difficult," said Jack, with an arch motion of his head. "Look here at these large tubs. Why cannot each of us get into one of them, and float to the land? I remember I succeeded very well in this manner on the water when I was visiting Grandfather last summer."

Every hint is good for something, and I began to think that what Jack had suggested was worth a trial.

"Quick, then, Jack. Give me the saw, the auger, and some nails, and we will see what is to be done."

I recollected having seen some empty casks in the hold. We went down, and found them floating about in the water, which almost filled the vessel. It cost us but little trouble to hoist them up and place them on the lower deck, which was at this time scarcely above water. We saw with delight that they were all made of excellent wood, well guarded by iron hoops, and in sound condition. They were exactly suited for our purpose, and with the assistance of my sons I instantly began to saw them in two. In a certain time I had produced eight tubs of equal size and of suitable height, which I contemplated with perfect satisfaction. My wife, however, sighed deeply as she looked at them.

"Never, never," cried she, "can I venture to get into one of these."

"Do not decide so hastily, my dear," said I. "My plan is not yet complete, and you will soon see that it is more worthy of our confidence than at present may appear."

I then sought for a long plank capable of being a little curved at the ends. I fastened my eight tubs together, and then fixed on the plank by way of a keel. The tubs were nailed to each other, and, to make them the firmer, two other planks of the same length as the first were fixed on each side of the tubs. When all this was finished, we found we had produced a kind of boat divided into eight compartments, which I had no doubt would be able to perform a short course in calm water.

But, unfortunately, our marvellous craft proved so heavy, that with the strength of all united we were not able to move it an inch from its place. I bade Fritz fetch me a crowbar, who soon returned with it. I sawed a thick round pole into several pieces for rollers, and easily raised the foremost part of our boat with the crowbar, while Fritz placed one of the rollers under it.

I tied a long cord to its stern, and the other end of it to one of the timbers of the ship which appeared to be still firm, so that the cord, being left loose, would serve to guide and restrain the craft when launched. We now put a second and a third roller under, and, applying the crowbar, to our great joy our contrivance descended into the water with such a velocity, that if the rope had not been well fastened it would have gone far out to sea. But now a new misfortune presented itself: it leaned so much on one side that my boys all exclaimed they could not venture to get into it. I was for some moments in the most painful perplexity, but it suddenly occurred to me that ballast only was wanting to set it straight. I threw everything I could find that was weighty and of small size into the tubs, and at length our quaint home-made boat floated quite straight and firm in the water, and seemed to invite us to take refuge in its protection. All now would have thrown themselves at once into it, and the boys began to push each other, and dispute which should get in first. I, however, drew them back, plainly perceiving that at best the voyage would be hazardous, and that the least motion of even one of these boisterous children might upset it and cause us to be all drowned. In seeking for a remedy for this difficulty, I recollected that some savage nations make use of a paddle fore and aft to help balance their canoes. With this thought I once more set to work to make a paddle of a kind.

I took two of the smaller yards, upon which the sails of the ship had been stretched, and fixed one of them at the bow and the other at the stern of my floating machine in such a manner as to enable us to turn them at pleasure to right or left, as should best answer the purpose of steadying and guiding our craft.

There remained nothing more for me to do but to find out in what way I could get clear from the wreckage that lay around us. I got into the first tub, and steered the head of our craft so as to make it enter the breach in the ship's side. I then got on board the ship again, and with saw and hatchet cleared away everything that could obstruct our passage. That being effected, we next secured some oars for our voyage.

We had spent the day in laborious exertions; it was already late, and as it would not have been possible to reach the land that evening, we were obliged to pass a second night in the wrecked vessel, which at every instant threatened to fall to pieces. We now refreshed ourselves by a regular meal, for during the day's work we had scarcely allowed ourselves to take a bit of bread or a glass of water. Being in a more tranquil frame of mind than on the preceding day, we all abandoned ourselves to sleep; not, however, till I had used the precaution of tying the swimming belts round my three youngest boys and my wife, as a means of safety if the storm should again come on and should put the finishing stroke to the destruction of the vessel. Our arrangements being now as complete as our united foresight could make them, we one and all crept into our separate hammocks, where a delicious repose prepared us for the renewal of our labours.

CHAPTER TWO

A LANDING, AND CONSEQUENT OCCUPATIONS

~

By break of day we were all awake and alert, for hope as well as grief is unfriendly to lengthened slumbers. When we had finished our morning prayer, I said:

"We now, with the assistance of Heaven, must enter upon the work of our deliverance. The first thing to be done is to give to each poor animal on board, before we leave them, a hearty meal; we will then put food enough before them to last for several days. We cannot take them with us, but we will hope it may be possible, if our voyage succeeds, to return and fetch them. Are you now all ready? Bring together whatever we mean to take, whatever is absolutely necessary for our wants."

I decided that our first cargo should consist of a barrel of gunpowder, three fowling-pieces, and three carbines, with as much small shot and lead and as many bullets as our boat would bear; two pair of pocket pistols and one of large ones, not forgetting a mould to cast balls in. I told each of the boys and their mother also to take a game-bag. We added a chest containing cakes of portable soup, another full of hard biscuits, an iron pot, a fishing-rod, a chest of nails and another of different tools, such as hammers, saws, pincers, hatchets, augers, &c., and lastly some sail-cloth to make a tent. In short, the boys brought so many things that we were obliged to reject some of them, though I had already exchanged the worthless ballast for articles of use for our subsistence.

When all was ready, we stepped bravely each into a tub. At the moment of our departure we heard all the cocks and hens begin to crow, as if they were conscious that we had deserted them, yet willing to bid us a sorrowful adieu. This suggested to me the idea of taking the geese, ducks, fowls, and pigeons with us, observing to my wife that if we could not find means to feed them, at least they would feed us.

We accordingly executed this plan. We put ten hens and an old and a young cock into one of the tubs, and covered it with planks. We set the rest of the poultry at liberty, in the hope that instinct would direct them towards the land – the geese and the ducks by water, and the pigeons by the air.

We were waiting for my wife, who had the care of this last part of our embarkation, when she joined us loaded with a large bag, which she threw into the tub which already contained her youngest son. I imagined that she intended it for him to sit upon, and also to confine him so as to prevent his being tossed from side to side. I therefore asked no questions concerning it. The order of our departure was as follows:

In the first tub, at the boat's head, my wife;

In the second, our little Francis, a lovely boy, six years old, full of the happiest dispositions;

In the third, Fritz, our eldest boy, between fourteen and fifteen years of age, a handsome, curl-pated youth, full of intelligence and vivacity;

In the fourth was the barrel of gunpowder, with the cocks and hens and the sail-cloth;

In the fifth, the provisions for the support of life;

In the sixth, my son Jack, a light-hearted, enterprising, audacious, generous lad, about ten years old;

In the seventh, my son Ernest, a boy of twelve years old, of a rational, reflecting temper, well informed, but somewhat disposed to indolence;

In the eighth, a father, to whose paternal care the task of guiding the craft for the safety of his beloved family was entrusted.

Each of us had useful implements within reach; the hand of each held an oar, and near each was a swimming belt in readiness for what might happen. The tide was already at half its height when we left the ship, and I had counted on this circumstance as favourable to our want of strength. We held the two paddles longways, and thus we passed without accident through the breach in the ship. The boys devoured with their eyes the blue land they saw at a distance (for to us it appeared to be of this colour). We rowed with all our strength, but long in vain, to reach it; the boat only turned round and round. At length, however, I had the good fortune to steer in such a way that she proceeded in a straight line. The two dogs we had left on board, perceiving that we had abandoned them, plunged immediately into the sea and swam to the boat. They were too large for us to think of giving them admittance, and I dreaded lest they should jump in and upset us. Turk was an English dog, and Ponto of the Danish breed. I was in great uneasiness on their account, for I feared it would not be possible for them to swim so far. The dogs, however, managed the affair with perfect intelligence. When they found themselves fatigued they rested their fore-paws on the paddles, which were now turned crossways.

Our voyage proceeded securely, though slowly; but the nearer we approached the land the more gloomy and unpromising we thought its aspect appeared. The coast was occupied by barren rocks, which seemed to offer nothing but hunger and distress. The sea was calm; the waves, gently agitated, washed the shore, and the sky was serene. In every direction we perceived casks, bales, chests, and other vestiges of shipwrecks floating round us. In the hope of obtaining some good provisions, I determined on endeavouring to secure two of the casks. I bade Fritz have a rope, a hammer, and some nails ready, and to try to seize them as we passed. He succeeded in laying hold of two of them, and in such a way that we found it easy to draw them after us to the shore. Now that we were close on land, its hideous aspect was considerably softened; the rocks no longer appeared one undivided chain. Fritz with his hawk's eyes already descried some trees, and exclaimed that they were palm-trees. Ernest expressed his joy that he should now get much larger and better coco-nuts than those to be had in Europe. I for my part was venting audibly my regret that I had not thought of bringing with us a telescope that I knew was in the captain's cabin, when Jack drew a small spy-glass from his pocket, and, with a look of triumph that he was able to compensate this neglect, instantly presented it to me.

In reality the glass was of great service, for with its aid I was able to see which was the best route to take. I remarked that the shore before us had a savage aspect, but that towards the left the scene was more agreeable. But when I attempted to steer in that direction a current carried me towards the coast that was rocky and barren. By and by we perceived a little opening between the rocks, near the mouth of a creek, towards which all our geese and ducks betook themselves; and I followed in the same course. This opening formed a little bay, the water of which was calm, and neither too deep nor too shallow to receive our boat. I entered it, and cautiously put on shore on a spot where the coast was about the same height above the water as our tubs, and where at the same time there was a quantity sufficient to keep us afloat. The shore extended inland in a shelving declivity in the form of a triangle, the upper angle of which terminated among the rocks, while the margin of the sea formed the base.

All that had life in the boat jumped eagerly on land. Even little Francis, who had been wedged in his tub like a potted herring, now got up and sprang forward; but, with all his efforts, he could not succeed without his mother's help. The dogs, who had swum on shore, received us as if they were appointed to do the honours of the place; the geese kept up a loud continual cackling, to which the ducks with their broad yellow beaks contributed a perpetual thorough bass; the cocks and hens, which we had already set at liberty, clucked; the boys chattering all at once, produced altogether an overpowering confusion of sounds. To this was added the disagreeable scream of some penguins and flamingoes, which we now perceived, some flying over our heads, others sitting on the points of the rocks. By and by the notes of the latter had the ascendant from the superiority of their numbers; and their society became the more unpleasant, from a comparison we could not avoid making between the sounds they uttered with the harmony of the feathered musicians of our own country. I had, however, one advantage in prospect; it was that these very birds might serve for our subsistence.

The first thing we did on finding ourselves safe on terra firma, was to fall on our knees, and return thanks to the Supreme Being who had preserved our lives, and to recommend ourselves with entire resignation to the care of His paternal kindness.

We next employed our whole attention in unloading the boat. Oh, how rich we thought ourselves in the little we had been able to rescue from the merciless waters! We looked everywhere for a convenient place to erect a tent under the shade of the rocks; and having agreed upon a place, we set to work. We drove one of our poles firmly into a fissure of the rock – this formed the ridge of our tent. We rested upon it another pole, and thus formed a frame. We next threw some sail-cloth over the ridge, and stretching it to a convenient distance on each side, fastened its extremities to the ground with stakes. By way of precaution we left the chests of provisions and other heavy things on the shore, and fixed some tenter-hooks near the edge of the sail-cloth in front, that we might be able to close the entrance during night. I next desired my sons to collect grass and moss, and spread it to dry in the sun, as it would then serve us for beds. During this occupation, in which even the little Francis could take a share, I erected at a small distance from the tent, and near a river, a kind of little kitchen. A few flat stones that I found in the bed of the river served for a fire-place. I got a quantity of dry branches: with the largest I made a small enclosure round it; and with the little twigs, added to some of our turf; I made a brisk, cheering fire. We put some of the soup-cakes, with water, into our iron pot, and placed it over the fire; and my wife, with her little Francis for a scullion, took charge of preparing the dinner. Francis, from their colour, had mistaken the soup-cakes for glue.

"Why, Mother," said he, "what are you going to use glue for?"

"I am going to make some soup of it," said his mother, laughing.

"That is droll enough," answered he; "for how shall we get any meat to put into it here, where there is nothing like a shop?"

"My boy," said I, "what you have been thinking was glue is in reality excellent meat, reduced to a jelly by the process of cookery, and which, being dried, is in no danger of becoming stale. In this state it will bear long voyages, where it would be difficult to take sufficient animals for the use of the ship's company, who would otherwise be kept constantly on a less wholesome soup made from salted meat; but ours, I assure you, Francis, will be excellent."

In the meanwhile Fritz had been reloading the guns, with one of which he had wandered along the side of the river. He had proposed to Ernest to accompany him, but Ernest replied that he did not like a rough and stony walk, and that he should go alone to the sea-shore. Jack took the road towards a chain of rocks which jutted out into the sea, with the intention of gathering some of the mussels which grew upon them. My own occupation was now an endeavour to draw the two floating casks on shore. But I did not succeed, for our place of landing, though convenient enough for our craft, was too steep for the casks. While I was looking about to find a more favourable spot, I heard loud cries proceeding from a short distance, and recognized the voice of Jack. I snatched my hatchet, and ran to his assistance. I soon perceived him up to his knees in water, and that a large sea-lobster had fastened his claws in his leg. The poor boy screamed pitiably, and made useless efforts to disengage himself. I jumped instantly into the water, and the enemy was no sooner sensible of my approach than he let go his hold, and would have scampered out to sea, but that I indulged the fancy of a little malice against him. I turned quickly upon him, and took him up by the body and carried him off, followed by Jack, who shouted our triumph all the way. He begged me at last to let him hold the animal in his own hand, that he might himself present so fine a booty to his mother. Accordingly, having observed how I held it to avoid the gripe, he laid his own hand upon it in exactly the same manner; but scarcely had he grasped it than he received a violent blow on the face from the lobster's tail, which made him lose his hold, and the animal fell to the ground. Jack again began to bawl out, while I could not refrain from laughing heartily. I picked up the lobster, and on Jack's entreaty let him carry it to the kitchen, which he entered, triumphantly exclaiming:

"Mamma, Mamma, a sea-lobster! Ernest, a sea-lobster! Where is Fritz? Where is Fritz? Take care, Francis, he will bite you!"

Ernest, ever eager about his meals, now bawled out that the lobster had better be put into the soup, which would give it an excellent flavour; but this his mother opposed, observing that we must be more economical of our provisions than that, for the lobster of itself would furnish a dinner for the whole family. I now left them, and walked again to the scene of this adventure and examined the shallow. I then made another attempt upon my two casks, and at length succeeded in getting them into the shallow, and in fixing them there securely on their ends.

On my return I complimented Jack on his being the first to have procured us an animal that might serve for our subsistence.

"Ah! but *I* have seen something too that is good to eat," said Ernest; "and I should have got it if it had not been in the water, so that I must have wetted my feet – "

"Oh, that is a famous story!" said Jack. "I can tell you what he saw – some nasty mussels. Why, I would not eat one of them for the world. Think of my lobster!"

"That is not true, Jack; it was oysters and not mussels that I saw," said Ernest. "I am sure of it, for they stuck against the foot of the rock, and I know they must be oysters."

"Fortunate enough, my dainty gentleman!" cried I, addressing myself to Ernest; "and since you are so well acquainted with the place where these shell-fish can be found, you will be so obliging as to dismiss your fears about wetting your feet, and to return and procure us some. In such a situation as ours, every member of the family must be actively employed for the common good."

"I will do my best with all my heart," answered Ernest; "and at the same time I will bring home some salt, of which I have seen immense quantities in the holes of the rocks, where I suppose it is dried by the sun. I tasted some of it, and it was excellent. Papa, is it not left there by the sea?"

"No doubt it is, Mr. Reasoner, for where else do you think it could come from? You would have done more wisely if you had brought us a bag of it, besides spending your time in such profound reflections; and if you do not wish to dine upon a soup without flavour, you had better run and fetch us a little immediately."

He set off, and soon returned. What he brought back was so mixed with sand that I was on the point of throwing it away. My wife, however, prevented me; and by dissolving and filtering it through a piece of muslin, we found it admirably fit for use.

After adding the salt, my wife tasted the soup, and pronounced that it was all the better for the salt, and now quite ready.

"But," said she, "Fritz is not come in. And then, how shall we manage to eat our soup without spoons or dishes? Why did we not remember to bring some from the ship?"

"Why did we not think of them? Because, my dear, one cannot think of everything. We shall be lucky if we do not discover that we have forgotten even more important things."

"But indeed," said she, this is a matter which cannot easily be set to rights. How will it be possible for each of us to raise this large boiling pot to our lips?"

A moment's further reflection convinced me my wife was right. We all cast our eyes upon the pot with perplexity, and we looked a little like the fox in the fable, when the stork desires him to help himself from a vessel with a long neck. Silence was at length broken by all bursting into a laugh at our want of every kind of utensil, and at our own folly in not recollecting that spoons and forks were things of absolute necessity.

Ernest observed that if we could but get some coco-nuts, we might use the pieces of the shells for spoons.

"Yes, yes, that is true enough," replied I, "but we have them not."

"But at least," said the boy, "we can use some oyster-shells."

"Why, this is well, Ernest," said I, "and is what I call a useful thought. Run, then, quickly and get us some of them. But no one of you must give himself airs because his spoon is without a handle, or if he should chance to grease his fingers in the soup."

Jack ran the first, and was up to his knees in the water before Ernest could reach the place. Jack tore off the shell-fish and threw them to the slothful Ernest, who put them into his handkerchief; having first secured in his pocket one shell he had met with of a large size. The boys came back together with their booty.

Fritz not having yet returned, his mother was beginning to be uneasy, when we heard him shouting to us from no great distance, and shouted in reply. In a few minutes he was among us; his two hands behind him, and with a sort of would-be melancholy air, which none of us could well understand.

"What have you brought?" asked his brothers.

"Nothing at all," said he.

But now, on fixing my eye upon him, I perceived a smile through his assumed dissatisfaction. At the same instant Jack, having stolen behind him, exclaimed, "A little pig! A little pig!" Fritz, finding his trick discovered, now proudly displayed his prize, which I immediately perceived, from the description I had read in different books of travels, was an agouti, and not a pig, as the boys had supposed.

"Where did you find him? How did you get at him? Did he make you run a great way?" asked all at once the young brothers.

I for my part assumed a serious tone. "I should have preferred," said I, "that you had in reality brought us nothing rather than to have heard you assert a falsehood. Never allow yourself; even in jest, my dear boy, to assert an untruth. By such trifles as these, a habit of lying, the most disgusting and frightful of vices, may be induced. Now, then, that I have given you this caution, let us look at the animal. Where did you find it?"

Fritz related that he had passed over to the other side of the river. "Ah!" continued he, "it is quite another thing from this place; the shore is low, and you can have no notion of the quantity of casks, chests, and planks, and different sort of things washed there by the sea. Ought we not to go and try to obtain some of these treasures?"

"Certainly we must do so," said I. "And we ought also to make a voyage back to the vessel and fetch away our animals; at least you will all agree that of the cow we are pretty much in want."

"If our biscuit were soaked in milk it would not be so hard, but much improved," said our greedy Ernest.

"I must tell you too," said Fritz, "that over on the other side there is as much grass for pasturage as we can desire, and, besides, a pretty wood, in the shade of which we could shelter. Why then should we remain on this barren desert side?"

"Patience, patience!" replied I. "There is a time for everything, friend Fritz; we shall not be without something to undertake to-morrow. But, above all, I am eager to know if you discovered any traces of our ship companions."

"Not the smallest trace of man; but I have seen some other animals that more resembled pigs than the one I have brought you, but with paws more like those of the hare. The animal I am speaking of leaps from place to place on the grass, now sitting on his hind legs rubbing his face with his front feet, and then seeking for roots and gnawing them like the squirrel. If I had not been afraid of his escaping me, I should have tried to catch him with my hands, for he appeared almost tame."

Ernest now turned the agouti backwards and forwards to examine him on all sides. After a long silence, he said with importance: "I cannot be sure that this animal, as you all believe, is a pig. His hair and his snout pretty much resemble, it is true, those of a pig; but look at his teeth, he has but four incisors in front similar to the genus Voracious animals. In general he has a greater resemblance to the rabbit than to the hare. I have seen an engraving of him in our book of natural history; if I am not mistaken he is the *agouti*."

"Ah ha!" said Fritz, "here is a learned professor!"

"And who this once is not mistaken!" cried I. "Spare your raillery, Fritz, for it is really an agouti. I have never myself seen the animal, and only know him by his description in books and from engravings, with which your supposed piggie perfectly corresponds. He is a native of America, lives underground on the roots of trees, and is, as travellers report, excellent food. But of this we will judge for ourselves."

While we were speaking, Jack was trying with all his might to open one of the oysters with his knife, but he could not succeed. I laughed heartily at his disappointment, and put a few of them on the fire, where they soon opened of themselves. Each then proceeded to dip his shell into the pot to get out a little soup; but, as I had foreseen, each drew out a scalded finger. Ernest was the only one who had been too cautious to expose himself to this misfortune; he quietly took his mussel-shell, as large and deep as a plate, from his pocket, and carefully dipping it into the pot, drew it out filled with as much soup as was his fair share, and casting a look of exultation on his brothers, he set it down to wait till it should be cold enough to eat.

"You have taken excellent care of yourself, I perceive," said I. "But now answer me, dear boy, is the advantage worth the pains you take to be better off than your companions? Yet this is the constant failing of your character. As your best friend, I feel it to be my duty to balk you. I therefore adjudge your dish of delicious soup to our followers, Turk and Ponto. For ourselves, we will all fare alike, you as well as the rest – we will simply dip our oyster-shells into the pot till hunger is appeased; but the picked dish for the dogs, Ernest, and all the rest *alike*!"

This gentle reproach sunk, I perceived, into his heart; he placed the shell, filled with soup, upon the ground, and in the twinkling of an eye the dogs had licked up every drop. We on our parts were almost as sharp set as they, and every eye was fixed on the pot, watching when the steam would subside a little that we might begin dipping, when, on looking round, we saw Turk and Ponto standing over the agouti, gnawing and tearing him fiercely. The boys all screamed together. Fritz seized his gun and struck them with it, called them the unkindest names, threw stones at them, and was so furious that, if I had not interfered, it is probable he would have killed them. He had already bent his gun with the blows he had aimed at them, and his voice was raised so high as to be re-echoed from the rocks.

When he had grown a little cool I remonstrated with him on his violence of temper. I represented to him what distress he had occasioned his mother and myself; that his gun, which might have been so useful, was now entirely spoiled; and that the poor animals, upon whose assistance we should probably so much depend, he had, no doubt, greatly injured.

"Anger," continued I, "is always a bad counsellor, and may even lead the way to crimes. You are not ignorant of the history of Cain, who in a moment of violent anger killed his brother."

"Say no more, my dearest father," interrupted Fritz.

"Happy am I to recollect on this occasion," resumed I, "that they were animals and not human creatures you treated thus. But an angry person never reasons; he scarcely knows whom he attacks. Confess, too, that it was vanity which excited the furious temper you exhibited. If another than yourself had killed the agouti you would have been more patient under the accident."

Fritz agreed that I was right.

Soon after we had taken our meal the sun began to sink into the west. Our little flock of fowls assembled round us, pecking what morsels of our biscuit had fallen to the ground. Just at this moment my wife produced the bag she had so mysteriously huddled into the tub. Its mouth was now opened; it contained the various sorts of grain for feeding poultry – barley, peas, oats, &c., and also different kinds of seeds of vegetables for the table. In the fullness of her kind heart she scattered several handfuls at once upon the ground. I complimented her on the benefit her foresight had secured for us, but I recommended a more sparing use of so valuable an acquisition, observing that the grain, if kept for sowing, would produce a harvest, and that we could fetch from the ship spoiled biscuit enough to feed the fowls. Our pigeons sought a roosting-place among the rocks; the hens, with the two cocks at their head, ranged themselves in a line along the ridge of the tent; and the geese and ducks betook themselves in a body, cackling and quacking as they proceeded, to a marshy bit of ground near the sea, where some thick bushes afforded them shelter.

A little later we ourselves began to follow the example of our winged companions by beginning our preparations for repose. First we charged our guns and pistols, and laid them carefully in the tent; next we assembled all together, and joined in offering up our thanks to the Almighty for the succour afforded us. With the last ray of the sun we entered our tent, and laid ourselves close to each other on the grass and moss we had collected in the morning.

CHAPTER THREE

VOYAGE OF DISCOVERY

~

I was awaked at dawn by the crowing of the cocks. I awoke my wife, and we consulted as to our occupation for the day. We both agreed that the thing of the most importance was to seek for such traces as might be found of our late ship companions, and at the same time to examine the soil on the other side of the river before we came to a determination about a fixed place of abode. My wife perceived that such an excursion could not be undertaken by all the members of the family; and, full of confidence in the protection of Heaven, she consented to my proposal of my leaving her with the three youngest boys, and proceeding myself with Fritz on a journey of discovery. I entreated her not to lose a moment in giving us our breakfast. She gave us notice that the share of each would be but small, there being no more soup prepared.

"What then," I asked, "is become of Jack's lobster?"

"That he can best tell you himself," answered his mother. "But now, pray step and awake the boys, while I make a fire and put on some water."

The children were soon roused: even our slothful Ernest submitted to the hard fate of rising so early in the morning. When I asked Jack for his lobster, he ran and fetched it from a cleft in the rock in which he had carefully concealed it.

"I was determined," said he, "that the dogs should not treat my lobster as they did the agouti."

"I am glad to see, son Jack," said I, "that that giddy head upon your shoulders can be prevailed upon to reflect. But will you not kindly give Fritz the great claw which bit your leg (though I promised it to you), to carry with him for his dinner on our journey?"

"What journey?" asked all the boys at once. "Ah! we will go too. A journey! a journey!" repeated they.

"For this time," said I, "it is impossible for all of you to go. Your eldest brother and myself shall be better able to defend ourselves in any danger without you; besides, with so many persons we could proceed but slowly. You will, then, all three remain with your mother in this place, which appears to be one of perfect safety, and you shall keep Ponto to be your guard, while we will take Turk with us. With such a protector, and a gun well loaded, who shall dare treat us with disrespect? Fritz, make haste and tie up Ponto, that he may not follow us; and have your eye on Turk, that he may be at hand to accompany us, and get the guns ready."

At the word "guns" the colour rose in the cheeks of my poor boy. His gun was so curved as to be of no use; he took it up, and tried in vain to straighten it. I let him alone for a short time, but at length I gave him leave to take another. A moment after he attempted to lay hold of Ponto to tie him up; but the dog, recollecting the blows he had so lately received, began to snarl, and would not go near him. Turk behaved the same, and I found it necessary to call with my own voice to induce them to approach us. Fritz then entreated for some biscuit of his mother, declaring that he would willingly go without his breakfast to make his peace with the dogs. He accordingly carried them some biscuit, stroked and caressed them, and in every motion seemed to ask their pardon.

We now prepared for our departure. We took each a game-bag and a hatchet; I put a pair of pistols in the leather band round Fritz's waist in addition to the gun, and provided myself with the same articles, not forgetting a stock of biscuit and a flask of fresh riverwater. My wife now called us to breakfast, when all attacked the lobster; but its flesh proved so hard that there was a great deal left when our meal was finished, and we packed it for our journey without further regret from anyone.

In about an hour we were ready to set out. I had loaded the guns we left behind, and I now enjoined my wife to keep by day as near the boat as possible, which, in case of danger, was the best and most speedy means of escape.

The river we were about to pass was on each side so steep as to be inaccessible, except by one narrow slip near the mouth on one side, whence we had already drawn our supply of fresh water; but there was no means of effecting a passage across from this place, the opposite shore being an unbroken line of perpendicular rocks. We therefore walked on, following the river till we arrived at an assemblage of rocks at which the stream formed a cascade; a few paces beyond we observed some large fragments of rock which had fallen into the bed of the river. By stepping upon these, and making some hazardous leaps, we at length contrived to reach the other side. We had proceeded a short way along the rock we ascended in landing, forcing ourselves a passage through overgrown grass mixed with other plants, and rendered more capable of resistance by being half dried up by the sun. Perceiving, however, that walking on this kind of surface, joined to the heat, would soon exhaust our strength, we looked for a path by which we might descend and proceed along the river, in which direction we hoped to meet with fewer obstacles, and perhaps discover traces of our ship companions.

When we had walked about a hundred paces we heard a loud noise behind us, and perceived a rustling motion in the grass, which was almost as tall as ourselves. I was a good deal alarmed, thinking that it was probably occasioned by some serpent, a tiger, or other ferocious animal, which might devour us. But I was well satisfied with the courage of Fritz, who, instead of running away, stood firm to face the danger; the only motion he made being that of seeing that his piece was fit to be discharged, and turning himself to front the spot whence the noise proceeded. Our alarm, however, was of short duration; for what was our joy on seeing rush out, not an enemy, but our faithful Turk, whom in the moment of departure we had quite forgotten, and whom no doubt our anxious relatives had sent on to us! I received the poor fellow with lively joy, and did not fail to commend both the bravery and discretion of my son, in not yielding to even a rational alarm, and for waiting till he was sure of the object before he resolved to fire.

We again pursued our way. On our left was the sea, and on our right, at the distance of half a league, the continuation of the ridge of rocks, which extended from the place of our debarkation in a direction nearly parallel with the shore, the summit everywhere adorned with a fresh verdure and a great variety of trees; and the space between partly covered with tall grass and partly with small clumps of bushes, which on one side extended to the rocks, and on the other to the sea. We were careful to proceed on a course as near the shore as possible, fixing our eyes rather upon its smooth expanse than upon the land, in hopes to see something of the boats. We did not, however, wholly neglect the shore, where we looked about in all directions; but our endeavours were all in vain.

Fritz proposed to fire his gun from time to time, suggesting, that should they be anywhere concealed near us, they might thus be led to know of our pursuit.

"This would be very well," answered I, "if you could contrive for our friends to hear the report of the gun, and not the savages, who are most likely not far distant."

When we had gone about two leagues we entered a wood situated a little farther from the sea. Here we threw ourselves on the ground, and under the shade of a tree, by the side of a clear running stream, took out some provisions and refreshed ourselves. We heard on every side around us the chirping, singing, and the motion of birds, which in reality were more attractive by their splendid plumage than by any charm of note. Fritz assured me that between the branches of the bushes he saw some animals like apes. This indeed was further confirmed by the restless movements we had observed in Turk, who began to smell about, and to bark so loud that the wood resounded with the noise. Fritz stole softly about, and, raising his head to spy into the branches above his height, he stumbled on a small round body which lay on the ground. He took it up and brought it to me, observing that he thought it must be the nest of some bird.

"What makes you of that opinion?" said I.

"But I have read that there are some kinds of birds who build their nests quite round. And look, Father, how the outside is crossed and twined!"

"That is true, Fritz, but do you not perceive that what you take for straws crossed and twined by a bird is in fact a coat of fibres formed by nature? Do you not remember that the nut is enclosed within a round fibrous covering, which again is surrounded by a skin of a thin and fragile texture? I see that in the one you hold in your hand this skin has been destroyed by time, and this is the reason why the twisted fibres are so apparent. But now let us break the outside covering, and you will see the nut inside."

We soon accomplished this, but the nut, alas! from lying on the ground, had perished, and appeared but little different from a bit of dried skin, and not the least inviting to the palate.

Fritz was much amused at this discovery.

"How I wish Ernest could have been here!" cried he. "How he envied me the fine large coco-nuts I was to find, and the whole tea-cupful of sweet delicious milk, which was to spring out upon me from the inside! But, Father, I really believed that the coco-nut contained a sweet refreshing liquid, a little like the juice of almonds; travellers surely tell untruths!"

"Travellers do sometimes tell untruths, Fritz, but on the subject of the coco-nut I believe them to be innocent. The coco-nut is known to contain the liquid you describe, just before a state of ripeness. It is the same with our European nuts, with only the difference of quantity: and the circumstance is common to both, that as the nut ripens the milk diminishes by becoming the same substance as the nut. If you put a ripe nut under the earth in a good soil, the kernel will shoot and burst the shell; but if it remain above-ground, or in a place that does not suit its nature, the nut rots and perishes as you have seen."

After looking for some time, we had at length the good luck to find another coco-nut. We opened it, and finding it sound we sat down and ate it for our dinner, by which means we were enabled to husband the provisions we had brought. The nut, it is true, was a little oily and rancid; yet, as this was not a time to be nice, we made a hearty meal, and then continued our route. We did not quit the wood, but pushed our way through it, being often obliged to cut a path through the bushes. At length we reached a plain, which afforded a more extensive prospect and a path less intricate.

We next entered a forest to the right, and soon observed in it some trees of a particular species. Fritz, whose sharp eye was continually on a journey of discovery, remarked that some of them were of so very extraordinary an appearance that he could not resist the curiosity he felt to examine them closely.

"Look here, Father!" he next exclaimed. "What a singular kind of tree, with wens growing all about the trunk!"

We walked up to some of them, and I perceived with surprise and satisfaction that they were of the gourd-tree kind, the trunks of which bear fruit. Fritz could not conceive the meaning of what he saw, and asked me if the fruit was a sponge or a wen.

"We will see," I replied, "if we cannot unravel the mystery. Try to get down one of them, and we will examine it minutely."

"I have got one," cried Fritz, "and it is exactly like a gourd, only the rind is thicker and harder."

"It then, like the rind of that fruit, can be used for making various utensils," observed I; "plates, dishes, basins, and flasks. We will give this tree the name of the gourd-tree."

"Hurrah!" cried he in ecstasy. "How happy Mother will be! She will no longer have the vexation when she makes soup of thinking that we shall scald our fingers."

"What, my boy, do you think is the reason that this tree bears its fruit only on the trunk and on its topmost branches?"

"I think it must be because the middle branches are too feeble to support such a weight."

"You have guessed exactly right."

"But are these gourds good to eat?"

"At worst they are, I believe, harmless; but they have not a very tempting flavour. The savages set as much value on the rind of this fruit as on gold, for its use to them is indispensable. These rinds serve them to keep their food and drink in, and sometimes they even cook their victuals in them."

"Oh, Father! it must be impossible to cook their victuals in them, for the heat of the fire would soon consume such a substance."

"I did not say the rind was put upon the fire, Fritz."

"Pray, how are the victuals to be cooked without fire?"

"Nor did I say that victuals could be cooked without a fire, and my meaning was, that there is no need to put the vessel that contains the food upon the fire."

"I have not the least idea of what you mean; there seems to be a miracle."

"So be it, my son. A little tincture of enchantment is the lot of man. Let me help you to understand this amazing phenomenon. When it is intended to dress food in one of these rinds, the process is to cut the fruit into two equal parts and scoop out the whole of the inside. Some water is put into one of the halves, and into the water some fish, a crab, or whatever else is to be dressed; then some stones red hot, beginning with one at a time, are thrown in, which impart sufficient heat to the water to dress the food, without the smallest injury to the pot."

"But is not the food spoiled by ashes falling in, or by pieces of the heated stones separating in the water?"

"Certainly it would not be very easy to make fine sauces or ragouts in such a vessel, but a dressing of the meat is actually accomplished, and the negroes and savages are not very delicate."

We next proceeded to the manufacture of our plates and dishes. I taught my son how to divide the gourd with a bit of string, which would cut more equally than a knife. I tied the string round the middle of the gourd as tight as possible, striking it pretty hard with the handle of my knife, and I drew tighter and tighter till the gourd fell apart, forming two regular-shaped bowls. Fritz, who had used a knife for the same operation, had entirely spoiled his gourd by the irregular strokes of his instrument. I recommended his making some spoons with the spoiled rind, as it was good for no other purpose. I on my part had soon completed two dishes, and some plates.

Fritz was in the utmost astonishment at my success. "I cannot imagine, Father," said he, "how this way of cutting the gourd could occur to you."

"I have read the description of such a process," replied I, "in books of travels, and also, that such of the savages as have no knives, and who make a sort of twine from the bark of trees, are accustomed to use it for this purpose."

"And the flasks, Father; in what manner are they made?"

"For this branch of their ingenuity the savages make preparation a long time beforehand. If a negro wishes to have a flask or bottle with a neck, he ties a very young gourd round in the proper place with a piece of string, of linen, bark of a tree, or anything he can get hold of; he draws this bandage so tight, that the part at liberty soon forms itself to a round shape, while the part which is confined contracts, and remains ever after narrow. By this method it is that they obtain flasks or bottles of a perfect form."

"Are then the bottle-shaped gourds I have seen in Europe trained by a similar preparation?"

"No, they are not; they are of another species, and what you have seen is their natural shape."

Our conversation and our labour thus went on together. Fritz had completed some plates, and was not a little proud of the achievement. "Ah, how delighted my mother will be to eat upon them!" cried he. "But how shall we convey them to her?"

"We must leave them here on the sand for the sun to dry them; this will be accomplished by the time of our return, and we can then carry them with us; but care must be taken to fill them with sand, that they may not shrink or warp in so ardent a heat."

My boy did not dislike this task, for he had no great fancy to the idea of carrying such a load. Our service was accordingly spread upon the shore.

We amused ourselves as we walked along in endeavouring to fashion some spoons from the fragments of the gourd-rinds. I had the fancy to try my skill upon a piece of coco-nut; but I must needs confess that what we produced had not the least resemblance to those I had seen in the Museum at London, and which were shown there as the work of some of the islanders of the Southern Seas. A European without instruments must always find himself excelled by the superior adroitness and patience of savages; in this instance, too, we had the assistance of knives, while the savages have only sharp flat stones to work with.

"My attempt has been scarcely more successful than your own," I cried; "and to eat soup with either your spoon or mine, we ought to have mouths extending from ear to ear."

"True enough, Father," answered Fritz; "but it is not my fault. In making mine, I took the curve of my bit of rind for a guide; if I had made it smaller, it should have been too flat, and it is still more difficult to eat with a shovel than with an oyster-shell. But I am thinking that they may serve till I have learned to improve, and I am quite sure of the pleasure they will afford Mother."

While these different conversations and our labours had been going on, we had not neglected the great object of our pursuit – the making every practicable search for our ship companions. But all, alas! was in vain.

After a walk of about four leagues, we arrived at a spot where a slip of land, on which we observed a hill of considerable height, reached far out into the sea. We determined to ascend to its summit, which could not fail to give us a clear view; this would save us farther rambles.

We did not reach the top of the hill without much hard climbing, but when there it presented a magnificent scene over a vast extent of land and water. It was, however, in vain that we made use of our spyglass; no trace of man appeared. The shore, rounded by a bay of some extent, the bank of which ended in a promontory on the farther side; the blue tint of its surface; the sea, gently agitated with waves; the woods of variegated hues and verdure, formed altogether a picture of such new and exquisite delight, that if the recollection of our unfortunate companions had not intervened, we should have yielded to the ecstasy the scene was calculated to inspire. In reality, from this moment we began to lose the hope we had entertained, and a certain sadness stole into our hearts. We, however, became but the more sensible of the goodness of the Divine Being in the special protection afforded us, in permitting us to find a home where there seemed to be no cause for fear of danger from without, where we had not experienced even the want of food, and where there seemed to be a prospect of future safety for us all. I remarked to Fritz that we seemed destined to a solitary life, and that it was a rich country which appeared to be allotted us for a habitation; at least our habitation it must be, unless some vessel should happen to put on shore on the same coast.

"Having left our native country, fixed on the intention of inhabiting some more propitious soil, it was natural to expect that we must at first encounter difficult adventures. Let us therefore consider our present situation as no disappointment in any essential respect. We can pursue our scheme for agriculture. We shall learn to invent arts. Our only want is numbers."

"We, however, of ourselves," observed Fritz, "form a larger society than was the lot of Adam before he had children; and as we grow older, we will perform all the necessary labour, while you and Mother enjoy a serene repose."

"Your assurances are as kind as I can desire, and they encourage me to struggle with what hardships may present themselves. Who can foresee in what manner it may be the will of Heaven to dispose of us?"

We descended from the hill, and having regained the shore we made our way to the wood of palms, which I had just pointed out to Fritz; but not without considerable difficulty, for our path lay through a quantity of reeds, entwined with other plants, which greatly obstructed our march. We advanced slowly and cautiously, fearing at every step we might receive a bite from some serpent. We made Turk go before us, to give us timely notice of anything dangerous. I also cut myself a reed of uncommon length and thickness, the better to defend myself. It was not without astonishment that I perceived a glutinous kind of sap proceed from the divided end of the stalk. Prompted by curiosity, I tasted the sap, and found it sweet and of an agreeable flavour, so that not a doubt remained in my mind that we were passing through a fine plantation of sugar-canes. I determined not to tell Fritz immediately of the fortunate discovery I had made, preferring that he should find the pleasure out for himself. As he was at some distance on before, I called out to him to cut a reed for his defence. This he instantly did, and, without any remark, used it simply for a stick, striking lustily with it on all sides to clear a passage. This motion occasioned the sap to run out abundantly upon his hand, and he stopped to examine so strange a circumstance. He lifted it up, and still a larger quantity escaped. He now tasted what was on his fingers. Oh! then for the exclamations. "Father, Father! I have found some sugar! some syrup! I have a sugar-cane in my hand!"

In the meantime Fritz eagerly devoured the cane he had cut, till his relish for it was appeased.

"I will take home a good provision. I shall only just taste of them once or twice as I walk along. But it will be so delightful to regale my mother and my little brothers with them!"

"Certainly, Fritz; but do not take too heavy a load, for recollect you have other things to carry, and we have yet far to go."

Counsel was given in vain. He persisted in cutting at least a dozen of the largest canes, tore off their leaves, tied them together, and, putting them under his arm, dragged them as well as he was able through thick and thin to the end of the plantation. We arrived without accident at the wood of palms, which we entered in search of a place of shade, where we might stretch our limbs on the ground and finish our repast. We were scarcely settled, when a great number of large monkeys, terrified by the sight of us and the barking of Turk, stole so nimbly and quietly up the trees, that we scarcely perceived them till they had reached the topmost parts. From this height they fixed their eyes upon us, grinding their teeth, making most horrible grimaces, and saluting us with frightful screams. I observed that the trees were

"We held the two paddles longways, and thus we passed without accident through the breach in the ship." (Chapter 2)

"The young monkey, on perceiving Fritz, sprang nimbly onto his shoulders." (Chapter 4)

palms, bearing coco-nuts, and I instantly conceived the hope of obtaining some of this fruit by help of the monkeys. Fritz on his part prepared to shoot at them. He threw his burdens on the ground, and it was with difficulty I could prevent him from firing.

"What are you going to do," said I, "in this youthful ardour of yours? What use or what pleasure can it be to you to destroy one of these monkeys?"

"Ah, Father, why did you not let me kill him? Look how they raise their backs in derision of us!"

"And is it possible that this can excite your vengeance, my most reasonable Mr. Fritz? As long as an animal does no injury, or that his death can in no shape be useful in preserving our own lives, we have no right to destroy it, and still less to torment it for our amusement, or from an insensate desire of revenge."

"We could roast a monkey, could we not, Father?"

"Many thanks for the hint. A fine repast you would have provided us! Thanks to our stars, too, we are each too heavily loaded to have carried the dead body to our kitchen. Does not your large bundle of sugar-canes convince you that I speak the truth? But the living monkeys we may perhaps find means to make contribute to our service. See what I am going to do; but step aside for fear of your head. If I succeed, the monkeys will furnish us with plenty of coco-nuts."

I now began to throw stones at the monkeys; and though I could not make them reach to half of the height at which they had taken refuge, they showed every mark of excessive anger. With their accustomed habit of imitation they furiously tore off, nut by nut, all that grew upon the branches near them, to hurl them down upon us, and in a short time a large quantity of coco-nuts lay round us. Fritz laughed heartily at the excellent success of our stratagem, and as the shower of coco-nuts began to subside we set about collecting them. We chose a place where we could repose at our ease to regale ourselves on this rich harvest. We opened the shells with a hatchet, but not without having first enjoyed the sucking of some of the milk through the three small holes, round which we found it easy to insert a knife and let the milk escape. The milk of the coco-nut has not a very pleasant flavour, but it is excellent for quenching thirst. What we liked best was a kind of solid cream which adheres to the shell, and which we scraped off with our spoons. We mixed with it a little of the sap of our sugar-canes, and it made a delicious repast. Turk obtained for his share what remained of the lobster, to which we added a small quantity of biscuit. All this, however, was insufficient to satisfy the hunger of so large an animal, and he sought about for bits of the sugar-canes and of the coco-nuts.

Our meal being finished, we prepared to leave the place. I tied together such of the coco-nuts as had retained the stalks, and threw them across my shoulder. Fritz resumed his bundle of sugar-canes. We divided the rest of the things between us, and continued our way towards home.

CHAPTER FOUR

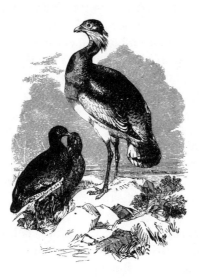

RETURN FROM THE VOYAGE OF
DISCOVERY — A NOCTURNAL ALARM
~

My poor boy now began to complain of fatigue. At last he stopped to take breath.

"I never could have thought," cried he, "that a few sugar-canes could be so heavy. I should, however, be so glad to get them home to Mother and my brothers."

"A little patience and a little courage, dear Fritz," replied I, "will enable you to accomplish this wish. Recollect Æsop's breadbasket, which at first was so overwhelming a burden, but which at last became so light. We can cause it to be the same with your sugar-canes if we diminish them by sucking a number on the road. As a beginning, you may give one to me. Take you one also; the rest we will bind together and put at your back, hanging them upon the barrel of your gun, by which means you will carry them more easily.

"But I am not without apprehensions, Fritz, that of our acquisition we shall carry them only a few sticks for firewood, for I must bring to recollection the circumstance that the juice of the sugar-cane is apt to turn sour soon after cutting. We may suck them, therefore, without compunction, and without regret at the diminution of our number of canes."

"Well, then, if we can do no better with the sugar-canes," said Fritz, "at least I will take them a good supply of the milk of coco-nuts, which I have here in a tin bottle."

"In this, too, my boy, I fear you will also be disappointed. You talk of milk, but the milk of the coco-nut, when exposed to the air and heat, turns soon to vinegar."

"Oh, dear, how provoking!" groaned poor Fritz. "I must taste it this very minute."

The tin bottle was lowered from his shoulder in the twinkling of an eye, and he began to pull the cork with all his strength. As soon as it was loose the liquid flew upwards in a brisk stream, and with a loud noise and frothing like champagne.

"Bravo, Mr. Fritz! You have manufactured a wine of some mettle. I must caution you not to let it make you tipsy."

"Oh, taste it, Father, pray taste it! It is really like wine; its taste is sweet, and it is so sparkling! Do take a little, Father! Is it not good? If all the milk remains in this state the treat will be better even than I thought."

"I wish it may prove so, but I have my fears. Its present state is what is called the first degree of fermentation. The same thing happens to honey dissolved in water, of which a beverage called hydromel is made. When this first fermentation is past and the liquid is clear, it is become a sort of wine, the quality of which depends on the materials used. By the application of heat there next results a second fermentation, which turns the fluid into vinegar. But this may be prevented by great care, and by keeping the vessel in a cool place. Lastly, a third fermentation takes place in the vinegar itself, which changes its character, and deprives it of its taste, its strength, and its transparency. In the intense temperature of this climate this triple fermentation comes on very rapidly, so that it is not improbable that, on entering our tent, you might find your liquids turned to vinegar, or even to a thick liquid of ill odour. We may therefore refresh ourselves with a portion of our booty, that it may not all be spoiled. Come then, I drink your health and that of our dear family. I find the liquor at present both refreshing and agreeable. But I am pretty sure that if we would arrive sober we must not venture on frequent libations."

The coco-nut wine gave our exhausted frames an increase of strength and cheerfulness, and we pursued our way with briskness to the place where we had left our gourd utensils. We found them perfectly dry, as hard as bone, and not the least misshapen. We now, therefore, could put them into our game-bags conveniently enough; and this done, we continued our way. Scarcely had we passed through the little wood in which we breakfasted, when Turk sprang furiously away to seize upon a troop of monkeys, who were skipping about and amusing themselves without observing our approach toward the place of their merriment. They were thus taken by surprise; and before we could get to the spot our ferocious Turk had already seized one of them. It was a female monkey, who held a young one in her arms, which she was caressing almost to suffocation, and which encumbrance deprived her of the power of escaping. The poor creature was killed, and afterwards devoured by Turk. The young one hid himself in the grass and looked on, grinding his teeth all the time.

Fritz flew like lightning to force the ferocious Turk from his prey. He lost his hat, threw down his tin bottle, canes, and other burdens, but all in vain.

The next scene was of a different nature, and comical enough. The young monkey, on perceiving Fritz, sprang nimbly on his shoulders, and fastened his feet securely in the stiff curls of his hair; nor could the squalls of Fritz, nor all the shaking he gave, make the little creature let go. I ran to Fritz, laughing heartily, for I saw that the animal was too young to be capable of doing him any injury, while the expression in the features of the boy made the most diverting contrast with the grimaces of the monkey, whom I in vain endeavoured to disengage.

"There is no remedy, Fritz," said I, "but to submit quietly and carry him. The conduct of the little animal displays a very surprising intelligence; he has lost his mother, and he adopts you for his father. Perhaps he discovered in you something of the air of a father of a family."

"But I assure you, Father," cried Fritz, "he is giving me some terrible twitches. Do try once more to get him off!"

With a little gentleness and management I at last succeeded. I took the creature in my arms as one would an infant, and I confess I could not help pitying and caressing him.

"Father," cried Fritz, "do let me have this little animal in my own keeping. I will take the greatest care of him. I will give him all my share of the milk of the coconuts till we get our cows and goats. And, who knows? his monkey instinct may one day assist us in discovering some different kinds of wholesome fruits."

"I have not the least objection," answered I. "By and by we shall see whether he will be fittest to aid us with his intelligence, or to injure us by his malice."

We now again thought of resuming our journey, and accordingly left the ferocious Turk to finish his meal. The little orphan jumped again on the shoulder of his protector, while I on my part relieved my boy of the bundle of canes. Scarcely had we proceeded a quarter of a league when Turk overtook us full gallop. He showed no sign of giving himself any concern about his cannibal feast, but fell quietly behind Fritz with an air of cool and perfect satisfaction. The young monkey appeared uneasy from seeing him so near, and passed round and fixed himself on his protector's bosom, who did not long bear with so great an inconvenience without having recourse to his invention for a remedy. He tied some string round Turk's body, in such a way as to admit of the monkey's being fastened on his back with it, and then in a tone really pathetic addressed the dog as follows: "Now, Mr. Turk, since it was you who had the cruelty to destroy the mother, it is for you to take every care of her child." At first the dog was restive and resisted; but by degrees, partly by menaces and partly by caresses, we succeeded in gaining his goodwill, and he quietly consented to carry the little burden. The young monkey found himself perfectly happy. Fritz put another string round Turk's neck, by which he might lead him.

In happy expectation of our return we forgot the length of our journey, and found ourselves on the bank of the river before we were aware. Ponto on the other side announced our approach by a violent barking, and Turk replied so heartily, that his motions disturbed the tranquillity of his little burden, who, in his fright, jumped the length of his string from Turk's back to Fritz's shoulder, which he could not afterwards be prevailed upon to leave. Turk ran off to meet his companion and announce our arrival; and shortly after our much-loved family appeared in sight on the opposite shore. They advanced along by the course of the river, till they on one side and we on the other had reached the place where we had crossed it in the morning. We repassed it again in safety and greeted each other with joy. Scarcely had the young ones joined their brother than they began their exclamations of surprise.

"A monkey, a live monkey! Oh, how delightful! How did you catch him? What a droll face he has!"

"He is very ugly!" said little Francis, half afraid to touch him.

"He is much prettier than you!" retorted Jack. "Only see, he is laughing! I wish I could see him eat!"

"Ah! If we had but some coco-nut!" said Ernest. "Could you not find any? Are they nice?"

"Have you brought me any milk of almonds?" said Francis.

"Have you met with any adventure?" asked my wife.

At length, when all became a little tranquil, I answered them thus: "Most happy am I to return to you again, and God be praised, without having encountered any new misfortune. We have even the pleasure of presenting you with many valuable acquisitions. But in the object nearest my heart, the discovering what has become of our ship companions, we have entirely failed."

"Since it pleases God that it should be so," said my wife, "let us endeavour to be content, and let us be grateful to Him for having saved us from their unhappy fate, and for having once more brought us all together. I have laboured this day under great uneasiness about your safety, and imagined a thousand evils. The day appeared an age. But now I see you once more safe and well, I am as happy as could be. Put down your burdens, we will all help you; for though we have not, I assure you, spent the day in idleness, we are less fatigued than you. Now then, sit down and tell us your adventures."

Jack received my gun, Ernest the coco-nuts, Francis the gourd-rinds, and my wife my game-bag. Fritz distributed the sugar-canes, and put his monkey on the back of Turk, at the same time begging Ernest to relieve him of his gun. But Ernest assured him that the large heavy bowls with which he was loaded were the most he had strength to carry. His mother, a little too indulgent to his lazy humour, relieved him of them. Thus we proceeded, all together, to our tent.

Fritz whispered me, that if Ernest had known what the large heavy bowls were he would not so readily have parted with them. "Why, Ernest," cried he, "do you know that these bowls are coco-nuts, your dear much-desired coco-nuts, and each containing the sweet nice milk you have so much wished to taste?"

"Are they indeed? Are they really and truly coco-nuts? Oh, Mother, return them to me quickly! I will carry them, if you please; and I can carry the gun too without finding it heavy!"

"No, no, Ernest," answered his mother. "I am certain you would begin to complain again before we had gone a hundred paces."

Ernest would willingly have asked his mother to give him the coco-nuts and take the gun herself, but this he dare not do. "I have only," said he, "to get rid of these sticks, and carry the gun."

"I would advise you not to give up the sticks either," said Fritz drily. "For the sticks are sugar-canes!"

"Sugar-canes!" cried Ernest. "Sugar-canes!" exclaimed they all; and, surrounding Fritz, made him give them full instructions on the sublime art of sucking sugar-canes.

My wife was perfectly astonished, and earnestly entreated we would explain to her all about it. I instantly complied with her request, giving her every explanation and particular respecting our journey, and our new acquisitions, which I alternately exhibited for her inspection, no one of which afforded her more pleasure than the plates and dishes. We now adjourned to our little kitchen, and with great delight observed the preparations going forward in it for supper. On one side of the fire we saw a turn-spit, which my wife had contrived by driving two forked pieces of wood into the ground, and placing a long even stick sharpened at one end across them. By this invention she was enabled to roast different kinds of fish or other food, with the help of little Francis, who was entrusted with the care of turning it round from time to time. On the occasion of our return she had prepared us the treat of a goose, the fat of which ran down into some oyster-shells placed there to serve the purpose of a dripping-pan. There were also a dish of fish which the little ones had caught, and the iron pot was upon the fire, provided with a good soup. By the side of these most exhilarating preparations stood one of the casks which we had recovered from the waves, the head of which my wife had knocked out, so that it exposed to our view a cargo of the finest Dutch cheeses contained in round tins.

"You indeed but barely did yourselves justice, my dear ones, in saying that you had not been idle during our absence," cried I. "I see before me what must have cost you great labour. I am, however, a little sorry that you have killed one of our geese so soon; we must employ the utmost economy in the use of our poultry, which may be of service in a time of need."

"Do not make yourself uneasy on this subject," said my wife; "for what you see is not one of our geese, but a kind of wild bird, and is the booty of your son Ernest, who calls him by a singular name, and assures me that it is good to eat."

"Yes, Father. I believe that the bird is a kind of penguin, or we might distinguish him by the surname of *Stupid.* He showed himself to be a bird so wanting in intelligence, that I killed him with a single blow with my stick."

"What is the form of his feet, and of his beak?" asked I.

"His feet were webbed; the beak was long, small, and a little curved downwards.

I have kept his head and neck. The bird reminds me exactly of the penguin, described as so stupid a bird in my book of natural history."

"I am glad you have read to such good purpose, my son. But now let us see what we can do with the coco-nuts. But first you will be obliged to learn from Fritz the best manner of opening them, so as to preserve the milk, and I recommend to you not to forget the young monkey."

We seated ourselves; my wife had placed each article of the repast in one of our newly-manufactured dishes. My sons had broken the coco-nuts, and already convinced themselves of their delicious flavour; and then they fell to making spoons with the shells. The little monkey had been served the first, and each amused himself with making him suck the corner of his pocket-handkerchief dipped in the milk of the coco-nut.

The boys were preparing to break some more of the nuts with the hatchet, after having drawn out the milk through the three little holes. I pronounced the word *halt*, and bade them bring me a saw. The thought struck me that by dividing the nuts carefully, the two halves when emptied would remain with the form of some well-looking tea-cups or basins already made to our hands. Jack, who was on every occasion the most active, brought me a saw. I performed my undertaking in the best manner I could, and in a short time each of us was provided with a convenient receptacle for food. Accordingly my wife put the share of soup which belonged to each into those basins. Fritz asked me if he might not invite our company to taste his fine champagne, which he said would not fail to make us all the merrier. "I have not the least objection," answered I, "but remember to taste it yourself before you serve it to your guests."

He ran to draw out the stopple, and to taste it. . . . "How unfortunate!" said he. "It is already turned to vinegar!"

"What is it? – vinegar did you say?" exclaimed my wife. "How lucky! It will make the most delicious sauce for our bird, mixed with the fat which has fallen from it in roasting, and will be as good a relish as a salad." No sooner said than done. This vinegar, produced from coco-nut, proved a most agreeable corrective of the wild and fishy flavour of the penguin, and without it I am afraid we should have found it not very palatable. The same sauce considerably improved our dish of fish also. Each boasted most of what he himself had been the means of procuring; it was Jack and Francis who had caught the fish, while Ernest was employed in securing his penguin. My dear wife herself performed the most difficult task of all, that of rolling the cask of Dutch cheeses into the kitchen, and then knocking out its head.

By the time we had finished our meal the sun was retiring from our view, and recollecting how quickly the night would fall upon us, we were in the greatest haste to regain our place of rest. Our whole flock of fowls placed themselves as they had done the preceding evening; we said our prayers, and with an improved serenity of mind lay down in the tent, taking the young monkey with us, who was become the little favourite of all. Fritz and Jack contended for a short time which should enjoy the honour of his company for the night, and it was at last decided that he should be laid between them, after which each would have a hand in covering him carefully that he might not catch cold. We now all lay down upon the grass in the order of the night before, myself remaining last to fasten the sail-cloth in front of the tent, when I as well as the rest soon fell into a profound and refreshing sleep.

But I had not long enjoyed this pleasing state, when I was awakened by the motion of the fowls on the tent, and by a violent barking of the dogs. I rushed out instantly; my wife and Fritz, who had also been alarmed, followed my example, we each taking a gun.

"Shall you, my dearest, have the courage to fire if it should be necessary?" said I to my wife.

"Most certainly," said she, "if, as you say, it should be necessary. At the same time it would perhaps be better that I should leave to you the task of firing, while I can undertake to load your guns, and to hand them to you as fast as you may want them."

"That is best," said I, "so let us not lose a moment in examining what enemy it is we have to deal with."

Our dogs continued barking with the same violence, and at intervals even howled. We had not proceeded many steps from the tent, when, to our great astonishment, we perceived by the light of the moon a terrible combat. At least a dozen of jackals had surrounded our brave dogs, who defended themselves with an almost unexampled courage.

I had apprehended something much worse than jackals, and felt relieved. "We shall soon manage to set these gentlemen at rest," said I. "Let us fire both together, my boy; but let us take care how we aim for fear of killing the dogs." We fired, and two of the intruders fell instantly dead upon the sands. The others made their escape. My wife, seeing that all was now quiet, entreated us to lie down again and finish our night's sleep, but Fritz asked my permission to let him first drag the jackal he had killed towards the tent, that he might be able to exhibit him the next morning to his brothers. Having obtained my consent, he ran to fetch him, and with great difficulty succeeded in his plan, the animal being of the size of a large dog.

Having therefore nothing further to prevent us, we lay down till day began to break, and till the cocks awoke us both. The children being still asleep, afforded us an excellent opportunity to consult respecting the ensuing day.

CHAPTER FIVE

RETURN TO THE WRECK

~

I broke a silence of some moments with observing to my wife that I could not conquer my alarm at the view of so many cares and such a variety of exertions to be made. In the first place, a journey to the vessel. "This is of absolute necessity; at least, if we would not be deprived of the cattle and various other useful things, all of which from moment to moment we run the risk of losing by the first approach of a heavy sea. On the other hand, there are so many things to think of, and so much to be done here, for the comfort of all in this desert spot! What ought we to resolve upon? For example, is it not, above all, necessary to contrive a better kind of habitation, and also the means of procuring a more secure retreat from wild beasts for ourselves, and some separate place of accommodation for our provisions? I own I am at a loss what to begin upon first."

"All will fall into the right order by degrees," observed my wife. "I cannot, I confess, help shuddering at the thought of this voyage to the vessel; but if you judge it to be of absolute necessity, it appears to me that it cannot be undertaken too soon. In the meanwhile, nothing that is immediately under my own care shall stand still, I promise you. Let us not be over-anxious about the morrow: sufficient unto the day is the evil thereof."

"I will follow your advice," said I, "and without further loss of time. You shall stay here with the three youngest boys. Fritz, being so much older and stronger than the others, shall accompany me in the undertaking."

I now woke the children. Fritz sprang nimbly out of the tent, while his little brothers began to gape and rub their eyes, to get rid of their sleepiness. Fritz ran to visit his jackal, which during the night had become cold and perfectly stiff. He fixed him upon his legs, and placed him to look like a sentinel at the entrance of the tent, joyously expecting the wonder and acclamations of his little brothers at so singular and unexpected an appearance. But no sooner had the dogs caught a sight of him than they began a horrible barking, and set themselves in motion to fall upon him instantly, thinking he was alive. Fritz had enough to do to restrain them, and succeeded only by dint of coaxing and perseverance. In the meantime their barking had effectually awakened the younger boys, and they all ran out of the tent, curious to know what could be the occasion. Jack was the first who appeared, with the young monkey on his shoulders; but when the little creature perceived the jackal, he sprang away in terror, and hid himself at the farthest extremity of the grass which composed our bed.

The children were much surprised at the sight of a yellow-coloured animal standing without motion at the entrance of the tent.

"Oh, dear!" exclaimed Francis; "it is a wolf!"

"No, no," said Jack, going near the jackal and taking one of his paws; "it is a yellow dog, and he is dead."

"It is neither a dog nor a wolf," put in Ernest. "Do you not see that it is a golden fox?"

"Very near it, most learned professor!" exclaimed Fritz. "So you can tell an agouti when you see him, but you cannot tell a jackal. I killed him myself in the night."

"In the night, you say, Fritz? In your sleep, I suppose."

"No, Mr. Ernest, not in my sleep, as you suppose, but broad awake. But I cannot wonder at this mistake in one who does not know the difference between a jackal and a golden fox."

"Come, come, my lads, I will have no disputes," said I. "As to the animal, you all are right and all are wrong. He partakes at once of the nature of the dog, the wolf, and the fox; and for his skin, it is really of a *golden* tint."

The boys in an instant became friends; and then followed questions, answers, and wonder in abundance.

The next thing thought of was breakfast. To-day their mother had nothing to give them for their morning meal but some biscuit, which was so hard and dry that it was with difficulty we could swallow it. Fritz asked for a piece of cheese to eat with it, and Ernest spied about the second cask we had drawn out of the sea, and which was standing in our kitchen, to discover whether, as we had all imagined, it also contained some Dutch cheeses. In a minute or two he came up to us, joy sparkling in his eyes.

"Papa," said he, "if we had but a little butter spread upon our biscuit, do you not think it would improve it?"

"That indeed it would, Ernest."

"Perhaps, then, if we were to knock out the head of this cask, we might find some."

"What cask, my boy? And what are you talking of?"

"I am talking of this cask, which is filled with excellent salt butter. I made a little opening in it with a knife; and, see, I got out enough of it to spread nicely upon this piece of biscuit."

"That instinct of yours for once is of some general use," answered I, "and justice requires that I should also commend, with moderation, the excellence of your nose. But now let us profit by the event. Who will have some butter on their biscuits?"

The boys surrounded the cask in a moment, while I was in some perplexity as to the safest method of getting out its contents. Fritz proposed taking off the topmost hoop, by which means one of the ends could be got out. But this I objected to, observing that we should be careful not to loosen the staves, as the heat of the sun would not fail to melt the butter, which would run out. The idea occurred to me that I would make a hole in the bottom of the cask, sufficiently large to take out a small quantity of butter at a time; and I immediately set about manufacturing a little wooden shovel, to use it for the purpose. All this succeeded quite well, and we sat down to breakfast, some biscuits and a coco-nut shell full of salt butter being placed upon the ground, round which we all assembled. We toasted our biscuit, and while it was hot applied the butter, and contrived to make a hearty breakfast.

Meantime I did not fail to notice that their encounter with the jackals had not concluded without the dogs receiving several wounds. Fearing that the heat might bring on inflammation, I desired Jack, the valiant, to wash a small quantity of the butter thoroughly in fresh water, and then to anoint the wounds with it. This he effected with much skill and tenderness. The dogs did not attempt the least resistance, seeming to be sensible of the benefit he was conferring on them. They themselves assisted the cure by licking, so that in a few days they were as well as before.

"One of the things we must not forget to look for in the vessel," said Fritz, "is a spiked collar or two for our dogs, as a protection to them from wild beasts."

"Oh," says Jack, "I can make some spiked collars if Mamma will give me a little help."

"That I will most readily, my boy, for I should like to see what new fancy has come into your head," cried Mamma.

"Yes, yes," pursued I, "as many inventions as you please! But now we must think of setting ourselves to some occupation. You, Mr. Fritz, who, from your superior age and discretion, enjoy the high honour of being my privy counsellor, must make haste and get yourself ready, and we will undertake to-day our voyage to the vessel, to save and bring away whatever may be possible. You younger boys will remain under the wing of your mother. I hope I need not mention that I rely on your perfect obedience to her, and general good behaviour."

While Fritz was getting the boat ready I looked about for a pole, and put a piece of white linen to the end of it. This I drove into the ground, in a place where it would be visible from the vessel. I agreed with my wife that in case of any accident that should require my immediate presence, they should take down the pole and fire a gun three times as a signal of distress. But I gave her notice, that there being so many things to do on board the vessel, it was very probable that we should not be able to return the same day; in which case I, on my part, also promised to make them signals. My wife had the courage and the good sense to consent to my plan. She, however, extorted from me a promise that we should pass the night in our tubs, and not on board the ship. We took nothing with us but our guns and a supply of powder and shot, relying on it that we should find provisions on board. Yet I did not refuse to indulge Fritz in the wish he expressed to let him take the young monkey.

We embarked in silence, often looking back at the dear ones we were quitting. When we had reached to a considerable distance, I remarked that besides the opening by which we had the first time made land, there was another that formed the mouth of the river, running not far from that spot, the current of which was visible a good way into the sea.

To take advantage of this current was my first thought and my first care. Little as I knew of the management of sea affairs, I succeeded in keeping our boat in the direction in which the current ran, by which means we were drawn gently on, till the current had conducted us to within a short distance of the wreck. There we were again obliged to have recourse to our oars. But our arms having now rested for some time, we were ready for new exertions. A little afterwards we found ourselves safely arrived at the breach of the vessel, and fastened our boat securely to one of the timbers.

Scarcely had we got out of the boat than Fritz proceeded with his young monkey on his arm to the main deck, where he found all the animals we had left on board. I followed him, pleased to observe the impatience he betrayed to relieve the wants of the poor creatures, who all now saluted us by the cry or the sounds natural each to its species. It was not so much the want of food as the desire of seeing once more their accustomed human companions which occasioned them to manifest their joy, for they had a portion of the food and water we had left them still remaining. We next examined the food and water of the other animals, taking away what was half-spoiled and adding a fresh supply. Nor did we neglect the care of renewing our own strength by a plentiful repast.

While we were seated and appeasing the calls of hunger, Fritz and I consulted what should be our first occupation, when, to my great surprise, the advice he gave was that we should immediately contrive a sail for our boat. "What," cried I, "makes you think of such a thing at so critical a moment?"

"Father," said Fritz, "let me confess the truth, which is, that I found it very difficult to perform the task of rowing for so long a time, though I assure you I did my best, and did not spare my strength. I observed that, though the wind blew strong in my face the current nevertheless carried us on. Now, as we cannot be benefited on our return by the current, I was thinking that we might make the wind supply its place."

"Ah ha, Mr. Fritz! So you wish to spare yourself a little trouble, do you? But I perceive a great deal of good sense in your argument. The best thing we can do is to take care and not overload the boat, and thus avoid the danger of sinking, or of being obliged to throw some of our stores overboard. Come then, let us set to work upon your sail, and let us look about for what we want."

I assisted Fritz to carry a pole strong enough to serve for a mast, and another for a sail-yard. I directed him to make a hole in a plank with an auger, large enough for the mast. I then went to the sail-chamber, and cut off from an ample piece of sail-cloth enough to make a triangular sail: in the edges I made holes, and passed cords through them. I then sought for a pulley, that I might fasten it to the top of the mast, and thus be enabled to raise and lower my sail at pleasure. Thus prepared I hastened to join Fritz, who was earnestly working at the mast. As soon as he had done we placed the plank that he had perforated across the centre of our craft, and made it fast. The pulley was suspended from a ring at the top of the mast, and the cord, attached to the sharpest angle of the sail, was passed through it. The sail formed a right-angled triangle, one side of which touched the mast and was fastened to it. The shortest side was also fastened with cords to a pole, stretching from the mast beyond the circumference of our bark, and of which one end was fastened to the mast, while the other had a cord running to the stern to be held in my hand.

While I was thus occupied, Fritz had been taking observations through a telescope of what was passing on land. He imparted the agreeable tidings that all was still well. He soon after brought me a small streamer which he had cut from a piece of linen, and which he entreated me to tie to the extremity of the mast, and appeared as much delighted with the streamer as with the sail itself.

"But now, Father," said Fritz, looking kindly on me as he spoke, "as you have eased me of the labour of rowing, it is my turn to take care of you. I am thinking about making a better rudder."

"Your thought would be a very good one," said I, "but that I am unwilling to lose the advantage of being able to proceed this way and that, without being obliged to veer. I shall therefore fix our oars so as to enable me to steer from either end."

During these exertions the day became far advanced, and I perceived that we should be obliged to pass the night in our tubs. We had promised to hoist a flag if our intention was to pass the night from home, and we decided that our streamer was precisely the thing for this purpose.

We employed the rest of the day in emptying the tubs of the useless ballast of stone, and putting in their place what would be of service, such as nails, pieces of cloth, and different kinds of utensils, &c. The prospect of entire solitude, made us devote our principal attention to the securing as much powder and shot as might fall in our way, that we might thus secure the means of killing animals for food, and of defending ourselves against wild beasts. Utensils also for every kind of workmanship were also objects of incalculable value to us. The vessel, which was now a wreck, had been sent out as a preparation for the establishment of a colony in the South Seas, and for that reason had been provided with a variety of stores not commonly included in the loading of a ship. The quantity of useful things which presented themselves in the store-chambers made it difficult for me to select among them, and I much regretted that circumstances compelled me to leave some of them behind. Fritz, however, already meditated a second visit. We took good care not to lose the present occasion for securing knives and forks and spoons, and a complete assortment of kitchen utensils. In the captain's cabin we found some services of silver, dishes and plates of high-wrought metal, and a little chest filled with bottles of all sorts of excellent wine. Each of these articles we put into our boat. We next descended to the kitchen, which we stripped of gridirons, kettles, pots of all kinds, a small roasting-jack, &c. Our last prize was a chest of choice eatables, intended for the table of the officers, containing Westphalia hams, Bologna sausages, and other savoury food. I took good care not to forget some little sacks of maize, of wheat, and other grain, and some potatoes. We next added such implements as shovels, hoes, spades, rakes, harrows, &c., &c. Fritz reminded me that we had found sleeping on the ground both cold and hard, and prevailed upon me to increase our cargo by some hammocks and a certain number of blankets; and as guns had hitherto been the source of his pleasures, he added such as he could find of a particular costliness or structure, together with some sabres and clasp-knives. The last articles we took were a barrel of sulphur, a quantity of ropes, some small string, and a large roll of sail-cloth. The ship appeared to us to be in so wretched a condition, that with the least storm she would go to pieces.

Our cargo was so considerable that the tubs were filled to the very brim, and no inch of the boat's room was lost. The first and last of the tubs were reserved for Fritz and me to seat ourselves in and row the boat, which sunk so low that, if the sea had been otherwise than calm, we should have been obliged to ease her of some of the loading: we, however, used the precaution of putting on our swimming-jackets.

It will easily be imagined that every moment of the day had been employed. Night suddenly surprised us, and it was no longer possible to think of returning the same evening. A large fire on shore soon greeted our sight – the signal we had agreed upon for assuring us that all was well. We returned the compliment by tying four lanterns to the mast-head. This was answered on their part, according to agreement, by the firing of two guns; so that both parties had reason to be satisfied and easy.

After offering up our earnest prayers for the safety and happiness of all, yet not without some apprehension for the night, we resigned ourselves to sleep in our tubs. The night passed tranquilly enough: my boy Fritz slept as soundly as if he had been in a bed, while I, notwithstanding my fatigue, could neither close my eyes nor keep them from the direction of the shore, perpetually haunted by the recollection of the nocturnal visit of the jackals. I had, however, great reliance that our valiant dogs would do their duty, and was thankful to Heaven for having enabled us to preserve so good a protection.

CHAPTER SIX

A Troop of Animals in
Cork-jackets

~

Early the next morning, though it was scarcely light, I was already on deck, endeavouring to have a sight of the tent through a spying-glass. Fritz prepared a good breakfast of biscuit and ham; but before we sat down to this refreshment, we recollected that in the captain's cabin we had seen a telescope of a much superior size and power, and we hastily conveyed it upon the deck. While this was doing, the brightness of the day had succeeded to the imperfect light of an earlier hour. I eagerly fixed my eye to the glass, and discovered my wife coming out of the tent and looking attentively towards the vessel, and we at the same moment perceived the motion of the flag upon the shore. A load of care was thus taken from my heart. A great object of my anxiety now was to endeavour to save the livestock and get them to shore.

"Would it be impossible to construct a raft," said Fritz, "and sail them ashore upon it?"

"But think what a difficulty we should find in completing such a raft, and that a greater still would be to induce a cow, an ass, and a sow, either to get upon a raft, or, when there, to remain quiet. The sheep and goats one might perhaps find means to remove, but for the larger animals, I am quite at a loss how to proceed. Do consider the point, and tell me what occurs to your imagination."

"I think, Father, we should tie a long rope round the sow's neck and throw her into the sea. She is sure to be able to swim, and we can easily get hold of the other end of the rope and draw her after the boat. Then here is another idea, Father: let us tie a swimming-jacket round each animal, and throw them into the water; you will see that they will swim like fish."

We accordingly hastened to carry out our design. We fixed on a jacket to one of the lambs and threw it into the sea, and full of anxious curiosity, I followed the poor animal with my eyes. He sunk at first, and I thought he was drowned; but he soon reappeared, shaking the water from his head, and in a few seconds we perceived that he could swim quite well. After another interval he appeared fatigued, gave up his efforts, and suffered himself without resistance to be borne along by the current, which conducted and sustained him to our complete satisfaction. "Victory!" exclaimed I; "these useful animals are all our own! Let us not lose a moment in adopting the same measures with those that remain, but take care not to lose our little lamb." Fritz now would have jumped eagerly into the water to follow the poor creature, but I stopped him till I had seen him tie on one of the swimming-jackets, and then I suffered him to go. He took with him a rope, first making a slip knot in it, and, soon overtaking the lamb, threw the noose round his neck, and thus drew him to our boat, and lifted him out of the water.

We then went and looked out four small casks, such as had been used for keeping fresh water. I emptied their contents, and then closed them again. Then I bound them together with a piece of sail-cloth. I strengthened this with a second piece, and this contrivance I destined to support the cow and the ass, two casks to each, the animal being placed in the middle. The weight of the animal pressed down the sail-cloth, and would have brought the casks into close contact on each side, but that I took care to insert a wisp of hay or straw, to prevent friction or pressure. I added a thong of leather, stretching from the casks across the breast and haunches of the animal, to make the whole secure; and thus both my cow and my ass were equipped for swimming.

It was next the turn of the smaller animals. Of these, it was the sow who gave us the most trouble; we were first obliged to put a muzzle on her to prevent her biting, and this being done, we tied a large piece of cork under her body. The sheep and goats were more docile, and we had soon accoutred them. And now we had succeeded in assembling our whole company on the deck, in readiness for the voyage. We tied a cord to either the horns or the neck of each, and to the other end of the cord a piece of wood. We struck away some more of the shattered pieces of wood from the side of the vessel, which only served to encumber the breach by which we had entered, and were again to pass to put out to sea. We began our experiment with the ass, by conducting him as near as possible to the edge of the vessel, and then suddenly shoving him off. He fell into the water, and for a moment disappeared; but he soon rose again.

Next came the cow's turn. As she was infinitely more valuable than the ass, my fears increased in proportion. The ass had swam so courageously, that he was already at a considerable distance from the vessel, so that there was room for our experiment on the cow. We had more difficulty in pushing her overboard, but she reached the water in as much safety as the ass; she did not sink so low in it, and was perfectly sustained by the empty barrels; and she made her way on the surface with, if I may so express it, a dignified composure. According to this method we proceeded with our whole troop, throwing them one by one into the water, where by and by they appeared in a group floating at their ease, at a short distance from the vessel. The sow was the only exception; she became quite furious, set up a loud squalling, and struggled with so much violence in the water that she was carried to a considerable distance, but fortunately in a direction towards the landing-place. We had now not a moment to lose; our last act was to put on our cork-jackets, and then we descended through the breach, took our station in the boat, and were soon out to sea, surrounded by our troop. We carefully took up from the water each of the floating bits of wood which we had fastened to the ends of the ropes round the animals, and thus drew them all after us. When everything was adjusted and our company in order, we hoisted our sail, which, soon filling, conducted us and our escort safe to the land.

We now perceived how impossible it would have been for us to have executed our enterprise without the assistance of the sail; for the weight of so many animals sunk the boat so low that all our exertions to row to such a distance would have been ineffectual, while by means of the sail she proceeded to our satisfaction, bearing in her train our suite of animals, which produced the most singular effect. Proud of the success of so extraordinary an enterprise, we were in high spirits, and seated ourselves in the tubs, where we made an excellent dinner. Fritz amused himself with the monkey, while I was wholly occupied in thinking of those I had left on land, and of whom I now tried to take a view through my telescope. My last act on board the vessel had been to take one look more at them, and I perceived my wife and the three boys setting out on some excursion; but it was in vain that I endeavoured to conjecture what their plan might be. I therefore seized the first moment of quiet to make another trial with my glass, when a sudden exclamation from Fritz filled me with alarm. "Oh, Father," cried he, "look! A fish of an enormous size is coming up to the boat!"

"Be ready with your gun, Fritz, and the moment he is close upon us, let us both fire upon him at the same instant."

Our guns were each loaded with two balls, and we got up from our tubs to give the intruder a hearty reception. He had nearly reached the boat, and with the rapidity of lightning had seized the foremost sheep: at this instant Fritz aimed his fire so skilfully that the ball lodged in the head of the monster, an enormous shark. The fish half turned himself round in the water and hurried off to sea, leaving us to observe the lustrous smoothness of his belly, and that as he proceeded he stained the water red. I determined to have the best of our guns at hand the rest of the way, lest we should be again attacked.

Fritz had reason to be proud of his achievement, while I on my part felt surprise.

I had always understood that this kind of sea-monster was not easily frightened, and also that the heaviest load of shot was rarely known to do him any injury, his skin being so hard as to present an extraordinary degree of resistance. I resumed the rudder, and as the wind drove us straight towards the bay, I took down the sail and continued rowing till we reached a convenient spot for our cattle to land. I then untied the end of the cords, and they stepped contentedly on shore. Our voyage thus happily concluded, we followed their example.

I had already been surprised at finding none of my family looking out for us, and was at a loss to conjecture in what they could be occupied to prevent them. We could not, however, set out in search of them till we had disencumbered our animals of their swimming apparatus. Scarcely had we entered upon this employment, when I was agreeably relieved by the exclamation and joyful sounds which reached our ears. It was my wife and the youngest boys who uttered them, the latter of whom were soon close up to us, and their mother followed not many steps behind, each and all in excellent spirits. When the first burst of happiness had subsided, we all sat down on the grass, and I began to give them an account of our different plans and their success, in the order in which they occurred. My wife could find no words to express her surprise and satisfaction at seeing so many useful animals round us.

"I had been ransacking my poor brains," said she, "every moment of your absence, to conceive some means by which you might succeed in protecting the poor animals, but I could fix on none."

"Ha! ha!" cried little Francis suddenly, "what is that I see in your boat? Look, Mother, there is a sail and a new flag floating about in the air. How pretty they are!"

Ernest and Jack now ran to the boat, and bestowed no less admiration than Francis had done upon the mast, the sail, and the flag. In the meantime we began to unpack our cargo, while Jack stole aside and amused himself with the animals; took off the jackets from the sheep and goats, bursting from time to time into shouts of laughter at the ridiculous figure of the ass, who stood before them adorned with his two casks and his swimming apparatus, and braying loud enough to make us deaf. Jack tried a long time to disengage the ass, but found difficulties he knew not how to overcome; till at last, tired out and longing to be in some way a more effectual actor in the scene, he got upon the ass's back between the casks, and kicked so violently against his sides that he at last succeeded in causing the animal to advance to the place where we were all assembled.

We laughed heartily at the sight of so singular an equipage, when, as I was assisting him to get down from the ass's back, I perceived with surprise that he had round his waist a belt of metal covered with yellow skin, in which were fixed a pair of pistols.

"Hullo, Jack!" exclaimed I, "where did you procure this curious costume, which gives you the look of a smuggler?"

"From my own manufactory," replied he. "And if you cast your eyes upon the dogs you will see more of my specimens."

I looked at them, and perceived that each had on a collar similar to the belt round Jack's waist, with, however, the exception of the collars being armed with a number of nails, the points of which were outwards, and exhibited a most formidable appearance.

"But where did you get the metal, and the thread, and the needle?"

"Fritz's jackal furnished the first," answered my wife; "and as to the last, a good mother is always provided with them. Then have I not an enchanted bag, from which I draw out such articles as I stand in need of? So, if you have a fancy for anything, you have only to acquaint me with it."

Fritz was somewhat angry and discontented on finding that Jack had taken upon him to dispose of his jackal, and to cut his beautiful skin into slices. He, however, concealed his ill-humour as well as he could. But, as he stood quite near to his brother, he called out suddenly, holding his nose as he spoke:

"What a horrid smell! It is enough to give one the plague! Does it come from you, Mr. Currier?"

"It is rather yours than mine," replied Jack in a resentful tone, "for it was your jackal which you hung up in the sun to dry."

"And which would have been dried in a whole skin if it had not pleased your fancy to cut it to pieces."

"Fritz," said I, in a somewhat angry tone, "this is not generous on your part. Of what importance is it who cut up the skin of the jackal, if it has contributed to our use? My dear children, we are here in this desert island in just such a situation as that of our first parents when they were driven out of the garden of Eden. Let us then share one with the other in every benefit bestowed upon us, and from this moment may the words *yours* and *mine* be banished from our happy circle! It is quite certain, Jack, that the belt round your waist, not being dry, has an offensive smell. The pleasure of wearing what you had contrived makes you willing to bear with the inconvenience, but we should never make our own pleasures the pain of another. I therefore desire that you will take it off and place it in the sun to dry; and then you can join your brothers, and assist them to throw the jackal into the sea."

Fritz's ill-humour was already over; but Jack, whose temper was less docile, persisted in keeping on the belt, assuming an air which was meant to express that he was not disposed to yield. His brothers, however, continued their warfare by pretending to avoid him, and crying out "What a smell! What a smell!" till at length Jack, tired with the part he had been acting, stripped off the belt, and ran to assist his brothers in dragging the dead jackal to the sea.

Perceiving that no preparations were making for supper, I ordered Fritz to bring us the Westphalia ham. The eyes of all were now fixed upon me with astonishment, everyone believing I could only be in jest. Fritz returned, displaying with exultation a large and excellent ham, which we had begun to cut in the morning.

"A ham!" cried one and all, clapping their hands. "A ham! and ready dressed! What a nice supper we shall have!"

"It comes quite in the nick of time too," said I, "for, to judge by appearances, a certain careful steward I could name seems to have intended to send us supperless to bed."

"I will tell you presently," replied my wife, " what prevented me from providing a supper for you all. Your ham, however, makes you ample amends, and I have something which will make a pretty side-dish." She now showed us about a dozen of turtles' eggs, and then hurried away to make an omelette.

"Oh, look, Father!" said Ernest, "if they are not the very same sort which Robinson Crusoe found in his island! See, they are like white balls, covered with a skin like wetted parchment! We found them upon the sands along the shore."

"Your account is perfectly just, my dear boy," said I. "By what means did you make so useful a discovery?"

"Oh, that is a part of our history," called out my wife; "for I also have a history to relate, when you will be so good as to listen."

"Hasten then, my dear, and get your pretty side-dish ready, and we will have the history for the dessert. In the meanwhile I will relieve the cow and the ass from the encumbrance of their sea accoutrements. Come along, boys, and give me your help."

I got up, and they all followed me gaily to the shore, where the animals had remained. We were not long in effecting our purpose with the cow and the ass, who were both animals of a quiet and kind temper. But when it was the turn of the sow, our success was neither so easy nor so certain. We had no sooner untied the rope than she escaped from us. The idea occurred to Ernest of sending the two dogs after her, who caught her by the ears and brought her back, while we were half deafened with the hideous noise she made. At length, however, she suffered us to take off her cork-jacket quietly enough. We now laid the swimming apparatus across the ass's back and returned to the kitchen, Ernest particularly delighted at finding that we were to have our loads carried for us.

In the meanwhile my wife had prepared the omelette, and spread a table-cloth on the end of the cask of butter, upon which she had placed some of the plates and silver spoons we had brought from the ship. The ham was in the middle, and the omelette and the cheese opposite to each other. The whole made a figure not to be despised by the inhabitants of a desert island. By and by the two dogs, the fowls, the pigeons, the sheep, and the goats had all assembled round us, which gave us something like the air of sovereigns of the country. It did not please the geese and ducks to add themselves to the number of our subjects; they seemed to prefer their natural element, and confined themselves to a swamp, where they found a kind of little crab in great abundance.

When we had finished our repast, I bade Fritz present our company with a bottle of Canary wine, which we had brought from the captain's cabin, and I then desired that my wife should tell us the promised history.

CHAPTER SEVEN

SECOND JOURNEY OF DISCOVERY
PERFORMED BY THE
MOTHER OF THE FAMILY

~

"You pretend," said my wife, with a smile, "to be curious about our history. Well, then, on the first day of your absence nothing took place, except that we were anxious on your account. But this morning, after catching sight of the signal you had promised, and having set up mine in return, I looked about before the boys were up, in hopes to find a shady place in which I might sit down and rest myself; but the only bit of shade which presented itself was behind our tent. This occasioned me to reflect on our situation. 'It will be impossible,' said I to myself, 'to remain in this place, without any other shelter than a miserable tent, inside which the heat is even worse than outside. Courage then,' said I, 'my husband and my eldest son are at this moment actively employed for the general good, why then should not I be active also? Why not undertake, with my younger sons, to do something that shall add some comfort to our existence? I will pass over with them to the other side of the river, and examine the country respecting which my husband and Fritz related such wonders. I will try to find out some well-shaded, agreeable spot, in which we may all be settled.'

"In the course of the morning Jack had slipped away to the side of the tent where Fritz had hung his jackal, and cut some long slips of skin, lengthways, from the back of the animal, and afterwards set about cleaning them.

"Jack completed the cleaning of his skins very cleverly. When he had finished, he looked out from the chest of nails those that were longest, and which had the largest and flattest heads; these he stuck through the bit of skin intended for the collar. He next cut a strip of sail-cloth the same breadth as the skin, and laying it along on the heads of the nails, politely proposed to me the agreeable occupation of sewing them together to prevent the heads of the nails from injuring the dogs. I begged leave to be excused; but observing afterwards the good humour with which he set about trying to sew them for himself, I conquered my repugnance, and rewarded him by completing the job myself.

"The next thing was a belt for himself; it being intended to contain his two pistols. 'But, my dear Jack,' said I, 'you do not foresee what will happen – a piece of skin not entirely dry is always liable to shrink. So you will not be able to make use of it.' My little workman, as I said this, struck his forehead and betrayed other marks of impatience. 'What you say is true,' said he. 'But I know what to do.' He then took a hammer and some nails, and stretched his strips of leather on a plank, which he then laid in the sun to dry quickly, thus preventing their shrinking.

"I next assembled them all three round me, and informed them of my plans, and you may believe I heard nothing like a dissenting voice. They lost not a moment in preparing for our departure; they examined their arms, their game-bags, looked out the best clasp-knives, and cheerfully undertook to carry the provision-bags. I, for my share, was loaded with a large flask of water and a hatchet, for which I thought it likely we might find a use. I also took the light gun which belongs to Ernest, and gave him in return a carbine. Turk seemed well aware that he knew the way, and proceeded at the head of the party. We arrived at the place at which you had crossed the river, and succeeded in passing over as securely as you had done.

"Ernest was first in reaching the other side, and met with no accident. Little Francis entreated me to carry him on my back, which appeared difficult enough, but Jack relieved me of my gun and hatchet. I had great difficulty to keep myself steady with the little burden at my back, who leaned with all his weight upon my shoulders. After having filled my flask with river-water, we proceeded on our way; and when we had reached to the top of the ascent on the other side, which you described to us as so enchanting, I myself experienced the same delight from the scenery around.

"In casting my eyes over the vast extent before me, I had observed a small wood of the most inviting aspect. I had so long sighed for shade, that I resolved to take our course towards it. For this, however, it was necessary to go a long way through a strong kind of grass, which reached above the heads of the little boys; an obstacle which we found too difficult to overcome. We therefore resolved to pursue a direction along the river, till it was necessary to turn upon the wood. We found traces of your footsteps, and took care to follow them till we had come to a turn on the right, which seemed to lead directly to it. Here again we were interrupted by the grass, which we had great difficulty in getting through. Jack was now loitering a little behind, and I frequently turned round to observe what he could be doing. At last I saw him tearing off some handfuls of grass and wiping his clothes with it; and then I perceived him shake his pocket-handkerchief and lay it on his shoulders to dry. I hastened back to him to inquire what had happened.

"'Oh, Mother!' said he, 'I believe all the water of the river has got into my pockets. Only see, everything I had in them is wet – pistols, everything!'

"'Mercy on us!' interrupted I in great alarm, 'have you put your pistols in your pocket? They are not loaded, I hope?'

"'I do not know, Mother. I only put them there while my belt was drying, that I might always have them about me.'

"'Thoughtless, yet fortunate boy!' exclaimed I. 'If with the suddenness of your motions the pistols had gone off, they would infallibly have killed you. Take care, I entreat you, not to commit such an imprudence in future.'

"In reality I perceived that there was little danger of their going off. While we were conversing about what had happened, our attention was interrupted by a sudden noise, and we perceived a large bird issuing from the thickest part of the grass and mounting in the air. Each of the boys prepared to fire, but before they could be ready the bird was out of the reach of shot. Ernest was bitterly disappointed, and instantly changed the gun for the carbine I had given him, crying, 'What a pity! If I had but had the lightest gun! if the bird had not got away so fast, I am sure I should have killed him. Ah, if one would but come at this very moment!'

"'A good sportsman, Ernest,' said I, 'always holds himself in readiness, this being the great art of a sportsman; for you must know that birds never send messages to give notice of their coming.'

"'I wish I could but know,' said Jack, 'what bird it was.'

"'I am sure it was an eagle,' said Francis; 'for I have read that an eagle can carry off a sheep, and this bird was terribly large.'

"'Oh yes,' said Ernest mockingly; 'as if all large birds must be eagles! Why, do you not know that there are some birds much larger even than eagles? The ostrich, for example; and there are others.'

"The boys now scampered away to the place where the bird had risen, when a second like the first, rushed out with a great noise, and mounted above their heads.

"The boys remained stupid with astonishment, following him with their eyes and open mouths, while I could not help laughing heartily.

"'Oh, such fine sportsmen as we have here!' cried I. 'They will never let us be in want of game, I plainly perceive. *Ah, if one would but come at this very moment!* These were your own words, Ernest!'

"Jack, with a comic look on his face, darted his eager eyes upon the flying bird, and taking off his hat made a profound bow, roaring out:

"'Have the goodness, Mr. Traveller, to pay just one more little visit, only for a single minute. I beg that we may have the pleasure of seeing you once again –'

"We now examined the place from which the birds had mounted, and found a large nest formed of dried plants, the workmanship of which was clumsy enough.

The nest was empty, with the exception of some broken shells of eggs. I inferred from this that their young had lately been hatched, and observing at this moment a rustling motion at some distance, I concluded that the young covey were scampering away in that direction.

"Continuing our journey, we reached the little wood. A prodigious number of unknown birds were skipping and warbling on the branches of the trees without betraying the least alarm at our presence. My dear husband, you cannot possibly form an idea of the trees we now beheld! In my whole life I have never seen a tree so immense. What appeared to us at a distance to be a wood, was only a group of about fourteen, the trunks of which looked as if they were supported in their upright position by so many arches on each side, the arches being formed by portions of the roots of the trees, of great thickness and extent. Meanwhile the tree itself is further supported by a perpendicular root, placed in the midst of the others, and of a smaller compass.

"Jack climbed with considerable trouble upon one of these arch-formed roots, and with a packthread in his hand measured its circumference, which he found was some twenty-two inches and a half. I made thirty-two steps in going round one of those giant trees at the roots. The twigs are strong and thick; its leaves moderately large in size, and bearing some resemblance to the hazel-tree; but I was unable to discover that it bore any fruit. The soil immediately round the tree and under its branches produced in great abundance a short, thick kind of plant, and of a perfectly smooth surface. Thus every circumstance seemed inviting us to use this spot as a place of repose, and I resolved to go no farther, but to enjoy its delicious coolness till it should be time to return. I sat down in this verdant elysium with my three sons. We took out our provision-bags; a charming stream flowed at our feet. Our dogs were not long in reaching us. They had remained behind, about the skirts of the wood. To my great surprise they did not ask for anything to eat, but lay down quietly, and were soon asleep at our feet. I felt that I could never tire of this enchanting spot. It occurred to me that if we could but contrive a kind of tent that could be fixed in one of the trees, we might safely come and make our abode here. I had found nothing in any other direction that suited us so well. When we had shared our dinner, and rested, we set out on our return, again keeping close to the river, half expecting to see along the shore some other vestiges of the vessel.

"But before we left our enchanting retreat, Jack entreated me to stay a little longer and finish sewing the linen strips to his leather belt. The little coxcomb had so great an ambition to strut about in his belt, that he had taken the trouble to carry the piece of wood, on which he had nailed his skin to dry, along with him. Finding that the skin was really dry, I granted his request. When I had finished my task, he eagerly fastened the belt round him, and placed his pistols in it. He set himself before us in a marching step, with the knuckles of his hand turned back upon his hip, leaving to Ernest the care of putting on the dogs' collars, which he insisted should be done, for it would give them, he said, a martial air. The little hero was all impatience for you and Fritz to see him in his new accoutrement, so that I had enough to do to walk quick enough to keep sight of him. In a country where no track of the foot of man is to be found, we might easily lose each other. I became more tranquil respecting him when we had got once more all together on the sea-shore, for, as I expected, we found there pieces of timber, poles, large and small chests, and other articles from the vessel. None of us, however, was strong enough to bring them away. We therefore contented ourselves with dragging all we could beyond the reach of the highest tide. Our dogs were fully employed in fishing for crabs, which they drew with their paws to the shore as the waves washed them up, and on which they made an excellent repast. I now understood that it was this sort of prey which had appeased their hunger before they joined us at dinner.

"We now suddenly cast our eyes on Ponto, whom we perceived employed in turning over a round substance he had found in the sands, some pieces of which he swallowed from time to time. Ernest also perceived what he was about, and did us the favour, with his usual composure, to pronounce: 'They are turtles' eggs.'

"'Run, my children,' cried I, 'and get as many of them as you can. They are excellent, and I shall have the greatest pleasure in being able to regale our dear travellers with so delicious a dish.'

"We found it difficult to make Ponto come away from the eggs, to which he had taken a great fancy. At length, however, we succeeded in collecting nearly two dozen. When we had concluded this affair, we by accident cast our eyes upon the ocean, and to our great astonishment we perceived a sail, which seemed to be approaching the land. I knew not what to think. But Ernest, who always thinks he knows everything, exclaimed that it was you and Fritz. Little Francis was terribly afraid that it must be the savages come to eat us up, like those described in Robinson Crusoe's island. We soon, however, had the happiness of being convinced that Ernest was right. We ran eagerly towards the river, which Jack and Ernest recrossed as before, while I also resumed my burden of little Francis at my back, and in this manner soon arrived at the place of your landing, when we had nothing to do but to throw ourselves into your arms! This, my dear husband, is a faithful narration of our journey; and now, if you wish me happiness, you will conduct me and your sons, with our whole train of animals, to the spot I have described."

My dear wife's story finished, I assured her how much I admired her courage.

"Tell me," said I, "if I shall make you a balloon of sail-cloth, to enable you to arrive at your country-seat?"

"Yes, yes," said she, "laugh as much as you like, but I assure you my plan is not so silly as you imagine. One advantage, at least, it is certain we should derive – the being out of reach of wild beasts. Do you recollect the large lime-tree in the public walk of the town we lived in, and the pretty little room which had been built among its branches, and the flight of stairs which led to it? What should hinder us from effecting such a contrivance in one of my giant trees?"

"I think it is a very good idea," said I.

Having finished our conversation, we performed our devotions and retired to rest.

CHAPTER EIGHT

CONSTRUCTION OF A BRIDGE

~

When my wife and I were awake next morning we resumed the question of our change of abode. I observed to her that it was a matter of great difficulty.

"First," I said, "we must contrive a place among the rocks where we can leave our provisions and other things, which may serve both for a fortress and a storehouse, and to which, in case of any danger, we can retreat. The next thing is to throw a bridge across the river, if we are to pass it with all our family and baggage."

"A bridge!" exclaimed my wife; "can you possibly think of such a thing? What reason can there be that we should not cross the river as we did before? The ass and the cow will carry all our goods upon their backs."

"But do you recollect, that to preserve dry what they carry they must not perform their journey as they did from the vessel? For this reason, then, if for no other, we must contrive a bridge. We shall want also some sacks and baskets; you may therefore set about making these, and I will undertake the bridge, which the more I consider the more I think to be of indispensable necessity, for the stream will, no doubt, at times increase, and the passage become impracticable in any other way."

"Well, then, a bridge let there be," said my wife. "But let us not allow ourselves a moment of leisure till we have completed all that is necessary for our departure.

You will leave our stock of gunpowder here, I hope, for I am not easy with a large quantity of it so near us. A thunderstorm, or some thoughtless action of one of the boys, might expose us to serious danger."

"You are right, my dear; and I will carefully attend to your suggestion."

Thus, then, we decided the important question of removing to a new abode; after which we fixed upon a plan of labour for the day, and then awaked the boys. Their joy on hearing of our project may easily be conceived; but they expressed their fear that it would be a long while before a bridge could be built, a single hour appearing an age to them, with such a novelty in view as the prospect of removing to the wood. In the fullness of their joy they entreated that the place might be called *The Promised Land*.

We now began to look about for breakfast, Fritz taking care not to neglect his monkey, who sucked one of the goats as quietly and as contentedly as if she had been his mother. My wife undertook to milk another, and then the cow, and afterwards gave some of the milk to each of the children: with a part of what remained she made a sort of soup with biscuits, and the rest she put into one of the flasks, to accompany us in our expedition. During this time I was preparing the boat for another journey to the vessel, to bring away planks and timbers for the bridge. After breakfast we set out; and this time I took with me Ernest as well as Fritz, that we might accomplish our object in a shorter time. We rowed stoutly till we reached the current, which soon drew us on beyond the bay; but scarcely had we passed a little islet lying to one side of us, than we perceived a prodigious quantity of sea-gulls, whose various and discordant sounds so disagreeably assailed us that we were obliged to stop our ears. I had a great curiosity to discover what could possibly be the reason of so numerous an assembly of these creatures. I therefore steered to the spot, but finding that the boat made but little way, I hoisted my sail that we might have the assistance of the wind.

To Ernest our expedition afforded the highest delight. Fritz on his part did not for a moment take his eyes from the islet where the birds had assembled. Presently he suddenly exclaimed: "I see what it is! The birds are all pecking at a monstrous fish, which lies dead upon the soil!"

I approached sufficiently near to step upon the land, and after bringing the boat to an anchor with a heavy stone, we walked cautiously up to the birds. We soon perceived that the object which attracted them was in reality an enormous fish, which had been thrown by the sea upon the islet, and whose body lay there for the birds. Indeed, so eagerly were they occupied with the feast, that though we were within the distance of half gun-shot, not one of them attempted to fly off. We observed the extreme voracity of this plumed group; each bird was so intent upon its prey, that nothing could have been more easy than to have killed numbers of them with our sticks alone. We did not, however, envy them their prize. Fritz did not cease to express his wonder at the monstrous size of the animal, and asked me by what means he could have got there.

"I believe," answered I, "you were yourself the means; there is every appearance that it is the shark you wounded yesterday. See, here are the two balls which you discharged."

"I do believe it is the very same!" cried Fritz, skipping about for joy. "I well remember I had two balls in my gun, and here they are, lodged in his hideous head!"

"I grant it is hideous enough," continued I. "Its aspect even when dead makes one shudder. See what a horrible mouth he has, and what a rough and prickly skin! Nor is he small of his kind, for I fancy that he measures more than twenty feet. We ought to be thankful to Providence, and a little to our Fritz also, for having delivered us from such a monster! But let us each take away with us a bit of his skin, for I have an idea that it may be useful to us. But how to drive away these eager intruders so as to get at him is the difficulty."

Ernest instantly drew out the iron ramrod from his gun, and in a few moments killed several of the birds, while all the others took their flight. Fritz and I then cut several long strips of the skin from the head of the shark, with which we were proceeding to our boat, when I observed, lying on the ground, some planks and timbers which had recently been cast by the sea on this little island. I therefore made choice of such as seemed proper for my purpose; and, with the assistance of the crowbar and a lever which we had brought with us, I found means to get them into the boat, and thus spared ourselves the trouble of proceeding farther to the vessel. I bound the timbers together, with the planks upon them, in the manner of a raft, and tied them to the end of the boat; so that we were ready to return in about four hours after our departure, and might with justice boast of having done a good day's work. I accordingly pushed again for the current, which soon drove us out to sea. Then I tacked about, and resumed the direct route for the bay and for our place of embarkation, by this means avoiding the danger of touching upon shallows. All this succeeded to my utmost wishes; I unfurled my sail, and a brisk wind soon conveyed us to our landing-place.

While we were sailing, Fritz at my request had nailed the strips of skin we cut from the shark to the mast to dry. Before very long he took a look at the drying strips. "Look, Father," he said, "you were wrong in telling me to nail my skins to the mast, for they have curled round in drying."

"That was precisely my intention," replied I; "they will be much more useful to us round than flat. Besides, you have still some left which you may dry flat; and then we shall have a fine provision of shagreen, if we can find out a good method to rub off the sharp points, and afterwards to polish it."

Ernest asked his brother if he knew why the mouth of the shark is not, as in other animals, placed in the middle of the snout, but directly under. Fritz confessed his inability to answer this question. "All I know is how to kill them," he growled.

"I suppose," rejoined Ernest, "that the mouth of the shark is thus placed with the intention of preventing him from depopulating the sea. With so voracious an appetite, nothing would escape him if he had the power to seize his prey without turning his body. But, as it is, there is time enough for a smaller animal to make his escape."

Presently we were once more landed safely on our shore, but no one of our family appeared. We called out to them and were answered by the same sounds in return, but in a few minutes my wife appeared between her two little boys returning from the river, a rising piece of ground having concealed her from our sight.

After we had all partaken of refreshment, we proceeded with our plans. I imitated the example of the Laplanders in harnessing their reindeer for drawing their sledges. Instead of traces, halters, &c., I put a piece of rope with a running knot at the end round the neck of the ass, and to the other end, which I passed between its legs, I tied the piece of wood which I wished to be removed. The cow was harnessed in the same manner, and we were thus enabled to carry our planks from the boat, piece by piece, to the spot which our architect, Jack, had chosen at the river as the most eligible for our bridge; and, to say the truth, I thought his judgment excellent. It was a place where the shore on each side was steep and of equal height. There was even on our side an old trunk of a tree, on which I rested my principal timber.

"Now then, boys," said I, "the first thing is to see if our timbers are long enough. By my eye I should think they are."

"Mother has some balls of packthread with which she measured the height of the giant tree," interrupted Ernest, "and nothing would be more easy than to tie a stone to the end of one of them and throw it to the other side of the river; then we could draw it to the very brink, and thus obtain the exact length."

"Your idea is excellent," cried I. "Run quickly and fetch the packthread."

He returned without loss of time. The stone was tied to its end and thrown across as we had planned We drew it gently back to the river edge, marking the place where the bridge was to rest. We next measured the string, and found that the distance from one side to the other was eighteen feet. It appeared to me necessary, that to give a sufficient solidity to the timbers I must allow three feet at each end of extra length, amounting therefore in all to twenty-four feet; and I was fortunate enough to find that several of those we had brought did not fall short of this length. There now remained the difficulty of getting them across the stream; but we determined to discuss this part of the subject while we ate our dinner.

We all now proceeded homewards, and entering the kitchen we found our good steward had prepared a large dish of lobsters for us. But before she would let us taste them she insisted we should see another useful labour she had been employed about. She accordingly displayed two sacks intended for the ass, which she had seamed with packthread. The work, she assured us, had with difficulty been accomplished, since for want of a needle large enough to carry pack-thread, she had been obliged to make a hole with a nail for every stitch. We might therefore judge by her perseverance in such a task of the ardour with which she longed to see her plan of a removal executed. She received on this occasion, as was well her due, abundance of compliments and thanks, and also a little good-humoured raillery. For this time we hurried through our meal, all being deeply interested in the work we were about to undertake. The impatience we all felt to begin scarcely left us time to strip the lobsters of their shells, each thinking only of the part which might be assigned him towards the execution of the bridge.

Having consulted together as to the means of laying our timbers across the river, the first thing I did was to attach one of them to the trunk of the tree of which I have already spoken, by a strong cord, long enough to turn freely round the trunk. I then fastened another cord to the other end of the beam. This cord I fastened round a stone, and then threw the stone across the river. I next passed the river as I had done before, furnished with a pulley, which I secured to a tree. I passed my second cord through the pulley, and recrossing the river with this cord in my hand, I contrived to harness the ass and the cow to the end of the cord. I next drove the animals from the bank of the river. They resisted at first, but I made them go by force of drawing. I first fixed one end of the beam to the trunk of the tree, and then they drew along the other end, so as gradually to advance over the river. Presently, to my great joy, I saw it touch the other side, and at length become fixed by its own weight. In a moment Fritz and Jack leaped upon the timber, and, in spite of my paternal fears, crossed the stream with a joyful step upon this narrow bridge.

The first timber being thus laid, the difficulty of our undertaking was considerably diminished; a second and a third were fixed with the greatest ease. Fritz and I placed them at such distances from each other as was necessary to form a broad and handsome bridge. What now remained to be done was to lay some short planks across them quite close to each other, which we executed so expeditiously that our whole undertaking was completed in a much shorter time than I should have imagined possible. I had not fastened the cross planks to each other, for they appeared to be close and firm without it; and, besides, I recollected that in case of danger from any kind of invasion, we could with the greatest ease remove them, and thus render the passage of the river more difficult. Our labour, however, had occasioned us so much fatigue, that we found ourselves unable for that day to enter upon new exertions, and, the evening beginning to set in, we returned to our home, where we partook heartily of supper and went to bed.

CHAPTER NINE

CHANGE OF ABODE

~

As soon as we had breakfasted the next morning, I assembled all the family together, to take with them a solemn farewell of this our first place of reception from the horrible disaster of the shipwreck. I thought it right to represent strongly to my sons, particularly to the youngest, the danger of exposing themselves as they had done the evening before, along the river.

"We are now going," said I, "to inhabit an unknown country. We are unacquainted both with the soil and its inhabitants, whether human creatures or beasts. It is therefore necessary to use the utmost caution; to make it a rule never to remain separate from each other. Particularly you young ones must take care not to run on before or stray too far behind."

I directed my sons to assemble our animals, and to leave the ass and the cow to me, that I might load them with the sacks as we had planned. I had filled these at the two ends, and made a slit longways in the middle of each of them, and to each side of the slit I tied several long pieces of cord, which, crossing each other and being again brought round and fastened, served to hold the sacks firmly on the back of the animal. We next began to put together all the things we should stand most in need of, for the two or three first days, in our new abode. I put these articles into the two ends of each sack, taking care that the sides should be equally heavy, and then fastened them on. I next added our hammocks and other coverings to complete the load, and we were about to begin our march when my wife stopped me.

"I cannot prevail upon myself," said she, "to leave our fowls behind us to pass the night by themselves, for I fear they would become the prey of the jackals. We must contrive a place for them among the luggage, and also one for our little Francis, who cannot walk so far. There is also my enchanted bag, which I recommend to your particular care," said she smiling, "for who can tell what may yet pop out of it for your good pleasure!"

Fortunately I had already thought of making the ass's load as light as possible, foreseeing that it would be necessary he should carry our little one a part of the way. I now placed the child upon his back, fixing the enchanted bag in such a way as to support him; and I tied them together upon the ass with so many cords, that the animal might have galloped without his falling off.

In the meanwhile the other boys had been running after the cocks and hens and the pigeons, but had not succeeded in catching one of them. "Well," said their mother, "see how you have heated yourselves in running after the fowls. I could have put you in a way to catch them in a moment."

"Yes, yes, you may think so, Mother," said Jack, a little sulky, "but I will give you leave to roast me in the place of the first fowl that you shall be able to catch."

"Poor Jack!" said his mother laughing, "you will then soon be on the spit, which would be a pity, considering what better things we might do with you."

She now stepped into the tent, and brought out two handfuls of peas and oats, and calling to the birds in her accustomed tones, they flocked round her, in a moment. She then walked slowly before them, dropping the grain all the way, till they had followed her into the tent. When they were all in, and busily employed in picking up the grain, she shut the entrance, and caught one after the other without difficulty.

"Grant me a reprieve from the spit, Mother," cried Jack, "and I will do all I can to help you in securing your prisoners."

Accordingly he soon caught the whole of the fowls. They were then tied by the feet and wings, and in a basket covered with a net, placed on the top of our luggage. Ernest suggested placing two bent sticks archways across the basket, and throwing a blanket over it, that the want of light might incline them to sleep, for with the clatter they made it was impossible to hear each other speak.

We packed up everything we were obliged to leave and placed it in the tent, which we carefully closed, and for greater security fastened down the ends of the sail-cloth at the entrance by driving stakes through them into the ground. We ranged a number of vessels, both full and empty, round the tent to serve as a rampart, and thus we confided to the protection of Heaven our remaining treasures. At length we set ourselves in motion. Every one of us carried a gun upon his shoulder and a game-bag at his back. Children are always fond of a change of place; ours were full of joy and good-humour. Nor was their mother less affected with the same cause. She walked before with her eldest son, the cow and the ass being immediately behind them. The goat, conducted by Jack, came next. The little monkey was seated on the back of his nurse, and made a thousand grimaces. After the goats came Ernest, conducting the sheep; while I, in my capacity of general superintendent, followed behind and brought up the rear. Our march was slow, and there was something patriarchal in the spectacle we exhibited. I fancied we must resemble our forefathers journeying in the deserts.

"Now then, Fritz," cried I, "you have the specimen you wished for of the patriarchal mode of life; what do you think of it?"

"I like it much, Father," replied he. "I never read the Bible without wishing I had lived in those good times."

We had now reached our bridge and advanced halfway across it, when the sow for the first time took the fancy of joining us, and contributed to the pictorial effect of our procession. At the moment of our departure she had shown herself so restive and indocile, that we had been compelled to leave her behind us. But when she saw that we had all left the place, she set out to overtake us.

On the other side of the river we experienced an inconvenience wholly unexpected. The nutritious aspect of the grass was too strong a temptation for our animals, who strayed in every direction to feed upon it, so that, without the assistance of our dogs, we should not have been able to bring them back to the line of our procession. The dogs, indeed, were of great use to us, and when everything was restored to proper order we were able to continue our journey. For fear, however, of a similar occurrence, I directed our march along the seaside, where there was not sufficient grass to attract the animals.

Scarcely had we advanced a few steps on the sands, when our two dogs, which had stayed behind, set up a loud barking, mixed at intervals with howling, as if they had been wounded, or were engaged in an encounter with some formidable animal. Fritz in an instant lifted his gun to his cheek, and was ready to fire; Ernest, always somewhat timid, drew back a step; Jack ran bravely after Fritz with his gun upon his shoulder; while I prepared myself to run to their assistance. Youth is always full of ardour, and in spite of all my exhortations that they would advance with caution, my boys, eager for the event, made but three jumps to the place from which the noise proceeded. In an instant Jack had turned to meet me, clapping his hands and calling out, "Come quickly, Father, come quickly! Here is a monstrous porcupine!"

I soon reached the spot, and perceived that it was really as they said, bating a little exaggeration. The dogs were running to and fro with bloody noses; and when they approached too near him, he made a frightful noise, and darted his quills so suddenly at them, that a great number of them had penetrated the skins of our valiant dogs, and remained sticking in them.

While we were looking on, Jack determined on an attack, which succeeded marvellously well. He took one of the pistols which he carried in his belt, and fired it so exactly at the head of the porcupine that he fell dead at once.

The boys were absolutely at a loss what means to use for carrying away the carcass.

They thought of dragging it, but as often as they attempted to take hold there was nothing but squalling, and running to show the marks made by the quills on their hands. "We must leave him behind," said they.

"Not for an empire," cried Jack, "shall he be left there, for Mother must have a sight of him."

In saying this, he tied one corner of his handkerchief round the neck of the animal, and drew him by the other to the place where we had left the dear mother in care of our possessions.

"Here is the monster, Mother," said he, "armed with his hundred thousand spears. But I was a match for him, and at one shot too! His flesh is excellent food, at least Father says so."

Meanwhile my wife and I had hastened to relieve the dogs, by drawing out the quills and examining their wounds. Having done this, we joined the boys round the porcupine. Jack took upon him to do the honours, as if he was showing the animal at a fair.

"Observe," cried he, "what a terrible creature it is! How long and hard his quills are, and see what strange feet he has! I am sure he must have run like a hare, but I killed him for all that! And what a singular sort of crest he has on his head!"

"That," said I, "is the reason why naturalists call him the crested porcupine. But now tell me, were you not afraid in going so near him that he would dart some of his quills at you?"

"Oh no, Father; I knew that the stories about his shooting his quills at you were merely fabulous."

"But you saw that many of them had stuck in the dogs."

"That was because the dogs attacked the animal and ran against his quills."

"Well, Jack, what do you mean to do with your prize?"

"Oh, take it with us, take it with us, certainly, Father, for you say its flesh is good to eat."

I could not resist his importunity, and I resolved to lay the porcupine on the back of the ass, behind little Francis, first having wrapped his bloody head in a quantity of grass, and then rolled him up in a blanket to protect my boy from his quills. We now resumed our journey, but had not proceeded far when the ass began to kick furiously with his hind legs, tore himself away from my wife, who was guiding him, and set off full gallop, braying so loud as almost to deafen us, and scampering from side to side in so extraordinary a way that the boys were thrown into fits of laughter, in which my wife and I should probably have joined, if we had not conceived the idea that the situation of Francis was not quite safe. A sign we made to the dogs made them set off like lightning after the deserter, whom they in a moment overtook, and stopped his way with a tremendous barking. We took our boy from the ass's back, delighted to find that he had scarcely even experienced any alarm.

"But tell me, Francis," said I jocosely, "have you been clapping spurs to your horse?"

I no sooner pronounced these words than suddenly I recollected the porcupine. I immediately examined if the quills had not penetrated through the covering in which I wrapped it. This I found was actually the case; though I had folded it three times double, the quills had pierced through all, and produced the effect of the sharpest spur. I soon found a remedy for this, by placing my wife's enchanted bag, which was filled with articles of a nature to be absolutely impenetrable, between the ass's back and the dead animal. I now restored Francis to his place, and we then resumed our journey.

Fritz had run on before with his gun, hoping he should meet with prey. What he most desired, was to find one or two of those large bustards which his mother had described. We followed him at our leisure, till at last, without further accident or adventure, we arrived at the place of the giant trees. Such, indeed, we found them, and our astonishment exceeded all description. "What trees! what a height! what trunks! I never heard of any so prodigious!" exclaimed one and all. "I must confess I had not myself formed an idea of the reality. To you be all honour, my dear wife, for the discovery of this agreeable abode. The great point we have to gain, is to fix a tent large enough to receive us all in one of these trees."

We began now to release our animals from their burdens, having first thrown our own on the grass. We next used the precaution of tying their two forelegs together with a cord, that they might not go far away. We restored the fowls to liberty, and then, seating ourselves upon the grass, held a family council. I was myself somewhat uneasy on the question of our safety during the ensuing night. I accordingly observed to my wife, that I would make an endeavour for us all to sleep in the trees that very night. While I was deliberating with her on the subject, Fritz, who thought of nothing but his sporting, had stolen away to a short distance, and we heard the report of a gun. This would have alarmed me, if at the same moment we had not recognized Fritz's voice crying out "Hit! hit!" and in a moment we saw him running towards us, dragging a dead animal of uncommon beauty by the paws. "Father, Father, look! Here is a superb tiger-cat!" said he, proudly raising it off the ground.

"Bravo! bravo!" cried I; "bravo, Nimrod the undaunted! Your achievements will call forth the unbounded gratitude of our cocks and hens and pigeons, for you have rendered them important service. If you had not killed this animal, he would no doubt have destroyed our whole stock of poultry. I charge you look about in every direction, and try to destroy as many of the species as fall in your way, for we cannot have more dangerous intruders."

"How did you kill him, Fritz?"

"With my pistol, Father, as Jack killed the porcupine. What is the exact name of the animal, Father?"

"You may for the present give it the name of the tiger-cat. I do not, however, think that it is the animal which is so denominated at the Cape of Good Hope. I rather think it is the margay, a native of America, an animal of extremely vicious dispositions and singular voraciousness; he destroys the birds of the forest, and neither a man, a sheep, nor goat that should fall in his way would escape his rapacity. We ought to be thankful to you for having destroyed so formidable an enemy."

"All I ask, Father, is, that you will let me keep the skin, and I wish you would tell me what use I can make of it."

"One idea occurs to me, and it is this: you must skin the animal yourself, taking the greatest care not to injure it in the operation, particularly those parts which cover the fore-legs and the tail. If you will do this, you may make yourself a belt with it, like your brother Jack's, except that it will be much more beautiful. The odd pieces will serve admirably to make bags to contain our knives, forks, spoons."

"And I too, Father, will make some cases with the skin of my porcupine," said Jack.

"And why should you not, my boy? The skin of the tiger-cat can only furnish us with four, and we ought to have six at least. So set to work, and show us quickly what you can do. I should like you to preserve some of the quills for me, for I think I can contrive to convert them into packing-needles, or into arrows. Those bits of skin that are left may serve to repair the dogs' collars when they begin to wear, or might be joined together and made into a sort of coat of mail, as a protection to them when they have to encounter wild beasts."

The boys left me no moment of repose till I had shown them how to take off the skins of the animals. In the meanwhile Ernest looked about for a flat stone as a sort of foundation for a fireplace, and Francis collected some pieces of wood for a fire. Ernest was not long in finding what he wanted, and then he ran to join us and advise on the subject of skinning animals, and then on that of trees, making various comments and inquiries respecting the name of those we intended to inhabit. "It is my belief," said he, "that they are large hazel-trees. See if the leaf is not of the same form."

"But that is no proof," interrupted I, "for many trees bear leaves of the same shape, but nevertheless are of different kinds. Besides, it appears to me that there is not so great a resemblance as you think between the leaves of the trees which grow here and those of the hazel, the former being of a paler colour, and white underneath. I recollect, too, that there is the wild mango and also the fig-tree, whose roots grow in the same manner as our giant trees, forming a beautiful arch."

"I thought, Father, that the mango-tree only grew on the sea-shore, and in marshy soils?"

"You are not mistaken, Ernest; the black mango-tree loves the water. But there is, besides, the red mango, which bears its fruit in bunches, something like our currant-bushes. This kind of the mango-tree is found at a considerable distance from the sea, and its wood is used for a red dye. There is a third sort, which is called the mountain mango, or yellow wood, and this is the kind whose roots produce the beautiful arches you now see around us."

Little Francis presently came running loaded with dry branches for his mother, his mouth crammed full of something, and calling out, "Mamma, Mamma, I have found a nice fruit to eat, and I have brought you home some of it!"

His mother, quite alarmed, made him open his mouth, and took out with her finger what he was eating with so keen a relish. With some difficulty she drew out the remains of a fig.

"A fig!" exclaimed I. "Where did you find it? Thank God, this is no poison! But nevertheless remember, Francis, that you are never to put anything in your mouth without first showing it to your mother or to me. And tell us where you got this fig."

"I got it among the grass, Father, and there are a great many more. I thought it must be good to eat, for the fowls and the pigeons, and even the pig, came to the place and ate them."

"You see, then, my dear," said I to my wife, "that our beautiful trees are fig-trees, at least the kind which are thus named at the Antilles, though they do not in the least resemble the tree called by that name in Europe, except that they both bear a fruit having some resemblance to the European fig. I now recollect that the leaves of the mango-tree are round, and not oval like these."

I took this occasion to give the boys a lesson on the necessity of being cautious, and never to venture on tasting anything they met with till they had seen it eaten by birds and monkeys. At the word monkeys they all ran to visit the little orphan, whom they found seated on a root of a tree, and examining with the oddest grimaces the half-skinned porcupine and the tiger-cat. Francis offered him a fig, which he first turned round and round, then smelled at it, and concluded by eating it voraciously.

In the meanwhile my wife had been employed in making a fire, in putting on the pot, and preparing for our dinner. She had put a large piece of the porcupine into it, and the rest she had laid in salt for another time. The tiger-cat was bestowed upon the dogs. While our dinner was dressing, I employed my time in making some packing-needles with the quills of the porcupine. I put the point of a large nail into the fire till it was red-hot. Then taking hold of it, with some wet linen in my hand by way of guard, I perforated the thick end of the quills with it. I had soon the pleasure of presenting my wife with a large packet of long, stout needles, which were the more valuable in her estimation, as she had formed the intention of contriving some better harnessing for our animals. I recommended her to be frugal in her use of the packthread, for which I should soon have so urgent a need in constructing a ladder for ascending the tree we intended to inhabit. I had singled out the highest and thickest fig-tree, and while we were waiting for dinner, I made the boys try how high they could throw their sticks and stones in it. I also tried, but the very lowest branches were so far from the ground that none of us could touch them. I perceived, therefore, that we should be under the necessity of inventing some method to reach so far, as otherwise it would be impossible to fasten the ends of my ladder to them. I allowed a short pause to my imagination on the subject, during which I assisted Jack and Fritz in carrying the skins of the two animals to the adjacent stream, where we confined them under water with some large stones. By this time we were called to dinner, and we all partook with pleasure of our porcupine, which had produced an excellent soup, and had no fault but that of being a little hard. My wife, however, could not prevail upon herself to eat of it; which occasioned Jack a little mortification.

CHAPTER TEN

CONSTRUCTION OF A LADDER

~

Our repast being ended, I observed to my wife that I did not think it would be possible for us to sleep that night in the tree. I however desired her immediately to begin preparing the harness for the animals, that they might go to the seashore and fetch the pieces of wood and such articles as I might find necessary for enabling us to ascend the tree, if, contrary to my expectation, it should be found practicable. She lost not a moment in beginning her work. In the meantime I set about suspending our hammocks to some of the arched roots of the trees. I next spread over the same arched roots a piece of sail-cloth large enough to cover all the hammocks, to preserve us from the dew and from the insects. Having thus made the best provision I could for the night, I hastened with the two eldest boys to the seashore to examine what pieces of wood might have been thrown up by the waves, and to choose out such as were most proper for the steps of my ladder. The dry branches of the fig-tree I would not use, for they appeared to me too fragile; and I had not observed any other kind of wood growing near that was sufficiently solid. There were, no doubt, on the sands, numberless pieces, the quality of which was fit for my object. Unfortunately, however, there was none that would not require considerable labour to be adapted to my purpose, and thus my undertaking would have experienced a considerable delay, if Ernest had not been lucky enough to discover a number of bamboo-canes in a sort of bog. I took them out, and with the boys' assistance completely cleared them from the dirt, and stripping off their leaves, I found that they were precisely what I wanted. I then began to cut them with my hatchet in pieces of four or five feet long; the boys bound them together in faggots proportioned to their strength for carrying, and we prepared to return with them to our place of abode. I next secured some of the straight and most slender of the stalks to make arrows. At some distance I perceived a thicket, in which I hoped I might find some young twigs, which I thought might also be useful. We proceeded to the spot, but apprehending it might be the retreat of some dangerous reptile or animal, we held our guns in readiness. Ponto, who had accompanied us, went before. We had hardly reached the thicket when we observed him make several jumps, and throw himself furiously into the middle of the bushes. Instantly a troop of large-sized flamingoes sprang out, and mounted into the air. Fritz, always too ready with his gun, instantly fired, when two of the birds fell down among the bushes. One of them was quite dead, but the other, slightly wounded in the wing, soon got up, and giving himself a shake, and finding that he could not fly, began to make use of his long legs, and to run so fast towards the water that we were afraid he would escape us. Fritz, in the joy of his heart, ran to pick up the flamingo he had killed. He plunged up to his knees in the water, and with great difficulty was able to get out again. Warned by his example, I proceeded more cautiously in my pursuit of the wounded bird. Ponto came to my assistance, and without him I should have lost all trace of the creature; but Ponto ran on before, caught hold of the flamingo, and held him till I reached the spot. All this was effected with considerable trouble, for the bird made a stout resistance, flapping his wings with violence for some time. However, at last I succeeded in securing him.

Fritz was not long in extricating himself from the swamp. He now, appeared holding the dead flamingo by the feet, but I had more trouble in the care of mine, as I had a great desire to preserve him alive. I had tied his feet and his wings with my handkerchief, notwithstanding which he still continued to flutter about, and tried to make his escape. I held the flamingo under my left arm, and my gun in my right hand. I made the best jumps I was able to get to the boys, at the risk of sinking every moment into the mud, which was extremely deep.

The joy of the boys was excessive when they saw that my flamingo was alive. "If we can but cure his wound and contrive to feed him, what a happiness it will be!" said they. "Do you think that he will like to be with the other fowls?"

"I know," answered I, "that he is a bird that may be easily tamed. But he will not thank you for such food as we give our fowls; he will make his humble petition to you for some small fish, a few worms, or insects."

"Our river will furnish him with all these," said Ernest.

"I hope you will take great care of him, boys."

"How delightful it will be," said Fritz, "if we can catch some other sorts of wild birds, and have a yard to keep them in! But look, Father, he is web-footed like aquatic birds, while his legs are long like the stork. Is not this rare and extraordinary?"

"Not at all, Fritz; many birds are able to both run and swim."

"But, Father," said Ernest, "are all flamingoes like this, of such a beautiful red colour, and the wings with purple? I think I have seen the flamingo in my *Natural History,* and the colours were not like these, so perhaps this is not a flamingo at all."

"I believe it is a flamingo, Ernest, and that this difference in the plumage denotes the age; when very young they are grey, at a more advanced age, white, and it is only when they are full grown that they are adorned with this beautiful tinted plumage."

"This dead one, then, is an old fellow, Father, and I am afraid he will make a tough dish. 'Shall we take him home to Mother?"

"Yes, certainly. I leave to you the care of carrying him in the best manner you can; in the meantime I shall repeat my visit to the canes, for I have not done with them yet."

I accordingly selected now some of the oldest of the stalks, and cut from them their hard-pointed ends, which I thought would serve for the tips of my arrows.

When I had done all I wanted, I began to think of returning. Ernest took the charge of all the canes; Fritz carried the dead flamingo, and I took care of the living one. We had not gone far when Fritz, addressing himself to Ponto, said, "Oho, lazy bones! so you think you are to be excused from any part of the burden; have the goodness to carry my flamingo on your back."

As he said this, he tied the dead bird upon his back without the least resistance from the patient animal.

"So then," said I, "Mr. Fritz intends to return quite at his ease, and without any part of our load, while his old father and his young brother carry each a heavy portion!"

"Your reproach is very just, Father," said Fritz. "Give me your live bird, and I will take care of him. See, he already gives me a kind look!"

We were now returned to the spot where we had left the three bundles of bamboo-canes, and as my sons were sufficiently loaded, I took charge of them myself.

We were at length arrived once more at our giant trees, and were received with a thousand expressions of interest and kindness. All were delighted at the sight of our new conquests. My wife immediately asked where we should get food enough for all the animals we brought home. "You should consider," said I, "that some of them feed us instead of being fed, and the one we have now brought need not give you much uneasiness, if, as I hope, he proves able to find food for himself." I now began to examine his wound, and found that only one wing was injured by the ball, but that the other had also been slightly wounded by the dog's laying hold of him. I anointed them both with an ointment composed of a mixture of butter and wine, which seemed immediately to ease the pain. I next tied him by one of his legs with a long string to a stake driven into the ground, quite near to the stream.

I now set Fritz and Ernest to work to measure our stock of thick ropes, of which

I wanted no less than some eighty feet for the two sides of the ladder; the two youngest I employed in collecting all the small string we had used for measuring, and carrying it to their mother. For my own part, I began to make arrows with a piece of the bamboo and the short, sharp points of the canes. As the arrows were hollow, I filled them with moist sand to give them weight, and lastly I tipped them with a bit of feather from the flamingo to make them fly straight. Scarcely had I finished my work than the boys came jumping round me.

"A bow! a bow! and some real arrows!" cried they. "Tell us, Father," continued they, "what you are going to do with them? Do let me shoot one! And me; and me too!"

"Have patience, boys; I say, have patience. This once I must claim the preference for myself, in order to make trial of my work, which I undertook rather for use than for amusement."

"Have you, my dear, any strong thread?" said I to my wife.

"Come," said she, "my pretty bag, give me what I ask you for! My husband wants some thread, and it must be very strong – See now, did I not promise you should have your wish?"

Just at this moment Fritz joined us, having finished measuring the rope. He brought me the welcome tidings that our stock in all was about five hundred fathoms. I now tied the end of the ball of strong thread to an arrow, and fixing it to the bow, I shot it off in such a direction as to make the arrow pass over one of the largest branches and fall on the other side. By this method I lodged my thread across the main branch, while I had the command of the end and the ball below. It was now easy to tie a piece of rope to the end of the thread, and draw it upwards till the knot should reach the same branch. We were thus enabled to measure the height it was from the ground, and it proved to be forty feet. Having now made quite sure of being able to raise my ladder by means of the string already suspended, we all set to work with increased confidence. The first thing I did was to cut a length of about a hundred feet from my ropes an inch thick; this I divided into equal parts, which I stretched along on the ground in two parallel lines, at the distance of a foot from each other. I then directed Fritz to cut pieces of bamboo-cane, each two feet in length. Ernest handed them to me, one after another; and as I received them I inserted them into my cords at the distance of twelve inches respectively, fixing them with knots in the cord, while Jack, by my order, drove into each a long nail at the two extremities, to hinder them from slipping out again. Thus in a very short time I had formed a ladder of forty rounds in length, and in point of execution firm and compact. I now proceeded to fasten it firmly to one end of the rope which hung from the tree, and pulled it by the other till one end of our ladder reached the branch, and seemed to rest so well upon it that the joyous exclamations of the boys and my wife resounded from all sides. All the boys wished to be the first to ascend upon it, but I decided that it should be Jack, he being the nimblest and of the lightest among them. Accordingly the rest of us held the end of the rope with all our strength, while our young adventurer tripped up the ladder with as much ease as if he were a cat, and presently took his post upon the branch; but he had not strength enough to tie the rope firmly to the tree. Fritz now assured me that he could ascend the ladder as safely as his brother; but, as he was much heavier, I was not altogether without apprehension. I gave him instructions how to step in such a way as to divide his weight, by occupying four rounds of the ladder at the same time with his feet and hands. I made him take with him some large nails and a hammer, to nail the ladder firmly to the branch. He set out courageously upon the undertaking, and was almost instantly side by side with Jack, forty feet above our heads, and both saluting us with cries of exultation. Fritz immediately set to work to fasten the ladder by passing the rope round and round the branch, and this he performed with so much skill and intelligence, that I felt sufficient reliance to determine me to ascend myself, and conclude the business he had begun. But before I ascended I tied a large pulley to the end of the rope, and carried it with me. When I was at the top I fastened the pulley to a branch which was within my reach, that by this means I might be able to draw up the planks and timbers for building my aerial castle. I executed all this by the light of the moon, and felt the satisfaction of having done a good day's work. I now gently descended my rope-ladder, and joined my wife.

I had directed the boys to descend first. My astonishment, therefore, on reaching the ground and finding that neither Fritz nor Jack had made their appearance, it is easier to conceive than to describe, their mother having seen nothing of them since they ascended the ladder. While I was endeavouring to conjecture where they could be, we suddenly heard the sound of voices which seemed to come from the clouds, chanting the evening hymn. I soon recognized the trick our young rogues had played me. Seeing me busily employed in the tree, instead of descending, they had climbed upwards till they reached a great height. My heart was now lightened of my apprehensions for their safety, and I called out to them as loudly as I could to take great care in coming down. It was almost night, and the light of the moon scarcely penetrated the foliage. They presently descended without any accident. I now directed them to assemble all our animals, and to get together what dry wood we should want for making fires, which I looked to as our defence against the attacks of wild beasts.

When these preparations were finished, my wife presented me with the result of the day's work she had performed. It was a set of traces and a breast-leather each for the cow and the ass. I promised her, as a reward for her zeal, that we should all be settled in the tree the following day. And now we began to think of our supper, in which she and Ernest and little Francis had been busily engaged. Ernest had made two wooden forks, and driven them into the ground to support a spit, upon which was a piece of the porcupine, which he kept turning at the fire. Another piece of the animal was boiling for soup, and both exhaled an odour which gave us an excellent appetite.

All our animals had now come round us, one after the other. My wife threw some grain to the fowls, to accustom them to assemble in a particular spot, and when they had eaten it we had the pleasure of seeing our pigeons take their flight to the top of the giant tree, and the cocks and hens perching and settling themselves, and cackling all the time, upon the rounds of the ladder. The quadrupeds we tied to the arched roots of the tree, quite near to our hammocks, where they lay down on the grass to ruminate in tranquillity. Our flamingo was not forgotten, Fritz having fed him with crumbs of biscuit soaked in milk, which he ate heartily. Afterwards, putting its head under its right wing and raising its left foot, the beautiful bird gave itself with confidence to sleep.

At last we had notice that our supper was served. My wife, still keeping her resolution of not tasting the porcupine, contented herself with bread and cheese. The children brought us some figs for dessert, which they had picked up under the trees, and of which we all partook with pleasure. And now the gaping of one of the boys, and the outstretched arms of another, gave us notice that it was time for our young labourers to retire to rest. We performed our evening devotions. I set fire to several of the heaps of branches; and then threw myself contentedly upon my hammock. My young ones were already cased in theirs, and we were soon greeted with their murmurs at being obliged to lie so close to each other that they could not move their limbs.

"Ah, boys," cried I, "you must try to be contented. No sailor is ever better accommodated than you are now."

I then directed them how to put themselves in a more convenient posture, and to swing their hammocks gently to and fro.

They profited by my advice, and all except myself were soon asleep.

CHAPTER ELEVEN

THE SETTLING IN THE GIANT TREE

~

I had thought it necessary to keep watch during this first night. Every leaf that stirred gave me the apprehension that it was the approach of a jackal or a tiger, who might attack some member of my family. As soon as one of the heaps was consumed I lighted another. At length, finding that no animal appeared, I by degrees became assured, and at last fell into so sound a sleep that I did not awake early enough for the execution of my project of that day. The boys were all up and about me. We took our breakfast and fell to our work. My wife, having finished her daily occupation of milking the cow and preparing the breakfast, set off with Ernest, Jack, and Francis, attended by the ass, to the seashore. They had no doubt of finding some more wood, and thought it would be prudent to replenish our store. I ascended the tree with Fritz, and made preparations for my undertaking, for which I found the tree in every respect convenient. The branches grew extremely close to each other, and in an exactly horizontal direction. Such as grew in a manner to obstruct my design, I cut off either with the saw or hatchet, leaving none but what presented me with foundation for my work. I left those which spread themselves evenly away from the trunk, and had the largest circuit, as a support for my floor. Above these, at the height of forty-six feet, I found others upon which to suspend our hammocks; and higher still there was a further series, destined to receive the roof of our tent, which for the present was to be formed of a large surface of sail-cloth.

The progress of these preparations was slow. It was necessary to hoist up to this height of forty feet beams that were too heavy for my wife and her little assistants to raise from the ground without great effort. I had, however, the resource of my pulley, which served to excellent purpose. My wife and her little boys fastened the beams to pieces of cord, while Fritz and I contrived to draw them up to the elevation of the tent. When I had placed two beams upon the branches, I hastened to fix my planks upon them. I made the floor double, that it might have solidity if the beams should be in any way warped from their places. I then formed a wall something like a park-paling all round, to prevent accidents to ourselves or children. This operation, and a third journey to the sea-shore to collect timber, filled our morning so completely that not one of us thought about dinner. For this once it was requisite to be content with ham and milk. Dinner ended, we returned to finish our aerial palace, which now began to make an imposing appearance. We unhooked our hammocks, and by means of the pulley hoisted them up to our new habitation. The sail-cloth roof was supported by the thick branches above. As it was of great compass, and hung down on every side, the idea occurred to me of nailing it to the paling on two sides, and thus getting not only a roof, but two walls also; the immense trunk of the tree forming a third side, while the fourth side contained the entrance of our apartment. This I left open, both as a means of seeing what passed without, and as a means of admitting air. We enjoyed an extensive view of the ocean and shore. The hammocks were soon suspended, and now everything was ready for our reception. Well satisfied with the execution of my plan I descended with Fritz, who had assisted me through the whole. As the day was not far advanced, and I observed we had still some planks remaining, we set about contriving a table to be placed between the roots of the trees, and surrounded with benches; and this place, we said, should be our dining-parlour.

Entirely exhausted by the fatigues of the day, I threw myself at full length on a bank, saying to my wife that as I had worked like a galley-slave to-day, I should allow myself some rest to-morrow.

My wife answered, that not only was I entitled to a day of rest, but that it was a duty to take it on the following day. "For," said she, "I have calculated that to-morrow is Sunday."

Unfortunately we had already passed one Sabbath day without recollecting that it was so.

"I thank you, my dear," said I, "for making this discovery, and I promise you that the day shall be celebrated by us as it ought to be. Now that we seem to have surmounted many difficulties, and to have secured ourselves an habitation, we should indeed be culpable not to celebrate the day He has consecrated."

The little company was soon assembled round the supper-table. Their mother followed, holding in her hand an earthen pot, which we had before observed upon the fire, and the contents of which we were all curious to be informed of. She took off the cover, and with a fork drew out of it the flamingo which Fritz had killed. She informed us that she had preferred dressing it this way to roasting, because it was an old bird, which would prove tough. The bird was excellent, and was eaten up to the very bones.

While we were thus enjoying our repast, the live flamingo stalked up to the place where we were sitting, in the midst of our flock of fowls, to receive his part of the repast, little thinking that it was his late companion that had furnished it. The live flamingo had now become so tame that we had released him from the stake. He took his walks gravely from place to place, and looked perfectly contented with his company. His fine plumage was most pleasing to look upon; while, on the other hand, the sportive tricks and the grimaces of our little monkey afforded the most agreeable spectacle imaginable. The little animal had become quite familiar with us: jumped from the shoulder of one to that of another; always caught adroitly the meat we threw him, and ate it in so pleasant a way as to make us laugh heartily. To increase our merriment, the old sow, which hitherto had shown an unconquerable aversion to our society, and which we had missed for two whole days, was now seen advancing towards us, grunting at every step. For this time, however, her grunting indicated her joy at having found us once more: and the joy was mutual, of which my wife gave her a substantial proof, by serving her instantly with what remained of our daily allowance of milk.

I thought her too generous, till she explained that it was necessary to contrive some utensils for making butter and cheese, and that till this was done, it was better to turn the milk to profit, than to let it be spoiled. And it was the more necessary as our grain began to run short, and that, as pigs are very fond of milk, it might be a means of preventing her wandering from us again.

"I always find you right, my dear," said I. "It shall not be long ere we again undertake another visit to the vessel to fetch a new provision of grain for your poultry."

"Again the subject of the vessel!" said she. "I shall never enjoy a moment's happiness till it is gone to the bottom, and you have banished it from your thoughts! You never make a voyage that does not leave me filled with agonizing alarm.'"

"I cannot deny," replied I, "that there may be reason for this. But I must remind you that we always choose a day of calm weather for our excursion; and we should be unpardonable, if we allowed ourselves to neglect the means of obtaining a variety of useful things which Providence seems to have reserved for our use."

During this conversation the boys had lighted one of the heaps of wood. Everyone was now eager to retire to rest, and the signal for ascending the ladder was given. The three eldest boys were up in an instant; then came their mother's turn, who proceeded cautiously, and arrived in safety. My own ascension was the last. I carried little Francis on my back, and the end of the ladder had been loosened at the bottom, that I might be able to draw it up during the night. Every step, therefore, was made with the greatest difficulty, in consequence of the swinging motion. At last, however, I got to the top, and drew the ladder after me. It appeared to the boys that we were in one of the castles of the ancient chevaliers, in which, when the drawbridge is raised, the inhabitants are secured. Notwithstanding this apparent safety, I kept our guns in readiness. We now abandoned ourselves to repose; our hearts experienced a full tranquillity; and the fatigue we had all undergone induced so sound a sleep, that daylight shone full in the front of our habitation before our eyes were opened.

CHAPTER TWELVE

THE SABBATH

~

On awaking in the morning, we were all sensible of an unusual refreshment, and a new activity of mind.

"Well, young ones," cried I jocosely, "you have learned, I see, how to sleep in a hammock."

"Ah," answered they, stretching and yawning, "we were so fatigued yesterday that it is no wonder we slept so soundly."

"Here, then, my children, is another advantage derived from labour; that of procuring a sweet and peaceful sleep."

"Yes, yes, Father, that is very true," said they, "so let us go to work again to-day. What is there to do?"

"Nothing at all, my children."

"Oh, Father, you are joking."

"No, my boys, I am not joking. This day is Sunday, and God said *six days shalt thou labour, but the seventh is the Sabbath of the Lord thy God*; and we will therefore refrain from all serious labour. Now let us descend to breakfast, and see to our animals."

Accordingly, after saying our prayers, we descended the ladder, and breakfasted on warm milk.

All now standing up, I repeated aloud the church service, which I knew by heart, and we sung some verses from the hundred-and-nineteenth psalm, which the boys had before learned.

My wife then brought from her enchanted bag a copy of the Holy Bible, which, most thoughtful of women, she had brought with her from the wreck. I read some passages from it to my family. In this solitude, in which for so long a time we had heard only our own thoughts expressed in simple enough language, we were singularly affected with the words of Scripture. I explained as well as I could what I read, and I gave the book in turn to each of the boys that they might read for themselves. I chose in preference such passages as were applicable to our circumstances. We then raised our hearts to God to thank Him for so signal a benefit as the preservation of our Bible.

My young folks remained for a time thoughtful and serious, but by and by each slipped away to seek the recreation he liked best.

Jack desired me to lend him my bow and arrows. Little Francis laid my activity under contribution, by requesting me to make him a bow and arrows, he being yet too young to be entrusted with a gun. I began with giving Jack the bow and arrows, as he desired, and told him how to put on the sharp points, and tie them securely round with packthread, and then to dip them into glue.

"Yes, yes, I understand," said Jack. "I know how to do it very well, Father. But will you tell me where there is a glue-shop."

"I will show you," said little Francis, laughing as he spoke. "Ask Mamma to give you one of her soup-cakes, which are exactly like good strong glue."

"Oh indeed!" replied Jack. "I want glue, not soup."

"Jack," cried I, "you will do well to follow Francis's advice. I believe that one of the cakes, with a little water added, and afterwards melted upon the fire, would produce a good substitute for glue. Give yourself therefore the trouble of making the experiment."

While Jack was preparing his glue, and Francis, proud of being the inventor, was busied in assisting his brother, Fritz came to me for advice about the making of his case. "Run," said I, "and fetch your skin, and we will work at it together." I sat down on the grass, took up my knife, and with the remains of a bamboo-cane began to make a bow for Francis. I was well satisfied to observe the boys, one and all, take a fancy to shooting with the bow, having been desirous to accustom them to this exercise, which might possibly become our only means of protection and subsistence.

While these reflections were passing through my mind, we heard the firing of a gun from the tent in the tree, and two birds fell at our feet. We were at once surprised and alarmed, and all eyes were turned upwards to the place. There we saw Ernest standing outside the tent, a gun in his hand, and heard him triumphantly exclaim, "I have hit them! You see, I did not run away for nothing."

One of the dead birds proved to be a sort of thrush, and the other was a very small kind of pigeon, which in the Antilles is called an *ortolan*. They are very fat, and of a delicious taste. We now observed that the wild figs began to ripen, and that they attracted a great number of these birds. I foresaw, in consequence, that we were about to have our table furnished with a dish which even a nobleman might envy us. My wife set about stripping off the feathers of the birds to dress them for our supper. I proceeded in my work of arrow-making for Francis, and observed to my wife that she would find in the figs an excellent substitute for grain to feed our fowls.

Thus finished our day of rest. The birds proved excellent; but in point of quantity, we ran no risk of indigestion.

CHAPTER THIRTEEN

CONVERSATION, A WALK, AND
IMPORTANT DISCOVERIES

~

Jack had finished the trial of his arrows: they flew to admiration. Little Francis waited with impatience for the moment when he should do the same, and followed with his eyes everything I did. When I had finished my bow, and prepared some little arrows for him, I must next undertake to make him a quiver; "for," said he, "an archer can no more be without a quiver than a sportsman without a game-bag."

I found I must submit. I took some bark from the branch of a tree, and, folding the edges over each other, I stuck them together with glue produced from the soup-cakes. I next stuck on a round piece to serve for the bottom, and then tied on a loop of string, which I hung round his neck. He put his arrows into it, and took his bow to try his skill by the side of his brother. Fritz had also cleaned and prepared his materials for the cases, when his mother summoned us to dinner. We cheerfully placed ourselves round the table I had manufactured. At the end of the repast, I made the following proposition to the boys.

"What think you," said I, "of giving a name to our abode, and to the parts of the country which are known to us?"

They all exclaimed joyfully that the idea was excellent.

Jack. "Oh pray, Father, let us invent some very long names, and that are very

89

difficult to be pronounced. I should be glad that those who shall read about us should be a little puzzled to remember the names of the places and things that belonged to us. What pains has it not cost me to remember their *Monomotapa*, their *Zanguebar*, their *Coromandel*, and many other still more difficult names!"

Father. "This would all be very well, but you forget that our own tongues will be fatigued by pronouncing such names as you propose."

Jack. "What pretty names can we find?"

Father. "We will name the places by different words from our own language; that shall express some particular circumstance with which we have been concerned."

Jack. "Where shall we begin?"

Father. "We shall begin with the bay by which we entered this country. What shall we call it? What say you, Fritz? You must speak first, for you are the oldest."

Fritz. "Let us call it *Oyster Bay*: you remember what quantities of oysters we found in it?"

Jack. "Oh, no! let it be called *Lobster Bay*; you cannot have forgot what a large one caught hold of my leg."

Ernest. "Why, then, we may as well call it the *Bay of Tears*, for you must remember that you roared loud enough."

My Wife. "My advice would be that we ought to call it *Providence Bay*, or the *Bay of Safety*."

Father. "This name is both appropriate and pleasing. Let it be *Providence Bay*. But what name shall we give to the spot where we first set up our tent?"

Fritz. "Let us call it simply *Tent House*."

Father. "That name will do very well. And the little islet at the entrance of Providence Bay?"

Ernest. "It may be called *Sea-Gull Island* or *Shark Island*."

Father. "I am for the last of those names, *Shark Island*, and it will also be a means of commemorating the courage and the triumph of Fritz, who had killed the monster."

Jack. "For the same reason we will call the marsh, in which you cut the canes for our arrows, *Flamingo Marsh*."

Father. "Quite right, I think; and the plain through which we passed *Porcupine Field*. But now comes the great question — what name shall we give to our present abode?"

Ernest. "It ought to be called simply *Tree Castle*."

Fritz. "No, no; that will not do at all. That is the same as if, when we wanted to name a town, we called it *The Town*. Let us invent a more noble name."

Jack. "Yes, so we will. I say *Fig Town*."

Fritz. "Ha, ha, ha! a noble name! Let us call it *The Eagle's Nest*, which has a much better sound. Besides, our habitation in the tree is really much more like a nest than a town, and the eagle cannot but ennoble it."

Father. "Will you let me decide the question? I think our abode should be called

The Falcon's Nest; for, my boys, you are not arrived at the dignity of eagles. Like the falcon you are, I trust, obedient, docile, active, and courageous. Ernest can have no objection, for, as he knows, falcons nest in large trees."

All exclaimed, clapping their hands, "Yes, yes, we will have it *The Falcon's Nest*! So, health to *Falcon's Nest Castle*!" cried they all, looking up to the tree and making low bows.

"And how," said I, "shall we name the promontory where Fritz and I in vain wearied our eyes in search of our companions of the vessel? I think it may properly be called *Cape Disappointment*."

All. "Yes, this is excellent. And the river with the bridge?"

Father. "If you wish to commemorate one of the greatest events of our history, it ought to be called *The Jackal's River*. The bridge I should name *Family Bridge*, because we were all employed in its construction, and all crossed it together on our way to this place. It will be quite a pleasure to converse about the country we inhabit now that we have instituted names."

Ernest. "It will be just as if we had farms and country houses all dependent upon our castle."

Francis. "It is the same as if we were kings."

My Wife. "And the queen-mother is not without hope that her little slips of majesty will conduct themselves mercifully towards their subjects – the birds, the agoutis, the geese, and the flamingoes; the — What more shall I say, for I do not know the family names of all your vassals? Let me therefore end by hoping that you will not depopulate your kingdom."

Fritz. "No, Mother, we will take care of that. We will extirpate only those among our subjects who are wicked."

After dinner Jack ran off, and returned presently, dragging after him the skin of his porcupine. He spread it at my feet, entreating me to assist him in making some coats of mail or cuirasses of it for the dogs, as I had before recommended to him. After making him clean the skin completely on the inside with some cinders and sand mixed together, I assisted him in cutting it, and his mother helped him in the sewing. When this was done we put the first that was dried on the back of the patient Turk, which gave him a warlike appearance, and no one could doubt that he was sufficiently well armed to encounter even a hyena.

His companion Ponto had less reason to be pleased with this spiked accoutrement. Turk, unconscious of one particular quality in his new dress, approached near to Ponto, who sprang off in a fright, searching for some place where he might be sheltered from the perforating familiarities of his companion. Jack's concluding business was stripping the skin from the head of the porcupine, and stretching it on one of the roots of our trees to dry, intending to make a cap of it, like those worn by the savages.

During our employment Ernest and Francis had been exercising themselves in shooting their arrows. The evening was advancing, and the intense heat of the day began to diminish. "Leave your work for this time, my boys," said I, "and let us make a short excursion. Where shall we go?"

Fritz. "Let us go to Tent House, Father. We are in want of powder and shot."

My Wife. "I too vote for Tent House. My butter is nearly gone, for Fritz took an unreasonable share for his tanning."

Ernest. "If we go to Tent House, let us try to bring away some of the geese and ducks."

Father. "To Tent House, then, we will go. But we will not take our accustomed road along the seashore, but rather explore some other way. We will keep along our own little stream as far as the wall of rocks, whose shade will accompany us almost as far as the cascade formed by Jackal's River. We will return with our provisions by the road of Family Bridge, and along the seashore; the sun, if not gone down, will then be at our backs."

All was soon arranged for our setting out. Fritz was adorned with a fine belt, made from the skin of his tiger-cat. Jack walked gravely on, his porcupine cap upon his head, and his jackal belt, armed with his two pistols, round his waist. Each carried a gun and a game-bag. Even little Francis had his bow in his hand and his quiver on his shoulder. My wife was the only person not burdened with a gun, but she carried her large butter-pot. Turk marched before us with his coat of mail studded with spikes, but it was apparent that he felt ill at ease. The monkey also, having a great desire to accompany us, leaped without ceremony on his accustomed seat, the back of Turk. But when he perceived the projecting spikes, he sprang forward four times, making the most comical grimaces. He was not long, however, in deciding what to do. Ponto, he saw, was without such a frightful saddle. So he jumped upon him in a trice, and clung so closely to his back that the dog could not shake him off. Even our new friend, the flamingo, prepared to make one of the party. The pretty kind-tempered creature had become every day more tame, and attached himself to us with a confidence which increased our goodwill towards him. The boys all contended for being his companion; but the flamingo adopted the prudent measure of coming up to me, and showing his reliance on my protection by walking gravely by my side.

Our route at first lay along the stream, sheltered by the shade of large trees. To prolong the pleasure of our walk we proceeded slowly, amusing ourselves with looking about us. The eldest boys made frequent escapes, running on before so that we sometimes lost sight of them. In this manner we reached the end of the wood. The country now appearing to be less open, we thought it would be prudent to bring our whole company together. On looking forward we saw the boys approaching us full gallop, and this time, for a wonder, the grave Ernest was first. He reached me panting for breath, and so full of joy and eagerness that he could not pronounce a word distinctly. He held out his hand, which contained three little balls of a light green colour.

"We have found a prize, Father!" cried he at last when he had recovered his voice. "We have found some potato-seed!"

"What say you – potato-seed?" inquired I joyfully. "Come near, every one of you, and let me see what you have."

I scarcely dared believe in so happy an event.

Ernest explained where he had found the plants, and we all hastened to the place. With extreme joy we found there a large plantation of potato plants. A part of them were covered with their lilac and yellow blossoms, the sight of which conveyed more pleasure to our hearts than if they had been the most fragrant roses. Another portion of the plantation was in seed. And in several places some younger plants were pushing through the earth. Our petulant Jack bawled out, jumping for joy:

"They are really potatoes! and though it was not I who discovered them, at least it shall be I who will dig them up!"

Saying this, he knelt down and began to scratch up the earth with all his ten fingers. He would not, however, have made much progress, if the monkey, excited by his example, had not also set himself to work. He dug up several potatoes with great dexterity. After smelling at them he was going to throw them to a distance, but Jack snatched them out of his paws and gave them to his mother. Afterwards the monkey and he continued digging up the potatoes together, and soon obtained enough to serve up for a dinner. The rest of us, unwilling to be idle, set to work also. With our knives and sticks we soon procured a sufficient number to fill our bags and our pockets. When we were well loaded we again began to think of our walk to Tent House. Some of our company raised their voices in favour of returning immediately to Falcon's Stream to prepare our booty for a delicious meal. But so many motives presented themselves for proceeding to our store-house, that it was decided we should continue our route.

CHAPTER FOURTEEN

CONTINUATION OF THE PRECEDING CHAPTER, AND MORE DISCOVERIES

~

Presently we reached the long chain of rocks, over which our pretty Falcon's Stream made its escape in the form of a cascade. We kept along the chain of rocks which led to Jackal's River, and from thence to Tent House, having first with difficulty pushed through the high grass. We saw many specimens of the Indian fig, with its large broad leaf; aloes of different forms and colours; the superb prickly candle or cactus, bearing straight stalks, taller than a man, and crowned with long straight branches, forming a sort of star. The broad plantain spread along the rocks, its innumerable boughs twisted with each other, hanging down perpendicularly, and ornamented with flowers, which grew in large tufts, and were of the brightest rose-colour; while that which pleased us best, and which was found there in great abundance, was the king of fruits, both for figure and relish, the crowned pine-apple. We immediately fell on this fruit with avidity, because we knew its value. The monkey was not the last to seize one for himself; and as he could make higher jumps than the boys, they formed the scheme of making him angry by little tricks, so as to induce him to fling pine-apples at them. This game they continued so long that I thought it prudent to interrupt them, fearing that the unripe state of the fruit might affect their health.

Soon after, I was fortunate enough to discover, among the multitude of plants

95

which grew either at the foot or in the clefts of the rock, the karata, many of which were now in blossom, and of others the flowers had lately fallen off. Travellers have given so perfect a description of them in their books of natural history that it was impossible I should mistake them. But what further confirmed their identity was their straight slender stalk, crowned with blossoms, and proceeding from a tuft of leaves like the pine-apple, with its large foliage terminating in a sharp point, and forming altogether a plant remarkably pleasing to the eye. I pointed out to the boys the immense size of these leaves, which were hollowed in the middle like a saucer, in which the rain is for a long time preserved; and also its beautiful red flowers. As I was acquainted with the properties of this useful plant, the pith of which is used as tinder by the negroes, who also make a strong kind of thread from the fibres of its leaves, I was not less satisfied with my discovery than I had been with that of the potatoes. I did not hesitate to assure the boys that I preferred it to the pine-apples. All answered me, their mouths at the same time full of the fruit, that they would resign these trees with all their flowers to me if I would leave them the pine-apples.

"The pine-apples are better than all the rest," said they, "even than the potatoes."

For answer I called to Ernest.

"Here," said I, "take out my flint and steel and strike me a light."

Ernest. "But, Father, what am I to do for tinder?"

Father. "This is precisely to the purpose. When the tinder which we brought from the vessel is all consumed, how shall we be able to make a fire?"

Ernest. "Oh, do like the savages – rub two pieces of wood against each other till at length they catch fire."

Father. "I think I can show you a better way."

I then took a dried stalk of the tree, stripped off the bark, and disclosed a dry spongy pith, which I laid upon the flint. Striking a spark with a steel, the pith instantly caught fire. The boys began to caper about, exclaiming, "Long live the tinder-tree!"

"Here, then," said I, "we have an article of greater usefulness than if it served merely to gratify the appetite. Your mother will next inform us what she will use for sewing your clothes when her thread from the enchanted bag is exhausted."

My Wife. "I have long been uneasy upon this subject, and would give all the pine-apples in the world for hemp or flax."

"And your wish shall be accomplished," said I. "If you examine, you will find some excellent thread under the leaves of this extraordinary plant, where all-provident nature has placed a store-house of this valuable article." I accordingly examined one of the leaves, and drew out of it a strong piece of thread of a red colour, which I gave to my wife. "We shall put the leaves to dry," said I, "either in the sun, or by a gentle fire. The useless part of the leaf will then separate by being beaten, and the mass of thread will remain."

I next drew attention to a specimen of the Indian fig or prickly-pear, a tree of no common interest. It grows in the poorest soils, even upon the rocks; the poorer the

"We returned to finish our aerial palace, which now began to make an imposing appearance." (Chapter 11)

"I have caught him! – I touched him!" cried Fritz…
"The tortoise is ours!" (Chapter 18)

soil the more its leaves are thick and succulent. "I should be tempted," said I, "to believe that it was nourished by the air, rather than by the earth. This plant bears a kind of fig, which is said to be sweet and palatable when ripened in its native sun, and it is a wholesome and refreshing food." Scarcely had I pronounced these words, than our light-footed Jack was on the rock trying to gather some of the fruit; but this time he had reason to repent his precipitation, for the fruit of this tree is covered with fine prickles. Poor Jack soon came down again, shaking his hand with the pain the prickles occasioned. I showed how to gather the fruit without incurring such inconvenience. I threw up a stone and brought down a fig, which I caught upon my hat. I cut off its two ends, and was thus enabled to hold it, while I peeled off the skin. I then resigned it to the curiosity of my young companions.

The novelty rather than the taste of the fruit made them think it excellent. They all found means to gather the figs, each inventing the best method of taking off the skins.

In the meantime, I perceived Ernest holding a fig upon the end of his knife, turning it about in all directions, and bringing it close to his eye with a look of inquiry. "I wish I could know," said at length our young observant, "what little animals these are in the fig, which feed so eagerly upon it, and are as red as scarlet."

Father. "Ha, ha! This, too, will perhaps turn out an additional source of usefulness which this plant possesses. Let me look at your fig. I believe it is the insect called the cochineal."

Jack. "What is the cochineal, Father?"

Father. "It is an insect that feeds upon the Indian fig, which, no doubt, is the cause of his beautiful colour, which forms an object of considerable importance in the trade of the dyer, for nothing else produces so fine a scarlet.

"There is another respect in which the prickly-pear is of great value. It is used for making hedges, its prickly surface preventing the approach of animals. You see that, besides those prickles which took such a fancy to Jack's hand, there is a large thorn at each of the knots which appear in the plant."

"The largest serve very well for pins," said my wife, "and even for nails. See how they keep my gown fastened."

"This, then," I continued, "is still another usefulness the Indian fig-tree can boast. You must perceive of what importance these enclosures are, and the rather as they are made with so little trouble. If you plant only one of the leaves in the ground it immediately takes root, and grows with astonishing rapidity."

"Oh, Father," said Ernest, "do let us make such a hedge round our tree! We shall then have no further occasion to light fires to preserve us from wild beasts, or even from the savages, who from one day to another may arrive in their canoes."

"And we could then easily gather the cochineal," said Fritz.

Conversing thus we reached Jackal's River, which we crossed, and very shortly arrived at our old habitation. We immediately dispersed, each in quest of what he intended to take away. Fritz loaded himself with powder and shot. My wife and I and

Francis employed ourselves in filling our pot with butter, the carrying of which on our return it was agreed was to fall on me. Ernest and Jack looked about for the geese and ducks, but the boys did not succeed in catching one of them. The idea then occurred to Ernest of taking a small bit of cheese and tying it to the end of a piece of string, and holding it to float in the water. The voracious animals hastened eagerly to seize it. In this way Ernest drew them towards him, one by one, with the cheese in its mouth, till he had caught the whole. We tied their legs together and fastened them to our game-bags, so that each had his share in carrying them.

We had thought of taking a stock of salt, but could not carry so much as we wished, the sacks being occupied with potatoes. I, however, thought of throwing a quantity into one of the sacks to fill up the space between the potatoes. In this way we secured a supply, but it made the sack so heavy that no one was willing to be encumbered with it. Fritz proposed that Turk should carry it; and accordingly we took off his coat of mail and left it at Tent House, and the sack was tied on the back of the kind-tempered animal.

We set out on our return, loaded with treasures, and the appearance of our caravan was even more amusing than it had been before. The ducks and geese, with their heads and necks stretching out at our shoulders, cackling with all their might, gave us a truly singular and ludicrous appearance. We could not help laughing immoderately as we passed the bridge, one after the other, loaded in so strange a fashion. Our jokes, and the general good-humour which prevailed, served to shorten the length of the walk, and we none of us were sensible of fatigue till we were seated under our tree at Falcon's Stream.

Chapter Fifteen

The Sledge

~

I had remarked on our return to the seashore, a quantity of wood, of which I thought I could make a conveyance for our cask of butter and other provisions from Tent House to Falcon's Stream. I had determined to go early the next morning, before my family should be awake, to the spot. I had fixed upon Ernest for my assistant, thinking that his indolent temper required to be stimulated. He felt as a great favour the preference I gave him, and he promised to be ready at a very early hour.

As soon as I perceived the first dawn I quietly awoke Ernest. He raised himself, stretching and gaping in his hammock. We descended the ladder without being perceived by the rest of the family. The first thing we had to do was to loose the ass, who was to be of our party. That he might not go without a load, I made him draw a very large branch of a tree, which I wanted for my undertaking.

When we reached the seashore we found the wood in great abundance. I determined to cut pieces of the proper length, and to lay them cross-ways on the branches which the ass had drawn to the place, and make them serve as a kind of sledge. We lost no time in setting to work, and we added to the load a little chest which we found quite close to the waves. We also provided ourselves with some poles which lay there, that we might use them as rollers, should we stand in need of them for passing difficult places, and then we set out on our return. When we were within a certain distance of our abode we heard a loud firing, which informed us that the attack upon the ortolans was in good train. On seeing us approach, all ran to meet us. The chest was soon opened by a hatchet, for all were eager to see what was within. It contained only some sailor's suits of clothes and linen, which was quite wet with the sea.

I next inspected the booty of the three sportsmen, who had shot in all no less than fifty ortolans and thrushes. They had had various luck, now missing and now hitting, and had used so large a quantity of powder and shot, that when they were about to get up the tree and fire from thence, my wife and I stopped them, recommending a more frugal use of those materials. I taught them how to make snares to be suspended from the fig-tree, and advised them to use the thread of the karata for the purpose. What is new always amuses young persons, and the boys took a great fancy to this mode of sporting. Jack succeeded in his first attempt. I left Francis to assist him, and took Fritz and Ernest to help me in making the sledge. As we were all hard at work, for my wife had joined the youngest boys, we suddenly heard a prodigious clatter among the fowls; the cock crowed louder than all the rest together, and the hens ran to and fro as if they were pursued by a fox.

"I wonder what is the matter," said my wife, rising. "Every day I hear the hens clucking as if they had been laying eggs."

At this moment Ernest happened to look at the monkey, and remarked that he fixed his piercing eyes on the hens. When he saw my wife approaching, driving the hens before her, the young rascal jumped quickly into a hollow place under one of the roots of the tree, and hid himself. Ernest ran to the place as soon as he, and was fortunate enough to seize him, seeing that he held a new-laid egg in his paw. The monkey sprang immediately to another hole, and Ernest followed. Here also he found some eggs, and brought them in his hat to his mother. The monkey was so greedy of this food, that he was sure to seize the eggs as soon as the hens had laid them. We inflicted no other punishment upon him for this knavery than that of tying him up when the hens were about to lay. By this means my wife soon collected a considerable number of eggs.

Meantime I was busily employed upon my sledge, which was soon completed; and I found that necessity had converted a preacher of moderate talents into a tolerably good carpenter. Two bent pieces of wood, the segments of a circle, formed the outline of my machine, which I fixed in their places by a straight piece of wood, placed across and firmly fixed to the bent pieces in the middle and at the rear. I then fastened two ropes to the front of my work, and my sledge was finished. As I had not raised my eyes from my work, I did not know what my wife and the two youngest boys had been about. On looking up, I perceived that they had been stripping off the feathers from a quantity of birds which the boys had killed, and that they afterwards spitted them on an officer's sword, which my wife had turned into this useful kitchen utensil. I approved of the idea, but I remarked on her profusion in dressing more birds at once than we could eat. She reminded me that I had myself advised her to half-roast the birds before putting them into the butter, to be preserved for future use. She was in hopes, she said, that as I had now a sledge, I should not fail of going to Tent House after dinner to fetch the cask of butter, and in the meanwhile she was endeavouring to be ready with the birds. I had no objection to this, and immediately determined on going to Tent House the same day, and requested my wife to hasten the dinner for that purpose. She replied that this was already her intention, as she also had a little project in her head, which I should be informed of at my return. I, for my part, had one too, which was to take a bathe in the sea. I wished that Ernest should bathe also; while Fritz was to remain at home for the protection of the family.

CHAPTER SIXTEEN

A Bathing, a Fishing, the Jumping-hare, and a Masquerade

~

As soon as Ernest and I had dined, we prepared for our departure. Fritz presented each with one of the neat skin-bags of his own workmanship, which we hung to our belts, and which held nicely spoons and knives and forks.

We now set about harnessing the ass and cow to our sledge. Each of us took a piece of bamboo-cane in hand, to serve as a whip; and, resting our guns upon our shoulders, we began our journey. Ponto was to accompany us, and Turk to remain behind. We took the road by the seashore, where the sands afforded better travelling for our vehicle than did the thick wild grass. We reached Family Bridge on Jackal's River, and arrived at Tent House without adventure. We immediately unharnessed the animals to let them graze, while we set to work to load the sledge with the cask of butter, the cask of cheese, a small barrel of gunpowder, different instruments, some ball, some shot, and Turk's coat of mail. These exertions had so occupied our thoughts, that it was late when we first observed that our animals, attracted by the quality of the grass on the other side of the river, had repassed the bridge, and wandered out of sight. I was in hopes they would be easily found, and I directed Ernest to go with Ponto and bring them back, intending in the meantime to look for a convenient place to have our bathe. In a short time I found myself at the extremity of Providence Bay, which ended, as I now perceived, in a marsh producing the finest bulrushes. Farther on a chain of steep rocks advanced into the sea, forming a kind of creek as if expressly contrived for bathing. Enchanted with this discovery, I called out to Ernest to come and join me, and in the meantime I amused myself with cutting rushes. Ernest neither replied nor came, so I resolved to go in pursuit of him. I at length discovered him at a distance, extended at his length on the ground, in the shade of Tent House. I approached him with a beating heart, and was agreeably surprised at finding him in a sound sleep, while the ass and the cow were eating the grass close by.

"Come, come, you must awake," cried I, shaking him. "While you are sleeping, your animals may once more escape."

He instantly awoke starting, and was soon on his feet.

"Oh, but I defy them to cross the bridge," said he, rubbing his eyes; "for I have taken away some of the planks, and left a space which they will have no inclination to jump."

Father. "Since your idle fit has rendered you inventive, I forgive it. But did you not promise your mother to carry her some salt?"

Ernest. "But, Father, I was planning something."

Father. "Pray tell me what study made you go to sleep?"

Ernest. "I was thinking how difficult it would be to bring away from the vessel everything which it contains."

Father. "And did you hit upon some method?"

Ernest. "No, Father; I fell asleep in the middle of my reflections."

Father. "So this is the hard work your head was engaged in. Discovering a difficulty, and finding no means for conquering it!"

Ernest. "At this very moment an idea strikes me. We ought to have a raft; but the beams of the ship are too heavy for the purpose. I think it would be better to take a number of empty casks, and nail planks upon them to keep them together."

Father. "This is a sound idea, but for the present, my boy, we must make up for lost time. Run and fill this little bag with salt, which you will then empty into the large one that the ass is to carry. During this time I will take the refreshment of bathing, and then it will be your turn to bathe and mine to take care of the animals."

I returned to the rocks, and was not disappointed in my enjoyment; but I did not stay long, fearing my boy might be impatient. When I had dressed I returned to see if his work had advanced; but he was not there, and I supposed that he had again fallen asleep. Presently, however, I heard his voice calling out:

"Father, Father, a fish! A fish of monstrous size! Run quickly, Father, I can hardly hold him!"

I ran to the place from which the voice proceeded, and found Ernest lying along the ground on his face, upon the extremity of a point of land, and pulling in his line, to which a large fish was hanging, and beating about. I hastily snatched the rod out of his hand, for I had some apprehension that the fish would pull him into the water. I gave a certain liberty to the line, to calm the fish, and then contrived to draw him gently along till I had got him into a shallow, from which he could no longer escape. We examined him thoroughly, and it appeared to me that he could not weigh less than fifteen pounds; our capture would afford the greatest pleasure to our steward of provisions at Falcon's Stream.

"You have now really laboured," said I to Ernest, "not only with your head, but with your whole body, so I would advise you to wipe the perspiration from your face, and keep a little quiet before you venture into the water. You have procured us a dish of great excellence."

"It was at least fortunate," observed he in a modest tone, "that I thought of bringing my fishing-rod."

Father. "Certainly it was. But tell me how you came to see this large fish, and what made you think you could catch it?"

Ernest. "I used to remark that there were many fish just hereabouts. This made me determine to bring my fishing-tackle. On my way to the place where we keep the salt, I saw a great number of little crabs, upon which fishes feed, near the water's brink. I thought I would try to bait my hook with one of them. So I hurried my task of fetching the salt, and came to this spot, where at first I caught only some very little fish, which are there in my handkerchief. Then I remarked that these were chased in the water by fishes of larger size. This gave me the idea of baiting my hook with one of the small ones. I put a larger hook to my line, and in a short time the fish seized the bait."

We now examined the smaller fishes he had caught, which for the most part appeared to me little herrings, while I felt certain that the large one was a cod. I immediately cut them all open, and rubbed them in the inside with salt. While I was thus employed Ernest went to the rocks and bathed, and I had time to fill some more bags with salt before his return. We then resumed the road to Falcon's Stream.

When we had proceeded about half-way, Ponto suddenly escaped, and by his barking gave notice that he scented some game. We soon after saw him pursuing an animal which seemed endeavouring to escape, and made the most extraordinary jumps. The dog continuing to follow, the creature in trying to avoid him passed within gunshot of the place where I stood. I fired, but its flight was so rapid that I missed. Ernest, who was at a small distance behind, hearing the report of my gun, prepared his own, and fired at the instant the animal was passing near him. He aimed so well that the animal fell dead. I ran hastily to ascertain what kind of quadruped it might be. We found it most remarkable. It was of the size of a sheep, with a tail resembling that of a tiger. Both its snout and hair were like those of a mouse, and its teeth were like a hare's, but much larger. The fore-legs resembled those of the squirrel; and were extremely short. But to make up for this, its hind-legs were very long. Ernest, after a long and close examination, interrupted our silence by an exclamation of joy. "And have I really killed this extraordinary animal?" said he, clapping his hands together. "What do you think is its name, Father? I would give all the world to know."

"And so would I, my boy; but I am as ignorant as you. So let us both examine this interesting stranger with attention, that we may be certain to what family of quadrupeds it belongs."

Ernest. "I think it can hardly be a quadruped, for the little fore-legs look more like hands, as is the case with monkeys."

Father. "They are legs, nevertheless, I can assure you. Let us look for its name among the mammalia. On this point we cannot be mistaken. Now let us examine its teeth."

Ernest. "Here are the four incisor teeth, like the squirrel."

Father. "Thus we see that it belongs to the order of Nibblers. Now let us look for some names of animals of this kind."

Ernest. "Besides the squirrels, I recollect only the mice, the marmots, the hares, the beavers, the porcupines, and the jumpers"

Father. "The jumpers! That word furnishes the clue; the animal is completely formed like the gerboa or jumping-hare, except that it is twice the size of those. . . . Wait a moment, an idea strikes me. I will lay a wager that our animal is one of the large jumpers, called kangaroo; it belongs properly to the genus *Didelphis* or *Philander*, because the female, who never bears more than one young one, carries it in a kind of purse placed between her hind-legs. To the best of my knowledge this animal has never been seen but on the coast of New Holland, where it was first observed by the celebrated navigator Captain Cook."

I now tied the fore-legs of the kangaroo together, and by means of two canes, we contrived to carry it to the sledge.

Ponto was still scampering about in the tall grass. We called him to us, and having continued our road, Ernest entreated me to tell him all I knew about the kangaroo. "It is," said I, "a most singular creature. Its fore-legs, as you see, have scarcely the third part of the length of the hind ones, and the most it can do is to make them serve to help in walking. But the hind-legs enable it to make prodigious jumps. The food of the kangaroo consists of herbs and roots, which they dig up very skilfully with their fore-legs. They place themselves upon their hind-legs, which are doubled under them, as if on a chair, and by this means are able to look above even the tall kinds of grass. They rest too upon their tail, which is exceedingly strong, and is also of great use to them in jumping, by assisting the spring from the ground.

We at length arrived happily, though somewhat late, at Falcon's Stream, having heard from a great distance the kind welcome of the salutations of our family. Our companions all ran to meet us. But it was now, on seeing the ludicrous style of the dress of the three boys, our turn for laughter. One had on a sailor's shirt, which trained round him like the robe of a spectre. Another was buried in a pair of pantaloons, which were fastened round his neck and reached to the ground. The third had a long waistcoat which came down to the instep. They all tried to jump about, but finding this impossible from the length of their garments, they next resolved to carry off the whole with an air, by strutting slowly to and fro in the manner of a great personage in a theatre. After some hearty laughing, I inquired of my wife the cause of this masquerade, and whether she had assisted them in attempting to act a comedy. She disclosed the mystery by informing me that her three boys had also been into the water to bathe, and that while they were thus engaged she had washed all their clothes; but as they had not dried so soon as she expected, her little rioters had become impatient, and had fallen on the chest of sailor's clothes, and each had taken from it what article he pleased. "I preferred," said she, "that you should see them in this odd sort of a disguise rather than quite naked, like little savages." In which opinion I assured her that I heartily joined.

It was now our turn to give an account of our journey. In proportion as we advanced in our narrative, we presented, one after another, casks, bulrushes, salt, fish, and lastly, our beautiful kangaroo. In a trice it was surrounded, examined, and admired by all, and such a variety of questions asked, that Ernest and I scarcely knew which to answer first. Fritz was the only one who was a little silent. I saw plainly by his countenance what was passing in his mind. He was jealous of his brother Ernest. But I also saw that he was struggling manfully against so mean a passion. In a short time he had succeeded so completely that he joined frankly in our conversation, and I am persuaded no one but myself perceived what was passing in his mind. He came near the kangaroo and examined it with great attention. Then, turning to his brother, he observed to him in a kind tone that he had had good luck, and that he must be a good shot. "But, Father," said he, "when you go again to Tent House, or on any other excursion, will it not be my turn to go with you? For here at Falcon's Stream there is nothing new to amuse us; a few thrushes and some pigeons."

"I promise you what you desire, my dear boy," said I, "for you have valiantly combated the ill-humour which assailed you on witnessing your brother's success. I promise that you shall accompany me in my next excursion, which will probably take place to-morrow. It will be another journey to the vessel."

We concluded the day with our ordinary occupations. I gave some salt to each of our animals, to whom it was an acceptable treat. We next skinned our kangaroo, and put it carefully aside till the next day, when we intended to cut it to pieces, and lay such parts in salt as we could not immediately consume. We made an excellent supper on our little fish, to which we added some potatoes. The labours of the day had more than usually disposed us all to seek repose; we therefore said our prayers at an early hour, mounted our ladder, and were soon asleep.

CHAPTER SEVENTEEN

MORE STORES FROM THE WRECK

~

$\mathcal{I}$ rose with the first crowing of the cock, before the rest of the family were
awake, descended the ladder, and employed myself in carefully skinning
the kangaroo. This gave me so much trouble that all my little family were assembled
about me and their mother, and calling out "Famine!" before I had finished my work.
Having completed it, I went to the stream to wash, and then to the sailor's chest to
change my coat, that I might make a decent appearance at breakfast, and give my
sons an example of cleanliness. Breakfast over, I ordered Fritz to prepare everything
to go to Tent House, and prepare our boat, that we might proceed to the vessel. At
the moment of departure I found that Ernest and Jack were wanting. Their mother
knew no more than myself what was become of them, but she thought they were
gone to get some potatoes. I charged her to reprove them a little for this, to prevent
their accustoming themselves to stray from home alone and without leave in an
unknown country. But they had taken Turk along with them this time, and I was
therefore the less uneasy.

We began our journey after having taken an affectionate leave of my wife and of
my little Francis. I left Ponto with her, and I entreated her not to be uneasy, and to
commit herself to the care of Providence.

We soon reached and crossed the bridge. At this moment, to our astonishment, we heard the shrill sounds of human voices, and almost at the same time we saw Ernest and Master Jack come forth from a bush, delighted to have half-alarmed us. "Ah! did not you think we were savages?" said Jack.

"'Rather," said I, "two little rogues I am much inclined to chide for having left their home without permission."

"Oh, Father," said Ernest, "we do wish so much to go with you to the vessel, and we were afraid you would refuse us; but we thought that when you saw us so near, you would consent."

"Very badly argued, my young gentleman," replied I. "At Falcon's Stream I might perhaps have consented, although I have so many things to take that it would be wrong to let you occupy a place in the boat, but as it is, I would on no account leave your mother in anxiety the whole day as to what is become of you. I have a commission to give you for her that I have much at heart."

I then requested them to tell her that it was probable we should be forced to pass the night on board the vessel.

It was essential that we should get out of the vessel, if it yet remained afloat, all that could be saved, as every moment might complete its destruction. With this view I told my sons what they should say to their mother. I exhorted them to obey and assist her; and made them collect some salt, and I enjoined them to be at Falcon's Stream before noon. To be sure of the fulfilment of this order, I requested Fritz to lend Ernest his silver watch, and told him he would find a gold one in the vessel, in which case he would allow his brother to keep the one he lent him, and that we might perhaps get another for Jack. This hope consoled them for not going on with us.

After having bid adieu to our dear boys, we got into the boat, and we left the shore to gain the current. We quickly cleared Safety Bay, and reached the vessel. As soon as we had got on board and our boat was securely fastened, our first care was to look out for fit materials to construct a raft. I wished to begin by executing the idea suggested by Ernest. Our boat of staves had neither room nor solidity enough to carry a considerable burden. We soon found a sufficient number of water-casks, which appeared to me very proper for my new enterprise. We emptied them, then replaced the bungs, and threw the casks overboard, after securing them by means of ropes and cramps, so as to keep them together at the vessel's side. This completed, we placed planks upon them to form a firm and commodious platform, to which we added a gunwale of a foot in depth all round to secure the lading. Thus we contrived to possess a raft in which we could stow thrice as much as in our boat. This laborious task had taken up the whole day. We scarcely allowed ourselves a minute to eat a mouthful of cold meat we had provided for the expedition. In the evening Fritz and I were so weary that it would have been impossible for us to row back to land, even if our business had not detained us. We therefore came to the resolution of passing the night on board; and having taken all precautions in case of a storm, we reposed in the captain's cabin, on a good elastic mattress. In fact, it induced such sound repose, that our design to watch in turn quite escaped us, and we slept heavily side by side, till broad daylight opened our eyes, when we awoke with gratitude to that Providence to whom we were indebted for the quiet night. We rose and actively set to work to load our raft.

In the first place, we completely stripped the cabin which had been occupied by my family on board the vessel, removing everything it contained which belonged to us. Then we proceeded to the cabin in which we had slept and carried off the very doors and windows. Some valuable chests of the officers were there; but this discovery, and the rich lace clothes which seemed to court our grasp, were less acceptable to us than the carpenter's and gunner's chests, containing tools and implements. Those which we could remove with levers and rollers were put entire upon the raft, and we took out of the others the things that made them too heavy. One of the captain's chests was filled with costly articles, which no doubt he meant to dispose of to the opulent planters of Port Jackson, or among the savages. In the collection were several gold, and silver watches, snuff-boxes of all descriptions, buckles, shirt-buttons, necklaces, and rings – in short, an abundance of all the trifles of European luxury. There was also a strong-box full of louis d'or and dollars, which attracted our notice less than another containing a very pretty table-service of fine steel, which we had substituted for the captain's, that were silver, and for which my wife had shown no small regard. But the discovery that delighted me most, and for which I would readily have given the box of louis d'or, &c., was a chest containing some dozens of young plants of every species of European fruits. I perceived pear, plum, almond, peach, apple, apricot, chestnut-trees, and vine-shoots. I beheld with a feeling I cannot describe those productions of my dear country, which, if God vouchsafed to bless them, would thrive in a foreign soil. We discovered a number of bars of iron and large pigs of lead, grinding-stones, cartwheels ready for mounting, a complete set of farrier's instruments, tongs, shovels, ploughshares, rolls of iron and copper wire, sacks of maize, pease, oats, vetches, and even a little hand-mill. The vessel had been freighted with everything likely to be useful in an infant colony so distant. We found a saw-mill in a separated state, but each piece numbered and so accurately fitted that nothing was easier than to put it together.

I had now to consider what of all these treasures I should take. It was impossible to carry with us in one trip such a quantity, and to leave them in the vessel, threatened every moment with destruction, was exposing ourselves to be wholly deprived of them.

"Ah," said Fritz, "let us leave, in the first place, this useless money and the chest of trinkets."

"It gives me pleasure, my boy, to hear you speak thus. We will do, then, as you wish, and determine upon taking with us what is useful, such as the powder, lead, iron, the corn and the fruit-trees, implements for gardening and agriculture. Let us take as many as possible of these last. If we should have any room left, we can then select a few of the objects of luxury. However, begin by taking from the chest the two watches I have promised, and one for yourself."

We then loaded our raft, we, moreover, stowed away a large and handsome fishing-net, quite new, and the vessel's great compass. With the net, Fritz found luckily two harpoons and a rope windlass, such as they use in the whale fishery. Fritz asked me to let him place the windlass, with the harpoons attached to the end of the rope, over the bow of our tub-boat, and thus hold all in readiness in case of seeing any large fish. I indulged him in his innocent fancy.

It was afternoon before we had finished our lading, for not only our raft was as full as it could hold, but our boat likewise.

Having completely executed our undertaking, both as to construction and lading, we stepped into the tub-boat, and with some small difficulty pushed out for the current, drawing our raft triumphantly after us with a stout rope.

CHAPTER EIGHTEEN

THE TORTOISE HARNESSED

~

The wind was in a humour favourable to our undertaking, and briskly swelled our sail. The sea was calm, and we advanced at a considerable rate. Fritz had been looking steadfastly for some time at something of a large size which was floating on the water, and now desired me to take the glass and see what it could be. I soon perceived distinctly that it was a tortoise, which, agreeably to the habits of its singular species, had fallen asleep in the sun on the surface of the water. No sooner had Fritz learned this, than he earnestly entreated me to steer softly within view of so extraordinary a creature, that he might examine it. I readily consented. But as his back was towards me, and the sail was between us, I did not observe what he was about till I felt a violent jerk, a sudden turning of the windlass, accompanied by a rapid motion of the boat.

"Whatever are you about, Fritz?" exclaimed I.

"I have caught him! – I touched him!" cried Fritz, without hearing one word I had been saying. "The tortoise is ours! Is not this a valuable prize, for it will furnish dinners for weeks?"

I soon admitted that the harpoon had secured the animal, which thus agitated the vessel in its endeavours to be disengaged, for the rope of the harpoon was fastened to the windlass. I quickly pulled down the sail, and seizing a hatchet sprang to the boat's head to cut the rope and let the harpoon and the tortoise go; but Fritz caught hold of my arm, begging me to wait a moment, and not bring upon him the mortification of losing, at one stroke, the harpoon, the rope, and the tortoise. He proposed watching himself with the hatchet in his hand to cut the rope should any danger appear. I yielded to his entreaties, after a due exhortation to him to take care.

Thus then, we proceeded with a hazardous rapidity, and having no small difficulty to keep the head of the boat in a straight direction, and keep her steady. In a little time I observed that the creature was making for the sea. I therefore again hoisted the sail. As the wind was to the land, and very brisk, the tortoise found resistance of no avail. He accordingly fell into the track we desired to take, and we soon gained the current which had always received us. He drew us straight towards our usual place of landing, and by good fortune without striking upon any of the rocks. We, however, did not disembark without encountering one adventure. I perceived that the state of the tide was such that we should be thrown upon one of the sand-banks, which indeed took place. We were at this time within a gunshot of the shore. The boat, though driven with violence, remained upright in the sand. I stepped into the water for the purpose of conferring upon our conductor his reward for the alarm he had caused us, when he suddenly gave a plunge, and I saw him no more. Following the rope I however soon found the tortoise at the bottom, where it was so shallow that I was not long in finding means to put an end to his pain by cutting off his head with the hatchet. Being now near Tent House, Fritz gave a halloo and fired a gun, to apprise our relatives that we were arrived in triumph. The good mother and her three young ones soon appeared, running towards us. Upon which Fritz jumped out of the boat, placed the head of our prize on the muzzle of his gun, and walked to shore, which I reached at the same moment.

After some gentle reproaches from my wife for leaving her and the boys for so long a time, the history of the tortoise was related in due form. The tender-hearted mother began to shudder at the thought of the danger we had been exposed to. We all now fell to a new examination of the adventure, and were struck with surprise that Fritz should so exactly have hit the vulnerable part of the animal; next, that the tortoise should have gone to sleep and left this part exposed, contrary to his habit of drawing the neck within his shell; and lastly, that with the harpoon stuck in his flesh, and sunk still deeper by the act of drawing in his head to save himself, he should yet have been able to pull along a heavy-laden boat and a raft tied to it.

Our conversation being ended, I requested my wife to go with two of the younger boys to Falcon's Stream and fetch the sledge and the beasts of burden, that we might not fail of seeing at least a part of our booty put safely under shelter. A tempest, or even the tide, might sweep away the whole during the night. We took every precaution in our power against the latter danger by fixing the boat and the raft as securely as we could. I rolled two heavy masses of lead, with the assistance of levers, from the raft upon the shore, and then tied a rope to each, the other ends of which were fastened, one to the raft and the other to the boat.

While we were employed on this scheme the sledge arrived, and we immediately placed the tortoise upon it, and also some articles of light weight, such as mattresses, pieces of linen, &c. The strength of our whole party was found necessary to move it, we therefore all set out together to unload it at Falcon's Stream. We pursued our way thither with the utmost gaiety of heart, and Fritz and I found the time pass quickly in answering the questions with which the three youngest boys assailed us as to the nature and amount of the treasures we had brought. The chest containing the articles in silver, and another filled with trinkets and utensils, most powerfully excited their interest, for Fritz had dropped a hint of what was in them.

"Are they left on the raft or in the boat?" asked Ernest. "We will open them to-morrow and I shall have my watch."

Jack. "I assure you I shall not be content with only a watch. I must have, since I hear there are so many, a snuff-box also."

Francis. "And I shall ask for a pretty purse filled with louis."

Father. "Well imagined, my young ones. Jack intends, I presume, to take now and then a pinch of the snuff he has not got, and Francis means to sow his louis that they may produce a crop."

In this trifling kind of talk we beguiled the time till we reached the foot of our castle. Our first concern now was the tortoise, which we turned on his back that we might strip off the shell, and make use of some of the flesh.

My wife asked leave to take away the *green*-coloured part of the flesh, which she said she could not even look at without distaste. I answered that she was wrong in this. I informed her that the green was the fat, and would add to the fine flavour of the dish.

"But," added I, "if you think it is too abundant, you can take a part and preserve it by melting. We will then," said I, "put what we mean to keep in salt, and distribute the head, the entrails, and the feet to the dogs; for all, you know, must live."

"Oh," cried Francis, "do give me the shell, Father!"

"No, no!" bawled out another, all contending for preference.

I imposed silence, declaring that the right was entirely in Fritz, since it was he who had harpooned the animal. "But," continued I, "it may be well to ask what Fritz would think of doing with the shell."

"I thought, Father, of cleaning it and fixing it by the side of our river, and keeping it always full of pure water for my mother's use when she had to wash the linen or cook."

"Excellent, excellent, my boy! This is what I call *thinking for the general good.* And we will execute the idea as soon as we can prepare some clay as a foundation."

"Hah, hah!" cried Jack. "Now then, it is my turn, for I have got some clay."

"And where did you get it, my boy?" said I.

Mother. "Oh, to my cost I know where the clay was got. This morning early my young hero falls to digging on the hill you see to the right, and home he comes with the news that he has found a bed of clay, but so dirty himself that we were obliged to think next of the washing-tub."

Jack. "And if I had minded a little dirt, Mother, I should not have discovered this clay, which will be of great use to us. As I was returning from looking for potatoes I thought I would take the high path along the river. By and by I came to a large slope watered by the river. It was so slippery that I could not keep upon my legs, so I fell and dirtied myself all over. The ground was all of clay, and almost liquid, so I made some into balls and brought them home."

Ernest. "When the water-tub is complete I will put the roots I have found to soak a little in it, for they are now quite dry. I do not exactly know what they are – they look something like the radish or horseradish, but the plant from which I took them was almost the size of a bush. As I don't know its nature, I have not tasted the roots, though I saw our sow eat heartily of them."

Father. "It was quite right to be cautious, my son. But let me look at these roots. How did you first discover them?"

Ernest. "I was rambling about, Father, and met the sow, who was turning up the earth under the plant I have been speaking of, and stopped only to chew and swallow greedily something she seemed to find there. I drove her away, and on looking into the place I found a knot of roots, which I tore out and brought home."

Father. "If my suspicion is right you have made a discovery, which, with our potatoes, may furnish us the means of existence as long as we remain in this land. I am tolerably certain that these roots are *manioc*, of which the natives of the West Indies make a sort of bread which they call *cassave*. But if we would make this use of it we must first carry it through a certain preparation, without which these roots possess pernicious properties."

By the time of ending this discourse we had also finished unloading the sledge, and I bade the three eldest boys accompany me to fetch another load before dark. We left Francis and his mother busy in preparing a refreshing supper, the tortoise having presented itself most opportunely for this purpose.

When we reached the raft, we took from it as many effects as the sledge could hold, or the animals draw along. The first object of my attention was to secure two chests which contained the clothes of my family; which I knew would afford the highest gratification to my wife. I reckoned also on finding in one of the chests some books, and principally a large handsomely-printed Bible. I added to these four cart-wheels and a hand-mill for grinding, which, now that we had discovered the manioc, I considered of signal importance.

On our return to Falcon's Nest we found my wife looking anxiously for our arrival, and ready with the welcome of an ample and agreeable repast. Nor was her kind humour diminished by the acquisitions we now added to her store.

Before she had well examined them, she drew me, with one of her sweetest smiles, by the arm. "Step this way," said she, "and I too will produce something that will both refresh and please you." And leading to the shade of a tree, "This," continued she, "is the work I performed in your absence," pointing to a cask of tolerable size half-sunk into the ground, and the rest covered over with branches of trees. She then applied a small corkscrew to the side, and filling the shell of a coco-nut with the contents, presented it to me. I found the liquor equal to the best Canary.

"How then," said I, "have you performed this new miracle? I cannot believe the enchanted bag produced it."

"Not exactly," replied she, "for this time it was an obliging wave which threw on shore the agreeable liquid. I took a little ramble in your absence yesterday, and behold how well my trouble was rewarded! The boys ran for the sledge, and had but little difficulty in getting it to Falcon's Stream, where our next care was to dig a place in the earth to keep it cool. We guessed it must contain wine, but to be quite sure Ernest and Jack bored a small hole in the side, and inserting a hollow reed they contrived to taste it, and assured me the cask was filled with a most delicious beverage."

After supper I completed my day's work by drawing up the mattresses from the ship to our chamber in the tree. When I had laid them along to advantage, they looked so inviting that I was glad the time had come to commit ourselves to the kind relief they offered to our exhausted strength.

CHAPTER NINETEEN

ANOTHER TRIP TO THE WRECK

~

Irose before day to go to the sea-side and inspect our two vessels. My family did not hear me depart, and I was unwilling to disturb their sleep. I therefore gently descended the ladder. Above, the scene was all repose; below, I found everything in life and motion. The dogs jumped about me for joy, perceiving that I was going out; the cock and the hens flapped their wings and chuckled; and our goats shook their long beards as they browsed; but the ass, the only creature amongst them I was likely to want at that time, still lay stretched at full length on the grass, and discovered no inclination for the morning jaunt I designed for him. I quickly roused and harnessed him singly to the sledge. It was unnecessary to call the dogs after me. As I walked towards the shore I saw with pleasure that the boat and raft had resisted the tide. I got quickly on the raft, took a small loading, and returned to Falcon's Stream in time for breakfast. Judge of my surprise when arrived, that I neither saw nor heard a single creature of its inhabitants, though the sun had climbed high above the horizon. Thinking it time for our fellow-labourers to be stirring, I gave a shout as loud as a war-whoop. My wife awoke first, and wondered to see the day so far advanced.

"Really, my dear," said she, "I think it must be the magic charm of the good mattress you brought home yesterday that has lulled me into such a long, sound sleep, and that appears to be still exerting its influence upon our boys."

In fact, they yawned, stretched, turned round, and turned back again.

"Come, come, up, my lads!" exclaimed I once again. "Brave youths like you ought to awake at the first call and leap gaily out of bed."

After this short admonition all came down. Prayers and breakfast over, we returned to the sea-side to complete the unloading of the raft, that it might be ready for sea on the ebbing of the tide. I was not long, with the additional assistance I had, in taking two cargoes to Falcon's Stream. At our last trip the tide was nearly up to our craft. I immediately sent back my wife and three children, and remained with Fritz waiting till we were quite afloat, when, observing Jack hovering round us, I perceived his wish, and assented to his embarking with us. Shortly after the tide was high enough for us to row off. Instead of steering for Safety Bay to moor our vessels there, I was tempted by the fineness of the weather to go out again to the wreck, which it was with considerable difficulty we reached, though aided by a fresh sea-breeze. On our getting alongside it was too late to undertake much, and I was unwilling to cause my wife uneasiness by passing another night on board. I therefore determined to bring only what could be obtained with speed. In this intention we searched hastily through the ship for any trifling articles that might be readily removed. Jack was up and down everywhere, at a loss what to select. When I saw him again he drew a wheel-barrow after him, rejoicing at having found such a vehicle for our potatoes. Fritz next disclosed that he had discovered behind the bulkhead amidships a pinnace taken to pieces, with all its appurtenances, and even two small guns. This intelligence so delighted me that I ran to the bulkhead, when I was convinced of the truth of the lad's assertion. But I perceived that to put it together and launch it into the sea would be a Herculean task, which I relinquished for the present. I then collected some house utensils and whatever else I thought most useful, such as a large copper boiler, some plates of iron, tobacco-graters, two grinding stones, a small barrel of gunpowder, and another of flints. Jack's barrow was not forgotten. Two more were afterwards added. All these articles were hurried into the boat, and we re-embarked with speed to avoid meeting the land wind that invariably rose in the evening. As we were drawing near to shore, we were struck with the appearance of an assemblage of small figures ranged in a long line on the strand. They were dressed in black, and all uniform, with white waistcoats and full gravats. The arms of these beings hung down carelessly. Now and then, however, they seemed to extend them tenderly, as if they wished to embrace or offer us a token of friendship.

"I really think," said I to the boys, who were steadfastly gazing at so novel a spectacle, "that we are in the country of the pygmies."

"But I begin to see," said Fritz, "that the pygmies have beaks and short wings. What strange birds!"

"You are right, son; they are penguins or ruffs. They are of the *stupid* species.

Ernest killed one soon after our arrival. They are excellent swimmers, but cannot fly; and so confused are they when on land, that they run in the silliest way into danger."

While we were talking I steered gently towards the shore to enjoy the uncommon sight the longer. But the very moment we got into shallow water, my giddy boy Jack leaped out of his tub up to his waist, and was quickly on land battering with his stick among the penguins, so that half a dozen of them were immediately laid flat. They were not dead, but only stunned. The remainder plunged into the sea, dived, and disappeared.

Fritz murmured at his brother for having frightened them away before he could fire. I could not help laughing at this perpetual shooter of guns, who was so disposed to waste his powder on animals who were to be taken with the hand. I also taunted Jack a little for having jumped into the water at the risk of being drowned. While I was making these observations, the birds gradually recovered, rose upon their legs and began a tottering sort of march with a gravity which irresistibly excited our laughter. I did not allow Jack's game to escape. I took hold of them, tied their legs together with reeds without hurting them, and laid them on the beach while we were landing our treasures. But as the sun declined, and we despaired of finishing before night set in, each of us filled a barrow in order to take home something. I requested that the tobacco-graters and iron plates might be in the first load. To these we added the penguins, living and dead, and then set out. As we drew near Falcon's Stream I heard the watchful dogs proclaim our approach with loud barking. My wife was highly pleased with the wheel-barrows, and for the most part with their contents, but she had no partiality for the tobacco-graters.

"What is the use of these graters?" she exclaimed. "Are our four sons to become snuff-takers?"

"No, dear wife," I replied; "and pray do not be uneasy about them. These graters are not for the gratification of our noses. Come, children," said I, pointing to the penguins, "look after the newcomers to the poultry-yard."

I then directed them to fasten the birds one by one to a goose or a duck, as a means of taming them and inuring them to the society of their companions. This essay, however, was inconvenient to our feathered animals, who were but slowly reconciled to their singular companions. My wife now showed me a good store of potatoes which she had got in, and a quantity of the roots I had taken for manioc, and in which I was not mistaken.

"Father, we have worked very hard," said little Francis. "What will you say when we have a fine crop of maize, melons, dates, and gourds? Mother has planted all these in the potato holes."

Mother. "I took the grain and seeds from my enchanted bag, and your thirst after booty and your trips to the wreck are the sources of the resolution I formed to increase the number of your comforts at home, and thus render them the less necessary. I determined, then, to fit up a kitchen-garden."

Father. "This was well thought, my dear; but we must not despise the trips to the vessel either. This very day we discovered in her a handsome little pinnace, which may be of the greatest service to us."

Mother. "I cannot say that this discovery gives me pleasure. I have no desire to trust myself again on the sea. But should it at any time be necessary, I must confess I should prefer a well-made, solid vessel to our raft composed of tubs."

Father. "Well, this you shall possess, if you will consent to my returning once more to the wreck. In the meanwhile let us have supper, and then we will retire to rest. And if my little workmen should be industriously inclined to-morrow, I shall reward them with the novelty of a new trade to be learnt."

This did not fail to excite the curiosity of all. But I kept my word, and made them wait till the following day for the explanation I had to give.

CHAPTER TWENTY

THE BAKEHOUSE

~

I waked the boys very early, reminding them that I had promised to teach them a new trade.

"What is it? What is it?" exclaimed they all at once, springing suddenly out of bed and hurrying on their clothes.

Father. "It is the art of baking, my boys, which at present I am no more acquainted with than yourselves. But we will learn it together. Hand me those iron plates that we brought yesterday from the vessel, and the tobacco-graters also."

Mother. "I really cannot understand what tobacco-graters and iron plates can have to do with making bread. A good oven would afford me much better hopes."

Father. "These very iron plates you looked so disdainfully upon yesterday will serve the purpose. I cannot promise to produce light and handsome-looking bread; but I can answer that you shall have some excellent-tasted cakes, though they should be a little flat and heavy. Ernest, bring hither the roots found underground; but first, my dear, I must request you to make me a small bag of a piece of the strongest wrapper linen."

I spread a large piece of coarse linen on the ground, and assembled my young ones round me. I gave each of the boys a grater, and showed him how to rest it on the linen, and then to grate the roots of manioc, so that in a short time each had produced a considerable heap of a substance resembling pollard. The occupation proved infinitely amusing to them all, and they looked no further into the matter.

A very short time was sufficient for producing a considerable quantity of ground manioc. By this time my wife had completed the bag. I had it well filled with what we called our pollard, and she closed it effectually by sewing up the end. I was now to contrive a kind of press. I cut a long, straight, well-formed branch of considerable strength from a neighbouring tree, and stripped it of the bark. I then placed a plank across the table we had fixed between the arched roots of our tree, and which was exactly the right height for my purpose, and on this I laid the bag. I put other planks again upon the bag, and then covered all with the large branch, the thickest extremity of which I inserted under an arch, while to the other, which projected beyond, the planks, I suspended all sorts of heavy substances, such as lead, our largest hammers, and bars of iron, which, acting with great force as a press on the bag of manioc, caused the sap it contained to issue in streams.

Mother. "But, pray tell me, are we to prepare the whole of this manioc at once? If so, we have at least a whole day's work, and a great part must be spoiled at last."

Father. "Not so, my dear. When the pollard is dry it may be placed in casks, and it will keep for years; but you will see that the whole of this large heap will be so reduced in quantity by the operation we are going to apply of baking, that there will be no cause for your apprehension."

Fritz. "Father, it no longer runs a single drop. May we not now set about making the dough?"

Father. "I have no objections; but it would be prudent to make only a small cake at first which, as I said before, we will give to the monkey and the fowls, and wait to see the effect."

We now opened the bag, and took out a small quantity of the pollard, which already was sufficiently dry. We stirred the rest about with a stick, and then replaced it under the press. The next thing was to fix one of our iron plates, which was of a round form and rather convex, so as to rest upon two blocks of stone at a distance from each other. Under this we lighted a large fire, and when the iron plate was completely heated we placed a portion of the dough upon it with a wooden spade. As soon as the cake began to be brown underneath it was turned.

As soon as the cake was cold we broke some of it into crumbs, and gave it to two of the fowls, and a larger piece to the monkey, who nibbled it with a perfect relish.

"But what, I pray you, may there be in that boiling vessel yonder?" said I, turning to my wife.

"It is the penguin that Jack brought home," she replied.

To say the truth, the bird was of a strong and fishy flavour. Jack, however, was of a different opinion, and he was left at full liberty to regale himself to his appetite's content.

The first thing we did after dinner was to visit our fowls. Those among them which had eaten the manioc were in excellent condition, and no less so the monkey.

"Now then, to the bakehouse, young ones!" said I.

The grated manioc was soon emptied out of the bag, a large fire was quickly lighted, and when it was sufficiently hot I placed the boys where a flat surface had been prepared for them, and gave to each a plate of iron and the quantity of a coco-nut shellfull for them to make a cake apiece, and they were to try who could succeed the best. They were ranged in a half-circle round the place where I stood myself that they might the better be enabled to observe how I proceeded. The result was not discouraging, though we were now and then so unlucky as to burn a cake. My little rogues could not resist the pleasure of frequently tasting their cake, a little bit at a time, as they went on. At length the undertaking was complete. The cakes were put in a dish, and served in company with a handsome share of milk to each person. With this addition, they furnished us an excellent repast. What remained we distributed among our animals and fowls. I observed that the penguins which I had preserved alive accommodated themselves perfectly to this food, and that they began to lose their timid behaviour. I therefore ventured to disengage them from their comrades. This indulgence procured me the pleasure of seeing them in a state of newly-acquired content.

The rest of the day was employed in drawing to Tent House the remaining articles we had brought from the ship. When all this was done we retired to rest, having first made another meal on our cakes, and concluded all with pious thanks to God for the blessings His goodness thought fit to bestow upon us.

CHAPTER TWENTY-ONE

THE PINNACE AND THE CRACKER

~

From the time of discovering the pinnace, my desire of returning to the vessel grew every moment more irresistible. One thing I saw was absolutely necessary, which was to collect all my hands and go with sufficient strength to get her out from the situation where we had found her. I therefore thought of taking with me the three boys. I even wished that my wife should accompany us; but she assured me the very attempt would make her ill, and thus occasion her to be an additional trouble rather than of use. I had some difficulty to prevail upon her to let the children go.

After breakfast, then, we prepared for setting out. We took with us an ample provision of boiled potatoes and cassave, and, in addition, arms and weapons. We embarked and reached Safety Bay without the occurrence of any remarkable event. Here we thought it prudent to put on our cork-jackets. We then scattered some food for the geese and ducks which had taken up their abode there, and soon after stepped gaily into our tub-boat, at the same time fastening the new raft by a rope to her stern. We put out for the current, though not without fear of finding that the wreck had disappeared. We soon, however, perceived that she still remained. Having got on board, our first care was to load our craft with different stores, that we might not return without some acquisition of comfort. Then we repaired to that part of the vessel called the bulkhead, which contained the enviable prize, the pinnace. On further observation, it appeared to me that the plan we had formed was subject to at least two perhaps insurmountable difficulties. The one was the situation of the pinnace in the ship, and the other was the size and weight it would necessarily acquire when put together. The enclosure in which she lay in pieces was far back in the interior of the ship, and close upon the side which was in the water, immediately under the officers' cabin. Several inner timbers of prodigious bulk and weight separated this enclosure from the breach at which only we had been able to get on board, and in this part of the deck there was not sufficient space for us to work at putting the pinnace together, or to give her room should we succeed in completing our business. The breach also was too narrow and too irregular to admit of her being launched from this place, as we had done with our tub-raft. In short, the separate pieces of the pinnace were too heavy for the possibility of our removing them. What, therefore, was to be done? I stood on the spot absorbed in deep reflection, while the boys were conveying everything portable they could find, on board the raft.

The cabinet which contained the pinnace was lighted by several small fissures in the timbers, which, after standing in the place a few minutes to accustom the eye, enabled one to see sufficiently to distinguish objects. I discovered with pleasure that all the pieces of which she was composed were so accurately arranged and numbered, that I might flatter myself with the hope of being able to collect and put them together, if I could be allowed the necessary time and place. I therefore, in spite of every disadvantage, decided on the undertaking, and we immediately set about it. We proceeded, at first so slowly as to produce discouragement, if the desire of possessing a little vessel which might at some future day be the means of our deliverance, had not at every moment inspired us with new strength and ardour.

Evening, however, was fast approaching, and we had made but small progress when, with reluctance, we left our occupation and re-embarked. On reaching Safety Bay, we had the satisfaction of finding there our kind steward and little Francis. They had been during the day employed in some arrangements for our living at Tent House as long as we should have to continue the excursions to the vessel. This she did to shorten the length of the voyage, and that we might be always in sight of each other. This new proof of her attention affected me in a lively manner, and I could not sufficiently express the gratitude which I felt, particularly as I knew the dislike she had conceived to living in this spot. I made the best display I could of two casks of salted butter, three of flour, some small bags of millet seed and of rice, and a multitude of other articles of utility and comfort for our establishment. My wife rewarded me by the expression of her perfect satisfaction, and the whole was removed to our store-house at the rocks.

We passed an entire week in this arduous undertaking of the pinnace. I embarked regularly every morning with my three sons, and returned every evening, and never without some addition to our stores.

"We glided with the rapidity of a bird along the mirror of the waters." (Chapter 21)

"I counselled them… to add the exercises of running, jumping, getting up trees." (Chapter 22)

At length the pinnace was completed, and in a condition to be launched. The question now was, how to manage this remaining difficulty. She was an elegant little vessel, perfect in every part. She had a small neat deck; and her mast and sails were no less exact and perfect than those of a little brig. It was probable she would sail well from the lightness of her construction, and drawing comparatively little water. We had pitched and towed all the seams that she might be water-tight. We had even taken the superfluous pains of further embellishing by mounting her with two small cannon of about a pound weight, and, in imitation of larger vessels, had fastened them to the deck with chains. But in spite of the delight we felt in contemplating a commodious little vessel, yet the great difficulty still remained. The little vessel still stood fast, enclosed within four walls; nor could I conceive of a means of getting her out. To effect a passage through the outer side of the vessel by means of the utensils we had secured, seemed to present a prospect of exertions beyond our powers. We now examined if it might be practicable to cut away all intervening timbers to which, from the nature of the breach, we had easier access. But should we even succeed in this attempt, the upper timbers being, in consequence of the inclined position of the ship, on a level with the water, our labour would be unavailing; besides, we had neither strength nor time for such a proceeding. From one moment to another a storm might arise and engulf the ship – timber, pinnace, ourselves, and all. Despairing, then, of being able to find a means consistent with the sober rules of art, my impatient fancy inspired the thought of a project which must be attended with hazards.

I had found on board a strong iron mortar, such as is used in kitchens. I took a thick oak plank, and nailed to a certain part of it some large iron hooks: with a knife I cut a groove along the middle of the plank. I sent the boys to fetch some match-wood from the hold, and I cut a piece sufficiently long to continue burning at least two hours. I placed this train in the groove of my plank. I filled the mortar with gunpowder, and then laid the plank, thus furnished, upon it, having previously pitched the mortar all round; and, lastly, I made the whole fast to the spot with strong chains crossed by means of the hooks in every direction. Thus I accomplished a sort of cracker. I hung this infernally-contrived machine against the side of the bulkhead next the sea, having taken previous care to choose a spot in which its action could not affect the pinnace. When the whole was arranged I set fire to the match, the end of which projected far enough beyond the plank to allow us time to escape. I now hurried on board the raft, into which I had sent the boys before applying a light to the match. Though they had assisted in forming the cracker, they had no suspicion of the use for which it was intended.

On our arrival at Tent House, I immediately put the raft in a certain order, that she might be in readiness to return speedily to the wreck, when the noise produced by the cracker should have informed me that my scheme had taken effect. We set busily to work to empty her, when, during the occupation, our ears were assailed with the noise of an explosion of such violence, that my wife and the boys, who were ignorant of the cause, were dreadfully alarmed. "What can it be? What is the matter? What can have happened?" cried all at once.

Mother. "The sound appeared to come in the direction of the wreck; perhaps she has blown up. Were you careful of not leaving any light which could communicate with gunpowder?"

From the bottom of her heart she made this last suggestion, for she desired nothing more earnestly than that the vessel should be annihilated, and thus an end be put to our repeated visits.

Father. "If this is the case," said I, "we had better return and convince ourselves of the fact. Who will be of the party?"

"I, I, I!" cried the boys; and the three young rogues lost not a moment in jumping into their tubs, whither I soon followed them, after having whispered a few words to my wife, somewhat tending to tranquillize her mind during the trip we had now to engage in.

We rowed out of the bay with more rapidity than on any former occasion. Curiosity gave strength to our arms. When the vessel was in sight, I observed with pleasure that no change had taken place in the part of her which faced Tent House, and that no sign of smoke appeared. We advanced, therefore, in excellent spirits. But instead of rowing as usual straight to the breach, we proceeded round to the side on the inside of which we had placed the cracker. The scene of devastation we had caused now broke upon our sight. The greater part of the ship's side was shivered to pieces; innumerable splinters covered the surface of the water. The whole exhibited a scene of destruction, in the midst of which presented itself our elegant pinnace entirely free from injury! I could not refrain from the liveliest exclamations of joy, which excited the surprise of the boys. They fixed their eyes upon me with the utmost astonishment. "Now then, she is ours!" cried I – "the elegant little pinnace is ours! for nothing is now more easy than to launch her. Come, boys, jump upon her deck, and let us see how quickly we can get her down upon the water."

Fritz. "Ah! now I understand you, Father. You have yourself blown up the side of the ship with that machine you contrived in our last visit, that we might be able to get out the pinnace. But how does it happen that so much of the ship is blown away?"

Father. "I will explain all this to you, when I have convinced myself that the pinnace is not injured, and that there is no danger of any of the fire remaining on board. Let us well examine." We entered by the new breach, and had soon reason to be satisfied that the pinnace had escaped from injury, and that the fire was extinguished. The mortar, however, and pieces of the chain, had been driven forcibly into the opposite side of the enclosure.

I now perceived that it would be easy, with the help of the crowbar and the lever, to lower the pinnace into the water. In putting her together, I had used the precaution of placing the keel on rollers. Before letting her go, however, I fastened the end of a long thick rope to her head, and the other end to the most solid part of the wreck, for fear of her being carried out too far. We put our whole ingenuity and strength to this undertaking, and soon enjoyed the pleasure of seeing our pretty pinnace descend gracefully into the sea, the rope keeping her sufficiently near, and enabling us to draw her close to the spot where I was loading the tub-boat, and where for that purpose I had lodged a pulley on a projecting beam, from which I was enabled also to advance with the fixing of the masts and sails for our new barge. I endeavoured to recollect minutely all the information I had ever possessed on the art of equipping a vessel, and our pinnace was shortly in a condition to set sail.

On this occasion a spirit of military affairs was awakened in the minds of my young flock, which was never afterwards extinguished. We were masters of a vessel mounted with two cannon, and furnished amply with guns and pistols! This was at once to be invincible, and in a condition for resisting and destroying the largest fleet the savages could bring upon us! For my own part, I answered their young enthusiasm with pious prayers that we might ever escape such a calamity as being compelled to use our firearms against human beings. Night surprised us before we had finished our work, and we accordingly prepared for our return to Tent House, after drawing the pinnace close under the vessel's side. We arrived in safety, and took great care, as had been previously agreed on, not to mention our new and invaluable booty to the good mother, till we could surprise her with the sight of it in a state of entire completeness.

Two whole days more were spent in equipping and loading the little barge. When she was ready for sailing, I found it impossible to resist the earnest importunity of the boys, who, as a recompense for the industry and discretion they had employed, claimed my permission to salute their mother, on their approach to Tent house, with two discharges of cannon. These accordingly were loaded, and the two youngest placed themselves, with a lighted match in hand, close to the touch-holes, to be in readiness. Fritz stood at the mast to manage the ropes, while I took my station at the rudder. These matters being adjusted, we put off. The wind was favourable, and so fresh that we glided with the rapidity of a bird along the mirror of the waters.

Our old friend the tub-raft had been deeply loaded and fastened to the pinnace, and it now followed as an accompanying boat to a superior vessel. We took down our large sail as soon as we found ourselves at the entrance of the Bay of Safety, to have the greater command in directing the barge; and soon the smaller ones were lowered one by one. Thus, proceeding at a slower rate, we had greater facilities for managing the important affair of the discharge of the cannon. Arrived within a certain distance – "Fire!" cried commander Fritz. The rocks behind Tent House returned the sound. "Fire!" said Fritz again. Ernest and Jack obeyed, and the echoes again majestically replied. Fritz at the same moment had discharged his two pistols, and all joined instantly in three loud huzzas.

"Welcome, welcome, dear ones!" was the answer from the anxious mother, almost breathless with astonishment and joy. "Welcome!" cried also little Francis, as he stood clinging to her side, and not well knowing whether he was to be sad or merry!

We now tried to push to shore with our oars, that we might have the protection of a projecting mass of rocks, and my wife and little Francis hastened to the spot to receive us.

"Ah, dear ones!" cried she, heartily embracing me, "what a fright have you and your cannon and your little ship thrown me into! I saw it advancing rapidly towards us, and was unable to conceive from whence it could come, or what it might have on board. I stole with Francis behind the rocks, and when I heard the firing, I was near sinking to the ground with terror. If I had not the moment after heard your voices, God knows where we should have run to – but come, the cruel moment is now over, and thanks to Heaven I have you once again in safety! But tell me where you got so unhoped-for a prize as this charming little vessel? In good truth it would really almost tempt me to venture once more on a sea-voyage, especially if she would promise to convey us back to our dear country! I foresee of what use she will be to us, and for her sake I think that I must try to forgive the many sins of absence you have committed against me."

Fritz now invited his mother to get on board, and gave her his assistance. When they had all stepped upon the deck, they entreated for permission to salute by again discharging the cannon, and at the same moment to confer on the pinnace the name of their mother – *The Elizabeth.*

My wife was particularly gratified by these our late adventures. "But do not," said she, "imagine that I bestow so much commendation without the hope of some return. On the contrary, it is now my turn to claim from you, for myself and little Francis, the same sort of agreeable recompense. For we have not, I assure you, remained idle. No, not so; little Francis and his mother found means to be doing something also, though not at this moment prepared to furnish such unquestionable proofs as you, by your salutations of cannon and pistols. But wait a little, and our proofs shall hereafter be apparent in some dishes of excellent vegetables. It depends, to say the truth, only on yourselves to go with me and see what we have done."

We did not hesitate to comply, and jumped briskly out of the pinnace. Taking little Francis by the hand she led the way, and we followed in the gayest mood. She conducted us up an ascent of one of the rocks, and stopping at the spot where the cascade is formed from Jackal's River, she displayed a commodious kitchen-garden, laid out in beds and walks, and, as she told us, everywhere sowed with the seed of useful plants.

"This," said she, "is the pretty exploit we have been engaged in, if you will kindly think so of it. In this spot the earth is so light, that Francis and I had no difficulty in working it, and then dividing it into different beds – one for potatoes, one for manioc, and other smaller shares for lettuces of various kinds, not forgetting to leave a due proportion to receive some plants of the sugar-cane. You, dear husband, and Fritz will easily find means to conduct sufficient water hither from the cascade, by means of pipes of bamboo, to keep the whole in health and vigour, and we shall have a double source of pleasure from the general prosperity, for both the eyes and the palate will be gratified. But you have not yet seen all. There, on the slope of the rock, I have transplanted some plants of the ananas. Between these I have sowed some melon-seeds. Here is a plot allotted to pease and beans, and this other for all sorts of cabbage. Round each bed or plot I have sowed seeds of maize, to serve as a border, while on account of its tall and bushy form it will protect my young plants from the scorching heat of the sun."

I stood transported in the midst of so perfect an exhibition of such persevering industry. I could only exclaim that I should never have believed in the possibility of such a result in so short a time, and particularly with so much privacy as to leave me wholly unsuspicious of the existence of such a project.

Mother. "To confess the truth, I did not myself expect to succeed, for which reason I resolved to say nothing of the matter, that I might not be put to the blush for my presumption. But as I found my little calculations answer better than I expected, I was encouraged, and the hope of surprising you so agreeably gave me new strength. I had my suspicions that your visits to the wreck were connected with some great mystery, which at a certain time you would unfold. So, mystery for mystery, thought I, and thus it has turned out."

"I had almost forgotten though," said my wife after a short pause, "one little reproach I had to make you. Your trips to the vessel have made you neglect the bundle of fruit-saplings we laid together in mould at Falcon's Stream. I fear they by this time must be dying for want of being planted, though I took care to water and cover them with branches. Let us go and see about them."

I should have been no less grieved than my wife to see this charming acquisition perish for want of care. We had reason on many accounts to return quickly to Falcon's Stream, where different matters required our presence. We had now in possession the greater part of the cargo of the vessel, but almost the whole of these treasures were at present in the open air, and liable to injury.

My wife prepared with alertness for our walk, and the rather from the aversion she had ever entertained, on account of the intense heat, for Tent House. We hastened to unload the boat, and to place the cargo safely under shelter along with our other stores.

The pinnace was anchored on the shore, and fastened with a rope to a stake. When all our stores were thus disposed of, we began our journey to Falcon's Stream, but not empty-handed. We took with us everything absolutely wanted for comfort; and when brought together, it was really so much that both ourselves and our beasts of burden had no easy task to perform.

CHAPTER TWENTY-TWO

GYMNASTIC EXERCISES – VARIOUS DISCOVERIES – SINGULAR ANIMALS, ETC.

~

I had recommended to the boys to continue the exercise we began upon the first Sunday of our abode in these regions – the shooting of arrows; for I had an extreme solicitude about increasing their strength and agility. Nothing tends more to the extinction of courage than the consciousness of wanting that strength of limb, or that address, which may be necessary to aid us in defending ourselves or in escaping from dangers. I counselled them, therefore, to add the exercises of running, jumping, getting up trees, both by means of climbing by the trunk, or by a suspended rope, as sailors are obliged to do to get to the masthead. We began at first by making knots in the rope at a foot distance from each other, then we reduced the number of knots, and before we left off we contrived to succeed without any. I next taught them an exercise of a different nature, which was to be effected by means of two balls made of lead, fastened one to each end of a string about a fathom in length. While I was preparing this all eyes were fixed upon me. "What can it be intended for?" "How can we use, it?" "Will it soon be ready?"

Father. "Have patience, boys. This is nothing less than an imitation of the arm used by a valiant nation remarkable for their skill in the chase, and whom you have heard of. I mean the Patagonians, inhabitants of the most southern point of America. Every Patagonian is armed with this simple instrument. If they desire to kill or wound an enemy or an animal, they fling one of the ends of this cord at him, and draw it back by the other, which they keep carefully in their hand, to be ready for another throw if necessary. But if they wish to take an animal alive, and without hurting it, they possess the singular art of throwing it in such a way as to make it run several times round the neck of the prey, occasioning a perplexing tightness. They then throw the second stone, and with so certain an aim that they scarcely ever miss their object. The operation of the second is the so twisting itself about the animal as to impede his progress, even though he were at a full gallop. The stones continue turning, and carrying with them the cord. The poor animal is at length so entangled he falls a prey to the enemy."

This was heard with much interest by the boys, who now all entreated I would that instant try the effect of my own instrument upon a small tree. My throws entirely succeeded, and the string with the balls at the end so completely surrounded the tree that the skill of the Patagonian huntsmen required no further illustration. Each of the boys must then needs have a similar instrument, and in a short time Fritz became quite expert in the art, as indeed he was in every kind of exercise that required strength or address.

The next morning, as I was dressing, I remarked from my window in the tree that the sea was violently agitated, and the waves swelled with the wind. I rejoiced to find myself in safety in my home. Though such a wind was in reality quite harmless for skilful sailors, for us it might be truly dangerous, from our ignorance in these matters. I observed then to my wife that I should not leave her the whole day, and should therefore hold myself ready to execute any little concerns she found wanting in our domestic arrangement. We now fell to a more minute examination than I had hitherto had time for of all our possessions. She showed me many things she had herself found means to add to them during my repeated absences from home. Among these was a large barrel filled with small birds half-roasted and stowed away in butter to preserve them fresh. This she called her *game*, which she had found means to ensnare with bird-lime. Next she showed me a pair of young pigeons which had been lately hatched, and were already beginning to try their wings, while their mother was again sitting on her eggs. From these we passed to the fruit-trees we had laid in earth to be planted, and which were in real need of our assistance, being almost in a dying state. I immediately set myself to prevent so grievous a mishap. I had promised the boys the evening before to go all together to the wood of gourds, for the purpose of providing ourselves with vessels of different sizes. They were enchanted with the idea, but I bargained that they must first assist me to plant all the young trees.

When we had finished, a little disappointment, however, occurred. The evening seemed too far advanced for so long a walk, especially as my wife and little Francis were to be of the party. We accordingly postponed the excursion till the following day, when we made the necessary preparations for leaving Falcon's Stream very early in the morning. By sunrise all were on foot. The ass was harnessed to the sledge. In the journey out he carried our dinner, and some powder and shot. I took with me a double-barrelled gun, one barrel loaded with shot and one with ball.

Turning round Flamingo Marsh we soon reached the pleasant spot which before had so delighted us. Fritz took a direction a little farther from the seashore, and sending Turk into the tall grass, he followed himself, and both disappeared. Soon, however, we heard Turk barking loud, a large bird sprang up, and almost at the same moment a shot from Fritz brought it down. But the bird, though wounded, was not killed; it raised itself and ran off with incredible swiftness. Turk pursued with eagerness. Fritz followed; and Ponto threw the monkey off his back and fell speedily into the same track. It was Ponto that seized the bird, and held it fast till Fritz came up. But now a different sort of scene succeeded from that which took place at the capture of the flamingo. The legs of that bird are long and weak, and it was able to make but a poor resistance. The present captive was large in size, and proportionately strong. It struck the dogs, or whoever came near, with its legs with so much force, that Fritz, who had received a blow or two, retired from the field of battle, and dared not again approach. Turk was also discouraged by some severities applied to his head by his sturdy combatant, and yielded the contest. The brave Ponto alone withstood the animal's attacks. He seized one of its wings, and did not let it go till I reached the spot, which I was long in doing on account of the height of the grass. When I was near enough to distinguish the bird as it lay on the ground, I was overjoyed to see that it was a female bustard of the largest size. I had long wished to possess and to tame for our poultry-yard a bird of this species, which closely resembles the turkey.

To effect the complete capture of the bird without injury, I took out my pocket-handkerchief and threw it over its head. It could not disengage itself, and its efforts only served to entangle it the more. As in this situation it could not see me, I got sufficiently near to pass a string with a running knot over its legs, which I then drew tight. I gently released the wing from Ponto, and tied that and its fellow close to the bird's body. The bustard was at length vanquished, though not till most of us had felt the powerful blows it was capable of inflicting.

We fixed the bustard on the sledge, and then pursued our way towards the wood where Fritz and I had seen such troops of monkeys. Fritz again recounted the adventure to his mother, and during this recital Ernest was wandering a little from us in every direction, in admiration of the height and beauty of the trees. He stopped in delight at the sight of one in particular which stood alone, gazing with wonder at the prodigious distance from the root to the nearest bunches of coco-nuts, which he saw hanging in clusters under their crown of leaves, and which excited an eager desire to possess some of them.

Father. "Yes, Ernest, they are indeed at a most unaccommodating height, and not a monkey in the way to throw them down to you. Even were I to set Knips at liberty, besides that he is not in the habit of giving away what he might keep for himself, he would perhaps take it into his head to stay in the tree. It is a pity, and I am sure you are of my opinion, that those fine coco-nuts cannot find a way to drop down into your mouth."

Scarcely had I ended my sentence when a nut fell down. Ernest stepped aside and looked up at the tree; another fell, and almost near enough to touch me, so that I was no less surprised than he. Not the smallest sign of a living creature appeared.

Ernest ventured to take up the nuts. We found them too unripe to be made use of, and were more than ever at a loss to account for their falling from the tree. In vain we strained our eyes; we saw nothing but now and then a slight motion of the leaves.

Fritz at this moment came up, and we told him what had passed. "I shall soon," said he, "see what it all means," raising his face to gaze at the tree. "If one would but fall at this moment, I would soon tell you who threw it."

At the very instant two nuts fell, and so near to the speaker as to bruise his lip and his chin. Ernest could not refrain from laughing heartily. "The magician is at least polite," said he; "he conducts his gift to your very mouth. It is no fault of his if your mouth is not quite large enough to receive it. But look, look! there are two more falling close to our mother and Francis! Let us quickly open one of them, and refresh ourselves with the liquor it contains in drinking to the health of our unknown friend."

We did this, and all called out together as they drank it, looking up at the tree, "Long life and thanks to the good magician!"

"Ah, ah! I see him! There he is!" exclaimed Jack suddenly. "What a hideous creature! What an ugly shape! He is as large as my hat, and has two monstrous pincer-claws!"

"Where is he then?" said I. "I do not see him."

"There, that is he, Father; crawling slowly down the tree. Do you see him now?"

It was a land-crab — an animal that, to say the truth, fully deserved Jack's description of him. The land-crab resembles the sea-crab, but is ten times more hideous. The one we now met with was of the kind called coco-crab, on account of its fondness for that fruit. It crawls up the trunk of the tree. When it has reached the clumps of leaves at the top, it falls to pinching off the bunches of coco-nuts at the stalks. It separates the nuts in the bunch and then throws them down one by one, which often bruises them considerably. The crab then descends, and finds below a plentiful repast. It is said by some that their claws are strong enough to break the shell of the nut. But for myself, I doubt this. I expect the animal sucks the milk by means of the small hole found near the stalk. The land-crab is not dangerous unless you are within reach of its claws, or, which is rarely the case, when they are found together in great numbers. Little Francis on seeing the animal was terribly frightened, and hid himself behind his mother. Even Ernest drew back. Jack raised the butt of his gun, and all of us cast looks of curiosity as the creature slowly descended. The moment he was on the ground the intrepid Jack aimed a blow at him with his gun, which missed him. The crab, finding himself attacked, turned round and advanced with his claws stretched open towards his enemy. My little ruffian defended himself valiantly. He did not retreat a single step, but his attempts to strike entirely failed, for the crab was perfect in the art of evading every blow. I, however, determined not to interfere. I saw that there could be no danger to the boy, and that the scene would conclude by his subduing the animal, if he conducted the affair with address.

After some time, being tired out with so many fruitless attempts, and perhaps recollecting that the pinches he might get from the animal's claws would not be very agreeable, Jack suddenly gave him the slip and ran off. The other boys now burst into peals of laughter, bawling out, "So the magician has conquered you! He has made you run away! Poor Jack! But why did you engage with a magician, Jack?" On this, the lad, piqued by their jeers, stopped short, threw his gun and his game-bag on the ground, stripped off his coat, spread it before him, and made a stand at his adversary, who was making up to him with his claws stretched out. Jack quickly threw his coat upon the creature and wrapped him round in it. Then tapping on the outside upon his shell, "Wicked magician," cried he, "I have you at last! I will teach you to brandish your horns at me another time!"

I laughed so heartily at this scene that I had not the power to give him any assistance. I saw by the motion under the coat that the crab was still alert and angry. I therefore took my hatchet and applied two or three powerful blows with it on the coat, which I took for granted would finish the affair at once. I lifted up the coat, and, as I expected, the terrible animal was practically dead, but still preserved a menacing posture.

I put the animal along with the coco-nuts together on the sledge, and we resumed our march. As we advanced the wood became thicker and more difficult to pass. I was frequently obliged to use the hatchet to make a free passage for the ass. The heat also increased, and we were all complaining of thirst, when Ernest, whose discoveries were generally of a kind to be of use, made one at this moment. He has already been described as a great lover of natural history, and now he was continually gathering such plants as he met with. He found a kind of hollow stalk of a tolerable height, which grew at the foot of the trees, and frequently entangled our feet. He cut some of the plants with his knife, and was much surprised to see a drop of pure fresh water issue from them. He showed it to us, put it to his lips, and found it perfectly agreeable, and felt much regret that there was no more. I then fell to examining the phenomenon myself, and soon perceived that the want of air prevented a more considerable issue of water. I made some more incisions, and presently water flowed out as if from a small conduit. Ernest, and after him the other boys, refreshed themselves and quenched their thirst at this new fountain.

I tried the experiment of dividing the plants longways, and they soon gave out water enough to supply even the ass, the monkey, and the wounded bustard. We were still compelled to fight our way through thick bushes, till at length we arrived at the wood of gourds, and we were not long in finding the spot where Fritz and I had once before enjoyed so agreeable a repose. Our companions had not soon done wondering at the magnificence of the trees they now beheld, and the prodigious size of the fruit which grew in so singular a manner. Fritz performed the office of lecturer to the rest, as I before had done to him. I strolled about the wood, choosing among the gourds such as were suited for our necessities, and marking the places in my mind's eye.

I found Jack and Ernest actively employed in collecting dried branches, while their mother was attending to the poor bustard, which was not materially injured. She remarked to me that it was cruel to keep her any longer blinded and her legs tied together. To please her, I took off the covering and loosened the string, but still left it so as to be a guard against its running away or inflicting blows. I contented myself with tying her by a long string to a tree. She had by no means the savageness of manners I should have expected, excepting when the dogs went near her. She did not appear to have any dread of man; which confirmed my previous belief that the island had no human inhabitants but ourselves.

The boys now amused themselves with making a large fire, which they joyously surrounded. I took the liberty to laugh at them, and asked if they had become salamanders, or inhabitants of the planet Mercury, who, it is said, make fires to refresh themselves from the burning heat of the sun.

"The fire, Father, is to enable us to cook the magician."

"Ah, hah! that is quite another thing," replied I. "It was for the same purpose, I suppose, that I saw you picking up shells. You mean no doubt to use them in the cooking, instead of the rind of the gourds, which would not bear sufficient heat."

They all agreed to my conclusion.

"I require also," said my wife, "some vessels to contain milk, and a large flat spoon to cut out my butter, and next some pretty plates for serving it at table."

Father. "You are perfectly reasonable in your demand, dear wife," said I, "and for me there must be manufactured some nests for pigeons, some baskets for eggs, and some hives for bees."

Jack. "But first, Father, let me make a dish for my crab. The heat would certainly make him unfit to be eaten by the evening. I should soon have finished if you will tell me how to divide one of the rinds with a string."

Father. "Well, well, it is but fair to allow you to enjoy the fruit of your victory. As to the cutting with a string, it was good for something when we had no saw. I will, however, show you how to do it, though I took care to bring here the instruments I thought we might want. Gather then a sufficient quantity of the gourds, of different sizes, and you shall see how soon we will cut them."

They all began to gather, and we were soon in possession of a sufficient number. We now began our work. Some had to cut; others to saw, scoop out, and model into agreeable forms. It was a real pleasure to witness the activity exhibited in this manufacture: each tried what he could present for the applause of his companions. For my own part, I made a pretty basket, large enough to carry eggs, with one of the gourds, leaving an arch at the top to serve as a cover. I likewise accomplished a certain number of vessels, also with covers, fit to hold our milk, and then some spoons to skim the cream. My next attempt was to execute some bottles large enough to contain a supply of fresh water, and these occasioned me more trouble than all the rest. It was necessary to empty the gourd through the small opening of the size of one's finger, which I had cut in it. I was obliged, after loosening the contents by means of a stick, to get them out by the friction of shot and water well shaken on the inside.

Lastly, to please my wife I undertook the labour of a set of plates. Fritz and Jack engaged to make the hives for the bees, and nests for the pigeons and hens. For this last object they took the largest gourds, and cut a hole in front, proportioned to the size of the animal for whose use it was intended. The pigeons' nests were intended to be tied to the branches of our tree; those for the hens, the geese, and the ducks were to be placed between its roots or on the sea-shore, and to represent a sort of hen-coop. When the most essential of the utensils were finished, I allowed the boys to add a dish to dress their crab in. This also was soon accomplished. But when the cooking was completed they discovered that they had no water. We found nothing on this spot like our providential *fountain* plants, as we had named them. The boys entreated me to go about with them in different directions and try to find water, as I would not allow them to venture farther into the woods alone.

I was therefore of necessity compelled to accompany them. Ernest had gone on a little ahead of us. It was not long before we heard him calling to us, and saw him returning in great alarm.

"Run quick, Father," said he, "here is an immense wild boar! I heard him grunting, and then he scampered away to the woods, and I hear him at this very moment."

"Here, here!" I then called out to the boys. "Call the dogs quickly. Halloo here! Turk! Ponto!"

The dogs arrived full gallop. Ernest was our leader, and conducted us to the place where the boar had approached him. But he was gone, and we saw nothing but a plot of potatoes, which had the appearance of having been ransacked by the animal. The ardour for the chase had been somewhat checked in Jack and Ernest, when they considered for a moment that they had so formidable a creature as a boar to encounter. They stopped short and began to dig potatoes, and left it to Fritz and me to follow the traces of the dogs. We soon heard their cry, and advanced with caution to the spot, holding our guns in readiness to fire. Presently the spectacle of the two brave creatures attacking him on the right and left presented itself. Each held one of his ears between their teeth. But the beast was not a boar, as the account of Ernest had made me suppose, but a pig of the true common breed, which on our approach appeared rather to ask for our assistance than to have any inclination to attack us. Fritz and myself also suddenly lost the relish for the sport, for we immediately recognized in the supposed boar our own sow which had run away and had so long been lost. After the first surprise we could not resist a hearty laugh, and then we hastened to disencumber our old friend of the teeth of her two adversaries. Her frightful squalling resounded through the wood and drew the attention of our companions, who now ran to the place, where a warfare of banter and accusation went round. Fritz knew certain persons whose passion for the chase ended in digging potatoes! Jack and Ernest returned the sally by complimenting Fritz on the wild boar he had been so fortunate as to make captive!

The attention of all was attracted to what looked like a kind of small potato which we observed lying thick on the grass around us, and which had fallen from some trees loaded with the same production. Our sow devoured them greedily, thus consoling herself for the fright she had been put into, and the pain the dogs had occasioned her.

The fruit was of different colours, and extremely pleasing to the eye. Fritz expressed his apprehension that it was a pernicious kind of apple called the Mancenilla. But the sow ate them with so much eagerness, and the tree which bore them being neither so high, and having neither the form nor foliage ascribed by naturalists to the Mancenilla, made me doubt of the truth of his idea. I desired my sons to put some of the fruit in their pockets, to make an experiment with them upon the monkey. We now again, from extreme thirst, recollected our want of water, and determined to seek for some in every direction. Jack sprang off and sought among the rocks, hoping, and with reason, that he should discover some little stream; but scarcely had he left the wood, than he bawled to us that he had found a crocodile.

"A crocodile!" cried I, with a hearty laugh. "Whoever saw a crocodile on such scorching rocks as these, and with not a drop of water near? Now, Jack, you are surely dreaming."

"Not so much of a dream as you may think, Father," answered Jack, trying to speak in a low voice. "Fortunately he is asleep; he lies here on a stone at his full length; he is exactly like Mother."

Father. "This is excellent, upon my word! So then your mother is like a crocodile?"

Jack. "I meant, Father, that the crocodile is about as long as the height of Mother; I had not, I assure you, the least idea of a joke. It is certainly a crocodile, though perhaps only a young one. Do, Father, step here and look at it."

I knew not what to think. We stole softly to the place where the animal lay, but instead of a crocodile, I saw before me an individual of a large sort of lizard, named by naturalists *Yguana*, the flesh of which is considered in the West Indies as the greatest delicacy. I explained this to my sons, and tranquillized them as to the danger of approaching this animal, of a mild character, and excellent as food. All were then seized with the hope of seizing the lizard and presenting a prize to their mother. Fritz had his gun ready, and was taking aim, but I was in time to prevent him.

"Let us try another way, as he is asleep," I said. "We need not be in a hurry; only a little contrivance is necessary to have him safe in our power alive."

I cut a stout stick from a bush, to the extremity of which I tied a string with a running knot. I guarded my other hand simply with a little switch, and thus with cautious steps approached the sleeping animal. When I was very near to him I began to whistle a lively air, taking care to make the sounds low at first, and to increase in loudness till the lizard was awaked. The creature appeared entranced with pleasure as the sounds fell upon his ear. He raised his head to receive them still more distinctly, and looked round on all sides to discover from whence they came. I now advanced by a step at a time, without a moment's interval in the music, which fixed him like a statue to the place. At length I was near enough to reach him with my switch, with which I tickled him gently, still continuing to whistle. The lizard was bewildered by the music. He stretched himself at full length, made undulating motions with his long tail, threw his head about, raised it up, and by this sort of action disclosed the range of his sharp-pointed teeth. I quickly seized the moment of his raising his head to throw my noose over him. When this was accomplished the boys drew near also, and wanted to draw it tight and strangle him; but this I forbade. I had used the noose only to make sure of him in case it should happen that a milder mode of killing him, which I intended to try, failed of success. Continuing to whistle, I seized a favourable moment to plunge my switch into one of his nostrils. The blood flowed in abundance, and soon deprived him of life, without his exhibiting the least symptom of being in pain; on the contrary, to the last moment he seemed to be still listening to the music.

As soon as he was dead I allowed the boys to come quite near. My sons were delighted with the means I had used for killing him.

"Little praise is due to me," I replied, "for I have often read the description of the manner of destroying this animal, so well known in the West Indies. But now let us consider of the best way for transporting him to Falcon's Stream."

I perceived that I had better carry him across my shoulders. The figure I made with so singular an animal on my back, with his tail dragging on the ground, was not the least amusing circumstance of the adventure. Fritz and Jack presented themselves as pages, contending which should support my train, as they called the tail, which, independently of the good-humour inspired amongst us, considerably eased me of the weight, and gave me the air of an old Chinese emperor habited in a superb royal mantle of many colours, for those of the lizard shone like precious stones in the eyes of the sun.

We were already far advanced in our return, when we distinguished the voice of my wife calling upon my name in a tone which indicated great uneasiness, and in addition we heard loud sobs from little Francis. Our long absence had excited painful apprehensions concerning us. No sooner, however, did our cheerful notes in speaking reach their ear, than their fears were changed to joy, and we soon found ourselves assembled together under a large gourd-tree, where we related to our dear companions every particular of the excursion we had made, not forgetting Jack's fancy of finding a resemblance between his mother and the lizard. We had so many things to inform her of that we lost sight of the principal object which caused our separation. Till she reminded us with some regret at our ill success, we forgot that we had failed of procuring any water. My sons had taken out some of the unknown apples from their pockets, and they lay on the ground by our side. Knips soon scented them, and according to custom he came slily up and stole several, and fell to chewing them with great eagerness. I myself threw one or two to the bustard, who also ate them without hesitation. Being now convinced that the apples were not poisonous, I announced to the boys, who had looked on with envy all the time, that they also might now begin to eat them, and I myself set the example. We found them excellent, and I began to suspect that they might be the sort of fruit called *guava*. The tree which bears them is sometimes twenty feet in height; no doubt, therefore, those from which we procured the fruit were too young to have attained their full stature.

This feast of guavas had in some measure relieved our thirst. On the other hand, it had increased our hunger; and as we had not time for preparing a portion of the lizard, we were obliged to content ourselves with the cold provisions we had brought with us. But we contrived to have an excellent dessert of potatoes, which the boys had had the foresight to lay under the cinders of the fire they had made to cook their crab.

We had scarcely finished before my wife entreated that we might begin our journey home, to be sure of arriving before dark. In fact, it appeared to me, as the evening was so far advanced, that it would be prudent to return without the sledge, which was heavy laden, and the ass would have driven it but slowly. I was, besides, inclined to take a shorter road by a narrow path that divided a plantation of thick bushes, which would have been too difficult a passage for the ass burdened with the sledge. I therefore determined to leave it till the following day, when I could return for it, contenting myself with loading the ass for the present with the bags which contained our new sets of porcelain and the lizard. Francis, who began to complain of being tired, I also placed on the back of the ass. I took these arrangements upon myself, and left to my wife and Fritz the care of confining the bustard in such a manner that she could walk without danger of escaping.

On leaving the wood of gourds, we arrived at a spot where we found more of the guava-trees, and could not resist the temptation to secure a new supply. The course of our route lay next along a majestic wood of oaks, interspersed with fig-trees of luxuriant growth, and of the same species as those at Falcon's Stream. The ground in this place was absolutely covered with acorns. My young travellers, ever on the watch for something gratifying to the palate, could not refrain from tasting them.

I more than ever admired the magnificence of the trees which at this moment covered us with their shade. On considering, I recognized that they were a kind of oak which remains always green, and are a common production of the woods in Florida, and that the Indians of North America extract from its fruit an excellent kind of sweet oil, which they use in cooking their rice. Numerous kinds of birds subsist upon these acorns. This we were led to remark by the wild and discordant cries of several sorts of jays and parrots. The boys would have fired their guns, and I could only prevail upon them to desist by observing how late it was, and promising that we would return another time.

We arrived sooner than we expected at Falcon's Stream. The path we had taken had so considerably lessened the distance, that we were in time to employ ourselves in some trifling arrangements before it was completely dark. My wife had great pleasure in taking out her service of porcelain and using some of the articles, particularly the egg-basket and the vessels for the milk. Fritz was instructed to dig a place in the ground to serve for a cooler, the better to preserve the milk, and we covered it with boards and put heavy stones to keep them down. Jack took the pigeons' nests and scampered up the tree, where he nailed them to the branches. He next laid some dry moss within, and placed one of the female pigeons we had contrived to tame, and which at the time was brooding, upon it. He put the eggs carefully under the mother, who seemed to accept his services, and to coo with gratitude.

My own employment was to clean the lizard and prepare a piece for our supper. My wife having expressed an extreme repugnance to both the lizard and the crab, we added some potatoes and some acorns, and dressed them together, and thus suited every palate. Francis had the care of turning the spit, and liked his office all the better for its allowing of his being near his mother. We all drew near a clear brisk fire while the supper was in hand. We concluded the exertions of the day by contriving a comfortable bed for the bustard by the side of the flamingo, and then hastened to stretch our limbs upon the beds, rendered by fatigue luxurious, that waited for us in the giant tree.

CHAPTER TWENTY-THREE

EXCURSION INTO UNKNOWN COUNTRIES

~

It is scarcely necessary to relate that my first thought the next morning was to fetch the sledge. I had a double motive for leaving it there, which I had refrained from explaining to my wife to avoid giving her uneasiness. I had formed a wish to penetrate a little farther into the soil, and ascertain whether anything useful would present itself beyond the wall of rocks. I was, besides, desirous to be better acquainted with our island. I wished Fritz only to accompany me. We took Turk with us. We set out very early in the morning, and drove the ass before us for the purpose of drawing home the sledge.

On reaching the wood of evergreen oaks, we found the sow feeding upon the acorns under the trees. We wished her a good appetite, and begged her to admit us to the honour of partaking her breakfast. Accordingly Fritz filled the pockets of his waistcoat with some of them. As we were quietly picking up the acorns, we observed some birds flying towards us. Some of them were clothed with a plumage of exquisite beauty, and for this once I could not refuse Fritz the pleasure of firing upon them, that we might in consequence obtain a nearer view, and inform ourselves respecting their species. He brought down three. I recognized one to be the great blue Virginia jay, and the other two were parrots. One of the two was a superb red parrot, the other was green and yellow.

We soon arrived at the guava-trees, and a little after at the spot where we had left the sledge, when we found our treasures in the best possible condition. As the morning was not far advanced, we entered upon our project of penetrating beyond the wall of rocks.

We pursued our way in a straight line at the foot of these massy productions of nature, every moment expecting to reach their extremity, or to find some turn, or breach, or passage through them, that should conduct us into the interior of the island, if, as I presumed, it was not terminated by these rocks. We walked on, continually looking about, that nothing worthy of notice might escape us, or to be enabled to anticipate and avoid such dangers as should threaten. Turk as usual took the lead, the ass followed with lazy steps, shaking his long ears, and Fritz and I brought up the rear. We met from time to time with some small streams, which afforded a most agreeable refreshment. We passed a wood of guava-trees, and fields of potatoes and manioc, the stalks of which perplexed our way; but we were recompensed by the fine views which everywhere presented themselves, and which the low stature of the plants enabled us to see in perfection. To the right, on the high grounds, we saw hares and agoutis amusing themselves in the morning sun. Fritz mistook them for marmots, but not one of them made the whistling kind of sound which is customary with these animals when they see a strange object.

We next entered a pretty little grove, the trees of which were unknown to us. Their branches were loaded with large quantities of berries of an extraordinary quality, being entirely covered with a wax which stuck to our fingers as we attempted to gather them. I knew of a sort of bush producing wax that grows in America, and named by botanists *Myrica cerifera*. I had no doubt that this was the plant, and the discovery gave me great pleasure. "Let us stop here," said I to Fritz, "for we cannot do better than collect a great quantity of these berries as a useful present to your mother."

A short time after another kind of object presented itself with equal claims to our attention. It was the singular behaviour of a kind of bird scarcely larger than a chaffinch, and clothed in feathers of a common brown colour. These birds appeared to exist as a republic, there being among them one common nest, inhabited at pleasure by all their tribes. We saw one of these nests in a tree in a somewhat retired situation. It was formed of platted straws and bulrushes intermixed. It appeared to us to enclose great numbers of inhabitants, and was constructed in an irregular form round the trunk of the tree where the branches sprout. It appeared to us to have a kind of roof formed of roots and bulrushes, but more carefully knit than the rest of the structure. In the sides, which were unequally formed, we observed a quantity of small apertures, seemingly intended as doors and windows to each particular cell. From a few of these apertures issued small branches, which served the birds as points of rest. The external appearance of the whole excited the image of an immensely large, open sponge. The birds which inhabited it were very numerous. They passed in and out continually, and I estimated that it might contain at least a million. The males were somewhat larger than the females, and there was a trifling difference in their plumage.

While we were examining this interesting little colony, we perceived a very small kind of parrot, not much larger than the birds themselves, hovering about the nest. Their gilded green wings and the variety of their colours produced a beautiful effect. They seemed to be perpetually disputing with the colonists, and not unfrequently endeavoured to prevent their entrance. They attacked them fiercely, and even endeavoured to peck at us if we but advanced our hand to the structure. Fritz, who was well trained in the art of climbing trees, was earnestly desirous to take a nearer view of such extraordinary beings, and to secure, if possible, a few individuals. He threw his bundles to the ground, and climbed till he reached the nest. He then tried to introduce his hand into one of the apertures, and to seize whatever living creature it should touch in that particular cell. What he most desired was to find a female brooding hen, and to carry both her and the eggs away. Several of the cells were empty, but by perseverance he found one in the situation he wished. But he did not pursue his plan without meeting with the punishment of his curiosity. He received so violent a stroke from the beak of an invisible bird, that his only care was now to withdraw his hand. But though punished he was not cured. No sooner had the pain subsided, than he ventured a second time to pass his hand into the nest, and succeeded in seizing his prey, which he laid hold of by the middle of the body, and in spite of the bird's resistance, its cries and wailings, he drew it through the aperture and squeezed it into his breast-pocket, and buttoning his coat securely, he slid down the tree and reached the ground in safety. The signals of distress sent forth by the prisoner collected a multitude of birds from their cells, who all surrounded him, uttering piteous cries and flying at him with their beaks, till he had made good his retreat. The birds pursued him till he was quite close to my side, when, by making a loud noise and waving my pocket-handkerchief; I succeeded in driving them away. Fritz now released the prisoner, and we discovered him to be a beautiful little green parrot, which Fritz entreated he might be allowed to preserve and make a present of to his brothers. I did not oppose his request, but thinking we had spent too much time upon this singular bird-colony, I bade him prepare for returning home. The birds were naturally the subject of our conversation on the road. It was the first time I had ever witnessed such a spectacle as a swarm of birds living together in one nest, and I was surprised at it. From the circumstance of so young a bird being nestled within the structure, it appeared probable that the true right of property was in this species, and that the brown-coloured birds we at first observed were intruders endeavouring to deprive them of it.

We had proceeded a considerable way, and had reached a wood, the trees of which were unknown to us, though they in a small degree resembled the wild fig-tree – at least the fruit they bore, like the fig, was round in form, and contained a soft juicy substance full of small grains. It had, however, a sharpness and sourness in the taste.

We took a nearer view of these trees, so remarkable for their height. The bark of the trunk was prickly or scaly, like the pine-apple, and wholly bare of branches, except at the very top, where they are loaded with them. The leaves of these trees, at the extremity of the branches, are very thick. In substance tough, like leather, their upper and under surfaces presented different tints. But what surprised us the most was a kind of gum, or bituminous matter, which appeared to issue in a liquid state from the trunk of the tree, and to become immediately hardened by the air. This discovery awakened Fritz's whole attention. In Europe he had often made use of the gum produced by cherry-trees, either as a cement or varnish, and the thought struck him that he could do the same with what he now saw. He accordingly collected with his knife a certain quantity.

As he continued walking he looked frequently at his gum, which he tried to soften with his breath or with the heat of his hand, as he had been accustomed to do with that from the cherry-trees, but he found he could not succeed. On the other hand, his endeavours revealed a still more singular property in the substance – that of stretching considerably on being pulled by the two hands at its extremities, and, on letting go, of reducing itself instantly by the power of an elastic principle. He was struck with surprise and sprang towards me, exclaiming, "Look, Father! if this is not the very kind of India rubber we formerly used to rub out the bad strokes in our drawings. See! I can stretch it, and it instantly shrinks back when I let go!"

"Ah! what do you tell me?" cried I with joy. "The best thanks of all will be due to you if you have discovered the true caoutchouc-tree which yields the Indian rubber. Quick, hand it here that I may examine it."

Fritz. "Look, Father, how it will stretch! Can it be made to serve any other purpose than rubbing out a pencil-mark? Nor am I quite sure that it is the very same ingredient. Why is it not black, like that we used in Europe?"

Father. "Caoutchouc is a milky sap which runs from certain trees. This liquid is received by those who collect it in vessels placed for the purpose. It is afterwards made to take the form of dark-coloured bottles of different sizes, such as we have seen them, in the following manner. Before the liquid which runs out has time to coagulate, small earthen bottles are dipped into it a sufficient number of times to form the thickness required. These vessels are then hung over smoke, which dries them, and gives the dark colour you allude to. Before they are entirely dry a knife is drawn across them, which produces the lines or figures with which you have seen them marked. The concluding part of the operation is to break the bottle which has served for a mould, and to get out the pieces by the passage of the neck, when the ingredient remains in the complete form of a bottle, soft to the touch, firm in substance, yet flexible and convenient to carry about, from being not liable to break, and may be even used as a vessel to contain liquid if necessary.

Fritz. "The fabrication seems simple, so let us try to make some bottles of it."

Father. "Its quality is admirable, too, Fritz, for being made into shoes and boots without seams. There is, besides, another use for which this substance is both fit and excellent. It renders waterproof any kind of linen or woollen production to which it may be applied."

Well satisfied with the discovery we had made, we continued our way, endeavouring still farther to explore the wood. After passing through it, we rested ourselves with great pleasure for a few minutes, and were regaled with two coco-nuts, which Turk had forced from two little monkeys, which were playing on the ground like children. After this refreshment we resumed our route. We were determined to reach the farthest outlet of this great wood to examine the dimensions of our empire. In a short time we had taken some observations to ascertain this point, and, looking attentively, we recognized the great bay on the right, and on the left Cape Disappointment, which latter had been the farthest point of our earliest excursion.

In this spot alone, and mixed with a quantity of coco-trees, I discovered a tree of smaller growth, which I presumed must be the sago palm. One of these had been thrown down by the wind, so that I was able to examine it. I perceived that the trunk contained a quantity of a mealy substance; I therefore with my hatchet laid it open longways, and cleared it of the whole contents, and on tasting the ingredient I found it was exactly like the sago I had often eaten in Europe.

We began to consider how much farther we would go. The thick bushes of bamboo, through which it was impossible to pass, seemed to furnish a natural conclusion to our journey. We were therefore unable to ascertain whether we should have found a passage beyond the wall of rocks. We perceived, then, no better resource than to turn to the left towards Cape Disappointment, where the luxurious plantations of sugar-canes again drew our attention. That we might not return empty-handed to Falcon's Stream, we each took the pains to cut a large bundle of the canes, which we threw across the ass's back, not forgetting the ceremony of reserving one apiece to refresh ourselves. We soon reached the wood of gourds, where we found our sledge as we had left it the night before. We took the sugar-canes from the ass and fastened them to the sledge, and then we harnessed the ass, and the patient animal began to draw towards home.

We arrived at Falcon's Stream rather early in the evening. Each of the boys seized a sugar-cane and began to suck it, as did their mother also. Nothing could be more amusing than to hear Fritz relate the recent discoveries we had made. Then came the history of the colony of birds and their singular habitation, and of the green parrot, all of which was listened to with the delight excited by a fairy tale. Fritz showed them the handsome red parrot, dead, also the great blue jay, both of which they did not cease to admire. But when he took out of his pocket the little parrot all alive, there were no bounds to their ecstasy. At length the bird was fastened by the leg to one of the roots of the trees till a cage could be made, and was fed with acorns, which he appeared to relish. My wife was delighted with the prospect of the candles I assured her I was now able to furnish. Fritz took a bit of the rubber from his pocket and drew it to its full length, and then let it suddenly go, to the great amusement of little Francis.

Soon after nightfall, after partaking of a hearty supper, we all mounted the ladder, and, having carefully drawn it up, we fell, exhausted, into sound and peaceful slumbers.

CHAPTER TWENTY-FOUR

USEFUL OCCUPATIONS AND LABOURS – EMBELLISHMENTS – A PAINFUL BUT NATURAL SENTIMENT

~

On the following day, neither my wife nor the boys left me a moment's tranquillity till I had put my manufactory of candles in some forwardness. I soon perceived that I should be at a loss for a little suet or mutton-fat to mix with the wax from the berries, for making the light burn clearer. But as I had neither of these articles, I was compelled to proceed without them. I put as many berries into a vessel as it would contain, and set it on a moderate fire. My wife in the meantime employed herself in making some wicks with the threads of sail-cloth. When we saw an oily matter of a pleasing smell and light-green colour rise to the top of the liquid, we skimmed it off and put it into a separate vessel, taking care to keep it warm. We continued this process till the berries had produced a considerable quantity of wax. We next dipped the wicks one by one into it while it remained liquid, and then hung them on the bushes. In a short time we dipped them again, and continued till the candles were increased to the proper size. They were then put in a place and kept till sufficiently hardened for use. We were all eager to judge of our success that very evening by burning one of the candles, and we had reason to be well satisfied. We should now be able to sit up later, and consequently spend less of our time in sleep. But independently of this advantage, the mere sight of a candle, which for so long a time we had been deprived of, caused ecstasies of joy to all.

Our success in this last enterprise encouraged us to think of another, the idea of which had long been cherished – it was the construction of a cart. I tried earnestly and long to accomplish my object, but for long did not succeed, and wasted both time and timber. I, however, at last produced what from courtesy we called a cart, but I would not advise my readers to take it for a model, though it answered the purpose.

While I was thus engaged, the boys and their mother were no less busy, and I now and then left my cart to assist them with my advice; though I must say they seldom stood in need of it. They undertook to transplant the greatest part of the European fruit-trees, to place them where they would be in a better situation for growth, according to the properties of each. They planted vineshoots round the roots of the magnificent tree we inhabited, and round the trunks of some other kinds of trees which grew near. We watched them, in the fond anticipation that they would in time ascend to a height capable of being formed into a sort of trellis, and help to cool us by their shade. In the climate we inhabited, the vine requires the protection of the larger trees against the rays of the sun. Lastly, we planted two parallel lines of saplings, consisting of chestnut, cherry, and the common nut trees, to form an avenue from Family Bridge to Falcon's Stream, which would hereafter afford us a cool shade in our walks to Tent House. This last undertaking was not to be effected without labour and fatigue. The ground was to be cleared, and a certain breadth covered with sand, left higher in the middle than on the sides, for the sake of being always dry. The boys fetched the sand from the sea-shore in their wheelbarrows, and I nailed together a few pieces of wood, in the form of a tub, which could be harnessed to the ass to ease in some measure their fatigue.

Our next concern was to introduce, if possible, some shade, and other improvements on the barren site of Tent House, and to render our visits there more secure. We began by planting all those sorts of trees that thrive best in the sun, such as lemon, pistachio, almond, mulberry, and lime trees; lastly, some of a kind of orange-tree which attains to a prodigious size, and bears a fruit as large as the head of a child, and weighs not less than twelve or fourteen pounds. The commoner sorts of nut-trees we placed along the shore. The better to conceal and fortify our tent, which enclosed all our stores, we formed on the accessible side a hedge of orange and lemon trees, which produce an abundant prickly foliage. To add to the agreeableness of their appearance, we introduced here and there the pomegranate. Nor did I omit to make a little arbour of the guava-shrub, which bears a small fruit rather pleasant to the taste. We also took care to introduce at proper places a certain number of the largest sorts of trees, which in time would serve the purpose of shading annual plants, and, with benches placed under them, be a kind of private cabinet. Should any accident or alarm compel us to retire to Tent House, a thing of the first importance would be to find there food for our cattle. For the greater security I formed a plantation of the thorny fig-tree, of sufficient breadth to occupy the space between our fortress and the river, thus rendering it difficult for an enemy to approach.

The curving form of the river having left some elevations of the soil within the enclosure, I found means to work them into slopes and angles so as to serve as bastions to our two cannon and our other firearms, should we ever be attacked. My concluding labour was to plant some cedars along the usual landing-places, to which we might fasten our vessels.

We employed many weeks in effecting what for the present it was possible to effect, of these arrangements. The exercise of mind and body they imposed contributed to the health of the boys, and to the support of cheerfulness in ourselves. The more we embellished our abode by the work of our own hands, the more it became dear to our hearts. The strict observance of the Sabbath-day afforded such an interval of rest as could not fail to restore our strength and inspire us with the desire of new exertions.

Our labours wore out our clothes so fast that another trip to the vessel was absolutely necessary. We had exhausted the stock we had brought away, and were now in rags. We feared we saw the time when we should be compelled to renounce European dress. I had also another reason for wishing to visit the ship. The cart I had just completed disclosed a defect which it was scarcely possible to endure. It was a violent creaking of the wheels at every turn, and in addition the wheels moved so imperfectly round the axle-tree, that the united strength of the ass and the cow could scarcely drag the machine along. It was in vain that, in spite of my wife's reproofs, I applied a little butter; in an hour or two the butter was dried, and the wheels remained the same.

These two circumstances compelled us, then, once more to have recourse to the vessel. We knew there remained on board five or six chests containing apparel, and we suspected there were also some tubs of pitch and grease for wheels in her hold. To these motives were added that of an earnest desire to take another look at her, and, if practicable, to bring away a few pieces of cannon which might be fixed on the new bastions at Tent House.

The first fine day I assembled my three eldest sons, and put my design into execution. We reached the wreck and found her still fixed between the rocks. We did not lose a moment in searching for the tubs of pitch, which, with the help of the pulley, we soon conveyed into the pinnace; we next secured the chests of clothes, and whatever remained of ammunition stores – powder, shot, and even such pieces of cannon as we could remove, while those that were too heavy we stripped of their wheels.

But to effect our purpose it was necessary to spend several days in visits to the vessel, returning constantly in the evening, enriched with everything of a portable nature which the wreck contained; doors, windows, locks, bolts, nothing escaped our grasp, so that the ship was now entirely emptied, with the exception of the heavy cannon and three or four immense copper caldrons, which were too heavy. We by degrees contrived to tie these heavy articles to two or three empty casks well pitched, which would effectually sustain themselves and the cannon above water. When these measures were taken, I came to the resolution of blowing up the wreck. I directed my views to that part of the vessel which had been entirely stripped of everything; I supposed that the wind and tide would convey the beams and timbers ashore, and thus with little pains we should be possessed of materials for erecting a building.

We accordingly prepared a cask of gunpowder, which we left on board. We made a small opening in its side, and at the moment of quitting the vessel we inserted a piece of match-wood, which we lighted at the last moment, as before. We then sailed with all possible expedition for Safety Bay. We could not, however, withdraw our thoughts from the wreck and from the expected explosion. I had cut the match a sufficient length for us to hope that she would not go to pieces before dark. I proposed to my wife to have our supper carried to a little point of land from whence we had a view of her, and here we waited for the moment of her destruction.

About the time of nightfall, a majestic rolling sound like thunder, accompanied by a column of fire and smoke, announced that the ship was that instant annihilated, and withdrawn for ever from the face of man! At this moment, love for the country that gave us birth, that most powerful sentiment of the human heart, sunk with a new force into ours. Could we hope ever to behold that country more?

My wife was the only person who was sensible of consolation. She was now relieved from all the fears for our safety in our visits to the wreck. From this moment she conceived a stronger partiality for our island. A night's repose relieved the melancholy of the preceding evening, and I went early in the morning with the boys to make further observations as to the effects of this remarkable event. We perceived in the water and along the shore abundant vestiges of the departed wreck, and among the rest, at a certain distance, the empty casks, caldrons, and cannon, all tied together, and floating. We jumped instantly into the pinnace, with the tub-boat fastened to it, and made a way towards them, and in a little time reached the object of our search, which from its great weight moved slowly upon the waves. With this rich booty we returned to land.

We performed three more trips for the purpose of bringing away more cannon, caldrons, fragments of masts, &c., all of which we deposited in Safety Bay. And now began our most fatiguing operations, the removing such numerous and heavy stores from the boats to Tent House. We separated the cannon and the caldrons from the tub-raft and from each other, and left them in a place which was accessible for the sledge and the beasts of burden. With the help of the crowbar we succeeded in getting the caldrons upon the sledge, and in replacing the four wheels we had before taken from the cannon, which we found it easy to make the cow and the ass draw. We in the same manner conveyed away all the wood we wished to preserve dry, and what stores remained we tied with cords to stakes to protect them from the tide.

The largest of the boilers or copper caldrons, which had been intended as utensils for a manufactory of sugar, we now found of the most essential use. We brought out all our barrels of gunpowder, and placed them on their ends in three separate groups at a short distance from our tent; we dug a little ditch round the whole to draw off the moisture from the ground, and then put one of the caldrons turned upside down upon each group of barrels, which answered the purpose of an out-house. The cannon were covered with sail-cloth, and upon this we laid heavy branches of trees. The larger casks of gunpowder we removed under a projecting rock, where, should they even blow up, no mischief could arise to the inhabitants of Tent House.

My wife made the agreeable discovery that two of our ducks and one of the geese had been brooding under a large bush, and at the time were conducting their little families to the water. The news produced general rejoicings. Fritz and Ernest looked forward to some luxurious Sunday dinners, and Jack and Francis wondered what the young birds could think when they first saw human creatures! We in a short time found means to tame them by throwing them crumbs of manioc. This last employment, together with the gambols of the little creatures, so forcibly carried our thought to Falcon's Stream, that we all conceived the desire of returning to the society of the old friends we had left there. One sighed for his monkey, another for his flamingo; Francis for his parrot, and his mother for her poultry-yard, her various housewifery accommodations, and her comfortable bed. We therefore fixed the next day for our departure, and set about the necessary preparations.

CHAPTER TWENTY-FIVE

A New Excursion –
Palm-tree Wine

~

On entering our new plantation of fruit-trees forming the avenue to Falcon's Stream, we observed that they inclined to droop. We therefore immediately resolved to support them with sticks, and I proposed a walk to the vicinity of Cape Disappointment for the purpose of cutting some bamboos. I had no sooner pronounced the words than the three eldest boys and their mother exclaimed at once that they would accompany me. Our provision of candles was nearly exhausted, and a new stock of berries must therefore be procured, for my wife now repaired our clothes by candle-light, while I employed myself in composing a journal of the events of every day; then, the sow had again deserted us, and nothing could be so probable as that we should find her in the acorn wood; Jack would fain gather some guavas for himself, and Francis must needs see the sugar-canes. In short, all would visit this land of Canaan.

We accordingly fixed the following morning, and set out in full procession. For myself, I had a great desire to explore this part of our island, and to reap some more substantial advantages from its produce. I therefore made some preparations for sleeping, should we find the day too short. I took the cart instead of the sledge, having fixed some planks across it for Francis and his mother to sit upon when they should be tired. I was careful to be provided with the different implements we might want; some rope machinery I had contrived for rendering the climbing of trees more easy; and lastly, provisions, consisting of a piece of the salted tortoise, water in a gourd-flask, and one bottle of wine. When all was placed in the cart, I for this occasion harnessed to it both the ass and the cow, as I expected the load would be increased on our return. We set out, taking the road of the potato and manioc plantations. Our first halt was at the tree of the colony of birds. Close upon the same spot were also the trees whose berries produced the wax, and intermixed with these some of the guava kind. On this second occasion of seeing the birds, I recollected to what species they belonged, which by naturalist is named *Loxia gregaria* (Sociable Grossbeak).

It was not without difficulty that we conducted the cart through the thick bushes. We succeeded tolerably well at last, and that the poor animals might have time to rest, we determined to pass several hours in this place. We began by gathering a bagful of the guavas, and after regaling ourselves put the remainder into the cart. We next examined anew the structure of the nest inhabited by the colony of birds, and concluded, contrary to the opinion I had formerly entertained, that the little green parrot was an invader, for numerous flocks of the brown-coloured birds now passed in and out, rested upon the bushes which produced the wax, and devoured large quantities of the berries, which explained the reason of their building their abode in this particular spot. We claimed the same privilege as the birds, and had soon filled another bag. Seeing them so greedily consumed by those little creatures, the boys desired to follow their example, and tasted them, but found them insipid.

We continued our way, and soon arrived at the caoutchouc or gum-elastic trees. I thought we could not do better than to halt here and collect a sufficient quantity of the sap to make the different kinds of utensils, and the impermeable boots and shoes, as I had before proposed. It was with this design that I had taken care to bring with me several gourd rinds. I made deep incisions in the trunks, and fixed some large leaves of trees, partly doubled together length-ways, to the place, to serve as a sort of channel to conduct the sap to the vessels. We had not long begun this process before we perceived the sap begin to run out as white as milk, and in large drops, so that we were not without hopes by the time of our return to find the vessels full.

We pursued our way to the wood of coco-trees. Thence we passed to the left, and stopped half-way between the bamboos and sugar-canes, to furnish ourselves with a provision of each. We aimed our course so that on clearing the skirts of the wood we found ourselves in an open plain, with the sugar-cane plantations on our left, and on our right those of bamboo interspersed with various kinds of palm-trees, and in front the magnificent bay formed by Cape Disappointment.

The prospect that now presented itself to our view was of such exquisite beauty that we determined to choose it for our resting-place, and to make it the central point of every future excursion. We were even more than half disposed to desert our pretty Falcon's Stream. A moment's reflection, however, betrayed the folly of quitting the thousand comforts we had assembled there.

Our next proceeding was to divide amongst us the different occupations which were the objects of our walk. Some scampered away to the right to cut bamboos, others to the left to secure the sugar-canes, of both of which a large bundle was collected. The exertions made by the boys again excited their desire to eat. They sucked some of the canes, but their hunger was not appeased. Their mother, however, refused to let them have the remainder of the provisions, and they therefore cast a longing eye to the tops of the trees, where they saw a great number of coco-nuts. After a short deliberation it was determined that two of them should venture on climbing to the top, a height of from sixty to eighty feet, and with the hatchet, which would be fastened to his waist, should beat them down. Fritz and Jack had no hesitation. They selected the trees for their attempt, and proceeded a considerable way. But the trunks were too thick to be easily grasped by their legs and arms, and they were obliged to come down again much quicker than they had ascended. It was now my part to suggest something. "I have something here," said I, "which may help. Here are some pieces of prepared shagreen, which must be tied round your legs. Then with this cord I shall fasten you by the body to the trunk of the tree, but so loosely that it will move up and down when you do. By sitting occasionally on this cord you will be enabled to rest when necessary, and so push on by little and little. This manner of climbing trees is practised by savages with success."

The boys had listened with entire attention. Excited by the description, they demanded to be equipped for the experiment, and their success exceeded our expectation. They with tolerable ease reached the top, where the thick-tufted foliage furnished a seat, whence they sent forth exulting salutations. They now set to work, when presently a shower of coco-nuts descended. The monkey took the fancy of imitating his masters, and springing into one of the trees, he with his teeth and his paws sent down as many nuts as the hatchet. He then came down with equal swiftness, and seating himself on the ground began to crack one of the nuts, making all the time such strange grimaces as to occasion us all much merriment.

Ernest was the only person who took no part in this animated scene. His brothers began to banter him on the old subject of his indolence. They gravely offered him some coco-nut, *to refresh him after so much fatigue.* He made no reply, and pushed the offering aside. He then rose from his seat, and began to examine the trees one by one with deep attention. He requested me to saw off the top of a coco-nut for him, which he emptied, and fastened round it cross-ways a string with a loop to hang it to the button of his waistcoat. Not one of us could imagine what he was going to do. He placed a small hatchet in his girdle, and then advancing a few paces out of the group we formed, he in a graceful manner pronounced the following little address:

"I am sensible, my dear parents, that in our republic, or rather in our kingdom, I am, I say, sensible that here, as in Europe, he who has sufficient talent to raise himself above the rest is held in high consideration and esteem. For my own part, I must confess I had more pleasure in remaining in tranquillity without endeavours to obtain distinction. I have but little ambition, and am fond of quiet, and therefore the greater will be my desert if I, like the rest, resolve to contribute to the general good of this our country, by executing, as the other subjects have done, the task of climbing trees, well satisfied if, like them, I should obtain the applauses of my king and of my fellow-citizens! To the tree then, since climbing is the question!" said he, saluting us with his hand as he sprang away to a high palm-tree of the cabbage species.

I looked with extreme curiosity, but when I saw him courageously grasp the trunk with his legs and arms, and proceed to climb, I approached the tree and offered him the shagreen and the cord. He accepted the first but refused the cord. "I am naturally somewhat awkward," observed he, "and to have to draw a cord after me would only add to my difficulty; besides, I think I have no occasion for it." In fact, he exerted his limbs with so much spirit, that I was astonished at the rapidity of his ascent, and conceived at every remove the most alarm, since the farther from the ground the more danger would attend him should any slip or other accident occasion him to fall. When Ernest now showed himself at the very top of the tree, Fritz and Jack burst into an immoderate fit of laughter. "Pains enough for nothing, Master Ernest!" bawled they as loud as they could. "In your wisdom you have chosen a tree which has no fruit upon it. Not a single coco-nut will you bring down, your most devoted fellow-subjects can truly assure you!"

"Not a coco-nut, certainly," replied Ernest in his loudest voice; "but, brothers, you shall receive a crown instead!" and at the same instant he with his hatchet cut off the tufted summit of the palm-tree, and a large mass of tender leaves fell at our feet.

"Mischievous boy!" cried his mother. "Disappointed of his coco-nuts, see if he has not cut off the head of this magnificent palm-tree, and it will perish in consequence!"

"I am happy, Mother, to be able to correct your mistake!" cried Ernest from his stately column, where he stood erect and looked like a statue. "What I have done was from a desire to procure you one of the finest kinds of food this country affords. The tree is the cabbage palm-tree, and, believe me, you will find it a more valuable acquisition than even our coco-nuts!"

"A cabbage!" exclaimed Fritz. "Ah, ah, Master Ernest, so you would make us believe that cabbages grow on palm-trees!"

"Examine this production, to which the name of palm-cabbage has been given by naturalists," said I. "It has not the shape of our European cabbage, but, as Ernest tells you, it is a most delicious food. He has also had the merit of distinguishing this tree from others. And let me seize the present occasion, young ones, to reprove you for the taunting spirit in which you viewed your brother's proceedings, who, though less enterprising and less alert than you, so far surpasses any one of you in observation and reflection. To him we are indebted for the most useful of the discoveries which have been made – the potatoes and the manioc."

We now looked up to invite Ernest to come down. We beheld him in a fixed erect position in the very centre of the palm-tree which he had stripped of its crown, as motionless as if he had become a cabbage. The effect of this spectacle was irresistibly ludicrous; and accordingly the boys, in spite of the lecture I had that moment concluded, burst into a fit of laughter.

I now called out to Ernest. "Do you mean," said I, "to stay all night in your tree, or are you afraid to come down?"

"Far from it, Father," answered he, "but I am engaged in preparing you here some good sauce for the cabbage, and the operation takes a longer time than I imagined."

"What can he mean?" asked little Francis. "Do you know, Papa, I have been thinking that this must be an enchanted forest, like those I have read about. Perhaps some of these trees are all the time princes and princesses. Do you think it very likely, Fritz?" said the young innocent, with so real and fearful a persuasion that we all laughed heartily as we answered his question.

By this time Ernest had finished his work, and was descending cautiously from the tree. When he reached the ground he released the coco-shell from his button, held it delicately in one hand, while with the other he drew from his pocket a small bottle, and pulling out the cork he emptied the contents into the shell and presented it to his mother, saying:

"Most gracious sovereign, permit your devoted cup-bearer to present you with a specimen of a new and choice beverage; may it be pleasing to your royal taste. It is called palm-wine, and your slave waits but your commands to obtain a larger supply!"

The other boys looked on in astonishment. I was myself less surprised, having read accounts of this production in different books.

"It is excellent, my boy," said my wife, smiling at her son's quaint address, "and we shall unite in drinking to your health."

I now made some inquiries of Ernest as to his previous knowledge of the tree and its properties.

"I knew," continued he, "that there was a sort of palm which bore a cabbage at the top; I thought that the tree which had no coco-nuts was most likely to be the sort; and you see I was lucky in my guess." He then related his expectation of finding some of our famous palm-wine also. "When I had cut off the cabbage," said he, "a quantity of juice issued from the place, which I tasted and found first-rate. You know the rest, Father," added he, "and I have only to regret that I had not a larger bottle to receive it; but now that we know the means, we can obtain the liquor when we please."

"A small quantity at a time," observed I, "will always be best; for the juice, though so like to champagne in flavour, and which would, perhaps, affect our heads as soon if we were to use it freely, would by to-morrow be quite sour. As there are abundance of the trees, we can, as you say, procure the liquor at pleasure, only taking care to be moderate; for if the cabbage at the top is cut off the tree dies. There are other sorts of palm-trees besides those we have noticed; one in particular, which yields a kind of oil which burns whatever it is applied to. In the meantime let us render thanks to Providence for the benefits He has bestowed."

It was now past noon. As we had determined to pass the night in this enchanting spot, we began to think of forming some large branches into a sort of hut. I accordingly set to work. I had brought a piece of sail-cloth with me from Falcon's Stream, and I drove some stakes into the ground, and covered them with it, filling the opening in the front with branches. While we were engaged in our work, which was nearly completed, we were suddenly roused by the loud braying of the ass, which we had left to graze at a distance. As we approached, we saw him throwing his head in the air and kicking and prancing about in a most extraordinary manner; and while we were thinking what could be the matter, he set off on a full gallop. Unfortunately, Turk and Ponto, whom we sent after him, took the fancy of entering the plantation of the sugar-canes, while the ass had preferred the direction of the bamboos. In a little time the dogs returned, and showed no signs, by scenting the ground or otherwise, of any pursuit. I made a turn round the hut to see that all was well, and then sallied forth with Fritz and the two dogs in the direction the ass had taken, hoping the latter might be enabled to trace him. But the dogs could not be made to understand our meaning. As night was coming on, I gave up the pursuit and returned to my companions.

Fatigued, and vexed with the loss of the ass, I entered the hut, which I found complete with branches strewed on the ground for sleeping, and with some reeds for making a fire. After supper we were glad to enjoy the blessing of sleep. When all was safe, I watched and replenished the fire till midnight, rather from habit than the fear of wild beasts, and then took possession of the little corner assigned me.

CHAPTER TWENTY-SIX

A NEW COUNTRY DISCOVERED – THE TROOP OF BUFFALOES – A PRECIOUS ACQUISITION

~

The following morning found us all in good health, and thankful for the Divine protection we had enjoyed. We breakfasted on milk, boiled potatoes, and a portion of Dutch cheese, and formed during our meal the plan of the business for the day. It was decided that one of the boys and myself, attended by the two dogs, should seek the ass in every direction. As I was to take both the dogs, I left the two eldest boys to protect little Francis and his mother, and took for my own escort the agile Jack.

We took our hatchets, firearms, a saw for coco-nuts, and began our course with the dawn. We soon reached the bamboo plantation, and found means to force ourselves along its intricate entanglements. After the most exhausting fatigue, and when we were on the point of relinquishing all hope, we discovered the print of the ass's hoofs, which inspired us with new ardour. After spending a whole hour in further endeavours, we at length, on reaching the skirts of the plantation, perceived the sea, and soon after found ourselves in an open space which bounded the great bay. A considerable river flowed into the bay, and we perceived that the ridge of rocks which we had invariably observed to the right extended to the shore, terminating in a precipice, leaving only a narrow passage, which during every flux of the tide must necessarily be under water, but which at that moment was dry and passable. The probability that the ass would prefer passing by this narrow way to the hazard of the water, determined us to follow in the same path. We had also some curiosity to ascertain what might be found on the other side of the rocks, for as yet we were ignorant whether they formed a boundary to our island or divided it into two portions. We continued to advance, and at length reached a stream which issued foaming from a large mass of rock and fell in a cascade into the river. The bed of this stream was so deep, and its course so rapid, that we were a long time finding a place to cross. When we had got to the other side, we found the soil again sandy and mixed with a fertile kind of earth. In this place we no longer saw naked rock, and here we again discovered the print of the ass's hoof.

We beheld with astonishment that there were the prints of the feet of other animals also, that they were somewhat different from those of the ass, and much larger. Our curiosity was so strongly excited that we resolved to follow the tracks. They conducted us to a plain at a great distance, which presented to our eyes the image of a terrestrial paradise. We ascended a hill which partly concealed from our view this scene, and then with the glass looked down upon a range of country exhibiting every rural beauty that the mind could conceive. To our right appeared the majestic wall of rocks, some of which appeared to touch the heavens, while mists partially concealed their tops. To the left a chain of gently rising hills stretched as far as the eye could discern, and were interspersed with little woods of palm-trees of every kind. The river we had crossed flowed in a serpentine course through this exquisite valley. I could with difficulty take my eyes from this enchanting spectacle, and seated myself on the ground to enjoy it at leisure. Neither on the plain nor on the hills was there the smallest trace of man.

By straining our eyes, however, we perceived at a great distance some specks that seemed to be in motion. We hastened towards the spot, and as we drew nearer, to our surprise discovered a group of animals, which presented something like the outline of a troop of horses or of cows. I observed them sometimes run up to each other, and then suddenly stoop to graze. Though we had not lately met with traces of the ass, I was not without hope of finding him among this group. We accordingly drew near by a path we found in a plantation of reeds, that we might not give notice of our approach, being ignorant of the kind of animal we were about to meet. We had not gone far when the soil became so marshy, and the reeds entangled to such a degree, that we were obliged to get out of the plantation and wind along on the outside. We were soon near the animals, which we perceived consisted of rather a numerous troop of wild buffaloes. This animal is formed at first sight to inspire the beholder with terror. It is endowed with extraordinary strength, and two or three of them were capable of destroying us in a moment. My alarm was so great that I remained for a few moments fixed to the spot like a statue. By good luck the dogs were far behind us, and the buffaloes, having never beheld the face of man, gave no sign of fear or of displeasure at our approach. They stood perfectly still, with their large round eyes fixed upon us in astonishment. Those which were lying down got up slowly, but not one seemed to have any hostile disposition towards us. We drew back quietly, and prepared our firearms. It was not, however, my intention to make use of them but for defence. I therefore thought only of retreating, and with Jack, for whom I was more alarmed than for myself, was proceeding in this way, when unfortunately Turk and Ponto ran up to us, and we could see were noticed by the buffaloes. The animals instantly and altogether set up such a roar as to make our nerves tremble with the shock of so terrible a noise. They struck their horns and their hoofs upon the ground, which they tore up and scattered in the air. I with horror foresaw the moment when, confounding us with the dogs, which no doubt they mistook for jackals, they would rush upon us and trample us. Our brave Turk and Ponto, fearless of danger, ran among the troop in spite of all our efforts to detain them, and, according to their manner of attacking, laid hold of the ears of a young buffalo which happened to be standing a few paces nearer to us than the rest. Although the creature began a tremendous roar and motion with his hoofs, they held him fast, and were dragging him towards us. Thus hostilities had commenced, and unless we could resolve to abandon our valiant defenders, we were now forced upon the measure of open war, which, considering the strength and number of the enemy, wore a face of the most pressing and inevitable danger. Our every hope seemed now to be in the chances of the terror the buffaloes would feel at the noise of our musketry. With a palpitating heart and trembling hands, we fired both at the same moment. The buffaloes, terrified by the sound and by the smoke, remained for an instant motionless, and then one and all betook themselves to flight with such rapidity that they were soon beyond our sight. We heard their loud roaring from a considerable distance, which by degrees subsided into silence, and we were left with only one of their terrific species near us. This one, a cow, was no doubt the mother of the young buffalo which the dogs still kept a prisoner. She had drawn near on hearing its cries, and had been wounded by our guns, but not killed. The creature was in a furious state. After a moment's pause she took aim at the dogs, and with her head down was advancing in her rage, and would have gored them to death, if I had not prevented her by firing upon her with my double-barrelled gun, and thus putting an end to her existence.

We now began to breathe. We might now hope that danger was over. I was enchanted with the behaviour of Jack, who had stood in a firm posture by my side, and had fired with a steady aim. I bestowed on him the commendation he deserved, but I had not time for a long discourse. The young buffalo still remained a prisoner, with his ears in the mouths of the dogs, and I was fearful he might do them some injury. I therefore determined to give them what assistance I might find practicable. I scarcely knew in what way to effect this. The buffalo, though young, was strong enough to revenge himself if I were to give the dogs a sign to let go his ears. I had the power of killing him with a pistol, but I had a great desire to preserve him alive and to tame him, that he might be a substitute for the ass. I found myself altogether in a state of indecision, when Jack unexpectedly interposed a most effective means for accomplishing my wishes. He had his string with balls in his pocket. He drew it out, and making a few steps backward, threw it so skilfully as to entangle the buffalo completely, and throw him down. As I could then approach him safely, I tied his legs together with a very strong cord. The dogs released his ears, and we considered the buffalo as our own. Jack was almost mad with joy. "What a magnificent creature! How much better than the ass he will look harnessed to the cart! How my mother and the boys will be surprised and stare at him as we draw near!" cried he.

Father. "Ah, ha! What, already you have harnessed him to the loaded cart, while for my part I have not yet been able to conceive a means for even removing him from this place! Will you carry him upon your back?"

Jack. "If I were Samson or Hercules I would most willingly; but, Father, he will be able to walk if we untie his legs."

Father. "And if we bid him do so, you think he will obey us?"

Jack. "The dogs would make him get on."

Father. "And the buffalo might kill the dogs, Jack. On reflection, the best way, I think, will be to tie his two fore-legs together, so tight that he cannot run, and loose enough for him to walk. I will assist the scheme by trying a method which is practised in Italy for subduing the buffalo. You will think it cruel, but success is probable. It shall afterwards be our study to make him amends by the kindest treatment. Hold you the cord which confines his legs with all your strength."

I then called Turk and Ponto, and made each again take hold of the ears of the animal, who was now keeping his head quite still. I took my knife, and held a piece of string in my hand. I placed myself before the buffalo, and taking hold of his snout I made a hole in his nostril, into which I quickly inserted the string, which I immediately tied so closely to a tree that the animal was prevented from the least motion of the head, which might have increased his pain. I drew off the dogs the moment the operation was performed. The first attempt I made to pull the cord found him docile, and I perceived that we might now begin our march. I left him for a short time to make some other preparations.

I was unwilling to leave so fine a prey as the dead buffalo. I therefore, after considering what was to be done, began by cutting out the tongue, which I sprinkled with some of the salt we had in our provision bag. I next took off the skin from the four feet, taking care not to tear it in the operation. I remembered that the Americans use these skins, which are of a soft and flexible quality, as boots and shoes. I lastly cut some of the flesh of the animal with the skin on, and salted it.

We now seated ourselves under the shade of a large tree, and as we ate we amused ourselves with a review of the scene which had been passing.

As we were not disposed to leave the spot in a hurry, I desired Jack to take the saw and cut down a small quantity of reeds, which, from their size, might be of use to us. We set to work, but I observed that he took pains to choose the smallest."

"What shall we do," said I, "with these small-sized reeds? You were thinking, I presume, of providing a bagpipe to announce a triumphal arrival to our companions!"

"You are mistaken, Father," answered Jack; "I am thinking rather of some candlesticks to present to Mother."

"This is a good thought, my boy," said I. "I am well pleased both with the kindness and the readiness of your invention, and I will give you my assistance in trying to empty the reeds without breaking them."

I now helped him, and soon after we set out on our return.

We had so many heavy articles to remove, that I did not hesitate to dismiss, for that day, all thoughts of looking further for the ass, that we might return the sooner to our companions. I began now to think of untying the young buffalo, and on approaching him perceived with pleasure that he was asleep, a proof that his wound was not extremely painful. When I awoke him he gave a start as I began to pull him gently with the string. But he seemed to forget his pain, and followed me without resistance. I fastened another string to his horns, and led him on by drawing both together, and he performed the journey with little inconvenience, and with so unexpected a docility, that to ease ourselves of a part of the heavy burdens we had to carry, we even ventured on fastening the bundles of reeds upon his back, and upon these we laid the salted buffalo meat. The creature did not seem aware that he was carrying a load. He followed as before, and thus on the first day of our acquaintance he rendered an essential service.

In a short time we found ourselves once more at the narrow passage between the torrent and the precipice which I have already mentioned. Near this spot we met with a large jackal, who on perceiving us slunk away, but was stoutly pursued by our dogs, who overtook him at the entrance of a cavern, and forced him to give battle. The fight, however, was unequal; the dogs were two to one, besides being protected by their pointed collars. When we got up to them the jackal was already killed. On examining our prey we found it was a female, and we concluded that she probably had her young in the cavern. Jack would instantly have entered to search, but I prevented him, from the apprehension that the male jackal might also be there. I accordingly used the precaution of shooting off my piece into the cavern, when, finding all quiet, I gave Jack leave to enter.

For some moments after entering the cavern the complete darkness prevented Jack from seeing anything, but when his eyes had become accustomed to it, he discerned in a corner a litter of young jackals. The dogs had discovered them by the smell. They flew upon the creatures, and with the exception of one, which Jack found means to preserve, put an end to their existence. He came out of the cavern with the young jackal in his arms, asking if he might have leave to rear it as Fritz had done the monkey. To this I made no objection, as I felt disposed to make an experiment on the effects of training on the wild creature. At all events it seemed worth while to try. Jack therefore promised to bestow upon him so faultless an education that he should become the gentlest little creature in the world.

We now left the cavern. I had fastened the young buffalo to a tree, without remarking of what species it might be. When I went to release him, I saw that it was a kind of small palm-tree, and on looking about me I observed also some other kinds of the palm which I had not before met with. One of the kinds was from ten to twelve feet in height. Its leaves were armed with thorns, and it bore a fruit resembling a small cucumber, but which was immature, so that we could not taste it. The second, smaller, was also thorny. It was now in blossom, and had no fruit. I suspected that the first of these was the *little royal palm,* sometimes called *awiva* or *Adam's needle,* and the other the *dwarf* palm. I resolved to avail myself of both for further fortifying my enclosure at Tent House, and also to protect the outer side of the narrow pass over the torrent of the cascade. I determined to return and plant a line of them there.

We repassed the river and regained the hazardous and narrow pass at the turn of the rocks. We proceeded with caution, and finding ourselves safe on the other side, thought of quickening our pace to arrive the sooner at the hut. We accordingly had the happiness to rejoin our friends before evening; and though we were somewhat fatigued, yet were well satisfied with the success of our undertakings. We were received with demonstrations of joy, and, as usual, a thousand questions.

CHAPTER TWENTY-SEVEN

THE SAGO MANUFACTORY

~

My wife the next morning began the conversation. She told me the children had been good and diligent, and had ascended Cape Disappointment together; that they had gathered wood and made some torches for the night, and had ventured to fell an immense palm-tree. During labours a somewhat unfortunate visit took place. A numerous group of monkeys had found their way to the hut. Every drop of the palm-wine these intrusive gentry contrived to swallow. They had upset and thrown about all the potatoes, stolen the coco-nuts, and almost wholly demolished the order of the branches and other contrivances we had recourse to for our hut, so that my children on their return were employed a full hour in repairing the damage.

When we had all finished our narratives, my wife began her usual lamentations upon the subject of so many animals being brought, which she said must, from the food they required, become burthensome to us. I consoled her by observing that the buffalo would be a good substitute for the ass, and I established as an invariable law, that he who wished to have a useful animal in his service should also have the care of it.

I next had a fire lighted and a quantity of green wood put on it, for raising a thick smoke, over which I meant to hang the buffalo meat, to preserve it. The young buffalo was beginning to browse, but the cow's milk was still given it. Jack succeeded also in making his little jackal drink some. We added to the buffalo's meal, whose appetite we found to be enormous, a heap of sliced potatoes, the whole of which he devoured, which led us to conclude that the pain from his nose was subsided, and that he would soon become tame.

Supper-time now arrived, and we did not fail to acquit ourselves at it, as well, to say the least, as our cattle, seasoning our repast with affectionate conversation. The combat with the buffaloes excited much raillery, which we saw was none the less intended for compliment. The candle-moulds, too, came in for a share in these playful attacks upon what they called the wonderful feats we had performed. Jack persisted in defending himself, and this he did so cleverly as to point the laughter at the adversary. The arrangements for this night were much the same as for the preceding. We tied the young buffalo by the side of the cow, and were pleased to see them agree and bid fair to live in peace together. The dogs were set upon the watch. The time of repose elapsed so calmly that none of us awoke to keep in the torch-lights. Directly after breakfast I chanted the summons for our setting out, but my young ones had some projects in their heads, and neither they nor their mother were just then in the humour to obey me.

"Let us reflect a little first," said my wife. "As we had so much difficulty in felling the palm-tree, would it not be a pity to lose our labour by leaving it in this place? It is the one from which Ernest cut the famous cabbage. Ernest assures me it is a sago-tree. If so, the pith would be an excellent ingredient for our soups. I hope you will see if we can turn it to account."

I found Ernest was right; the tree was a sago-palm. To extract the sago would employ fully a day, since to open the trunk sixty feet long was not a trivial task. I assented, however, with some readiness, as, apart from the pith, I could, by emptying the halves of the trunk, obtain two troughs for the conveyance of water from Jackal's River to my wife's kitchen-garden at Tent House, and to my plantations of trees.

Fritz. "One of the halves, Father, will answer that purpose, and the other will serve as a conduit for our little stream from Falcon's Nest into my pretty basin lined with tortoise-shell. We shall then be constantly regaled with the agreeable view of a fountain."

"And I, for my part," said Ernest, "long for a sight of the sago formed into small grains as I have seen it in Europe. Can you, Father, make it up into that sort of composition."

"With your help I think I could. But let us first make the sago-paste. Have we one of our manioc-graters at hand?"

"Yes, certainly," replied Ernest. "We were even thinking of making some graters here for our amusement, but we found we were not likely to want employment." He accordingly scampered off to fetch the grater to me, while the rest crowded round.

"Patience, children, patience!" exclaimed I. "We are not yet in readiness to use the grater. Many other matters are previously requisite. In the first place, you must first assist me to raise this palm-tree from the ground, and it must be done by fixing at each end two small cross-pieces or props to support it. To split it open as it lies would be a work of too much labour. This done, I shall want several wooden wedges to keep the cleft open while I am sawing it, and afterwards a sufficient quantity of water."

"There is the difficulty," said my wife. "Our Falcon's Stream is too far off."

Ernest. "That is of no consequence, Mother. I have seen hereabouts so great an abundance of the plants which contain water that we need not be at a loss. They will fully supply us, if I could only contrive to get vessels enough to hold the water."

We now produced the enormous reeds we had brought home, which would answer the purpose of vessels for water; and as some time was required to draw off the water from such small tubes, Ernest and Francis set to work. They cut a number of the plants, which they placed slantingly over the brim of a vessel, and whilst that was filling they were preparing another. The rest of us, with our united strength, soon succeeded in raising the heavy trunk, and the top of it was then sawed off. We next began to split it through the whole length, and this the softness of the wood enabled us to effect with little trouble. We soon reached the pith that fills up the middle of the trunk. When divided, we laid one half on the ground, and we pressed the pith together with our hands so as to make temporary room for the pith of the other half of the trunk, which rested still on the props. We wished to empty it entirely, that we might employ it as a kneading trough, leaving merely enough of the pith at both ends to prevent it running out. We then proceeded to form our paste. We had fastened the grater at one end, for the purpose of squeezing the paste through the small holes as soon as it was made.

My young manufacturers, with stripped arms, joyfully fell to work, and really surpassed my expectation. They brought water in succession and poured it gradually into the trough, whilst we mixed it with the flour. In a short time the paste appeared sufficiently fermented. I then made an aperture at the bottom of the grater on its outside, and pressed the paste strongly with my hand. The farinaceous parts passed with ease through the small holes of the grater, and the fibrous parts were thrown aside in a heap. My boys were in readiness to receive in the reed vessels what fell from the grater, and conveyed it directly to their mother, whose business was to spread out the small grains in the sun upon sail-cloth for the purpose of drying them. The subsequent process was the making of vermicelli, by working up the paste into a thicker consistence and pressing it more forcibly against the perforations of the grater. It passed through in slender rolls of different lengths, which were quickly dried by means of a gentle fire. To reward our toil my wife promised to dress us a dish of this new manufacture, with some Dutch cheese. Thus we procured a good supply of a wholesome and pleasant food, and should have had a larger stock had we not been restricted as to time. But the privilege of renewing the process at pleasure, by felling a sago-tree, added to impatience to take home our two pretty conduits and employ them as proposed, prompted us to expedite the business.

We employed ourselves the remainder of the evening in loading the cart with our tools and two halves of the tree. Night coming on, we retired to our hut, where we enjoyed our usual repose, and next morning were ready to return to Falcon's Stream.

Our buffalo now commenced his service yoked with the cow. He was very tractable. It is true I led him by the cord which passed through his nose, and thus I restrained him within the bounds of his duty.

We returned the same way as we came, in order to load the cart with a provision of berries, wax, and elastic gum. I sent forward Fritz and Jack with one of the dogs. They were to cut a commodious road through the bushes. My sons well performed their task, and we reached without any serious accident the wax and gum-trees, where we halted to place our sacks filled with berries in the cart. The elastic gum had not yielded as much as I expected, from the too rapid thickening caused by an ardent sun, and an incrustation formed over the incision. We obtained, however, about a quart.

We set out again, still preceded by our pioneers, who cleared the way for us through the little wood of guavas. Suddenly we heard a dreadful noise which came from our vanguard, and beheld Fritz and Jack hastening towards us. I began now to fear a tiger or panther was near at hand, or had perhaps attacked them. Turk began to bark so frightfully, and Ponto, running up to him, joined in so hideous a yell, that I prepared myself; not without terror, for a bloody conflict. I advanced at the head of my troop, who expressed their determination to follow me, and my high-mettled dogs ran furiously up to a thicket, where they stopped and, with their noses to the ground, strove to enter. I had no doubt some terrible animal was lurking there, and Fritz, who had seen it through the leaves, confirmed my suspicion. He said it was about the size of the young buffalo, and that its hair was black and shaggy. I was going to fire, when Jack, who had thrown himself on his face on the ground to have a better view of the animal, got up in a fit of laughter. "It is only," exclaimed he, "dame pig that has played us another trick – our old sow." He had hardly spoken when the grunting of the monster justified the assertion. Half-vexed, half-laughing, we broke into the midst of the thicket, where we found our sow stretched on the earth, but by no means in a state of dreary solitude; the good matron had round her seven little creatures, which had been littered a few days. This discovery gave us considerable satisfaction, and we all greeted the creature, who seemed to welcome us with a sociable kind of grunting. We rewarded her docility with potatoes, sweet acorns, and manioc bread; for the boys readily consented to go without. A general consultation took place. Should this swinish family be left where we found it or conveyed to Falcon's Stream? Fritz voted for their being all left to run at large like the wild boars in Europe, that he might have the sport of hunting them. My wife proposed that two of them at least should be domesticated for breeding; and as to the old sow, as she was always running away, we could kill her later on, and she would afford a large provision of salt-meat. We decided upon this course. For the moment they were suffered to keep quiet possession of their retreat.

We then, so many adventures ended, pursued our road to Falcon's Stream, and arrived there in safety and content.

We all passed an excellent night in our green castle and in our good beds, which we returned to with abundant satisfaction.

Origin of some European
Fruit-trees – Bees

~

We commenced the next day a business which we had long determined to engage in, to plant bamboos close to all the young trees, to support them. We quitted our tree with great alertness, having our cart loaded with canes and a large pointed iron to dig holes in the ground. We left my wife with only her little Francis, requesting them to prepare a plentiful dinner, and to include the palm-tree cabbage and the sago-macaroni mixed with some Dutch cheese. In addition, they volunteered the melting some of the wax berries for candles.

We did not take the buffalo with us, as I wished to give it a day's rest for its nose to heal up, and the cow was sufficient for drawing the load of light bamboo canes. Before setting out we gave the buffalo a few handfuls of salt to ingratiate ourselves with our horned companion.

We began our work at the entrance of the avenue which we had formed, and nearest to Falcon's Stream. The walnut, chestnut, and cherry trees we had planted in a regular line and at equal distances we found disposed to bend considerably. I took upon myself the task of making holes which I easily performed, taking care to go deep enough to fix the stake firmly. In the meantime the boys selected the bamboos, cut them of equal lengths, and pointed the ends to go into the ground. When they were all fixed we threw up the earth compactly about them, and fastened the saplings to them with some long tendrils of a plant. In the midst of our exertions we entered into a conversation respecting the culture of trees.

After much arduous labour we got to the end of our alley of trees, which looked all the better. This accomplished, we crossed Family Bridge on our way to the southern plantation of trees, in order to raise and prop them also. We were delighted with the view of beautiful orange, citron, and pomegranate trees, that were thriving to our satisfaction, as well as the pistachio and mulberry trees.

We quickly set to work and towards noon a keen appetite hastened our return to Falcon's Stream, where we found an excellent and plentiful dinner prepared by our good and patient steward, of which the palm-tree cabbage was the chief dish. Ernest, who had procured it, received the thanks of all the table.

When the sharpness of hunger was appeased, a new subject was introduced which I and my wife had been seriously revolving for some time. She found it difficult and even dangerous to ascend and descend our tree by the rope-ladder. We never went there but on going to bed, and each time felt an apprehension that one of the children might make a false step. Bad weather might come on and compel us for a long time together to seek an asylum in our aerial apartment, and consequently to ascend and descend oftener.

A staircase on the outside was not to be thought of; the considerable height of the tree rendered that impracticable, as I had nothing to rest it on, and should be at a loss to find beams to sustain it. But I had for some time formed the idea of constructing winding stairs within the immense trunk of the tree, if it should happen to be hollow, or I could contrive to make it so. Francis had excited this idea in speaking of the bees.

"Did you not tell me, dear wife," said I, "that there is a hole in this tree of ours, in which a swarm of bees is lodged?"

"Without doubt," answered she. "It was there little Francis was stung in attempting to thrust in a stick."

"Then," replied I, "we have only to examine how far this excavation goes, whether it extends to the roots, and what the circumference of it is."

All my children seized the idea with ardour. They sprang up, and prepared themselves to climb the tops of the roots like squirrels, to succeed in striking at the trunk with axes, and to judge from the sound how far it was hollow. But they soon paid dearly for their attempt. The whole swarm of bees, alarmed at the noise, issued forth, buzzing with fury, attacked the little disturbers, began to sting them, stuck to their hair and clothes, and soon put them to flight. My wife and I had some trouble to stop the course of this uproar, and cover the stings with fresh earth to allay the smart. Jack had struck exactly upon the bees' nest, and was more severely attacked by them than the rest. It was necessary, so serious was the injury, to cover the whole of his face with linen. The less active Ernest got up the last, and was the first to run off when he saw the consequences, and thus avoided any further injury than a sting or two. But some hours elapsed before the other boys could open their eyes or be relieved from the pain. When they grew a little better, the desire of being avenged of the insects had the ascendant in their minds. They teased me to hasten the measures for getting everything in readiness for obtaining possession of their honey. The bees in the meantime were still buzzing furiously round the tree. I prepared tobacco, a pipe, some clay, chisels, hammers, &c. I took the large gourd long intended for a hive, and I fitted a place for it by nailing a piece of board on a branch of the tree. I made a straw roof for the top to screen it from the sun and rain. As all this took up more time than I was aware of, we deferred the attack on the fortress to the following day, and got ready for a sound sleep, which completed the cure of the wounded patients.

CHAPTER TWENTY-NINE

VICTORY OVER THE BEES — WINDING STAIRCASE — TRAINING OF VARIOUS ANIMALS — DIVERS MANUFACTURES — FOUNTAIN, ETC.

~

Next morning, almost before dawn, all were up and in motion. The bees had returned to their cells, and I stopped the passages with clay, leaving only a sufficient aperture for the tube of my pipe. I then smoked as much as was requisite to stupefy the little warlike creatures. At first a humming was heard in the hollow of the tree, and a noise like a gathering tempest, which died away by degrees. All was calm, and I withdrew my tube without the appearance of a single bee. Fritz had got up by me. We then began with a chisel and a small axe to cut out of the tree, under the bees' entrance, a piece three feet square. Before it was entirely separated I repeated the fumigation, lest the stupefaction produced by the first smoking should have ceased, or the noise we had been just making revived the bees. As soon as I supposed them lulled again, I separated from the trunk the piece I had cut out, producing as it were the aspect of a window, through which the inside of the tree was laid entirely open to view, and we were filled with astonishment on beholding the wonderful work of this colony of insects. There was a stock of wax and honey that we feared our vessels would be insufficient to contain. The whole interior of the tree was lined with honeycombs. I cut them off with care, and put them in the gourds the boys constantly supplied me with. When I had somewhat cleared the cavity, I put the upper combs, in which the bees had assembled in clusters and swarms, into the gourd which was to serve as a hive, and placed it on the plank I had raised. I came down, bringing with me the rest of the honeycombs, with which I filled a small cask, previously well washed in the stream. Some I kept out for a treat at dinner, and had the barrel carefully covered with cloths and planks, that the bees might be unable to get at it. We then sat round the table, and regaled ourselves with the delicious honey. Having finished our meal, my wife put by the remainder, and I proposed to my sons to go back to the tree, to prevent the bees from swarming again there on being roused from their stupor, as they would not have failed to do but for the precaution I took of passing a board at the aperture and burning a few handfuls of tobacco on it, the smell and smoke of which drove them back from their old abode whenever they attempted to return to it. At length they became reconciled to their new residence, where their queen, no doubt, had settled herself.

I resolved to take full possession next day. The cask of honey was emptied into a kettle, except a few prime combs, which we kept for daily consumption. The remainder, mixed with a little water, was set over a gentle fire and reduced to a liquid consistence, strained and squeezed through a bag, and afterwards poured back into the cask, which was left upright and uncovered all night to cool. In the morning the wax was entirely separated, and had risen to the surface in a compact and solid cake that was easily removed; beneath was the purest, most beautiful, and delicate honey. The cask was then carefully headed again, and put into cool ground near our wine vessels. This task accomplished, I mounted to revisit the hive, and found the bees going forth in swarms and returning loaded, from which I judged they were forming fresh edifices in their new dwelling-place. I was surprised to see the numbers that had occupied the trunk of the tree find room in the gourd, but on looking round me I perceived a part of them collected in a cluster upon a branch, and I then concluded a young queen was amongst them. On perceiving this I procured another gourd, into which I shook them, and placed it by the former; thus I had the satisfaction of obtaining at an easy rate two fine hives of bees in activity.

We soon after these operations proceeded to examine the inside of the tree. I sounded it with a pole from the opening I had made, and a stone fastened to a string served us to sound the bottom. To my surprise, the pole penetrated to the branches on which our dwelling rested, and the stone descended to the roots. The trunk, it appeared, had wholly lost its pith, and most of its wood internally; nothing, therefore, was more practicable than to fix winding stairs in this capacious hollow. I determined to begin our construction that very day. The undertaking appeared at first beyond our powers, but patience, time, and a firm resolution vanquished all obstacles. We were not disposed to relax in any of these requisites; and I was pleased to find opportunities to keep my sons in continual action.

We began to cut into the side of the tree towards the sea a doorway equal in dimensions to the door of the captain's cabin, which we had removed with all its framework and windows. We next cleared away from the cavity all the rotten wood, and rendered the interior even and smooth, leaving sufficient thickness for cutting out resting-places for the winding stairs. I then fixed in the centre the trunk of a tree ten or twelve feet high and a foot thick, completely stripped of its branches, in order to carry my winding staircase round it. On the outside of this trunk, and the inside of the cavity of our own tree, we formed grooves, so calculated as to correspond with the distances at which the boards were to be placed to form the stairs. These were continued till I had got to the height of the trunk round which they turned. The window I had opened at the top to take out the honey gave light enough. I made a second aperture below, and a third above it, and thus completely lighted the whole ascent. I also effected an opening near our room, that I might more conveniently finish the upper part. A second trunk was fixed upon the first, and firmly sustained with screws and transverse beams. It was surrounded, like the other, with stairs cut slopingly. Thus we eventually effected the undertaking of conducting a staircase to our bed-chamber. To render it more solid I closed the spaces between the steps with boards. I then fastened two strong ropes, the one descending the length of the little tree, the other along the side of the large one, to assist in case of slipping. I fixed the sash-windows taken from the captain's cabin in the apertures we had made to give light to the stairs. When the whole was complete, it was so pretty, solid, and convenient that we were never tired of going up and coming down it.

A few days after the commencement of our staircase, the two she-goats gave us two kids, and our ewes five lambs, so that we now saw ourselves in possession of a pretty flock. But lest the domestic animals should follow the example of the ass, and run away from us, I tied a bell to the neck of each. We had found a sufficient number of bells in the vessel, which had been shipped for trading with the savages, it being one of the articles they most value. We could now immediately trace a deserter by the sound.

Next to the winding stairs my chief occupation was the young buffalo, whose nose was quite healed, so that I could lead it at will with a cord or stick passed through the orifice. I preferred the latter method, which answered the purpose of a bit, and I resolved to break in this spirited beast for riding as well as drawing. It was already used to the shafts, and very tractable in them. But I had more trouble in inuring him to the rider and to wear a girth, I having made one out of the old buffalo's hide. I formed a sort of saddle with sail-cloth, and tacked it to the girth. Upon this I fixed a burthen, which I increased progressively. I was indefatigable in the training of the animal, and soon brought it to carry, without fear or repugnance, large bags full of potatoes, salt, and other articles. The monkey was his first rider, who stuck so close to the saddle, that in spite of the plunging and kicking of the buffalo it was not thrown. Francis was then tried, as the lightest of the family. Throughout his excursion I led the beast with a halter. Jack now showed some impatience to mount the animal. Some restraint was requisite. I passed a piece of wood through the buffalo's nose, and tied strong pack-thread at each end of the stick, bringing the threads together over the neck of the animal. I then put this new-fashioned bridle into the hands of the young rider, directing him how to use it. For a time the lad kept his saddle, notwithstanding the repeated jumps of the horned steed; but at length a side jolt threw him on the sand, without his receiving much injury. Ernest, Fritz, and lastly myself got on successively, with more or less effect. His trotting shook us badly, the rapidity of his gallop turned us giddy, and our lessons in horsemanship were reiterated many days before the animal could be ridden with either safety or pleasure. At last, however, we succeeded without any serious accident. The strength and swiftness of our buffalo were prodigious; it seemed to sport with the heaviest loads. My three eldest boys mounted it together now and then, and it ran with them with the swiftness of lightning. By continued attentions it at length became extremely docile. It was not in the least apt to start, and I really felt satisfaction in being thus enabled to make my sons expert riders, so that if they should ever have horses, they might ride without fear. Fritz and Jack, with my instructions, amused themselves in training the animal as horses are exercised in a riding-house, and by means of the little stick through the nose they were able to do what they pleased with him.

Our whole company, including even Ernest, was infected with the passion of becoming instructors. Ernest tried his talents with the monkey. It was no poor specimen of the ludicrous to see the lad; he whose movements were habitually slow and studied, now constrained to skip, jump, and play a thousand antics with his pupil during training hours, and all the time deeply interested in carrying forward the lesson the grotesque mimic was condemned to learn, of carrying small loads, climbing the coco-trees, and to find and fetch the nuts. He and Jack made a little hamper of rushes, very light. They put three straps to it, two of which passed under the fore, and one between the hind legs of the animal, and were then fastened to a belt in front to keep the hamper steady. This apparatus was at first intolerable to poor Knips. He gnashed his teeth, rolled on the ground, jumping like a mad creature, and did everything to get rid of it; but all in vain, and he soon found he must submit. The hamper was left on day and night; his sole food was what was thrown into it, and in a short time Knips was so much accustomed to the burden, that he began to spit and growl whenever we attempted to take it off. Knips became at length a useful member of our society. But he would only obey Ernest. Jack was less successful with his little jackal, which he had named *Hunter*, hoping that its qualities would justify the name. He made continual attempts to induce the animal to go after game, but for the first six months he advanced no further in the lesson than teaching him to bring what was thrown to him; and when it was dead game, Hunter was sure to devour it on the way, and to bring home the skin alone. But it was nevertheless so pretty and tractable a creature, that I entreated the boy not to relinquish a task that would prove so beneficial to us, and he persevered with considerable zeal.

These different occupations filled up several hours of the day, and after working at our stairs, we assembled in the evening round our never-failing constant friend, the good mother, to rest ourselves. Forming a little circle, every individual of which was affectionate and cheerful, it was her turn to give us some agreeable and less fatiguing occupation; such, for example, as endeavouring to improve our candle-manufactory, by blending the berry and the bees'-wax and employing the reed-moulds invented by Jack. Having found some difficulty in taking out the candles when cold, I adopted the plan of dividing the moulds, cleaning the inside, and rubbing it over with butter to prevent the wax from adhering. I rejoined both halves with a band that could be loosened at pleasure to facilitate the extraction of the candles. The wicks gave us most trouble, as we had no cotton. We tried with moderate success the fibrous threads of the karata, and those of the algava or flame-wood, but each had the inconvenience of becoming a sort of cinder. The substance which gave us the most satisfaction was the pith of a species of elder. It did not, however, lessen our desire to discover the only really appropriate substance, namely, the cotton-tree.

We had also been engaged in the construction of our fountain, which afforded a perpetual source of pleasure. In the upper part of the stream we built with stakes and stones a kind of dam, that raised the water sufficiently to convey it into the palm-tree troughs, and afterwards, by means of a gentle slope, to our habitation, where it fell into the tortoise-shell basin. It was so contrived that the surplus water passed off through a cane-pipe fitted to it. I placed two sticks athwart each other for the gourds, that served as pails, to rest on. We thus produced, close to our abode, an agreeable fountain, delighting with its rill, and supplying us with a pure crystal fluid. The only inconvenience was, that the water flowing in this open state was heated, and not refreshing when it reached us. I resolved to obviate this inconvenience by employing instead of the uncovered conduits, large bamboo-canes fixed deep enough in the ground to keep the water cool.

CHAPTER THIRTY

THE WILD ASS – DIFFICULTY IN BREAKING IT – PREPARING WINTER QUARTERS

~

We were scarcely up one morning, and had got to work in putting the last hand to our staircase, when we heard at a distance two strange voices that resembled the howlings of wild beasts, mixed with hissings and sounds of some creature at its last gasp, which I was at a loss to explain. Our dogs, too, pricked up their ears, and seemed to whet their teeth.

We loaded our guns and pistols, placed them together within our castle in the tree, and prepared to repel vigorously any hostile attack. The howlings having ceased an instant, I descended from our citadel, and put on our two faithful guardians their spiked collars and side-guards. I assembled our cattle about the tree to have them in sight, and reascended to look around for the enemy's approach.

At this instant the howlings were renewed quite close to us. Fritz got as near as he could, listened attentively, then threw down his gun and burst into laughter, exclaiming: "Father, it is our ass – the deserter comes back to us, chanting the hymn of return! Listen! do you not hear his melodious braying?" We lent an ear; our doubts ceased, and we felt somewhat mortified at our preparations of defence against such an ignoble foe.

I was, however, soon reconciled to the offence against our pride, since it also insured our safety. And a fresh roar, in sounds unquestionable, raised loud peals of laughter among us. Then followed the usual train of jests and mutual banter at the alarm we had all betrayed. Shortly after, we had the satisfaction of seeing among the trees our old friend Grizzle, moving towards us leisurely, and stopping now and then to browse. But to our great joy we perceived in his train one of the same species of very superior beauty, and when it was nearer I knew it to be a fine onagra or wild ass, which I conceived a strong desire to possess. Without delay I descended the ladder with Fritz, desiring his brothers to keep still. I consulted my privy-councillor on the means of taking the stranger captive. I got ready a long cord with a running knot, one end of which I tied fast to the root of a tree. The noose was kept open with a little stick slightly fixed in the opening so as to fall of itself on the cord being thrown round the neck of the animal, whose efforts to escape would draw the knot closer. I also prepared a piece of bamboo about two feet long, which I split at the bottom, and tied fast at the top to serve as nippers. Fritz attentively examined my contrivance, without seeing the use of it. Prompted by the impatience of youth, he took the ball-sling and proposed aiming at the wild ass with it. I declined adopting this Patagonian method, fearing the attempt might fail, and the beautiful creature avail itself of its natural speed to evade us beyond recovery. I told him my project of catching it by the noose, which I gave him to manage, as being nimbler and more expert than myself. The two asses drew nearer and nearer to us. Fritz, holding in his hand the open noose, moved softly on from behind the tree where we were concealed, and advanced as far as the length of the rope allowed him. The onagra was extremely startled on perceiving a human figure; it sprung some paces backward, then stopped as if to examine the unknown form. As Fritz now remained quite still, the animal resumed its composure and continued to browse. Soon after Fritz approached the old ass, hoping that the confidence that would be shown by it would raise a similar feeling in the stranger. He held out a handful of oats mixed with salt; our ass instantly ran up to take its favourite food; this was quickly perceived by the other. It drew near, raised his head, breathed strongly and came up so close, that Fritz succeeded in throwing the rope round its neck. The motion and stroke so affrighted the beast that it instantly sprang off, but was checked by the cord. It could go no farther, and after many exhausting efforts, it sank panting for breath upon the ground. I hastened to loosen the cord and prevent its being strangled. I then quickly threw our ass's halter over its head. I fixed the nose in my split cane, which I secured at the bottom with packthread. I wholly removed the noose that seemed to bring the creature into a dangerous situation. I fastened the halter with two long ropes to two roots near us, on the right and left, and let the animal recover itself, noticing its actions, and devising the best way to tame it in the completest manner.

The rest of my family had by this time come down from the tree, and beheld the fine creature with admiration, its graceful shape and well-turned limbs, which placed it so much above our ass, and nearly raised it to the noble structure of the horse. In a few moments the onagra got up, kicked out furiously, and seemed resolved to free itself from its bonds. But the pain of its nose, which was grasped and violently squeezed in the bamboo, forced it to lie down again. My eldest son and I now gently undid the cords, and half-led, half-dragged it between two adjoining roots, to which we fastened it afresh. We also guarded against Master Grizzle playing truant again, and tied him fast with a new halter, confining his fore-legs with a rope. I then fastened him and the wild ass side by side, and put before both plenty of good provender.

We had now the additional occupation of training the onagra for our service or our pleasure. My boys exulted in the idea of riding it. I did not conceal that we should have many difficulties in taming it. I let the nippers remain on its nose, which appeared to distress it, though we could plainly perceive the good effect in subduing the creature, for without them no one could have ventured to approach it. I took them off, however, at times when I gave it food, to render eating easier; and I began, as with the buffalo, by placing a bundle of sail-cloth on its back to inure it to carry. When it was accustomed to the load, I strove to render the beast still more docile by hunger and thirst, and I observed that when it had fasted a little, and I supplied it with food, its actions were less wild. I also compelled the animal to keep erect on its four legs, by drawing the cords closer that fastened it to the roots, in order to subdue by fatigue its natural ferocity. The children came in turns to play with it and scratch its ears gently, which were remarkably tender, and it was on these I resolved to make my last trial if all other endeavours failed. For a long time we despaired of success. The onagra made furious starts and leaps when any of us went near it, kicked with its hind-feet, and even attempted to bite those who touched it. This obliged me to have recourse to a muzzle, which I managed with rushes, and put on when it was not feeding. To avoid being struck by its hind-feet, I partially confined them by fastening them to the fore-feet with cords, which, however, I left moderately loose, that we might not encroach too much upon the motion necessary for its health. It was at length familiarized to this discipline, and was no longer in a rage when we approached, but bore to be handled and stroked.

At last we ventured to free it by degrees from its restraints, and to ride it as we had done with the buffalo, still keeping the fore-feet tied. But notwithstanding this precaution it proved as unruly as ever for the moment. The monkey, who was first put on its back, held on pretty well by clinging to its mane, from which it was suspended as often as the onagra furiously reared and plunged. It was therefore for the present impracticable for either of my sons to get upon it. The perverse beast baffled all our efforts, and the perilous task of breaking it was still to be persevered in with apprehension. In the stable it seemed tolerably quiet, but the moment it was in any degree unshackled, it became wholly unmanageable.

I was at length reduced to my last expedient, but not without much regret, as I resolved, if it did not answer, to restore the animal to full liberty. I tried to mount the onagra, and just as in the act of rearing up violently to prevent me, I seized with my teeth one of the long ears of the enraged creature, and bit it till it bled. Instantly it stood almost erect on its hind-feet, motionless. It soon lowered itself by degrees, while I still held its ear between my teeth. Fritz seized the moment and sprang on its back. Jack, with the help of his mother, did the same, holding by his brother, who on his part clung to the girth. When both assured me they were firmly seated, I let go the ear. The onagra made a few springs less-violent than the former, and, checked by the cords on its feet, gradually submitted, began to trot up and down more quietly, and ultimately grew so tractable that riding it became one of our chief pleasures. My lads were soon expert horsemen, and their horse, though rather long-eared, was very handsome and well broken-in.

"Wherever," said my wife to me, "did you learn this strange notion of biting the animal's ear?"

"I learned it," replied I, "from a horse-breaker. He had lived long in America, and employed half-tamed horses of the southern provinces. They are at first unruly and resist burthens, but as soon as the hunter bites one of their ears they become submissive."

In a few weeks the onagra was so tamed that we all could mount it without fear. I still, however, kept his two fore-legs confined together with the cord, to moderate the extreme swiftness of its running. In the room of a bit I contrived a curb, and with this and a good bite applied as wanted to the ear, it went to right or left at the will of the rider.

During the training of the wild ass, which we named *Lightfoot*, a triple brood of our hens had given us a crowd of little feathered beings. Forty of these at least were chirping and hopping about us, to the great satisfaction of my wife.

"Here," she said, "are animals of real utility in a family, far beyond your monkeys and jackals, that do nothing but eat, and are unfit to be eaten." The buffalo was not found fault with, because it brought her the provisions; nor the onagra, on which she liked to see her sons gallop. From the time we had trained it to this, the rough-paced buffalo that shook us to pieces was no longer used for riding, but kept entirely for drawing.

This increase of our poultry reminded us of the necessity of an undertaking we had long thought of, and was not in prudence to be deferred any longer. This was the building between the roots of our great tree covered sheds for all our bipeds and quadrupeds. The rainy season, which is the winter of these countries, was drawing near, and it was requisite to provide shelter.

We began by forming a roof above the arched roots of our tree, and employed bamboo canes for the purpose. The longest and strongest supported the roofing in the place of columns, the smaller composed the roof. I filled up the interstices with moss and clay, and I spread over the whole a thick coat of tar. I then made a railing round it, which gave the appearance of a pretty balcony, under which, between the roots, were various stalls that could be easily shut and separated from each other by means of planks nailed upon the roots. Part of them were to serve as a stable and yard, part as an eating-room, a store-room, &c., and as a hay-loft.

This work was soon completed. But afterwards it was necessary to fill these places with stores of every kind.

One evening, on our return from digging up potatoes, as our cart, loaded with bags, drawn by the buffalo, ass, and cow, was gently rolling along, seeing still a vacant place in the vehicle, I advised my wife to go home with the two youngest boys whilst I went round by the wood of oaks with Ernest and Fritz to gather sweet acorns. We had still some empty sacks. Ernest was accompanied by the monkey, who seldom left him, and Fritz was on the onagra. Notwithstanding the onagra was so well broken-in for riding, it continued to be very mettlesome and restive in the shafts, to which we could not inure it. Occasionally it submitted to our putting a loaded sack or two on its back, but we could seldom prevail even in this without Fritz being seated in front.

When we reached the oaks, Lightfoot was tied to a bush, and we set actively to work to gather the acorns that had dropped from the trees. And now Ernest came forward, driving the monkey before him, and carrying his hat with the utmost care. He had stuck his girdle full of narrow sharp-pointed leaves, which reminded me of the production named sword-grass.

"I am going to take them home, they will please Francis," said he. "They are like swords, and will be the very thing he will like."

I applauded Ernest's idea, and encouraged him and Fritz to be thus ever considerate for the absent. It was now time to think of moving homeward. My two sons filled the bags with acorns and put them on Lightfoot. Fritz mounted, and we proceeded to Falcon's Stream, followed by our train-wagon. Fritz could not refrain from trotting on briskly, but he went rather faster than he intended. He had taken a handful of the pointed leaves with him, which he whisked before the eyes of the onagra till the animal was frightened, lost all restraint, and darting forward, hurried away at such a rate that we soon lost sight of them. Anxious for his safety, we followed as fast as possible, but on our arrival at Falcon's Stream we had the satisfaction of finding him there in perfect safety. His mother, indeed, had been somewhat alarmed in seeing him dash in like a thunderbolt, but firmly seated betwixt the bags on Master Lightfoot, who stopped short with wonderful precision at his stable door.

CHAPTER THIRTY-ONE

FLAX, AND THE RAINY SEASON

~

Francis for a short time was highly amused with his sword-leaves, and then grew weary of them, and they were thrown aside. Fritz picked up some of them that were quite soft and withered. He held up one which was pliable as a riband.

"My little fellow," said he to his brother, "you can make whips of your sword-grass. Take the leaves and keep them, they will be of use in driving your goats and sheep." It had been decided that it should be the business of Francis to lead these to pasture.

"Well then, help me to make, them," said the child.

They sat down together. Francis divided the leaves into long slips, and Fritz platted them into whip-cords. As they were working, I saw the flexibility and strength of the bands. I examined them closely, and found they were composed of fibres. This discovery led me to surmise that this might be the flax-plant of New Zealand. This was a valuable discovery in our situation. I knew how much my wife wished for the production, and that it was the article she felt most the want of. I therefore hastened to communicate the intelligence to her, upon hearing which she expressed the liveliest joy.

"This," said she, "is the most useful thing you have found. I entreat you lose not a moment in searching for more of these leaves. I will make you stockings, shirts, clothes, thread, ropes. . . . In short, give me flax, looms, and frames, and I shall be at no loss in the employment of it."

I could not help smiling at the scope she gave to her imagination on the mention of flax, though so much was to be done between the gathering the leaves and having the cloth she was already sewing in idea. Fritz whispered a word in Jack's ear. Both went to the stable, and without asking my leave, one mounted Lightfoot, the other the buffalo, and galloped off towards the wood. They were already out of sight. Their eagerness to oblige their mother in this instance pleaded their forgiveness, and I suffered them to go on without following them, purposing to proceed and bring them back if they did not soon return.

In waiting for them I conversed with my wife, who pointed out to me the various machinery I must contrive for spinning and weaving her flax for the manufactory of cloths, with which she said she should be able to equip us from head to foot, in speaking of which her eyes sparkled with the love of doing good, the purest kind of joy, and I promised her all she desired of me.

In a quarter of an hour our deserters came back on a full trot. Like true hussars they had foraged the woods and heavily loaded their cattle with the precious plant, which they threw at their mother's feet with joyful shouts. Jack made us laugh in recounting with his accustomed vivacity and drollery at what a rate he had trotted his buffalo to keep up with Lightfoot, and how his great horned horse had thrown him by a side leap.

Fritz. "How is flax prepared, Father, and what is meant by steeping it?"

Father. "Steeping flax or hemp is exposing it in the open air, by spreading it on the ground to receive the rain, the wind, and the dew in order in a certain degree to liquefy the plant. By this means the ligneous parts of the flax are separated with more ease from the fibrous; a kind of vegetable glue that binds them is dissolved, and it can then be perfectly cleaned with great facility, and the parts selected which are fit for spinning."

My wife suggested that we should soak the flax in Flamingo Marsh, and begin by making up the leaves in bundles, as they do hemp in Europe. We joined in this previous and necessary preparation of the flax during the rest of the day.

Next morning the ass was put to the small light car, loaded with bundles of leaves. Francis and the monkey sat on them, and the remainder of the family gaily followed with shovels and pick-axes. We stopped at the marsh, divided our large bundles into smaller ones, which we placed in the water, pressing them down with stones and leaving them in this state.

A fortnight after my wife told us the flax was sufficiently steeped. We then took it out of the water and spread it on the grass in the sun, where it dried so well and rapidly that we were able to load it on our cart the same evening, and carry it to Falcon's Stream, where it was put by till we had time to attend further to it, and make beetles, wheels, reels, carding-combs, &c., as required. It was thought best to

"…the training of the wild ass, which we named lightfoot."
(Chapter 30)

"What say you, now, Father?" said Jack. "A single fish of this troop would fill a tub!" (Chapter 34)

reserve this task for the rainy season, and to get ready what would be then necessary during our confinement within doors. Uninformed as we were as to the duration of this season, it was highly important to lay in a competent stock of provisions. Occasional slight showers, the harbingers of winter, had already come on. The temperature, which hitherto had been warm and serene, became gloomy and variable. The sky was often darkened by clouds, the stormy winds were heard, and warned us to avail ourselves of the favourable moment.

Our first care was to dig up a full supply of potatoes and yams, for bread, with plenty of coco-nuts and some bags of sweet acorns. It occurred to us while digging, that the ground being thus opened and manured with the leaves of plants, we might sow in it to advantage the remainder of our European corn. Notwithstanding all the delicacies this stranger land afforded us, the force of habit still caused us to long for the bread we had been fed with from childhood. We had not yet laid ourselves out for regular tillage, and I was inclined to attempt the construction of a plough of some sort as soon as we had a sufficient stock of corn for sowing. For this time, therefore, we committed it to the earth with little preparation. The season, however, was proper for sowing and planting, as the ensuing rain would moisten and swell the embryo grain. We accordingly expedited the planting of the various palm-trees we had discovered in our excursions, at Tent House, carefully selecting the smallest and the youngest. In the environs we formed a large handsome plantation of sugar-canes.

These different occupations kept us several weeks. Our cart was incessantly in motion, conveying home our winter stock. Time was so precious that we could not even make regular meals, and limited ourselves to bread, cheese, and fruits.

Unfortunately the weather changed sooner than we had expected. Before we had completed our winter establishment, the rain fell in such heavy torrents that little Francis, trembling, asked me whether Father Noah's deluge was coming on again. And I could not myself refrain from painful apprehension in surmising how we should resist such a body of water, that seemed to change the whole face of the country into a perfect lake.

The first thing to be done was to remove our aerial abode, and to fix our residence at the bottom of the tree, between the roots and under the tarred roof I had erected; for it was no longer possible to remain above, on account of the furious winds that threatened to bear us away, and deluged our beds with rain through the large opening in front. Most fortunate did we deem ourselves in having made the winding stairs, which sheltered us during the operation of the removal. The stairs served afterwards for a kind of lumber-room. We kept in it all we could dispense with, and most of our culinary vessels, which my wife fetched as she happened to want them. Our little sheds between the roots, constructed for the poultry and the cattle, could scarcely contain us all, and the first days we passed in this manner were painfully embarrassing, crowded all together, and hardly able to move in these almost dark recesses, which the foetid smell from the close-adjoining animals rendered almost insupportable. In addition, we were half stifled with smoke whenever we kindled a fire, and drenched with rain when we opened the doors. For the first time since our disaster we sighed for the comfortable houses of our dear country. But what was to be done? I strove to raise the spirits of my companions and obviate some of the inconveniences. The now doubly-precious winding stair was, as I have said, every way useful to us. The upper part of it was filled with numerous articles that gave us room below. As it was lighted and sheltered by windows, my wife often worked there, seated on a stair, with her little Francis at her feet. We confined our live stock to a smaller number, and gave them a freer current of air, dismissing from the stalls those animals that would be at no loss in providing for themselves. That we might not lose them altogether, we tied bells round their necks. Fritz and I sought and drove them in every evening that they did not spontaneously return. We generally got wet to the skin and chilled with cold during the employment, which induced my wife to contrive for us a kind of clothing more suitable to the occasion. She took two seamen's shirts from the chest we had recovered from the wreck, and, with some pieces of old coats, she made us a kind of cloth hoods joined together at the back, and well formed for covering the head entirely. We melted some elastic gum, which, we spread over the shirts and hoods. The articles thus prepared answered every purpose of waterproof overalls. Our young rogues were ready with their derision the first time they saw us in them, but afterwards they would have been rejoiced to have had the same. This, however, the reduced state of our gum did not allow of, and we contented ourselves with wearing them in turn.

As to the smoke, our only remedy was to open the door when we made a fire. And we did without as much as we could, living on milk and cheese, and never making a fire but to bake our cakes. We then availed ourselves of the opportunity to boil a quantity of potatoes and salt meat enough to last us a number of days. Our dry wood was also nearly expended, and we thanked Heaven the weather was not very cold. A more serious concern was our not having provided sufficient hay and leaves for our European cattle, which we necessarily kept housed to avoid losing them. The cow, the ass, the sheep, and the goats, the two last of which were increased in number, required a large quantity of provender, so that we were ere long forced to give them our potatoes and sweet acorns. Milking, cleaning the animals, and preparing their food occupied us most of the morning, after which we were usually employed in making flour of the manioc root, with which we filled the large gourds, which were previously placed in rows. The gloom of the atmosphere and our low windowless habitation sensibly abridged our daylight. Fortunately we had laid in a huge store of candles. When darkness obliged us to light up, we got round the table, when a large taper fixed on a gourd gave us an excellent light, which enabled my wife to pursue her occupation with the needle; while I, on my part, was writing a journal, and recording what the reader has perused of our ship-wreck and residence in this island, assisted from time to time by my sons and my wife, who did not cease to remind me of various incidents. To Ernest, who wrote a fine hand, was entrusted the care of writing off my pages. Our kind and faithful steward often surprised us agreeably on our return from looking after the cattle, by lighting up a faggot of dried bamboo, and quickly roasting a chicken, pigeon, duck, or penguin from our poultry-yard, or some of the thrushes we had preserved in butter, which were excellent, and welcomed as a treat. Every four or five days she made us new fresh butter in the gourd churn. This, with some deliciously fragrant honey on our manioc cakes, formed a collation that would have raised the envy of European epicures.

The fragments of our meals belonged to our domestic animals. We had the two dogs, the young jackal, and the monkey to feed. They relied on the kindness of their masters, who certainly would have deprived themselves to supply their helpless dependants. If the buffalo, the onagra, and pig had not found sustenance abroad, they must have been killed or starved, and that would have given us much pain. In the course of these discomforts it was unanimously resolved on that we would not pass another rainy season exposed to the same evils. Even my beloved consort, who felt such a predilection for the abode at Falcon's Stream, was frequently a little ruffled and out of temper with our inconvenient situation, and insisted on the propriety of building a more spacious winter residence. She wished, however, to return to our castle in the tree every summer, and we all joined with her in that desire. The choice of a fresh abode now engrossed our attention, and Fritz in the midst of consultation came forward triumphantly with a book he had found in the bottom of our clothes-chest. "Here," said he, "is our best counsellor and model, *Robinson Crusoe.* Since Heaven has destined us to a similar fate," said he, "whom better can we consult? As far as I remember, he cut himself an habitation out of the solid rock. Let us see how he proceeded. We will do the same, and with greater ease, for he was alone. We are six in number, and four of us able to work."

We assembled, and read the famous history with an ardent interest. It seemed, though so familiar, quite new to us. We entered earnestly into every detail and derived considerable information from it, and never failed to feel lively gratitude towards God, who had rescued us all together, and not permitted one of us to be cast, a solitary being, on the island.

Francis repeated his wish to have a Man Friday; Fritz thought it better to be without such a companion, and to have no savages to contend with. Jack was for the savages, warfare and encounters. The final result of our deliberations was to go and survey the rocks round Tent House, and to examine whether any of them could be excavated for our purpose.

Our last job for the winter, undertaken at my wife's solicitation, was a beetle for her flax and some carding-combs. I filed large nails till they were even, round, and pointed. I fixed them at equal distances in a sheet of tin, and raised the sides of it like a box. I then poured melted lead between the nails and the sides, to give firmness to their points, which came out four inches. I nailed this tin on a board, and the contrivance was fit for work. My wife was impatient to use it, and the drying, peeling, and spinning her flax became a source of delight.

CHAPTER THIRTY-TWO

SPRING – SPINNING – SALT-MINE

~

I can hardly describe our joy when, after gloomy weeks of rain, the sky began to brighten, the sun to dart its rays on the earth, the winds to be lulled, and the state of the air became mild and serene. We issued from our hovels with joyful shouts, and walked round our habitation breathing the balmy air, while our eyes were regaled with the verdure beginning to shoot forth on every side. Reviving nature opened her arms, every creature seemed reanimated, and we felt the genial influence of that luminary which had been so long concealed, now returning like a friend who has been absent, to bring us back blessings and delight. We forgot the embarrassments and weary hours of the wet season, and with hopeful hearts looked forward to the toils of summer as amusements.

The vegetation of our trees was rapidly advancing. The seed we had thrown into the ground was sprouting in slender blades that waved luxuriantly, a pleasing tender foliage adorned the trees, the earth was enamelled with an infinite variety of flowers. Odorous exhalations were diffused through the atmosphere. The song of birds was heard around; they were seen between the leaves joyfully fluttering from branch to branch; their various forms and brilliant plumage heightened this delightful picture of spring, and we were at once struck with gratitude towards the Creator of so many beauties.

Our summer occupations commenced by arranging and thoroughly cleaning Falcon's Nest, the order and neatness of which the rain and dead leaves blown by the wind had disturbed. In other respects, however, it was not injured, and in a few days we rendered it fit for our reception. The stairs were cleared, the rooms between the roots reoccupied, and we were left with leisure to proceed to other employments. My wife lost not a moment in resuming the process of her flax industry. Our sons hastened to lead the cattle to the fresh pastures; whilst it was my task to carry the bundles of flax into the open air, where, by heaping stones together, I contrived an oven sufficiently commodious to dry it well. The same evening we all set to work to peel, and afterwards to beat it and strip off the bark, and lastly to comb it with my carding-machine. I took this laborious task on myself; and drew out such distaffsful of long soft flax ready for spinning, that my enraptured wife ran to embrace me, requesting me to make her a wheel without delay, that she might enter upon her favourite work.

At an earlier period of my life I had practised turnery for my amusement; now, however, I was unfortunately destitute of the requisite utensils. But as I had not forgotten the arrangement and component parts of a spinning-wheel and reel, I by repeated endeavours found means to accomplish those two machines to my wife's satisfaction, and she fell so eagerly to spinning as to allow herself no leisure even for a walk, and scarcely time to dress our dinners. Nothing so much delighted her as to be left with her little boy, whom she employed to reel as fast as she could spin, and sometimes the other three were also engaged in turns at the wheel to forward her business while she was occupied in culinary offices. Not one of them was found so tractable as the cool-tempered, quiet Ernest, who preferred this to more laborious exertions. Our first visit was to Tent House, as we were anxious to ascertain the ravages of winter there, and we found them much more considerable than at Falcon's Stream. The tempest and rain had beaten down the tent, carried away a part of the sail-cloth, and made such havoc amongst our provisions, that by far the largest portion of them was spotted with mildew, and the remainder could be saved only by drying them instantly. Luckily, our handsome pinnace had been spared, but our tub-boat was in too shattered a state to be of any further service.

In looking over the stores we were grieved to find the gunpowder most damaged, of which I had left three barrels in the tent. The contents of two were rendered wholly useless. I thought myself fortunate on finding the remaining one in tolerable condition, and derived from this great and irreparable loss a cogent motive to fix upon winter quarters where our stores and wealth would not be exposed.

Notwithstanding the gigantic plan suggested by the enterprising characters of Fritz and Jack, I had little hope of being able to effect the excavation of a dwelling in the rock. Robinson Crusoe found a spacious cavern that merely required enlarging and arrangement; no such cavity was apparent in our rock, which was of extreme hardness, so that it seemed that three or four summers would scarcely have sufficed to execute the design. Still, the earnest desire of a more substantial habitation perplexed me incessantly, and I resolved to make at least the attempt of cutting out a recess that should contain the gunpowder, the most valuable of all our treasures. With this resolution I set off one day, accompanied by my two valiant workmen, Fritz and Jack, leaving their mother at her spinning with her assistants, Ernest and Francis. We took with us pickaxes, chisels, hammers, and iron levers. I chose a part of the rock nearly perpendicular, and much better situated than our tent. The view from it was enchanting, for it embraced the whole range of Safety Bay, and the banks of Jackal River and Family Bridge. I marked out with charcoal the circumference of the opening we wished to make, and we began the heavy toil of piercing the quarry. We made so little progress the first day, that in spite of all our courage we were tempted to relinquish our undertaking. We persevered, however, and my hope was somewhat revived as I perceived the stone was of a softer texture as we penetrated deeper. We concluded from this, that the ardent rays of the sun striking upon the rock had hardened the external layer, and that the stone would increase in softness as we advanced. This proved to be the case, and when I had cut about a foot in depth we could loosen the rock with the spade. This determined me to proceed with double ardour, and my boys assisted me with a zeal beyond their years.

After a few days of labour we measured the opening, and found we had already advanced seven feet. Fritz removed the fragments in a barrow, and discharged them before the place to form a sort of terrace. I applied my own labour to the upper part to enlarge the aperture; Jack, the smallest of the three, was able to get in and cut away below. Jack worked a long iron bar sharpened at the end. When he was driving this in with a hammer, to loosen a particularly large piece of rock, he suddenly bawled out:

"It is pierced through, Father!"

"Ha, ha! Master Jack! What have you pierced? Is it the mountain? Not your hand or foot, is it, Jack?" cried I.

Jack. "No, no, it is the mountain! Huzza, huzza! I have pierced the mountain!"

Fritz now ran to him.

"Come, let us see," cried he. "You should have pushed on your tool boldly till you reached Europe, which they say is under our feet. I should have been glad to peep into that hole."

Jack. "Well then, peep you may; but I hardly know what you will see. Now, come and look how far the iron is gone in, and tell me if it is all my boasting. If there were not a hollow space behind, how could it penetrate the rock so easily?"

"Come here, Father," said Fritz. "This is really extraordinary. His iron bar seems to have got to a hollow place."

I approached, thinking the incident worth attention. I took hold of the bar, which was still in the rock, and pressing it forcibly from one side to another, I made a sufficient aperture for one of my sons to pass. I observed that in reality the rubbish fell within the cavity. My two lads offered to go in together to examine it. This, however, I firmly opposed. I even made them remove themselves from the opening, as I smelled the bad air that issued abundantly from it, and began myself to feel giddiness in consequence of having gone too near; indeed I was compelled to withdraw quickly, and inhale a purer air.

"Beware, my dear children," said I in terror, "of entering such a perilous cavern. Life might be suddenly extinguished there. I fear it is full with noxious vapours that would suffocate."

Jack. "Then all to be done is to be off quickly when one feels a stoppage of breath."

Father. "This is the natural course when it can be taken; but the suffocation in such air usually begins by a dizziness of the head, so violent as to intercept motion, which is followed by an insurmountable oppression; efforts are made to breathe, fainting follows, and without speedy help death takes place. But there is a test of bad air of the kind I believe this to be: fire does not burn in it. We must try to light a fire in this hole."

The boys now hastened to gather some dry moss, which they made into bundles. They then struck a light, and set fire to them, and then threw the moss blazing into the opening; the fire was extinguished at the very entrance. We then made a very large fire near the opening, which we hoped would set up a draught, and gradually draw out the bad and admit good air. We were the more confident of this taking place, as we already observed a current of air outwards at the bottom of our hole. We kept the fire burning for some hours. Then we again threw in some lighted straw into the cavern, and found, to our great satisfaction, the bundles were entirely consumed. We could accordingly hope nothing was to be feared from the air. There still remained the danger of plunging into some abyss, or of meeting with a body of water. From these considerations I thought it more prudent to defer our entrance into this unknown recess till we had lights. I dispatched Jack on the buffalo to Falcon's Stream, to impart our discovery to his mother and two brothers, directing him to return with them, and bring all the tapers that were left. My intention was to fasten them together on a stick to form a large torch, and thus illuminated proceed with our whole troop to examine the interior of this grotto. I had not sent Jack on his embassy without a meaning; the boy possessed from nature a lively and poetical imagination. I knew he would tell his mother such wonders of the grotto, that in spite of the charms of her spinning-wheel he would induce her to accompany him, and bring us lights to penetrate the obscure sanctuary.

Overjoyed at his commission, Jack sprang on the buffalo, which he had nearly appropriated to himself, cracked his whip, and set off boldly. The intrepid boy was unencumbered by fear, and made a racehorse of his horned steed.

In waiting his return I proposed to Fritz to widen the entrance to the grotto, and make a way for his mother to pass in. After labouring three or four hours we saw them coming up in our car of state – the one I had equipped for the potatoes, and which was now drawn by the cow and the ass, and conducted by Ernest. Francis, too, played his part in the cavalcade, and contended with his brother for the ropes that served as reins. Jack, mounted on his buffalo, came prancing before them, blew through his closed hand in imitation of a French horn, and now and then whipped the ass and cow to quicken their motion. When they had crossed Family Bridge he came forward on the gallop, and when he got up to us, jumped off the beast, shook himself, took a spring or two from the ground, and thus refreshed ran up to the car to hand his mother out like a true and gallant knight.

I immediately lighted the torches, but instead of tying them together, as I had intended, I preferred that each should take one in his right hand, an implement in his left in case of accident, a taper in his pocket, and flint and steel. Thus we entered the rock in procession. I took the lead, my sons followed me, and their beloved mother, with the youngest, brought up the rear. We had scarcely advanced four paces within the grotto when all was changed to more than admiration and surprise. The most beautiful and magnificent spectacle presented itself. The sides of the cavern sparkled like diamonds, the light from our six tapers was reflected from all parts, and had the effect of a grand illumination. Innumerable crystals of every length and shape hung from the top of the vault, which, uniting with those of the sides, formed pillars, altars, entablatures, and a variety of other figures, constituting the most splendid masses. We might have fancied ourselves in the palace of a fairy, or in an illumined temple. In some places all the colours of a prism were emitted from the angles of the crystals, and gave them the appearance of precious stones. The waving of the lights, their bright coruscations, dark points here and there occurring, the dazzling lustre of others — the whole, in short, enchanted the sight and the fancy.

The astonishment of my family was so great as to be almost ludicrous. They were all in a kind of stupor, half-imagining it was a dream. I had seen stalactites, and read the description of the famous grotto of Antiparos, far more considerable than this, which, however, gave an idea of it. The bottom was level, covered with white, fine sand, so dry that I could not see the least mark of humidity. All this led me to hope the spot would be eligible for our residence. I now formed a conjecture as to the nature of the crystallizations, namely, that I was in a grotto of rock-salt. The discovery of this fact pleased us all exceedingly. The shape of the crystals, their little solidity, and finally their saline taste, were decisive evidences.

How highly advantageous to us and our cattle was this superabundance of salt, pure and ready to be shovelled out for use!

As we advanced, remarkable figures formed by the saline matter everywhere presented themselves. Columns reaching from the bottom to the top of the vault appeared to sustain it, and some even had cornices and capitals; here and there undulating masses which at certain distances resembled the sea. From the whimsical forms we beheld, fancy might make a thousand creations at its pleasure; windows, large open cupboards, benches, church ornaments, grotesque figures of men and animals, some like polished crystals or diamonds, others like blocks of alabaster.

We viewed with unwearied curiosity this repository of wonders, and we had all lighted our second taper, when I observed on the ground in some places a number of crystal fragments that seemed to have fallen off from the upper part. Such a separation might recur at any moment, and therefore I thought it prudent to retire, as other loosened pieces might fall on us. I directed my wife and three of the children to place themselves in the entrance, while Fritz and I examined every part that threatened danger. We loaded our guns with ball and fired them in the centre of the cavern; one or two fell, the rest remained immovable, though we went round with long poles and struck all we could reach. We at length felt confident that there was nothing to fear, and that we might proceed to fit up our new habitation without dread. Many schemes were formed for converting this beautiful grotto into a mansion for our abode. All the force of our imagination was centred in that point. The greatest difficulty was removed; we had possession of the most eligible premises; the sole business now was to turn them to the best account and how to effect this was our unceasing theme. Some voted for our immediate establishment there, but they were opposed by more sagacious counsel, and it was resolved that Falcon's Stream should continue to be our headquarters till the end of the year.

CHAPTER THIRTY-THREE

HOUSE IN THE SALT-ROCK

~

The lucky discovery of a cavern in the rock had, as must be supposed, considerably lessened our labour. Excavation was no longer requisite. To render it habitable was the present object. The upper bed of the rock in front of the cavern, through which my little Jack had dug so easily, was of a soft nature, and to be worked with moderate effort. I. hoped also that, being now exposed, it would become by degrees as hard as the first layer. From this consideration I began, while it retained its soft state, to make openings for the door and windows. This I regulated by the measurement of those I had fixed in my winding staircase, which I had removed for the purpose of placing them in our winter tenement. Intending Falcon's Nest as a retreat for the hottest days, the windows became unnecessary. As to the door, I preferred making one of bark similar to that of the tree itself, as it would conceal our abode the better. The doors and windows were therefore taken to Tent House, and afterwards properly fixed. I had previously marked out the openings to be cut for the frames, which were received into grooves. I took care not to break up the stone taken from the apertures, or at least to preserve it in large pieces, and these I cut into oblongs an inch and a half in thickness to serve as tiles. I laid them in the sun, and was gratified in seeing they hardened quickly.

When I could enter the cavern freely through a good doorway, and it was sufficiently lighted by the windows, I erected a partition for the distribution of our apartments and other conveniences. I was cautious to injure as little as possible the natural embellishments of this new mansion. But I could not avoid demolishing them in the division allotted to the stables. Cattle are fond of salt, and would not have failed to eat away these ornaments. However, I preserved the finest of the pillars and the most beautiful pieces to decorate our saloon. The large ones served us as chairs and tables, and the brilliant pilasters at once enlivened and adorned the apartment, and at night multiplied the reflection of the lights. I laid out the interior in the following manner. A very considerable space was first partitioned off in two divisions; the one on the right was appropriated to our residence, that on the left was to contain the kitchen, stables, and workroom. At the end of the second division, where windows could not be placed, the cellar and storeroom were to be formed; the whole separated by partition boards, with doors of communication, so as to give us a comfortable abode.

The side we designed to lodge in was divided into three chambers; the first, next the door, was the bedroom for my wife and me, the second a dining-parlour, and the last a bed-chamber for the boys. As we had only three windows, we put one in each sleeping-room; the third was fixed in the kitchen. A grating for the present fell to the lot of our dining-room, which, when too cold, was to be exchanged for one of the other apartments. I contrived a good fireplace in the kitchen near the window; I pierced the rock a little above, and four planks nailed together and passed through this opening answered the purpose of a chimney. We made the workroom near the kitchen of sufficient dimensions for the performance of undertakings of some magnitude; it served also to keep our cart and sledge in. Lastly, the stables, which were formed into four compartments to separate the different species of animals, occupied all the bottom of the cavern on this side; on the other were the cellar and magazine.

The long stay we made at Tent House during these employments furnished us an opportunity of perceiving several advantages we had not reckoned upon, and which we did not defer availing ourselves of. Immense turtles were very often seen on the shore, where they deposited their eggs in the sand, and they regaled us with a rich treat. But, extending our wishes, we thought of getting possession of the turtles themselves for live stock, and of feasting on them whenever we pleased. As soon as we saw one on the sands, one of my boys was dispatched to cut off its retreat. Meanwhile we approached the animal, turned it on its back, passed a long cord through the shell, and tied the end of it to a stake which we fixed close to the edge of the water. This done, we set the prisoner on his legs again. It hastened into the sea, but could not go beyond the length of the cord. Apparently it was quite happy, finding plenty of food alongshore, and we enjoyed the idea of being able to take it when wanted. I say nothing of sea-lobsters, oysters, and many other small fishes which we could catch in any number.

At this time I likewise made some improvements in our sledge. I raised it on two beams or axle-trees, at the extremities of which I put on the four gun-carriage wheels I had taken off the cannon from the vessel. By this alteration I obtained a light and very convenient vehicle, of moderate height, on which boxes and casks could be placed. Pleased with the operations of the week, we set out all together with cheerful hearts for Falcon's Stream, to pass our Sunday there, and once more offer our pious thanks to the Almighty for all the benefits He had bestowed upon His defenceless creatures.

CHAPTER THIRTY-FOUR

New Fishery – New Experiments and Chase – New Discoveries and House

~

The arrangement of our grotto went on according to the importance of other concerns, and our progress was such as to afford the hope of our being securely established within it by the time of the rainy season.

I had made the fortunate discovery of a bed of gypsum in the neighbourhood of our grotto. I foresaw the great advantages I should derive from it, and tried to find a place in the continuation of the rock which I might be able to blow up. I had soon the good fortune to meet with a narrow slip between the rocks which I could easily convert into a passage that should terminate in our work-room. I found also a quantity of fragments of gypsum, and removed a number of them to the kitchen, where we did not fail to bake a few of the pieces at a time when we made a fire for cooking, which, thus calcined, rubbed into a powder when cold. We obtained a considerable quantity of it which I put carefully into casks for use when the time should come for finishing the interior of our dwelling. My notion was to form the walls for separating the apartments of squares of stone, and to unite them together with a cement of gypsum, which would be the means both of sparing our timber and increasing the beauty and solidity of the work.

About two months after the discovery of our grotto, we observed Safety Bay to be filled with large fishes, which seemed eager to push to the shore for the purpose of depositing their eggs. Jack was the first to discover this circumstance. He told me he had seen a number of whales swimming about in Jackal River. I replied that I could not conceive of a regiment of whales arriving in our diminutive rivulet.

It, however, appeared to me worth while to go and convince myself on the spot respecting these new-comers. Jack and I walked to the mouth of Jackal River, and perceived immense quantities of a large fish moving slowly towards the banks, and some of them from four to eight feet in length. By the pointed snout I supposed them to be sturgeons. "What say you, now, Father?" said Jack. "A single fish of this troop would fill a tub!"

"No doubt," answered I; and with great gravity I added, "Pr'ythee, Jack, step into the river, and fling them to me."

He looked at me for a moment with a sort of vacant doubt, then seizing suddenly a new idea, "Wait a moment, Father," cried he, "and I will do so!" and he sprang off towards the cavern, from whence he returned with a bow and arrows, the bladders of some fish, and a ball of string. I looked on with interest to mark what was next to happen. He tied the bladders round at certain distances with a long piece of string, to the end of which he fastened an arrow and a small iron hook. He placed the large ball of string in a hole in the ground, at a sufficient distance from the water's edge, and then he shot off his arrow, which the next instant stuck in one of the largest fishes. My young sportsman uttered a shout of joy. At the same moment Fritz joined us, and witnessed this unexpected feat without the least symptom of jealousy. "Well done, brother Jack!" cried he; "but let me too have my turn." Saying this he ran back and fetched the harpoon and the windlass, and returned to us accompanied by Ernest, who also desired to show his prowess in a contest with our newly-discovered mariners. We were well pleased with their arrival, for the fish Jack had pierced struggled so fiercely that we dreaded at every jerk to see it escape. By degrees, however, its strength was exhausted, and aided by Fritz and Ernest we succeeded in drawing it to a bank.

This fortunate beginning of a plan for a fishery inspired us all with hope and emulation. Fritz eagerly seized his harpoon and windlass. I, for my part, like Neptune, wielded a trident. Ernest prepared the large fishing-rod, and Jack his arrow, with the same apparatus as before, not forgetting the bladders, which were effectual in preventing the fish from sinking when struck. Such numbers of fishes presented themselves that we had only to choose. Accordingly we were soon loaded to our heart's content. Jack's arrow, after missing twice, struck the third time a large sturgeon, which was so untractable that we had great difficulty in securing him. I had caught two, and had been obliged to go up to the middle in the water to manage my booty. Ernest, with his rod and line and a hook, had also taken two fish. Fritz with his harpoon had struck a sturgeon at least eight feet in length, and the skill and strength of our whole company were found necessary to conduct him to shore.

Our first concern was to clean our fish thoroughly. I took care of the bladders, thinking it might be possible to make a glue from them. I advised my wife to boil some of the smaller fish in oil, similar to the manner of preparing tunny fish in the Mediterranean, and while she was engaged in this process I was at work upon the glue. For the first, I washed the berries in several waters, and then pressed them closely in gourd-rinds in which a certain number of holes had been bored. When the water had run off, the berries were taken out in a substance like cheese, which was then conveyed to the hut to be dried and smoked. For the second, we cut the bladders into strips, which we fastened firmly by one end to a stake, and taking hold of the other with a pair of pincers, we turned them round and round till the strip was reduced to a kind of knot, and these were then placed in the sun to harden, this being the simple and only preparation necessary for obtaining glue from the ingredient. When thoroughly dry, a small quantity is put on a slow fire to melt. We succeeded so well, and our glue was of so transparent a quality, that I could not help feeling the desire to manufacture some pieces large enough for panes to a window-frame.

When these various concerns were complete, we began to meditate a plan for constructing a small boat as a substitute for the tub raft. I had a great desire to make it as the savages do, of the rind of a tree; but the difficulty was to fix on one of sufficient bulk, for, though many were to be found, each was on some account or other of too much value to be spared. We therefore resolved to make a little excursion in pursuit of a tree of capacious dimensions, and in a situation where it was not likely to yield us fruit, to refresh us with its shade, or to adorn the landscape round our dwelling.

In this expedition we as usual aimed at more than one object. Eager as we were for new discoveries, we yet allowed ourselves the time to visit our different plantations and stores at Falcon's Stream. We were also desirous to secure a new supply of the wax berry, of gourds, and of elastic gum. Our kitchen-garden at Tent House was in a flourishing condition; nothing could exceed the luxuriance of the vegetation, and we had excellent roots and plants in abundance, which came in succession, and promised a rich supply of peas, beans, lettuces, &c. We had, besides, melons and cucumbers in great plenty, which, during the hottest weather, we valued more than all the rest. We reaped a considerable quantity of Turkey wheat from the seed we had sown, and some of the ears were a foot in length. Our sugar-canes were also in the most prosperous condition, and one plantation of pine-apples on the high ground was also in progress to reward our labour with delicious fruit.

This state of prosperity at Tent House gave us flattering expectations from our nurseries at Falcon's Stream. Full of these hopes, we one day set out for our former abode.

We arrived at Falcon's Stream, where we intended to pass the night. We visited the ground my wife had so plentifully sowed with grain, which had sprung up with an almost incredible rapidity and luxuriance, and was nearly ready for reaping. We cut down what was fairly ripe, bound it together in bundles, and conveyed it to a place where it would be secure from the attacks of more expert grain consumers than ourselves, of which thousands hovered round the booty. We reaped barley, wheat, rye, oats, peas, millet, lentils – only a small quantity of each, it is true, but sufficient to enable us to sow again plentifully at the proper season. The plant that had yielded the most was maize, a proof that it best loved the soil and climate. The moment we drew near, a dozen, at least, of large bustards sprang up with a loud rustling noise, which awakened the attention of the dogs. They plunged into the thickest parts, and routed numerous flocks of birds of all kinds and sizes. Among the fugitives were some quails, who escaped by running, and lastly some kangaroos, whose prodigious leaps enabled them to elude the pursuit of the dogs.

We were so overcome by the surprise such an assemblage occasioned as to forget the resource we had in our guns.

Jack alone thought of how to repair the error, and also the giving us a specimen of the happy effects of the education he had bestowed on the young jackal. He let him loose, and he slipped slily away after the birds we supposed were quails. The jackal soon overtook them, seized one of them by the wing, and brought it to his master. In the same manner he carried him at least a dozen.

At the conclusion of this adventure we hastened forward to Falcon's Stream. I threw a few more bundles of maize into the cart, and without further delay we arrived at our tree, one and all sinking with faintness from hunger, thirst, and fatigue. It was on such occasions that my wife evinced the superior fortitude and generosity of her temper. Though more a sufferer than any, her first thought was what she could administer to relieve us. She contrived to bruise some of the maize between two large stones, and then put it in a linen cloth, and with all her strength squeezed out the sap. She then added some juice from the sugar-canes, and in a few minutes presented us with a draught of a cool refreshing liquid, beautifully white in appearance and agreeable to the taste.

Jack had been able to preserve alive only two of the quails. All the others were put on the spit for supper. The rest of the day was employed in picking the grains of the different sorts of corn from the stalks. We put what we wished to keep for sowing into gourd shells, and the Turkey wheat was laid aside in sheaves till we should have time to beat and separate it. Fritz observed that we should also want to grind it, and I reminded him of the hand-mill we had secured from the wrecked vessel.

Fritz. "But, Father, the hand-mill is so small, and so subject to be put out of order. Why should we not contrive a water-mill? We have surely rapid streams of water in abundance."

Father. "This is true, but such a mechanism is more difficult than you imagine. In the meantime, let us be thinking, boy, of our proposed excursion for to-morrow, for we should set out at latest by sunrise."

We began our preparations accordingly. My wife chose some hens and two fine cocks, with the intention of taking them with us and leaving them at large to produce a colony of their species. I, with the same view, visited our stable, and selected four young pigs, four sheep, two kids, and one male of each species, our numbers having so much increased that we could afford to spare these.

The next morning, after loading the cart with all things necessary, not forgetting the rope-ladder and the tent, we quitted Falcon's Stream. The animals, with their legs tied, were all stationed in the vehicle. We left abundance of food for those that remained behind. The cow, the ass, and the buffalo were harnessed to the cart. Fritz, mounted on his favourite, the onagra, pranced along before us to ascertain the best and smoothest path.

We took this time a new direction, which was straight forward between the rocks and the shore, that we might make ourselves acquainted with everything contained in the island. In effect, the line proceeding from Falcon's Stream to the Great Bay might be said to be the extent of our dominions, for, though Jack and I had discovered the adjacent exquisite country of the buffaloes, yet the passage to it by the end of the rocks was so dangerous, and at so great a distance, that we could not hope to settle ourselves upon its soil. We found, as usual, much difficulty in pushing through the tall tough grass, and alternately through the thick prickly bushes. We were often obliged to turn aside while I cut a passage with my hatchet. But these accidents seldom failed to reward my toil by the discovery of additions to our comfort: among others, some roots of trees curved by nature to serve both for saddles and yokes for our beasts of burden.

When we had spent about an hour in getting forward, a most singular phenomenon presented itself to our view: a small plain, or rather a grove of small bushes, to appearance almost covered with flakes of snow, lay before us. Little Francis was the first to call our attention to it, he being seated in the cart.

"Look, Father," cried he, "here is a place quite full of snow!"

Though sure that what we saw could not be snow, yet I was at a loss to explain the nature of what bore so near a resemblance to it. Suddenly, however, a suspicion crossed my mind, and was confirmed by Fritz, who had darted forward and now returned with one hand filled with tufts of cotton, so that the whole surface of low bushes was in reality a plantation of that article. The pods had burst from ripeness, and the winds had scattered around their flaky contents, so that the ground was strewed with them. They had gathered in tufts on the bushes, and the air was full of the gently-floating down.

The joy of this discovery was almost too great for utterance. We collected as much cotton as our bags would hold, and my wife filled her pockets with the seed to raise it in our garden.

It was now time to proceed. We took a direction towards a point of land which skirted the wood of gourds, and, being high, commanded a view of the adjacent country. I conceived a wish to remove our establishment to the vicinity of the cotton plantation and the gourd wood, which furnished so many of our utensils. I pleased myself in idea with the view of the different colonies of animals I had imagined, both winged and quadruped; and in this elevation of my fancy I even thought it might be practicable to erect a sort of farmhouse on the soil, which we might visit occasionally, and be welcomed by the agreeable sounds of the cackling of our feathered subjects.

We accordingly soon reached the high ground, which I found in all respects favourable to my design.

My plan for a building was approved, and we lost no time in pitching our tent. When we had refreshed ourselves with a meal, we each took up some useful occupation. My wife and the boys went to work with the cotton, which they thoroughly cleaned, and which was then put into the bags and served at night for bolsters and mattresses. I for my part resolved to look about in all directions, that I might completely understand what we should have to depend upon in this place. I had also to find a tree that would suit for the construction of a boat; and lastly, to meet with a group of trees at such fit distances from each other as would assist me in erecting my farmhouse. I was fortunate enough to find in this last respect exactly what I wanted. But I was not equally successful as regards the boat, the trees in the vicinity being of too small a bulk. I returned to my companions, whom I found employed in preparing beds of the cotton, upon which at an earlier hour than usual we all retired to rest.

CHAPTER THIRTY-FIVE

COMPLETION OF TWO FARMHOUSES – A LAKE

~

The trees that I had chosen for the construction of my farm were all about one foot in diameter; their growth was regular, and they formed a rough parallelogram with the longer side to the sea, the length being twenty-four feet and the breadth sixteen. I cut little hollow places or mortises in the trunks, at the distance of ten feet, one above the other, to form two stories. The upper one I made a few inches shorter before than behind, that the roof might be in some degree shelving. I then inserted beams five inches in diameter in the mortises, and thus formed the skeleton of my building. We next nailed some laths from tree to tree at equal distances to form the roof, and placed on them a covering of pieces of bark cut into the shape of tiles, and in a sloping position for the rain to run off. As we had no great provision of nails, we used for the purpose the thorn of the acacia, which we had discovered the day before. The tree is known by the name of *Acacia with three thorns*, and exhibits, growing all together, three strong sharp-pointed thorns. We cut down a quantity of them and laid them in the sun, when they became as hard as iron, and of essential service.

On this occasion we made another agreeable discovery. My wife took up the remaining chips of the bark for lighting a fire, and we were surprised by a delicious aromatic odour which perfumed the air. On examining the half-consumed substance, we found some of the pieces to contain turpentine and others gum-mastich. It was less with a view to the gratifying our sense of smell, than with the hope of being able to secure a sort of pitch to complete our meditated boat, that we indulged our earnestness in the pursuit. The instinct of our goats, or the acuteness of their smell, discovered for us another acquisition. We observed with surprise that they ran from a considerable distance to throw themselves about on some particular chip of bark, and to chew it greedily. Jack seized a piece also, to find out what could be the reason of so marked a preference.

"Oh, it is indeed excellent," exclaimed he. "Only try this bit, brother Fritz, and tell us if it is not like cinnamon?"

Fritz was of Jack's opinion. My wife and I then followed and were convinced that it was cinnamon, though not so fine as that from Ceylon.

During our next meal we amused ourselves with a retrospect of the different discoveries we had made that day. I had to relate what I knew on the subject of the nature of these new productions: the turpentine, the mastich, and the cinnamon.

When our meal and the lecture were both ended, we resumed with ardour our undertaking of the farm.

We formed the walls of our building with matted reeds, interwoven with pliant laths to the height of six feet. The remaining space to the roof was enclosed with only a simple grating, that the air and light might be admitted. A door was placed in the front. We next arranged the interior, with as much convenience as the shortness of the time and our reluctance to use all our timber would allow. We divided it halfway up by a partition wall, into two equal parts. The largest was intended for the sheep and goats, and the smallest for ourselves. At the farther end of the stable we fixed a house for the fowls, and above it a sort of hay-loft for the forage. Before the door of entrance we placed two benches, contrived as well as we could of laths and odd pieces of wood, that we might rest under the shade of the trees and enjoy the exquisite prospect. Our own apartment was provided with a couple of the best bedsteads we could make of branches of trees raised upon four legs and these were destined to receive our cotton mattresses. Our aim was to content ourselves for the present with these slight hints of a dwelling, and to consider hereafter what additions could be made. All we were now anxious about was to provide a shelter for our animal colonists, which should encourage them in the habit of assembling every evening in one place. For several days at first we took care to fill their troughs with their favourite food mixed with salt, and we agreed that we would return frequently to repeat this mode of invitation till they should be fixed in their expectation of finding it.

I had imagined we could accomplish what we wished at the farm in three or four days. But we found that a whole week was necessary, and our victuals fell short before our work was done. I therefore decided that on this trying occasion I would invest Fritz and Jack with an important mission. They were accordingly dispatched to Falcon's Stream and to Tent House to fetch new supplies for our subsistence, and also to distribute food to the animals.

During the absence of our purveyors, I rambled with Ernest about the neighbouring soil, to make what new discoveries I could.

We followed the winding of a river we had remarked, and which conducted towards the centre of the wall of rocks. Our course was here interrupted by an extensive marsh which bordered a small lake, the aspect of which was enchantingly picturesque. I perceived with joyful surprise that the whole surface of this swampy soil was covered with a kind of wild rice, ripe on the stalk, which attracted large flocks of birds. As we approached a loud rustling was heard, and we distinguished on the wing bustards and great numbers of smaller birds. We succeeded in bringing down five or six of them, and I was pleased to remark in Ernest a justness of aim that promised well for the future. The habits of his mind discovered themselves on this as on many previous occasions. He betrayed no ardour, he did everything with a deliberation that almost seemed to imply sluggishness; yet the coolness and constancy he applied to every attempt he had to engage in, so effectually assisted his judgment, that he was sure to arrive at a more perfect execution than the other boys. He had practised but little in the study of how to fire a gun; but Ernest was a silent observer, and accordingly his first essays were generally crowned with success. In this affair, however, of the birds, his skill would have proved fruitless if Jack's young jackal, which had followed us, had not plunged into the swamp and brought out the birds as they fell.

At a small distance was also Knips, who had taken his post on Ponto's back. Presently we saw him jump off and smell along the ground among some thick-growing plants, then pluck off something and eat of it voraciously. We ran to the spot to see what it could be, when, to the relief of our parched palates, we found he had discovered there the largest kind of strawberry.

After pursuing our way farther along the marsh, we reached the lake which was situated in a deep and abrupt valley. No traveller who is not a native of Switzerland can conceive the emotion which trembled at my heart as I contemplated this limpid, azure, undulating body of water, the faithful miniature of so many grand originals, which I had probably lost sight of for ever! My eyes swam with tears! "How glad I am to see a lake! I could almost think myself in Switzerland, Father!" said Ernest.

Alas, a single glance upon the surrounding pictures, the different characters of the trees, the vast ocean in the distance, destroyed the momentary illusion, and brought back our ideas to the painful reality that we were strangers in a desert island!

Another sort of object now presented itself to confirm the certainty that we were no longer inhabitants of Europe. It was the appearance of a quantity of swans which glided over the lake; their colour was a jetty black; and their plumage had so high a gloss as to produce, reflected in the water, the most astonishing effect. The six large feathers of the wing of this bird are white, exhibiting a singular contrast to the rest of the body. In other respects these creatures were remarkably like those of Europe.

We now began to look for the shortest path for rejoining our companions at the farm, which we reached at the same time with Fritz and Jack, who had well performed the object of their journey. We produced our strawberries and our specimen of rice, which were welcomed with pleasure and surprise.

The following day we took a silent leave of our animals and directed our course towards Cape Disappointment. On entering Monkey Wood, innumerable animals of the species from which it derives its name began to scamper away. We pursued our way, and arrived shortly after at the eminence we were in pursuit of in the vicinity of Cape Disappointment. We ascended it, and found it in every respect adapted to our wishes. From this eminence we had a view over the country which surrounded Falcon's Stream in one direction, and in others of a landscape comprehending sea, land, and rocks. When we had paused for a short time upon the beauties of the scene, we agreed that it should be on this spot we would build our second cottage. A spring of the clearest water issued from the soil near the summit, forming in its rapid course agreeable cascades. "Let us build here," exclaimed I, "and call the spot *Arcadia*!" to which my wife and all agreed.

We lost no time in again setting to work upon this undertaking. Our experience enabled us to proceed with rapidity, and our success was in every respect complete. The building contained a dining-room, two bed-chambers, two stables, and a store-room. We formed the roof square, with four sloping sides, and the whole had really the appearance of a European cottage, and was finished in the short space of six days.

CHAPTER THIRTY-SIX

THE BOAT – PROGRESS IN THE ABODE OF ROCKS

~

Our Arcadia being entirely completed, what remained to be done was to fix on a tree fit for a boat. After much search, I at length found one in most respects suitable to my views.

It was, however, no very encouraging prospect I had before me, being nothing less than the stripping off a piece of the bark that should be eighteen feet in length and five in diameter. I now found my rope-ladder of signal service. We cut quite round the trunk in two places, and then took a perpendicular slip from the whole length between the circles. By this means we could introduce the proper utensils for raising the rest till it was entirely separated. We toiled with increasing anxiety, dreading that we should not be able to preserve it from breaking. When we had loosened about half, we supported it by means of cords and pulleys, and when all was at length detached we let it down gently, and with joy beheld it lying safe on the grass. Our business was next to mould it to our purpose while the substance continued moist and flexible.

The boys observed that we had now nothing more to do than to nail a plank at each end, and our boat would be complete. But I could not be contented with a mere roll of bark for a boat, and when I reminded them of the paltry figure it would make following the pinnace, they asked eagerly for my instructions. I made them assist me to saw the bark in the middle, the length of several feet from the ends. These two parts I folded over till they ended in a point, naturally raised. I kept them in this form by the help of the strong fish-glue, and pieces of wood nailed fast over the whole. This operation tended to widen the boat in the middle, and thus render it of too flat a form. This we counteracted by straining a cord all round, which again reduced it to the due proportion, and in this state we put it to the sun to harden and fix. Many things were still wanting to the completion of my undertaking, but I had not with me proper utensils. I therefore dispatched the boys to Tent House to fetch the sledge, and convey the boat there for our better convenience in finishing.

Before our departure for Tent House we collected several new plants. We also made another trip to the narrow strait at the end of the wall of rocks, resolved to plant there a sort of fortification of trees, which should produce the double effect of discouraging the invasion of savages and of allowing us to keep our pigs on the other side, and thus secure our different plantations from injury. We accomplished this to our satisfaction, and in addition we placed a slight drawbridge across the river beyond the narrow pass, which we could let down or take up at pleasure. We now hastened our return to Arcadia, and after a night's repose loaded the sledge with the boat and other things, and returned to Tent House.

As soon as possible we resumed the completion of the boat. In two days she had received a keel, a lining of wood, a flat floor, benches, a mast and triangular sail, a rudder, and a thick coat of pitch on the outside, so that the first time we saw her in the water we were all delighted at the appearance she made.

Our cow in the meantime had brought forth a bull calf. I pierced its nostrils, as I had so successfully practised with the buffalo, and the animal gave promise of future docility.

We had still two months before the rainy season, and we employed them in completing our grotto. We made the internal divisions of planks, and that which separated us from the stables of stone, to protect us from the smell of the animals. We took care to collect or manufacture a sufficient quantity of all sorts of materials, such as beams and planks, reeds and twigs for matting, pieces of gypsum for plaster, &c. At length the time of the rainy season was near at hand, and this time we thought of it with pleasure, as the period that would put us in possession of the enjoyments we had procured by unremitting industry and fatigue. We had an inexpressible longing to find ourselves domiciled and at leisure.

We plastered over the walls of the principal apartments with the greatest care, finishing them by pressure with a flat board. This work amused us all so much, that we began to think we might venture a step farther in luxury, and agreed that we would make carpets with the hair of our goats. To this purpose we smoothed the ground in the rooms. We then spread over it some sail-cloth, which my wife had joined in breadths, and fitted exactly. We next strewed the goats' hair, mixed with wool from the sheep, over the whole. On this surface we threw hot water, in which cement had been dissolved. The whole was then rolled up, and beaten for a considerable time with hard sticks. The sail-cloth was now unrolled, and the inside again sprinkled, rolled, and beaten as before. This process was continued till the substance had become a sort of felt, which could be separated from the sail-cloth. We put it in the sun to harden, and found we had produced a very tolerable substitute for a European carpet. We completed two of them, one for our parlour and the other for our drawing-room, as we jocosely named them, both of which were completely fit for our reception by the time the rains had set in.

All we had suffered during the preceding rainy season doubled the value of the comforts with which we were now surrounded. In the morning our first care was to feed the cattle and give them drink. After this we assembled in the parlour, where prayers were read, and breakfast immediately served. We then adjourned to the common room, where all sorts of industry went forward. After dinner our work was resumed till night, when we lighted candles, which, as they cost no more than our own trouble, we did not refuse ourselves the pleasure of using. We had formed a portion of our dwelling into a small chapel, in which we left the crystals as produced by nature, and they exhibited a truly enchanting spectacle. Divine service was performed in it regularly every Sunday. I had raised a sort of pulpit, from which I pronounced such discourses as I had framed for the instruction of my affectionate group of auditors.

Jack and Francis had a natural inclination for music. I did the most I could in making a flageolet apiece for them of two reeds, on which they attained a tolerable proficiency. They accompanied their mother, who had a sweet-toned voice, the volume of which was doubled by the echoes of the grottos, and they produced together a very pleasing little concert.

Thus, we had made the first steps towards civilization. Separated from society, condemned perhaps to pass the remainder of life in this desert island, we yet possessed the means of happiness. We had abundance of necessaries, and many comforts. We had fixed habits of industry; we were in ourselves contented; our health and strength increased from day to day; the sentiment of tender attachment was perfect in every heart; and we every day acquired some new channel for the exertion of our physical and moral faculties.

Nearly two years had elapsed without our perceiving the smallest trace of civilized or savage man, without the appearance of a vessel upon the vast sea by which we are surrounded. Ought we then to indulge a hope that we shall once again behold the face of a fellow-creature? We encourage serenity and thankfulness in each other, and wait with resignation!

POSTSCRIPT BY THE EDITOR

~

I have presented the public, and in particular the sons of families, with the part I had in my possession of the journal of the Swiss pastor, who, with his family, were shipwrecked on a desert island. It cannot escape the observation of the parents who will read the work, that it exhibits a lively picture of the happiness which does not fail to result from the practice of moral virtues. Thus, in a situation that seemed calculated to produce despair, we see piety, affection, industry, and a generous concern for fellow-sufferers, capable of forming the basis of an unexpected state of happiness. We also see the advantage of including in the education of boys such a knowledge of the natural productions of the earth, of the various combinations by which they may be rendered serviceable, and of the use of tools, as may qualify them to assist others or preserve themselves under every possible occurrence. It now remains for me to inform the reader by what means the journal of the Swiss pastor came into my possession.

Three or four years subsequent to the occurrence of the shipwreck of the pastor and his family, an English transport was driven by the violence of a tempest upon the same shore. The name of the vessel was the *Adventurer*, Captain Johnson. It was on a voyage from New Zealand to the eastern coast of North America, by Otaheite, in the South Seas, to fetch a cargo of skins and furs for China, and to proceed from

Canton to England. A violent tempest drove it from its track. The vessel beat about in unknown seas for many days, and was now so injured by the weather that the best hope of the captain and his company was to get into some port. They at length discovered a rocky coast, and as the wind had somewhat abated they made with all speed for the shore. When within a short distance they cast their anchor, and put out a boat to examine the coast and find a place for landing. They rowed backward and forward for some time without success, on account of the rocky nature of the coast. At length they turned a promontory, and perceived a bay whose calm water seemed to invite their approach. This was the *Safety Bay* of the wrecked islanders. The boat put on shore, and the officers beheld the traces of the abode of man. A handsome well-conditioned pinnace and a small boat were at anchor. Near the strand, under a rock, was a tent, and farther on in the rock a housedoor and windows announced European comforts and workmanship. The officers advanced towards the spot, and were met half-way by a man of middle age, dressed like a European and armed with a gun. The stranger accosted them with friendly tones and gestures. He spoke first German, and then some words in English. Lieutenant Bell, one of the English officers, who spoke German, answered. A mutual confidence immediately ensued. We need not add that the stranger was the father of the family whose adventures are narrated in the previous pages. His wife and children happened at the moment to be at Falcon's Stream. He had discovered the English ship with his glass, and, unwilling to alarm his family, had come, perceiving she bore that way, alone to the coast.

After an interchange of cordial greetings, and a hospitable reception of the officers at the grotto, the Swiss pastor put his journal into the hands of Lieutenant Bell, to be conveyed to Captain Johnson, that he also might become acquainted with the story of the islanders. After an hour's conversation the newly-made friends separated, in the expectation of meeting again on the following day. But Heaven had otherwise ordained.

During the night the tempest revived. The *Adventurer* dragged her anchor, and was obliged to steer to the bosom of the ocean. As there was no change of weather for several days, the vessel was driven so far from the coast of Safety Bay as to leave no possibility of returning, and Captain Johnson was compelled to renounce the gratification of seeing this most interesting family, or of proposing to convey them all to Europe.

Captain Johnson brought the journal of the Swiss pastor to England, from whence it was transmitted to a friend in Switzerland, who has deemed its contents an instructive lesson to the world.

At a later time the Pastor and his family were again heard of. Their island became a regular place of call for trading ships; and as prosperity increased, the Pastor was able to let his son Ernest proceed to Europe to pursue a course of professional study at one of the universities, where he attained distinction. The other sons married and remained with their parents as prosperous planters on their loved island home, to which Ernest also ultimately returned, bringing with him as wife his cousin Henrietta.

A word should be said about the title by which this entrancing record is known. Those who were responsible for publishing it, and giving the story to the world, could not but be struck by the many points of similarity between the adventures of the Swiss Pastor's family and those of the famous Robinson Crusoe. They therefore named the book *The Swiss Family Robinson Crusoe*, which in course of time became contracted to the title by which the book is now known, *The Swiss Family Robinson.*

Robinson Crusoe

~

Daniel Defoe

Robinson Crusoe

~

Daniel Defoe

Illustrated by
J. Ayton Symington

Colour Illustrations

I was born in the year 1632, in the city of York, of a good family, though not of that country, my father being a foreigner of Bremen, who settled first at Hull. He got a good estate by merchandise, and leaving off his trade, lived afterward at York, from whence he had married my mother, whose relations were named Robinson, a very good family in that country, and from whom I was called Robinson Kreutznaer; but by the usual corruption of words in England we are now called, nay, we call ourselves, and write our name, Crusoe, and so my companions always called me.

Being the third son of the family, and not bred to any trade, my head began to be filled very early with rambling thoughts. My father, who was very ancient, had given me a competent share of learning, as far as house-education and a country free school generally goes, and designed me for the law; but I would be satisfied with nothing but going to sea; and my inclination to this led me so strongly against the will, nay, the commands, of my father, and against all the entreaties and persuasions of my mother and other friends, that there seemed to be something fatal in that propension of nature tending directly to the life of misery which was to befall me.

My father, a wise and grave man, gave me serious and excellent counsel against what he foresaw was my design. He called me one morning into his chamber, where he was confined by the gout, and expostulated very warmly with me upon this subject.

He pressed me earnestly, and in the most affectionate manner, not to play the young man, not to precipitate myself into miseries which Nature and the station of life I was born in seemed to have provided against; that I was under no necessity of seeking my bread; that he would do well for me, and endeavour to enter me fairly into the middle station of life which he had been just recommending to me; and that if I was not very easy and happy in the world it must be my mere fate or fault that must hinder it, and that he should have nothing to answer for, having thus discharged his duty in warning me against measures which he knew would be to my hurt; in a word, that as he would do very kind things for me if I would stay and settle at home as he directed, so he would not have so much hand in my misfortunes, as to give me any encouragement to go away. And to close all, he told me I had my elder brother for an example, to whom he had used the same earnest persuasions to keep him from going into the Low Country wars, but could not prevail, his young desires prompting him to run into the army, where he was killed; and though he said he would not cease to pray for me, yet he would venture to say to me, that if I did take this foolish step, God would not bless me, and I would have leisure hereafter to reflect upon having neglected his counsel when there might be none to assist in my recovery.

I was sincerely affected with this discourse, as indeed who could be otherwise? and I resolved not to think of going abroad any more, but to settle at home according to my father's desire. But alas! a few days wore it all off; and, in short, to prevent any of my father's farther importunities, in a few weeks after I resolved to run quite away from him. However, I did not act so hastily neither as my first heat of resolution prompted, but I took my mother, at a time when I thought her a little pleasanter than ordinary, and told her, that my thoughts were so entirely bent upon seeing the world, that I should never settle to anything with resolution enough to go through with it, and my father had better give me his consent than force me to go without it; that I was now eighteen years old, which was too late to go apprentice to a trade, or clerk to an attorney; that I was sure if I did, I should never serve out my time, and I should certainly run away from my master before my time was out, and go to sea; and if she would speak to my father to let me go but one voyage abroad, if I came home again and did not like it, I would go no more, and I would promise by a double diligence to recover that time I had lost.

This put my mother into a great passion. She told me, she knew it would be to no purpose to speak to my father upon any such subject; that he knew too well what was my interest to give his consent to anything so much for my hurt, and that she wondered how I could think of any such thing after such a discourse as I had had with my father, and such kind and tender expressions as she knew my father had used to me; and that, in short, if I would ruin myself there was no help for me; but I might depend I should never have their consent to it; that for her part, she would not have so much hand in my destruction, and I should never have it to say, that my mother was willing when my father was not.

Though my mother refused to move it to my father, yet, as I have heard afterwards, she reported all the discourse to him, and that my father, after showing a great concern at it, said to her with a sigh, "That boy might be happy if he would stay at home, but if he goes abroad he will be the miserablest wretch that was ever born: I can give no consent to it."

It was not till almost a year after this that I broke loose, though in the meantime I continued obstinately deaf to all proposals of settling to business, and frequently expostulating with my father and mother about their being so positively determined against what they knew my inclinations prompted me to. But being one day at Hull, where I went casually, and without any purpose of making an elopement that time; but I say, being there, and one of my companions being going by sea to London, in his father's ship, and prompting me to go with them, with the common allurement of seafaring men, viz., that it should cost me nothing for my passage, I consulted neither father or mother any more, nor so much as sent them word of it; but leaving them to hear of it as they might, without asking God's blessing, or my father's, without any consideration of circumstances or consequences, and in an ill hour, God knows, on the first of September, 1651, I went on board a ship bound for London. Never any young adventurer's misfortunes, I believe, began sooner, or continued longer than mine. The ship was no sooner gotten out of the Humber, but the wind began to blow, and the waves to rise in a most frightful manner; and as I had never been at sea before, I was most inexpressibly sick in body, and terrified in my mind. I began now seriously to reflect upon what I had done, and how justly I was overtaken by the judgment of heaven for my wicked leaving my father's house, and abandoning my duty.

All this while the storm increased, and the sea, which I had never been upon before, went very high, though nothing like what I have seen many times since; no, nor like what I saw a few days after. But it was enough to affect me then, who was but a young sailor, and had never known anything of the matter. I expected every wave would have swallowed us up, and that every time the ship fell down, as I thought, in the trough or hollow of the sea, we should never rise more; and in this agony of mind I made many vows and resolutions, that if it would please God here to spare my life this one voyage, if ever I got once my foot upon dry land again, I would go directly home to my father, and never set it into a ship again while I lived; that I would take his advice, and never run myself into such miseries as these any more. Now I saw plainly the goodness of his observations about the middle station of life, how easy, how comfortably he had lived all his days, and never had been exposed to tempests at sea, or troubles on shore; and I resolved that I would, like a true repenting prodigal, go home to my father.

These wise and sober thoughts continued all the while the storm continued, and indeed some time after; but the next day the wind was abated and the sea calmer, and

I began to be a little inured to it. However, I was very grave for all that day, being also a little sea-sick still; but towards night the weather cleared up, the wind was quite over, and a charming fine evening followed; the sun went down perfectly clear, and rose so the next morning; and having little or no wind, and a smooth sea, the sun shining upon it, the sight was, as I thought, the most delightful that ever I saw.

I had slept well in the night, and was now no more sea-sick but very cheerful, looking with wonder upon the sea that was so rough and terrible the day before, and could be so calm and so pleasant in so little time after. And now lest my good resolutions should continue, my companion, who had indeed enticed me away, comes to me: "Well, Bob," says he, clapping me on the shoulder, "how do you do after it? I warrant you were frighted, wa'n't you, last night, when it blew but a capful of wind?" "A capful, d'you call it?" said I; "'twas a terrible storm." "A storm, you fool you," replies he; "do you call that a storm? Why, it was nothing at all; give us but a good ship and sea-room, and we think nothing of such a squall of wind as that; but you're but a fresh-water sailor, Bob. Come, let us make a bowl of punch, and we'll forget all that; d'ye see what charming weather 'tis now?" To make short this sad part of my story, we went the old way of all sailors; the punch was made, and I was made drunk with it, and in that one night's wickedness I drowned all my repentance, all my reflections upon my past conduct, and all my resolutions for my future. I found indeed some intervals of reflection, and the serious thoughts did, as it were, endeavour to return again sometimes; but I shook them off, and roused myself from them as it were from a distemper, and applying myself to drink and company, soon mastered the return of those fits, for so I called them, and I had in five or six days got as complete a victory over conscience as any young fellow that resolved not to be troubled with it could desire. But I was to have another trial for it still; and Providence, as in such cases generally it does, resolved to leave me entirely without excuse. For if I would not take this for a deliverance, the next was to be such a one as the worst and most hardened wretch among us would confess both the danger and the mercy.

The sixth day of our being at sea we came into Yarmouth roads; the wind having been contrary and the weather calm, we had made but little way since the storm. Here we were obliged to come to an anchor, and here we lay, the wind continuing contrary, viz., at south-west, for seven or eight days, during which time a great many ships from Newcastle came into the same roads, as the common harbour where the ships might wait for a wind for the river.

We had not, however, rid here so long, but should have tided it up the river, but that the wind blew too fresh; and after we had lain four or five days, blew very hard. However, the roads being reckoned as good as a harbour, the anchorage good, and our ground-tackle very strong, our men were unconcerned, and not in the least apprehensive of danger, but spent the time in rest and mirth, after the manner of the sea; but the eighth day in the morning the wind increased, and we had all hands at work to strike our topmasts, and make everything snug and close, that the ship might ride as easy as possible. By noon the sea went very high indeed, and our ship rid forecastle in, shipped several seas, and we thought once or twice our anchor had come home; upon which our master ordered out the sheet-anchor, so that we rode with two anchors ahead, and the cables veered out to the better end.

By this time it blew a terrible storm indeed, and now I began to see terror and amazement in the faces even of the seamen themselves. The master, though vigilant to the business of preserving the ship, yet as he went in and out of his cabin by me, I could hear him softly to himself say several times, "Lord be merciful to us, we shall be all lost, we shall be all undone"; and the like. During these first hurries I was stupid, lying still in my cabin, which was in the steerage, and cannot describe my temper; I could ill reassume the first penitence, which I had so apparently trampled upon, and hardened myself against; I thought the bitterness of death had been past, and that this would be nothing too, like the first. But when the master himself came by me, as I said just now, and said we should be all lost, I was dreadfully frighted; I got up out of my cabin, and looked out. But such a dismal sight I never saw; the sea went mountains high, and broke upon us every three or four minutes; when I could look about, I could see nothing but distress round us. Two ships that rid near us we found had cut their masts by the board, being deep loaden; and our men cried out, that a ship which rid about a mile ahead of us was foundered. Two more ships being driven from their anchors, were run out of the roads to sea at all adventures, and that with not a mast standing. The light ships fared the best, as not so much labouring in the sea; but two or three of them drove, and came close by us, running away with only their sprit-sail out before the wind.

Towards evening the mate and boatswain begged the master of our ship to let them cut away the foremast, which he was very unwilling to. But the boatswain protesting to him that if he did not the ship would founder, he consented; and when they had cut away the foremast, the mainmast stood so loose, and shook the ship so much, they were obliged to cut her away also, and make a clear deck.

Any one may judge what a condition I must be in at all this, who was but a young sailor, and who had been in such a fright before at but a little. But if I can express at this distance the thoughts I had about me at that time, I was in tenfold more horror of mind upon account of my former convictions, and the having returned from them to the resolutions I had wickedly taken at first, than I was at death itself; and these, added to the terror of the storm, put me into such a condition, that I can by no words describe it. But the worst was not come yet; the storm continued with such fury, that the seamen themselves acknowledged they had never known a worse. We had a good ship, but she was deep loaden, and wallowed in the sea, that the seamen every now and then cried out she would founder. It was my advantage in one respect, that I did not know what they meant by founder till I inquired. However, the storm was so violent, that I saw what is not often seen, the master, the boatswain, and some others more sensible than the rest, at their prayers, and expecting every moment when the ship would go to the bottom. In the middle of the night, and under all the test of our distresses, one of the men that had been down on purpose to see cried out we had sprung a leak; another said there was four foot water in the hold. Then all hands were called to the pump. At that very word my heart, as I thought, died within me, and I fell backwards upon the side of my bed where I sat, into the cabin. However, the men roused me, and told me, that I, that was able to do nothing before, was as well able to pump as another; at which I stirred up and went to the pump and worked very heartily. While this was doing, the master seeing some light colliers, who, not able to ride out the storm, were obliged to slip and run away to sea, and would come near us, ordered to fire a gun as a signal of distress. I, who knew nothing what that meant, was so surprised that I thought the ship had broke, or some dreadful thing had happened. In a word, I was so surprised that I fell down in a swoon. As this was a time when everybody had his own life to think of, nobody minded me, or what was become of me; but another man stepped up to the pump, and thrusting me aside with his foot, let me lie, thinking I had been dead; and it was a great while before I came to myself.

We worked on, but the water increasing in the hold, it was apparent that the ship would founder, and though the storm began to abate a little, yet as it was not possible she could swim till we might run into a port, so the master continued firing guns for help; and a light ship, who had rid it out just ahead of us, ventured a boat out to help us. It was with the utmost hazard the boat came near us, but it was impossible for us to get on board, or for the boat to lie near the ship's side, till at last the men rowing very heartily, and venturing their lives to save ours, our men cast them a rope over the stern with a buoy to it, and then veered it out a great length, which they after great labour and hazard took hold of, and we hauled them close under our stern, and got all into their boat. It was to no purpose for them or us after we were in the boat to think of reaching to their own ship, so all agreed to let her drive, and only to pull her in towards shore as much as we could, and our master promised them that if the boat was staved upon shore be would make it good to their master; so partly rowing and partly driving, our boat went away to the norward, sloping towards the shore almost as far as Winterton Ness.

While we were in this condition, the men yet labouring at the oar to bring the boat near the shore, we could see, when, our boat mounting the waves, we were able to see the shore, a great many people running along the shore to assist us when we should come near. But we made but slow way towards the shore, nor were we able to reach the shore, till being past the lighthouse at Winterton, the shore falls off to the westward towards Cromer, and so the land broke off a little the violence of the wind. Here we got in, and though not without much difficulty got all safe on shore, and walked afterwards on foot to Yarmouth, where, as unfortunate men, we were used with great humanity as well by the magistrates of the town, who assigned us good quarters, as by particular merchants and owners of ships, and had money given us sufficient to carry us either to London or back to Hull, as we thought fit.

Had I now had the sense to have gone back to Hull, and have gone home, I had been happy, and my father, an emblem of our blessed Saviour's parable, had even killed the fatted calf for me; for hearing the ship I went away in was cast away in Yarmouth road, it was a great while before he had any assurance that I was not drowned.

But my ill fate pushed me on now with an obstinacy that nothing could resist; and though I had several times loud calls from my reason and my more composed judgment to go home, yet I had no power to do it. I know not what to call this, nor will I urge that it is a secret overruling decree that hurries us on to be the instruments of our own destruction, even though it be before us, and that we rush upon it with our eyes open. Certainly nothing but some such decreed unavoidable misery attending, and which it was impossible for me to escape, could have pushed me forward against the calm reasonings and persuasions of my most retired thoughts, and against two such visible instructions as I had met with in my first attempt.

My comrade, who had helped to harden me before, and who was the master's son, was now less forward than I. The first time he spoke to me after we were at Yarmouth, which was not till two or three days, for we were separated in the town to several quarters – I say, the first time he saw me, it appeared his tone was altered, and looking very melancholy and shaking his head, asked me how I did, and telling his father who I was, and how I had come this voyage only for a trial in order to go farther abroad, his father turning to me with a very grave and concerned tone, "Young man," says he, "you ought never to go to sea any more, you ought to take this for a plain and visible token, that you are not to be a seafaring man. And, young man," said he, "depend upon it, if you do not go back, wherever you go you will meet with nothing but disasters and disappointments, till your father's words are fulfilled upon you."

We parted soon after; for I made him little answer, and I saw him no more; which way he went, I know not. As for me, having some money in my pocket, I travelled to London by land; and there, as well as on the road, had many struggles with myself what course of life I should take, and whether I should go home, or go to sea.

As to going home, shame opposed the best motions that offered to my thoughts; and it immediately occurred to me how I should be laughed at among the neighbours, and should be ashamed to see, not my father and mother only, but even everybody else; from whence I have since often observed how incongruous and irrational the common temper of mankind is, especially of youth, to that reason which ought to guide them in such cases, viz., that they are not ashamed to sin, and yet are ashamed to repent; not ashamed of the action for which they ought justly to be esteemed fools, but are ashamed of the returning, which only can make them be esteemed wise men.

It was my lot first of all to fall into pretty good company in London, which does not always happen to such loose and misguided young fellows as I then was; the devil generally not omitting to lay some snare for them very early; but it was not so with me. I first fell acquainted with the master of a ship who had been on the coast of Guinea, and who, having had very good success there, was resolved to go again; and who, taking a fancy to my conversation, which was not at all disagreeable at that time, hearing me say I had a mind to see the world, told me if I would go the voyage with him I should be at no expense; I should be his messmate and his companion; and if I could carry anything with me, I should have all the advantage of it that the trade would admit, and perhaps I might meet with some encouragement.

I embraced the offer; and, entering into a strict friendship with this captain, who was an honest and plain-dealing man, I went the voyage with him, and carried a small adventure with me, which, by the disinterested honesty of my friend the captain, I increased very considerably, for I carried about £40 in such toys and trifles as the captain directed me to buy. This £40 I had mustered together by the assistance of some of my relations whom I corresponded with, and who, I believe, got my father, or at least my mother, to contribute so much as that to my first adventure.

This was the only voyage which I may say was successful in all my adventures, and which I owe to the integrity and honesty of my friend the captain; under whom also I got a competent knowledge of the mathematics and the rules of navigation, learned how to keep an account of the ship's course, take an observation, and, in short, to understand some things that were needful to be understood by a sailor. For, as he took delight to introduce me, I took delight to learn; and, in a word, this voyage made me both a sailor and a merchant; for I brought home five pounds nine ounces of gold dust for my adventure, which yielded me in London at my return almost £300, and this filled me with those aspiring thoughts which have since so completed my ruin.

Yet even in this voyage I had my misfortunes too; particularly, that I was continually sick, being thrown into a violent calenture by the excessive heat of the climate; our principal trading being upon the coast, from the latitude of 15 degrees north even to the line itself.

I was now set up for a Guinea trader; and my friend, to my great misfortune, dying soon after his arrival, I resolved to go the same voyage again, and I embarked in the same vessel with one who was his mate in the former voyage, and had now got the command of the ship. This was the unhappiest voyage that ever man made; for though I did not carry quite £100 of my new-gained wealth, so that I had £200 left, and which I lodged with my friend's widow, who was very just to me, yet I fell into terrible misfortunes in this voyage; and the first was this, viz., our ship making her course towards the Canary Islands, or rather between those islands and the African shore, was surprised in the grey of the morning by a Turkish rover of Sallee, who gave chase to us with all the sail she could make. We crowded also as much canvas as our yards would spread, or our masts carry, to have got clear; but finding the pirate gained upon us, and would certainly come up with us in a few hours, we prepared to fight, our ship having twelve guns, and the rogue eighteen. About three in the afternoon he came up with us, and bringing to, by mistake, just athwart our quarter, instead of athwart our stern, as he intended, we brought eight of our guns to bear on that side, and poured in a broadside upon him, which made him sheer off again, after returning our fire and pouring in also his small-shot from near 200 men which he had on board. However, we had not a man touched, all our men keeping close. He prepared to attack us again, and we to defend ourselves; but laying us on board the next time upon our other quarter, he entered sixty men upon our decks, who immediately fell to cutting and hacking the decks and rigging. We plied them with small-shot, half-pikes, powder-chests, and such like, and cleared our deck of them twice. However, to cut short this melancholy part of our story, our ship being disabled, and three of our men killed and eight wounded, we were obliged to yield, and were carried all prisoners into Sallee, a port belonging to the Moors.

The usage I had there was not so dreadful as at first I apprehended, nor was I carried up the country to the emperor's court, as the rest of our men were, but was kept by the captain of the rover as his proper prize, and made his slave, being young and nimble, and fit for his business.

As my new patron, or master, had taken me home to his house, so I was in hopes that he would take me with him when he went to sea again, believing that it would some time or other be his fate to be taken by a Spanish or Portugal man-of-war; and that then I should be set at liberty. But this hope of mine was soon taken away; for when he went to sea, he left me on shore to look after his little garden, and do the common drudgery of slaves about his house; and when he came home again from his cruise, he ordered me to lie in the cabin to look after the ship.

Here I meditated nothing but my escape, and what method I might take to effect it, but found no way that had the least probability in it. Nothing presented to make the supposition of it rational; for I had nobody to communicate it to that would embark with me; so that for two years, though I often pleased myself with the imagination, yet I never had the least encouraging prospect of putting it in practice.

After about two years an odd circumstance presented itself, which put the old thought of making some attempt for my liberty again in my head. My patron lying at home longer than usual without fitting out his ship, which, as I heard, was for want of money, he used constantly, once or twice a week, sometimes oftener, if the weather was fair, to take the ship's pinnace, and go out into the road a-fishing; and as he always took me and a young Maresco with him to row the boat, we made him very merry, and I proved very dexterous in catching fish; insomuch, that sometimes he would send me with a Moor, one of his kinsmen, and the youth the Maresco, as they called him, to catch a dish of fish for him.

It happened one time that, going a-fishing in a stark calm morning, a fog rose so thick, that though we were not half a league from the shore we lost sight of it; and rowing we knew not whither or which way, we laboured all day, and all the next night, and when the morning came we found we had pulled off to sea instead of pulling in for the shore; and that we were at least two leagues from the shore. However, we got well in again, though with a great deal of labour, and some danger, for the wind began to blow pretty fresh in the morning; but particularly we were all very hungry.

But our patron, warned by this disaster, resolved to take more care of himself for the future; and having lying by him the long-boat of our English ship which he had taken, he resolved he would not go a-fishing any more without a compass and some provision; so he ordered the carpenter of his ship, who also was an English slave, to build a little state-room, or cabin, in the middle of the long-boat, like that of a barge, with a place to stand behind it to steer and haul home the main-sheet, and room before for a hand or two to stand and work the sails.

We went frequently out with this boat a-fishing, and as I was most dexterous to catch fish for him, he never went without me. It happened that he had appointed to go out in this boat, either for pleasure or for fish, with two or three Moors of some distinction in that place, and for whom he had provided extraordinarily; and had therefore sent on board the boat overnight a larger store of provisions than ordinary; and had ordered me to get ready three fuzees with powder and shot, which were on board his ship, for that they designed some sport of fowling as well as fishing.

I got all things ready as he had directed, and waited the next morning with the boat, washed clean, her ancient and pendants out, and everything to accommodate his guests; when by-and-by my patron came on board alone, and told me his guests had put off going, upon some business that fell out, and ordered me with the man and boy, as usual, to go out with the boat and catch them some fish, for that his friends were to sup at his house; and commanded that as soon as I had got some fish I should bring it home to his house; all which I prepared to do.

This moment my former notions of deliverance darted into my thoughts, for now I found I was like to have a little ship at my command; and my master being gone, I prepared to furnish myself, not for a fishing business, but for a voyage; though I knew not, neither did I so much as consider, whither I should steer; for anywhere, to get out of that place, was my way.

My first contrivance was to make a pretence to speak to this Moor, to get something for our subsistence on board; for I told him we must not presume to eat of our patron's bread. He said that was true; so he brought a large basket of rusk or biscuit of their kind, and three jars with fresh water, into the boat. I knew where my patron's case of bottles stood, which it was evident by the make were taken out of some English prize; and I conveyed them into the boat while the Moor was on shore, as if they had been there before for our master. I conveyed also a great lump of beeswax into the boat, which weighed above half a hundredweight, with a parcel of twine or thread, a hatchet, a saw, and a hammer, all which were great use to us afterwards, especially the wax to make candles. Thus furnished with everything needful, we sailed out of the port to fish. The castle, which is at the entrance of the port, knew who we were, and took no notice of us; and we were not above a mile out of the port

before we hauled in our sail, and set us down to fish. The wind blew from the N.N.E., which was contrary to my desire; for had it blown southerly I had been sure to have made the coast of Spain, and at least reached to the bay of Cadiz; but my resolutions were, blow which way it would, I would be gone from the horrid place where I was, and leave the rest to Fate.

After we had fished some time and catched nothing, for when I had fish on my hook I would not pull them up, that he might not see them, I said to the Moor, "This will not do; our master will not be thus served; we must stand farther off." He, thinking no harm, agreed, and being in the head of the boat set the sails; and as I had the helm I run the boat out near a league farther, and then brought her to as if I would fish; when giving the boy the helm, I stepped forward to where the Moor was, and making as if I stooped for something behind him, I took him by surprise with my arm under his twist, and tossed him clear overboard into the sea. He rose immediately, for he swam like a cork, and called to me, begged to be taken in, told me he would go all the world over with me. He swam so strong after the boat, that he would have reached me very quickly, there being but little wind; upon which I stepped into the cabin, and fetching one of the fowling-pieces, I presented it at him, and told him I had done him no hurt, and if he would be quiet I would do him none.

"But," said I, "you swim well enough to reach to the shore, and the sea is calm; make the best of your way to shore, and I will do you no harm; but if you come near the boat I'll shoot you through the head, for I am resolved to have my liberty." So he turned himself about, and swam for the shore, and I make no doubt but he reached it with ease, for he was an excellent swimmer.

I could have been content to have taken this Moor with me, and have drowned the boy, but there was no venturing to trust him. When he was gone I turned to the boy, whom they called Xury, and said to him, "Xury, if you will be faithful to me I'll make you a great man; but if you will not stroke your face to be true to me," that is, swear by Mahomet and his father's beard, "I must throw you into the sea too." The boy smiled in my face, and spoke so innocently, that I could not mistrust him, and swore to be faithful to me, and go all over the world with me.

While I was in view of the Moor that was swimming, I stood out directly to sea with the boat, rather stretching to windward, that they might think me gone towards the straits' mouth.

But as soon as it grew dusk in the evening, I changed my course, and steered directly south and by east, bending my course a little toward the east, that I might keep in with the shore; and having a fair, fresh gale of wind, and a smooth, quiet sea, I made such sail that I believe by the next day at three o'clock in the afternoon, when I first made the land, I could not be less than 150 miles south of Sallee; quite beyond the Emperor of Morocco's dominions, or indeed of any other king thereabouts, for we saw no people.

Yet such was the fright I had taken at the Moors, and the dreadful apprehensions I had of falling into their hands, that I would not stop, or go on shore, or come to an anchor, the wind continuing fair, till I had sailed in that manner five days; and then the wind shifting to the southward, I concluded also that if any of our vessels were in chase of me, they also would now give over; so I ventured to make to the coast, and came to an anchor in the mouth of a little river, I knew not what, or where; neither what latitude, what country, what nations, or what river. I neither saw, or desired to see, any people; the principal thing I wanted was fresh water. We came into this creek in the evening, resolving to swim on shore as soon as it was dark, and discover the country; but as soon as it was quite dark we heard such dreadful noises of the barking, roaring, and howling of wild creatures, of we knew not what kinds, that the poor boy was ready to die with fear, and begged of me not to go on shore till day.

Xury was dreadfully frighted, and indeed so was I too; but we were both more frighted when we heard one of these mighty creatures come swimming towards our boat; we could not see him, but we might hear him by his blowing to be a monstrous huge and furious beast. Xury said it was a lion, and it might be so for aught I know; but poor Xury cried to me to weigh the anchor and row away. "No," says I, "Xury; we can slip our cable with the buoy to it, and go off to sea; they cannot follow us far." I had no sooner said so, but I perceived the creature (whatever it was) within two oars' length, which something surprised me; however, I immediately stepped to the cabin door, and taking up my gun, fired at him, upon which he immediately turned about and swam towards the shore again.

But it is impossible to describe the horrible noises, and hideous cries and howlings, that were raised, as well upon the edge of the shore as higher within the country, upon the noise or report of the gun, a thing I have some reason to believe those creatures had never heard before. This convinced me that there was no going on shore for us in the night upon that coast; and how to venture on shore in the day was another question too; for to have fallen into the hands of any of the savages, had been as bad as to have fallen into the hands of lions and tigers; at least we were equally apprehensive of the danger of it.

Be that as it would, we were obliged to go on shore somewhere or other for water, for we had not a pint left in the boat; when or where to get to it, was the point. Xury said if I would let him go on shore with one of the jars, he would find if there was any water and bring some to me. I asked him why he would go? why I should not go and he stay in the boat? The boy answered with so much affection, that made me love him ever after. Says he, "If wild mans come, they eat me, you go way." "Well, Xury," said I, "we will both go; and if the wild mans come, we will kill them, they shall eat neither of us." So I gave Xury a piece of rusk bread to eat, and a dram out of our patron's case of bottles which I mentioned before; and we hauled in the boat as near the shore as we thought was proper, and so waded on shore, carrying nothing but our arms and two jars for water.

I did not care to go out of sight of the boat, fearing the coming of canoes with savages down the river; but the boy seeing a low place about a mile up the country, rambled to it; and by-and-by I saw him come running towards me. I thought he was pursued by some savage, or frighted with some wild beast, and I ran forward towards him to help him; but when I came nearer to him, I saw something hanging over his shoulders, which was a creature that he had shot, like a hare, but different in colour, and longer legs. However, we were very glad of it, and it was very good meat; but the great joy that poor Xury came with was to tell me he had found good water, and seen no wild mans.

As I had been one voyage to this coast before, I knew very well that the islands of the Canaries, and the Cape de Verde Islands also, lay not far off from the coast. But as I had no instruments to take an observation to know what latitude we were in, and did not exactly know, or at least remember, what latitude they were in, I knew not where to look for them, or when to stand off to sea towards them; otherwise I might now easily have found some of these islands. But my hope was, that if I stood along this coast till I came to that part where the English traded, I should find some of their vessels upon their usual design of trade, that would relieve and take us in.

Once or twice in the daytime I thought I saw the Pico of Teneriffe, being the high top of the Mountain Teneriffe in the Canaries, and had a great mind to venture out, in hopes of reaching thither; but having tried twice, I was forced in again by contrary winds, the sea also going too high for my little vessel; so I resolved to pursue my first design, and keep along the shore.

Several times I was obliged to land for fresh water after we had left this place; and once in particular, being early in the morning, we came to an anchor under a little point of land which was pretty high; and the tide beginning to flow, we lay still to go farther in. Xury, whose eyes were more about him than it seems mine were, calls softly to me, and tells me that we had best go farther off the shore; "For," says he, "look, yonder lies a dreadful monster on the side of that hillock fast asleep." I looked where he pointed, and saw a dreadful monster indeed, for it was a terrible great lion that lay on the side of the shore, under the shade of a piece of the hill that hung as it were a little over him. "Xury," says I, "you shall go on shore and kill him." Xury looked frighted, and said, "Me kill! he eat me at one mouth"; one mouthful he meant. However, I said no more to the boy, but bade him lie still, and I took our biggest gun, which was almost musket-bore, and loaded it with a good charge of powder, and with two slugs, and laid it down; then I loaded another gun with two bullets; and the third (for we had three pieces) I loaded with five smaller bullets. I took the best aim I could with the first piece to have shot him into the head, but he lay so with his leg raised a little above his nose, that the slugs hit his leg about the knee, and broke the bone. He started up growling at first, but finding his leg broke, fell down again, and then got up upon three legs and gave the most hideous roar that ever I heard. I was a little surprised that I had not hit him on the head. However, I took up the second piece immediately, and, though he began to move off, fired again, and shot him into the head, and had the pleasure to see him drop, and make but little noise, but lay struggling for life. Then Xury took heart, and would have me let him go on shore. "Well, go," said I; so the boy jumped into the water, and taking a little gun in one hand, swam to shore with the other hand, and coming close to the creature, put the muzzle of the piece to his ear, and shot him into the head again, which despatched him quite.

This was game indeed to us, but this was no food; and I was very sorry to loose three charges of powder and shot upon a creature that was good for nothing to us. However, Xury said he would have some of him; so he comes on board, and asked me to give him the hatchet. "For what, Xury?" said I. "Me cut off his head," said he. However, Xury could not cut off his head, but he cut off a foot, and brought it with him, and it was a monstrous great one.

I bethought myself, however, that perhaps the skin of him might one way or other be of some value to us; and I resolved to take off his skin if I could. So Xury and I went to work with him; but Xury was much the better workman at it, for I knew very ill how to do it. Indeed, it took us up both the whole day, but at last we got off the hide of him, and spreading it on the top of our cabin, the sun effectually dried it in two days' time, and it afterwards served me to lie upon.

After this stop we made on to the southward continually for ten or twelve days, living very sparing on our provisions, which began to abate very much, and going no oftener into the shore than we were obliged to for fresh water. My design in this was to make the river Gambia or Senegal – that is to say, anywhere about the Cape de Verde – where I was in hopes to meet with some European ship; and if I did not, I knew not what course I had to take, but to seek out for the islands, or perish there among the negroes. I knew that all the ships from Europe, which sailed either to the coast of Guinea or to Brazil, or to the East Indies, made this cape, or those islands; and in a word, I put the whole of my fortune upon this single point, either that I must meet with some ship, or must perish.

When I had pursued this resolution about ten days longer, as I have said, I began to see that the land was inhabited; and in two or three places, as we sailed by, we saw people stand upon the shore to look at us; we could also perceive they were quite black, and stark naked. I was once inclined to have gone on shore to them; but Xury was my better counsellor, and said to me, "No go, no go." However, I hauled in nearer the shore that I might talk to them, and I found they ran along the shore by me a good way. I observed they had no weapons in their hands, except one, who had a long slender stick, which Xury said was a lance, and that they would throw them a great way with good aim. So I kept at a distance, but talked with them by signs as well as I could, and particularly made signs for something to eat; they beckoned to me to stop my boat, and that they would fetch me some meat. Upon this I lowered the top of my sail, and lay by, and two of them ran up into the country, and in less than half an hour came back, and brought with them two pieces of dried flesh and some corn, such as is the produce of their country; but we neither knew what the one or the other was. However, we were willing to accept it, but how to come at it was our next dispute, for I was not for venturing on shore to them, and they were as much afraid of us; but they took a safe way for us all, for they brought it to the shore and laid it down, and went and stood a great way off till we fetched it on board, and then came close to us again.

I was now furnished with roots and corn, such as it was, and water; and leaving my friendly negroes, I made forward for about eleven days more, without offering to go near the shore, till I saw the land run out a great length into the sea, at about the distance of four or five leagues before me; and the sea being very calm, I kept a large offing, to make this point. At length, doubling the point, at about two leagues from the land, I saw plainly land on the other side, to seaward; then I concluded, as it was most certain indeed, that this was the Cape de Verde, and those the islands, called from thence Cape de Verde Islands. However, they were at a great distance, and I could not well tell what I had best to do; for if I should be taken with a fresh of wind, I might neither reach one or other.

In this dilemma, as I was very pensive, I stepped into the cabin, and sat me down, Xury having the helm; when, on a sudden, the boy cried out, "Master, master, a ship with a sail!" and the foolish boy was frighted out of his wits, thinking it must needs be some of his master's ships sent to pursue us, when I knew we were gotten far enough out of their reach. I jumped out of the cabin, and immediately saw, not only the ship, but what she was, viz., that it was a Portuguese ship, and, as I thought, was bound to the coast of Guinea, for negroes. But when I observed the course she steered, I was soon convinced they were bound some other way, and did not design to come any nearer to the shore; upon which I stretched out to sea as much as I could, resolving to speak with them, if possible.

With all the sail I could make, I found I should not be able to come in their way, but that they would be gone by before I could make any signal to them; but after I had crowded to the utmost, and began to despair, they, it seems, saw me by the help of their perspective glasses, and that it was some European boat which, as they supposed, must belong to some ship that was lost so they shortened sail to let me come up. I was encouraged with this; and as I had my patron's ancient on board, I made a waft of it to them for a signal of distress, and fired a gun, both which they saw; for they told me they saw the smoke, though they did not hear the gun. Upon these signals they were kindly brought to, and lay by for me; and in about three hours' time I came up with them.

They asked me what I was, in Portuguese, and in Spanish, and in French, but I understood none of them; but at last a Scots sailor, who was on board, called to me, and I answered him, and told him I was an Englishman, that I had made my escape out of slavery from the Moors, at Sallee. Then they bade me come on board, and very kindly took me in, and all my goods.

It was an inexpressible joy to me, that any one will believe, that I was thus delivered, as I esteemed it, from such a miserable, and almost hopeless, condition as I was in; and I immediately offered all I had to the captain of the ship, as a return for my deliverance. But he generously told me he would take nothing from me, but that all I had should be delivered safe to me when I came to the Brazils. "For," says he, "I have saved your life on no other terms than I would be glad to be saved myself; and it may, one time or other, be my lot to be taken up in the same condition. Besides," says he, "when I carry you to the Brazils, so great a way from your own country, if I should take from you what you have, you will be starved there, and then I only take away that life I have given. No, no, Seignior Inglese," says he, "Mr. Englishman, I will carry you thither in charity, and those things will help you to buy your subsistence there, and your passage home again."

As he was charitable in his proposal, so he was just in the performance to a tittle; for he ordered the seamen that none should offer to touch anything I had; then he took everything into his own possession, and gave me back an exact inventory of them, that I might have them, even so much as my three earthen jars.

As to my boat, it was a very good one, and that he saw, and told me he would buy it of me for the ship's use, and asked me what I would have for it? I told him he had been so generous to me in everything, that I could not offer to make any price of the boat, but left it entirely to him; upon which he told me he would give me a note of his hand to pay me eighty pieces of eight for it at Brazil, and when it came there, if any one offered to give more, he would make it up. He offered me also sixty pieces of eight more for my boy Xury, which I was loth to take; not that I was not willing to let the captain have him, but I was very loth to sell the poor boy's liberty, who had assisted me so faithfully in procuring my own. However, when I let him know my reason, he owned it to be just, and offered me this medium, that he would give the boy an obligation to set him free in ten years if he turned Christian. Upon this, and Xury saying he was willing to go to him, I let the captain have him.

We had a very good voyage to the Brazils, and arrived in the Bay de Todos los Santos, or All Saints' Bay, in about twenty-two days after. And now I was once more delivered from the most miserable of all conditions of life; and what to do next with myself, I was now to consider.

The generous treatment the captain gave me, I can never enough remember. He would take nothing of me for my passage, gave me twenty ducats for the leopard's skin, and forty for the lion's skin, which I had in my boat, and caused everything I had in the ship to be punctually delivered me; and what I was willing to sell he bought, such as the case of bottles, two of my guns, and a piece of the lump of beeswax – for I had made candles of the rest; in a word, I made about 220 pieces of eight of all my cargo, and with this stock I went on shore in the Brazils.

I had not been long here, but being recommended to the house of a good honest man like himself, who had an *ingeino* as they call it, that is, a plantation and a sugar-house, I lived with him some time, and acquainted myself by that means with the manner of their planting and making of sugar; and seeing how well the planters lived, and how they grew rich suddenly, I resolved, if I could get licence to settle there, I would turn planter among them, resolving in the meantime to find out some way to get my money which I had left in London remitted to me. To this purpose, getting a kind of a letter of naturalisation, I purchased as much land that was uncured as my money would reach, and formed a plan for my plantation and settlement, and such a one as might be suitable to the stock which I proposed to myself to receive from England.

I had a neighbour, a Portuguese of Lisbon, but born of English parents, whose name was Wells, and in much such circumstances as I was. I call him my neighbour, because his plantation lay next to mine, and we went on very sociably together. My stock was but low, as well as his; and we rather planted for food than anything else, for about two years. However, we began to increase, and our land began to come into order; so that the third year we planted some tobacco, and made each of us a large piece of ground ready for planting canes in the year to come. But we both wanted help; and now I found, more than before, I had done wrong in parting with my boy Xury.

I was in some degree settled in my measures for carrying on the plantation before my kind friend, the captain of the ship that took me up at sea, went back; for the ship remained there in providing his loading, and preparing for his voyage, near three months; when, telling him what little stock I had left behind me in London, he gave me this friendly and sincere advice: "Seignior Inglese," says he, for so he always called me, "if you will give me letters, and a procuration here in form to me, with orders to the person who has your money in London to send your effects to Lisbon, to such persons as I shall direct, and in such goods as are proper for this country, I will bring you the produce of them, God willing, at my return. But since human affairs are all subject to changes and disasters, I would have you give orders but for one hundred pounds sterling, which, you say, is half your stock, and let the hazard be run for the first; so that if it come safe, you may order the rest the same way; and if it miscarry, you may have the other half to have recourse to for your supply."

This was so wholesome advice, and looked so friendly, that I could not but be convinced it was the best course I could take; so I accordingly prepared letters to the gentlewoman with whom I had left my money, and a procuration to the Portuguese captain, as he desired.

I wrote the English captain's widow a full account of all my adventures; my slavery, escape, and how I had met with the Portugal captain at sea, the humanity of his behaviour, and in what condition I was now in, with all other necessary directions for my supply. And when this honest captain came to Lisbon, he found means, by some of the English merchants there, to send over not the order only, but a full account of my story to a merchant at London, who represented it effectually to her; whereupon, she not only delivered the money, but out of her own pocket sent the Portugal captain a very handsome present for his humanity and charity to me.

The merchant in London vesting this hundred pounds in English goods, such as the captain had writ for, sent them directly to him at Lisbon, and he brought them all safe to me to the Brazils; among which, without my direction (for I was too young in my business to think of them), he had taken care to have all sorts of tools, iron-work, and utensils necessary for my plantation, and which were of great use to me.

When this cargo arrived, I thought my fortune made, for I was surprised with joy of it; and my good steward, the captain, had laid out the five pounds, which my friend had sent him for a present for himself, to purchase and bring me over a servant under bond for six years' service, and would not accept of any consideration, except a little tobacco, which I would have him accept, being of my own produce.

Neither was this all; but my goods being all English manufactures, such as cloth, stuffs, baize, and things particularly valuable and desirable in the country, I found means to sell them to a very great advantage; so that I may say I had more than four times the value of my first cargo, and was now infinitely beyond my poor neighbour, I mean in the advancement of my plantation; for the first thing I did, I bought me a negro slave, and an European servant also; I mean another besides that which the captain brought me from Lisbon.

But as abused prosperity is oftentimes made the very means of our greatest adversity, so was it with me. I went on the next year with great success in my plantation. I raised fifty great rolls of tobacco on my own ground, more than I had disposed of for necessaries among my neighbours; and these fifty rolls, being each of above a hundredweight, were well cured, and laid by against the return of the fleet from Lisbon. And now, increasing in business and in wealth, my head began to be full of projects and undertakings beyond my reach, such as are, indeed, often the ruin of the best heads in business.

You may suppose, that having now lived almost four years in the Brazils, and beginning to thrive and prosper very well upon my plantation, I had not only learned the language, but had contracted acquaintance and friendship among my fellow-planters, as well as among the merchants at St Salvador, which was our port, and that in my discourses among them I had frequently given them an account of my two voyages to the coast of Guinea, the manner of trading with the negroes there, and how easy it was to purchase upon the coast for trifles – such as beads, toys, knives, scissors, hatchets, bit of glass, and the like – not only gold-dust, Guinea grains, elephants' teeth, &c., but negroes, for the service of the Brazils, in great numbers.

They listened always very attentively to my discourses on these heads, but especially to that part which related to the buying negroes; which was a trade, at that time, not only not far entered into, but, as far as it was, had been carried on by the *assiento,* or permission, of the Kings of Spain and Portugal, so that few negroes were brought, and those excessive dear.

It happened, being in company with some merchants and planters of my acquaintance, and talking of those things very earnestly, three of them came to me the next morning, and told me they had been musing very much upon what I had discoursed with them of, the last night, and they came to make a secret proposal to me. And after enjoining me secrecy, they told me that they had a mind to fit out a ship to go to Guinea; that they had all plantations as well as I, and were straitened for nothing so much as servants; that as it was a trade that could not be carried on because they could not publicly sell the negroes when they came home, so they desired to make but one voyage, to bring the negroes on shore privately, and divide them among their own plantations; and, in a word, the question was, whether I would go their supercargo in the ship, to manage the trading part upon the coast of Guinea; and they offered me that I should have my equal share of the negroes without providing any part of the stock.

This was a fair proposal, it must be confessed, had it been made to any one that had not had a settlement and plantation of his own to look after, which was in a fair way of coming to be very considerable, and with a good stock upon it. But for me, that was thus entered and established, and had nothing to do but go on as I had begun, for three or four years more, and to have sent for the other hundred pounds from England; and who, in that time, and with that little addition, could scarce have failed of being worth three or four thousand pounds sterling, and that increasing too – for me to think of such a voyage, was the most preposterous thing that ever man, in such circumstances, could be guilty of.

But I, that was born to be my own destroyer, could no more resist the offer than I could restrain my first rambling designs, when my father's good counsel was lost upon me. In a word, I told them I would go with all my heart, if they would undertake to look after my plantation in my absence, and would dispose of it to such as I should direct if I miscarried. This they all engaged to do, and entered into writings or covenants to do so; and I made a formal will, disposing of my plantation and effects, in case of my death; making the captain of the ship that had saved my life, as before, my universal heir, but obliging him to dispose of my effects as I had directed in my will; one half of the produce being to himself; and the other to be shipped to England.

In short, I took all possible caution to preserve my effects, and keep up my plantation. Had I used half as much prudence to have looked into my own interest, and have made a judgment of what I ought to have done and not to have done, I had certainly never gone away from so prosperous an undertaking, leaving all the probable views of a thriving circumstance, and gone upon a voyage to sea, attended with all its common hazards, to say nothing of the reasons I had to expect particular misfortunes to myself.

But I was hurried on, and obeyed blindly the dictates of my fancy rather than my reason. And accordingly, the ship being fitted out, and the cargo furnished, and all things done as by agreement by my partners in the voyage, I went on board in an evil hour, the [first] of [September 1659], being the same day eight year that I went from my father and mother at Hull, in order to act the rebel to their authority, and the fool to my own interest.

Our ship was about 120 tons burthen, carried six guns and fourteen men, besides the master, his boy, and myself. We had on board no large cargo of goods, except of such toys as were fit for our trade with the negroes – such as beads, bits of glass, shells, and odd trifles, especially little looking-glasses, knives, scissors, hatchets, and the like.

The same day I went on board we set sail, standing away to the northward upon our own coast, with design to stretch over for the African coast, when they came about ten or twelve degrees of northern latitude, which, it seems, was the manner of their course in those days. We passed the line in about twelve days' time, and were, by our last observation, in seven degrees twenty-two minutes northern latitude, when a violent tornado, or hurricane, took us quite out of our knowledge. It began from the south-east, came about to the north-west, and then settled into the north-east, from whence it blew in such a terrible manner, that for twelve days together we could do nothing but drive, and, scudding away before it, let it carry us wherever fate and the fury of the winds directed; and during these twelve days, I need not say that I expected every day to be swallowed up, nor, indeed, did any in the ship expect to save their lives.

In this distress we had, besides the terror of the storm, one of our men died of the calenture, and one man and the boy washed overboard. About the twelfth day, the weather abating a little, the master made an observation as well as he could, and found that he was gotten upon the coast of Guiana, or the north part of Brazil, beyond the river Amazon, toward that of the river Orinoco, commonly called the

Great River, and began to consult with me what course we should take, for the ship was leaky and very much disabled, and he was going directly back to the coast of Brazil.

I was positively against that; and looking over the charts of the sea-coast of America with him, we concluded there was no inhabited country for us to have recourse to till we came within the circle of the Carribbee Islands, and therefore resolved to stand away for the Barbadoes, which by keeping off at sea, to avoid the indraft of the Bay or Gulf of Mexico, we might easily perform, as we hoped, in about fifteen days' sail; whereas we could not possibly make our voyage to the coast of Africa without some assistance, both to our ship and to ourselves.

With this design we changed our course, and steered away N.W. by W. in order to reach some of our English islands, where I hoped for relief; but our voyage was otherwise determined; for a second storm came upon us, which carried us away with the same impetuosity westward, and drove us so out of the very way of all human commerce, that had all our lives been saved, as to the sea, we were rather in danger of being devoured by savages than ever returning to our own country.

In this distress, the wind still blowing very hard, one of our men early in the morning cried out, "Land!" and we had no sooner ran out of the cabin to look out, in hopes of seeing whereabouts in the world we were, but the ship struck upon a sand, and in a moment, her motion being so stopped, the sea broke over her in such a manner, that we expected we should all have perished immediately; and we were immediately driven into our close quarters, to shelter us from the very foam and spray of the sea.

It is not easy for any one, who has not been in the like condition, to describe or conceive the consternation of men in such circumstances. We knew nothing where we were, or upon what land it was we were driven, whether an island or the main, whether inhabited or not inhabited; and as the rage of the wind was still great, though rather less than at first, we could not so much as hope to have the ship hold many minutes without breaking in pieces, unless the winds, by a kind of miracle, should turn immediately about. In a word, we sat looking one upon another, and expecting death every moment, and every man acting accordingly, as preparing for another world; for there was little or nothing more for us to do in this. That which was our present comfort, and all the comfort we had, was that, contrary to our expectation, the ship did not break yet, and that the master said the wind began to abate.

Now, though we thought that the wind did a little abate, yet the ship having thus struck upon the sand, and sticking too fast for us to expect her getting off, we were in a dreadful condition indeed, and had nothing to do but to think of saving our lives as well as we could. We had a boat at our stern just before the storm, but she was first staved by dashing against the ship's rudder, and in the next place, she broke away, and either sunk, or was driven off to sea, so there was no hope from her; we had another boat on board, but how to get her off into the sea was a doubtful thing. However, there was no room to debate, for we fancied the ship would break in pieces every minute, and some told us she was actually broken already.

In this distress, the mate of our vessel lays hold of the boat, and with the help of the rest of the men they got her slung over the ship's side; and getting all into her, let go, and committed ourselves, being eleven in number, to God's mercy, and the wild sea; for though the storm was abated considerably, yet the sea went dreadful high upon the shore.

And now our case was very dismal indeed, for we all saw plainly that the sea went so high, that the boat could not live, and that we should be inevitably drowned. However, we committed our souls to God in the most earnest manner; and the wind driving us towards the shore, we hastened our destruction with our own hands, pulling as well as we could towards land.

What the shore was, whether rock or sand, whether steep or shoal, we knew not; the only hope that could rationally give us the least shadow of expectation was, if we might happen into some bay or gulf, or the mouth of some river, where by great chance we might have run our boat in, or got under the lee of the land, and perhaps made smooth water. But there was nothing of this appeared; but as we made nearer and nearer the shore, the land looked more frightful than the sea.

After we had towed, or rather driven, about a league and a half, as we reckoned it, a raging wave, mountain-like, came rolling astern of us, and plainly bade us expect the *coup de grâce.* In a word, it took us with such a fury, that it overset the boat at once; and separating us, as well from the boat as from one another, gave us not time hardly to say, "O God!" for we were all swallowed up in a moment.

Nothing can describe the confusion of thought which I felt when I sunk into the water; for though I swam very well, yet I could not deliver myself from the waves so as to draw breath, till that wave having driven me, or rather carried me, a vast way on towards the shore, and having spent itself, went back, and left me upon the land almost dry, but half dead with the water I took in. I had so much presence of mind, as well as breath left, that seeing myself nearer the mainland than I expected, I got upon my feet, and endeavoured to make on towards the land as fast as I could, before another wave should return and take me up again. But I soon found it was impossible to avoid it; for I saw the sea come after me as high as a great hill, and as furious as an enemy, which I had no means or strength to contend with. My business was to hold my breath, and raise myself upon the water, if I could; and so, by swimming, to preserve my breathing, and pilot myself towards the shore, if possible; my greatest concern now being, that the sea, as it would carry me a great way towards the shore when it came on, might not carry me back again with it when it gave back towards the sea.

The wave that came upon me again, buried me at once 20 or 30 feet deep in its own body, and I could feel myself carried with a mighty force and swiftness towards the shore a very great way; but I held my breath, and assisted myself to swim still forward with all my might. I was ready to burst with holding my breath, when, as I felt myself rising up, so, to my immediate relief, I found my head and hands shoot out above the surface of the water; and though it was not two seconds of time that I could keep myself so, yet it relieved me greatly, gave me breath and new courage. I was covered again with water a good while, but not so long but I held it out; and finding the water had spent itself, and began to return, I struck forward against the return of the waves, and felt ground again with my feet. I stood still a few moments to recover breath, and till the water went from me, and then took to my heels and ran with what strength I had farther towards the shore. But neither would this deliver me from the fury of the sea, which came pouring in after me again, and twice more I was lifted up by the waves and carried forwards as before, the shore being very flat.

The last time of these two had well near been fatal to me; for the sea, having hurried me along as before, landed me, or rather dashed me, against a piece of a rock, and that with such force, as it left me senseless, and indeed helpless, as to my own deliverance; for the blow taking my side and breast, beat the breath as it were quite out of my body; and had it returned again immediately, I must have been strangled in the water. But I recovered a little before the return of the waves, and seeing I should be covered again with the water, I resolved to hold fast by a piece of the rock, and so to hold my breath, if possible, till the wave went back. Now as the waves were not so high as at first, being near land, I held my hold till the wave abated, and then fetched another run, which brought me so near the shore, that the next wave, though it went over me, yet did not so swallow me up as to carry me away, and the next run I took I got to the mainland, where, to my great comfort, I clambered up the cliffs of the shore, and sat me down upon the grass, free from danger, and quite out of the reach of the water.

I was now landed, and safe on shore, and began to look up and thank God that my life was saved in a case wherein there was some minutes before scarce any room to hope.

I walked about on the shore, lifting up my hands, and my whole being, as I may say, wrapt up in the contemplation of my deliverance, making a thousand gestures and motions which, I cannot describe, reflecting upon all my comrades that were drowned, and that there should not be one soul saved but myself; for, as for them, I never saw them afterwards, or any sign of them, except three of their hats, one cap, and two shoes that were not fellows.

I cast my eyes to the stranded vessel, when the breach and froth of the sea being so big, I could hardly see it, it lay so far off, and considered, Lord! how was it possible I could get on shore?

After I had solaced my mind with the comfortable part of my condition, I began to look round me to see what kind of place I was in, and what was next to be done, and I soon found my comforts abate, and that, in a word, I had a dreadful deliverance; for I was wet, had no clothes to shift me, nor anything either to eat or drink to comfort me, neither did I see any prospect before me but that of perishing with hunger, or being devoured by wild beasts; and that which was particularly afflicting to me was, that I had no weapon either to hunt and kill any creature for my sustenance, or to defend myself against any other creature that might desire to kill me for theirs. In a word, I had nothing about me but a knife, a tobacco-pipe, and a little tobacco in a box. This was all my provision; and this threw me into terrible agonies of mind, that for a while I ran about like a madman. Night coming upon me, I began, with a heavy heart, to consider what would be my lot if there were any ravenous beasts in that country, seeing at night they always come abroad for their prey.

All the remedy that offered to my thoughts at that time was, to get up into a thick bushy tree like a fir, but thorny, which grew near me, and where I resolved to sit all night, and consider the next day what death I should die, for as yet I saw no prospect of life. I walked about a furlong from the shore, to see if I could find any fresh water to drink, which I did, to my great joy; and having drank, and put a little tobacco in my mouth to prevent hunger, I went to the tree, and getting up into it, endeavoured to place myself so, as that if I should sleep I might not fall; and having cut me a short stick, like a truncheon, for my defence, I took up my lodging, and having been excessively fatigued, I fell fast asleep, and slept as comfortably as, I believe, few could have done in my condition, and found myself the most refreshed with it that I think I ever was on such an occasion.

When I waked it was broad day, the weather clear, and the storm abated, so that the sea did not rage and swell as before. But that which surprised me most was, that the ship was lifted off in the night from the sand where she lay, by the swelling of the tide, and was driven up almost as far as the rock which I first mentioned, where I had been so bruised by the dashing me against it. This being within about a mile from the shore where I was, and the ship seeming to stand upright still, I wished myself on board, that, at least, I might have some necessary things for my use.

When I came down from my apartment in the tree I looked about me again, and the first thing I found was the boat, which lay as the wind and the sea had tossed her up upon the land, about two miles on my right hand. I walked as far as I could upon the shore to have got to her, but found a neck or inlet of water between me and the boat, which was about half a mile broad; so I came back for the present, being more intent upon getting at the ship, where I hoped to find something for my present subsistence.

A little after noon I found the sea very calm, and the tide ebbed so far out, that I could come within a quarter of a mile of the ship; and here I found a fresh renewing of my grief, for I saw evidently, that if we had kept on board we had been all safe, that is to say, we had all got safe on shore, and I had not been so miserable as to be left entirely destitute of all comfort and company, as I now was. This forced tears from my eyes again; but as there was little relief in that, I resolved, if possible, to get to the ship; so I pulled off my clothes, for the weather was hot to extremity, and took the water. But when I came to the ship, my difficulty was still greater to know how to get on board; for as she lay aground, and high out of the water, there was nothing within my reach to lay hold of. I swam round her twice, and the second time I spied a small piece of a rope, which I wondered I did not see at first, hang down by the fore-chains so low, as that with great difficulty I got hold of it, and by the help of that rope got up into the forecastle of the ship. Here I found that the ship was bulged, and had a great deal of water in her hold, but that she lay so on the side of a bank of hard sand, or rather earth, that her stern lay lifted up upon the bank, and her head low almost to the water. By this means all her quarter was free, and all that was in that part was dry; for you may be sure my first work was to search and to see what was spoiled and what was free. And first I found that all the ship's provisions were dry and untouched by the water; and being very well disposed to eat, I went to the bread-room and filled my pockets with biscuit, and eat it as I went about other things, for I had no time to lose. I also found some rum in the great cabin, of which I took a large dram, and which I had indeed need enough of to spirit me for what was before me. Now I wanted nothing but a boat, to furnish myself with many things which I foresaw would be very necessary to me.

It was in vain to sit still and wish for what was not to be had, and this extremity roused my application. We had several spare yards, and two or three large spars of wood, and a spare top-mast or two in the ship. I resolved to fall to work with these, and flung as many of them overboard as I could manage for their weight, tying every one with a rope, that they might not drive away. When this was done I went down the ship's side, and, pulling them to me, I tied four of them fast together at both ends as well as I could, in the form of a raft; and laying two or three short pieces of plank upon them crossways, I found I could walk upon it very well, but that it was not able to bear any great weight, the pieces being too light. So I went to work, and with the carpenter's saw I cut a spare top-mast into three lengths, and added them to my raft, with a great deal of labour and pains; but hope of furnishing myself with necessaries encouraged me to go beyond what I should have been able to have done upon another occasion.

My raft was now strong enough to bear any reasonable weight. My next care was what to load it with, and how to preserve what I laid upon it from the surf of the sea; but I was not long considering this. I first laid all the planks or boards upon it that I could get, and having considered well what I most wanted, I first got three of the seamen's chests, which I had broken open, and emptied, and lowered them down upon my raft. The first of these I filled with provisions, viz., bread, rice, three Dutch cheeses, five pieces of dried goat's flesh, which we lived much upon, and a little remainder of European corn, which had been laid by for some fowls which we brought to sea with us, but the fowls were killed. There had been some barley and wheat together, but, to my great disappointment, I found afterwards that the rats had eaten or spoiled it all. As for liquors, I found several cases of bottles belonging to our skipper, in which were some cordial waters, and, in all, about five or six gallons of rack. These I stowed by themselves, there being no need to put them into the chest, nor no room for them. While I was doing this, I found the tide began to flow, though very calm, and I had the mortification to see my coat, shirt, and waistcoat, which I had left on shore upon the sand, swim away; as for my breeches, which were only linen, and open-kneed, I swam on board in them, and my stockings. However, this put me upon rummaging for clothes, of which I found enough, but took no more than I wanted for present use; for I had other things which my eye was more upon, as first tools to work with on shore; and it was after long searching that I found out the carpenter's chest, which was indeed a very useful prize to me, and much more valuable than a ship-loading of gold would have been at that time. I got it down to my raft, even whole as it was, without losing time to look into it, for I knew in general what it contained.

My next care was for some ammunition and arms; there were two very good fowling-pieces in the great cabin, and two pistols; these I secured first, with some powder-horns, and a small bag of shot, and two old rusty swords. I knew there were three barrels of powder in the ship, but knew not where our gunner had stowed them; but with much search I found them, two of them dry and good, the third had taken water; those two I got to my raft with the arms. And now I thought myself pretty well freighted, and began to think how I should get to shore with them,

"If you come near the boat I'll shoot you" (page 242)

I guided my raft as well as I could (page 257)

having neither sail, oar, or rudder; and the least capful of wind would have overset all my navigation.

I had three encouragements. 1. A smooth calm sea. 2. The tide rising and setting in to the shore. 3. What little wind there was blew me towards the land. And thus, having found two or three broken oars belonging to the boat, and besides the tools which were in the chest, I found two saws, an axe, and a hammer, and with this cargo I put to sea. For a mile or thereabouts my raft went very well, only that I found it drive a little distance from the place where I had landed before, by which I perceived that there was some indraft of the water, and consequently I hoped to find some creek or river there, which I might make use of as a port to get to land with my cargo.

As I imagined, so it was; there appeared before me a little opening of the land, and I found a strong current of the tide set into it, so I guided my raft as well as I could to keep in the middle of the stream. But here I had like to have suffered a second shipwreck, which, if I had, I think verily would have broke my heart; for knowing nothing of the coast, my raft ran aground at one end of it upon a shoal, and not being aground at the other end, it wanted but a little that all my cargo had slipped off towards that end that was afloat, and so fallen into the water. I did my utmost by setting my back against the chests to keep them in their places, but could not thrust off the raft with all my strength, neither durst I stir from the posture I was in, but holding up the chests with all my might, stood in that manner near half-an-hour, in which time the rising of the water brought me a little more upon a level; and a little after, the water still rising, my raft floated again, and I thrust her off with the oar I had into the channel, and then driving up higher, I at length found myself in the mouth of a little river, with land on both sides, and a strong current or tide running up. I looked on both sides for a proper place to get to shore, for I was not willing to be driven too high up the river, hoping in time to see some ship at sea, and therefore resolved to place myself as near the coast as I could.

At length I spied a little cove on the right shore of the creek, to which, with great pain and difficulty, I guided my raft, and at last got so near, as that, reaching ground with my oar, I could thrust her directly in; but here I had like to have dipped all my cargo in the sea again; for that shore lying pretty steep, that is to say, sloping, there was no place to land but where one end of my float, if it run on shore, would lie so high and the other sink lower, as before, that it would endanger my cargo again. All that I could do was to wait till the tide was at the highest, keeping the raft with my oar like an anchor to hold the side of it fast to the shore, near a flat piece of ground, which I expected the water would flow over; and so it did. As soon as I found water enough, for my raft drew about a foot of water, I thrust her on upon that flat piece of ground, and there fastened or moored her by sticking my two broken oars into the ground; one on one side near one end, and one on the other side near the other end; and thus I lay till the water ebbed away, and left my raft and all my cargo safe on shore.

My next work was to view the country and seek a proper place for my habitation, and where to stow my goods to secure them from whatever might happen. Where I was, I yet knew not; whether on the continent, or on an island; whether inhabited or not inhabited; whether in danger of wild beasts, or not. There was a hill, not above a mile from me, which rose up very steep and high, and which seemed to overtop some other hills, which lay as in a ridge from it, northward. I took out one of the fowling-pieces and one of the pistols, and a horn of powder; and thus armed, I travelled for discovery up to the top of that hill, where, after I had with great labour and difficulty got to the top, I saw my fate to my great affliction, viz,, that I was in an island environed every way with the sea, no land to be seen, except some rocks which lay a great way off, and two small islands less than this, which lay about three leagues to the west.

I found also that the island I was in was barren, and, as I saw good reason to believe, uninhabited, except by wild beasts, of whom, however, I saw none; yet I saw abundance of fowls, but knew not their kinds; neither, when I killed them, could I tell what was fit for food, and what not. At my coming back, I shot at a great bird which I saw sitting upon a tree on the side of a great wood. I believe it was the first gun that had been fired there since the creation of the world. I had no sooner fired, but from all the parts of the wood there arose an innumerable number of fowls of many sorts, making a confused screaming, and crying everyone according to his usual note; but not one of them of any kind that I knew. As for the creature I killed, I took it to be a kind of a hawk, its colour and beak resembling it, but had no talons or claws more than common; its flesh was carrion, and fit for nothing.

Contented with this discovery, I came back to my raft, and fell to work to bring my cargo on shore, which took me up the rest of that day; and what to do with myself at night, I knew not, nor indeed where to rest; for I was afraid to lie down on the ground, not knowing but some wild beast might devour me, though, as I afterwards found, there was really no need for those fears. However, as well as I could, I barricaded myself round with the chests and boards that I had brought on shore, and made a kind of a hut for that night's lodging; as for food, I yet saw not which way to supply myself, except that I had seen two or three creatures like hares run out of the wood where I shot the fowl.

I now began to consider, that I might yet get a great many things out of the ship, which would be useful to me, and particularly some of the rigging and sails, and such other things as might come to land; and I resolved to make another voyage on board the vessel, if possible. And as I knew that the first storm that blew must necessarily break her all in pieces, I resolved to set all other things apart till I got everything out of the ship that I could get. Then I called a council, that is to say, in my thoughts, whether I should take back the raft, but this appeared impracticable; so I resolved to go as before, when the tide was down; and I did so, only that I stripped before I went from my hut, having nothing on but a chequered shirt and a pair of linen drawers, and a pair of pumps on my feet.

I got on board the ship as before, and prepared a second raft, and having had experience of the first, I neither made this so unwieldy, nor loaded it so hard; but yet I brought away several things very useful to me; as, first, in the carpenter's stores I found two or three bags full of nails and spikes, a great screw-jack, a dozen or two of hatchets, and above all, that most useful thing called a grindstone. All these I secured, together with several things belonging to the gunner, particularly two or three iron crows, and two barrels of musket bullets, seven muskets, and another fowling-piece, with some small quantity of powder more; a large bag full of small-shot, and a great roll of sheet lead; but this last was so heavy, I could not hoist it up to get it over the ship's side. Besides these things, I took all the men's clothes that I could find, and a spare fore-top sail, a hammock, and some bedding; and with this I loaded my second raft, and brought them all safe on shore, to my very great comfort.

I was under some apprehensions during my absence from the land, that at least my provisions might be devoured on shore; but when I came back, I found no sign of any visitor, only there sat a creature like a wild cat upon one of the chests, which, when I came towards it, ran away a little distance, and then stood still. She sat very composed and unconcerned, and looked full in my face, as if she had a mind to be acquainted with me. I presented my gun at her; but as she did not understand it, she was perfectly unconcerned at it, nor did she offer to stir away; upon which I tossed her a bit of biscuit, though, by the way, I was not very free of it, for my store was not great. However, I spared her a bit, I say, and she went to it, smelled of it, and ate it, and looked (as pleased) for more; but I thanked her, and could spare no more, so she marched off.

Having got my second cargo on shore, though I was fain to open the barrels of powder and bring them by parcels, for they were too heavy, being large casks, I went to work to make me a little tent with the sail and some poles which I cut for that purpose; and into this tent I brought everything that I knew would spoil either with rain or sun; and I piled all the empty chests and casks up in a circle round the tent, to fortify it from any sudden attempt, either from man or beast.

When I had done this I blocked up the door of the tent with some boards within, and an empty chest set up on end without; and spreading one of the beds upon the ground, laying my two pistols just at my head, and my gun at length by me, I went to bed for the first time, and slept very quietly all night, for I was very weary and heavy; for the night before I had slept little, and had laboured very hard all day, as well to fetch all those things from the ship, as to get them on shore.

I had the biggest magazine of all kinds now that ever was laid up, I believe, for one man; but I was not satisfied still, for while the ship sat upright in that posture, I thought I ought to get everything out of her that I could. So every day at low water I went on board, and brought away something or other; but, particularly, the third time I went I brought away as much of the rigging as I could, as also all the small ropes and rope-twine I could get, with a piece of spare canvas, which was to mend the sails upon occasion, the barrel of wet gunpowder; in a word, I brought away all the sails first and last, only that I was fain to cut them in pieces, and bring as much at a time as I could; for they were no more useful to be sails, but as mere canvas only,

But that which comforted me more still was, that at last of all, after I had made five or six such voyages as these, and thought I had nothing more to expect from the ship that was worth my meddling with; I say, after all this, I found a great hogshead of bread, and three large runlets of rum or spirits, and a box of sugar, and a barrel of fine flour; this was surprising to me, because I had given over expecting any more provisions, except what was spoilt by the water. I soon emptied the hogshead of that bread, and wrapped it up parcel by parcel in pieces of the sails, which I cut out; and, in a word, I got all this safe on shore also.

The next day I made another voyage. And now, having plundered the ship of what was portable and fit to hand out, I began with the cables; and cutting the great cable into pieces, such as I could move, I got two cables and a hawser on shore, with all the iron-work I could get; and having cut down the sprit-sailyard, and the mizzen-yard, and everything I could to make a large raft, I loaded it with all those heavy goods, and came away. But my good luck began now to leave me; for this raft was so unwieldy, and so overladen, that after I was entered the little cove where I had landed the rest of my goods, not being able to guide it so handily as I did the other, it overset, and threw me and all my cargo into the water. As for myself it was no great harm, for I was near the shore; but as to my cargo, it was great part of it lost, especially the iron, which I expected would have been of great use to me. However, when the tide was out I got most of the pieces of cable ashore, and some of the iron, though with infinite labour; for I was fain to dip for it into the water, a work which fatigued me very much. After this I went every day on board, and brought away what I could get.

I had been now thirteen days on shore, and had been eleven times on board the ship; in which time I had brought away all that one pair of hands could well be supposed capable to bring, though I believe verily, had the calm weather held, I should have brought away the whole ship piece by piece. But preparing the twelfth time to go on board, I found the wind begin to rise. However, at low water I went on board, and though I thought I had rummaged the cabin so effectually as that nothing more could be found, yet I discovered a locker with drawers in it, in one of which I found two or three razors, and one pair of large scissors, with some ten or a dozen of good knives and forks; in another, I found about thirty-six pounds value in money, some European coin, some Brazil, some pieces of eight, some gold, some silver.

I smiled to myself at the sight or this money. "O drug!" said I aloud, "what art thou good for? Thou art not worth to me, no, not the taking off of the ground; one of those knives is worth all this heap. I have no manner of use for thee; even remain where thou art, and go to the bottom as a creature whose life is not worth saving." However, upon second thoughts, I took it away; and wrapping all this in a piece of canvas, I began to think of making another raft; but while I was preparing this,

I found the sky overcast, and the wind began to rise, and in a quarter of an hour it blew a fresh gale from the shore. It presently occurred to me that it was in vain to pretend to make a raft with the wind off shore, and that it was my business to be gone before the tide of flood began, otherwise I might not be able to reach the shore at all. Accordingly I let myself down into the water, and swam across the channel, which lay between the ship and the sands, and even that with difficulty enough, partly with the weight of the things I had about me, and partly the roughness of the water; for the wind rose very hastily, and before it was quite high water it blew a storm.

But I was gotten home to my little tent, where I lay with all my wealth about me very secure. It blew very hard all that night, and in the morning, when I looked out, behold, no more ship was to be seen. I was a little surprised, but recovered myself with this satisfactory reflection, viz., that I had lost no time, nor abated no diligence, to get everything out of her that could be useful to me, and that indeed there was little left in her that I was able to bring away if I had had more time.

I now gave over any more thoughts of the ship, or of anything out of her, except what might drive on shore from her wreck, as indeed divers pieces of her afterwards did; but those things were of small use to me.

My thoughts were now wholly employed about securing myself against either savages, if any should appear, or wild beasts, if any were in the island; and I had many thoughts of the method how to do this, and what kind of dwelling to make, whether I should make me a cave in the earth, or a tent upon the earth; and, in short, I resolved upon both, the manner and description of which it may not be improper to give an account of.

I soon found the place I was in was not for my settlement, particularly because it was upon a low moorish ground near the sea, and I believed would not be wholesome; and more particularly because there was no fresh water near it. So I resolved to find a more healthy and more convenient spot of ground.

I consulted several things in my situation, which I found would be proper for me. First, health and fresh water, I just now mentioned. Secondly, shelter from the heat of the sun. Thirdly, security from ravenous creatures, whether men or beasts. Fourthly, a view to the sea, that if God sent any ship in sight I might not lose any advantage for my deliverance, of which I was not willing to banish all my expectation yet.

In search of a place proper for this, I found a little plain on the side of a rising hill, whose front towards this little plain was steep as a house-side, so that nothing could come down upon me from the top; on the side of this rock there was a hollow place, worn a little way in, like the entrance or door of a cave; but there was not really any cave, or way into the rock at all.

On the flat of the green, just before this hollow place, I resolved to pitch my tent This plain was not above an hundred yards broad, and about twice as long, and lay like a green before my door, and at the end of it descended irregularly every way down into the low grounds by the seaside. It was on the NNW. side of the hill, so that I was sheltered from the heat every day, till it came to a W. and by S. sun, or thereabouts, which in those countries is near the setting.

Before I set up my tent, I drew a half circle before the hollow place, which took in about ten yards in its semi-diameter from the rock, and twenty yards in its diameter from its beginning and ending. In this half-circle I pitched two rows of strong stakes, driving them into the ground till they stood very firm like piles, the biggest end being out of the ground about five feet and a half, and sharpened on the top. The two rows did not stand above six inches from one another.

Then I took the pieces of cable which I had cut in the ship, and laid them in rows one upon another, within the circle, between these two rows of stakes, up to the top, placing other stakes in the inside leaning against them, about two feet and a half high, like a spur to a post; and this fence was so strong, that neither man or beast could get into it, or over it. This cost me a great deal of time and labour, especially to cut the piles in the woods, bring them to the place, and drive them into the earth.

The entrance into this place I made to be not by a door, but by a short ladder to go over the top; which ladder, when I was in, I lifted over after me, and so I was completely fenced in, and fortified, as I thought, from all the world, and consequently slept secure in the night, which otherwise I could not have done; though as it appeared afterward, there was no need of all this caution from the enemies that I apprehended danger from.

Into this fence or fortress, with infinite labour, I carried all my riches, all my provisions, ammunition, and stores, of which you have the account above; and I made me a large tent, which, to preserve me from the rains that in one part of the year are very violent there, I made double, viz., one smaller tent within, and one larger tent above it, and covered the uppermost with a large tarpaulin, which I had saved among the sails. And now I lay no more for a while in the bed which I had brought on shore, but in a hammock, which was indeed a very good one, and belonged to the mate of the ship.

Into this tent I brought all my provisions, and everything that would spoil by the wet; and having thus enclosed all my goods, I made up the entrance, which, till now, I had left open, and so passed and repassed, as I said, by a short ladder.

When I had done this, I began to work my way into the rock; and bringing all the earth and stones that I dug down out through my tent, I laid them up within my fence in the nature of a terrace, so that it raised the ground within about a foot and a half; and thus I made me a cave just behind my tent, which served me like a cellar to my house.

It cost me much labour, and many days, before all these things were brought to perfection, and therefore I must go back to some other things which took up some of my thoughts. At the same time it happened, after I had laid my scheme for the setting up my tent, and making the cave, that a storm of rain falling from a thick dark cloud, a sudden flash of lightning happened, and after that a great clap of thunder, as is naturally the effect of it. I was not so much surprised with the lightning, as I was with a thought which darted into my mind as swift as the lightning itself. O my powder! My very heart sunk within me when I thought, that at one blast all my powder might be destroyed, on which, not my defence only, but the providing me food, as I thought, entirely depended. I was nothing near so anxious about my own danger; though had the powder took fire, I had never known who had hurt me.

Such impression did this make upon me, that after the storm was over I laid aside all my works, my building, and fortifying, and applied myself to make bags and boxes to separate the powder, and keep it a little and a little in a parcel, in hope that whatever might come it might not all take fire at once, and to keep it so apart, that it should not be possible to make one part fire another. I finished this work in about a fortnight; and I think my powder, which in all was about 240 pounds' weight, was divided in not less than a hundred parcels. As to the barrel that had been wet, I did not apprehend any danger from that, so I placed it in my new cave, which in my fancy I called my kitchen, and the rest I hid up and down in holes among the rocks, so that no wet might come to it, marking very carefully where I laid it.

In the interval of time while this was doing, I went out once, at least, every day with my gun, as well to divert myself, as to see if I could kill anything fit for food, and as near as I could to acquaint myself with what the island produced. The first time I went out, I presently discovered that there were goats in the island, which was a great satisfaction to me; but then it was attended with this misfortune to me, viz., that they were so shy, so subtle, and so swift of foot, that it was the difficultest thing in the world to come at them. But I was not discouraged at this, not doubting but I might now and then shoot one, as it soon happened; for after I had found their haunts a little, I laid wait in this manner for them. I observed if they saw me in the valleys, though they were upon the rocks, they would run away as in a terrible fright; but if they were feeding in the valleys, and I was upon the rocks, they took no notice of me, from whence I concluded that, by the position of their optics, their sight was so directed downward, that they did not readily see objects that were above them. So afterward I took this method; I always climbed the rocks first to get above them, and then had frequently a fair mark. The first shot I made among these creatures I killed a she-goat, which had a little kid by her, which she gave suck to, which grieved me heartily; but when the old one fell, the kid stood stock still by her till I came and took her up; and not only so, but when I carried the old one with me upon my shoulders, the kid followed me quite to my enclosure; upon which I laid down the dam, and took the kid in my arms, and carried it over my pale, in hopes to have bred it up tame; but it would not eat, so I was forced to kill it, and eat it myself. These two supplied me with flesh a great while, for I eat sparingly, and saved my provisions, my bread especially, as much as possibly I could.

And now being to enter into a melancholy relation of a scene of silent life, such, perhaps, as was never heard of in the world before, I shall take it from its beginning, and continue it in its order. It was, by my account, the 30th of September when, in the manner as above said, I first set foot upon this horrid island, when the sun being to us in its autumnal equinox, was almost just over my head, for I reckoned myself, by observation, to be in the latitude of 9 degrees 22 minutes north of the line,

After I had been there about ten or twelve days, it came into my thoughts that I should lose my reckoning of time for want of books and pen and ink, and should even forget the Sabbath days from the working days; but to prevent this, I cut it with my knife upon a large post, in capital letters; and making it into a great cross, I set it up on the shore where I first landed, viz., "I came on shore here on the 30th of September 1659." Upon the sides of this square post I cut every day a notch with my knife, and every seventh notch was as long again as the rest, and every first day of the month as long again as that long one; and thus I kept my calendar, or weekly, monthly, and yearly reckoning of time.

In the next place we are to observe, that among the many things which I brought out of the ship in the several voyages, which, as above mentioned, I made to it, I got several things of less value, but not all less useful to me, which I omitted setting down before; as in particular, pens, ink, and paper, several parcels in the captain's, mate's, gunner's, and carpenter's keeping, three or four compasses, some mathematical instruments, dials, perspectives, charts, and books of navigation, all which I huddled together, whether I might want them or no. Also I found three very good Bibles, which came to me in my cargo from England, and which I had packed up among my things; some Portuguese books also, and among them two or three Popish prayer-books, and several other books, all which I carefully secured. And I must not forget, that we had in the ship a dog and two cats, of whose eminent history I may have occasion to say something in its place; for I carried both the cats with me; and as for the dog, he jumped out of the ship of himself; and swam on shore to me the day after I went on shore with my first cargo, and was a trusty servant to me many years. I wanted nothing that he could fetch me, nor any company that he could make up to me; I only wanted to have him talk to me, but that would not do. As I observed before, I found pen, ink, and paper, and I husbanded them to the utmost; and I shall show that while my ink lasted, I kept things very exact; but after that was gone, I could not, for I could not make any ink by any means that I could devise,

And this put me in mind that I wanted many things, notwithstanding all that I had amassed together; and of these, this of ink was one, as also spade, pickaxe, and shovel, to dig or remove the earth, needles, pins, and thread; as for linen, I soon learned to want that without much difficulty,

This want of tools made every work I did go on heavily; and it was near a whole year before I had entirely finished my little pale or surrounded habitation. The piles or stakes, which were as heavy as I could well lift, were a long time in cutting and preparing in the woods, and more by far in bringing home; so that I spent sometimes two days in cutting and bringing home one of those posts, and a third day in driving it into the ground; for which purpose I got a heavy piece of wood at first, but at last bethought myself of one of the iron crows, which, however, though I found it, yet it made driving those post or piles very laborious and tedious work.

But what need I have been concerned at the tediousness of anything I had to do, seeing I had time enough to do it in? nor had I any other employment, if that had been over, at least, that I could foresee, except the ranging the island to seek for food, which I did more or less every day.

I now began to consider seriously my condition, and the circumstance I was reduced to, and I drew up the state of my affairs in writing; not so much to leave them to any that were to come after me, for, I was like to have but few heirs, as to deliver my thoughts from daily poring upon them, and afflicting my mind. And as my reason began now to master my despondency, I began to comfort myself as well as I could, and to set the good against the evil, that I might have something to distinguish my case from worse; and I stated it very impartially, like debtor and creditor, the comforts I enjoyed against the miseries I suffered, thus:

Evil.	*Good.*
I am cast upon a horrible desolate island, void of all hope of recovery.	But I am alive, and not drowned, as all my ship's company was.
I am singled out and separated, as it were, from all the world to be miserable.	But I am singled out, too, from all the ship's crew to be spared from death; and He that miraculously saved me from death, can deliver me from this condition.
I am divided from mankind, a solitaire, one banished from human society.	But I am not starved and perishing on a barren place, affording no sustenance.
I have not clothes to cover me.	But I am in a hot climate, where if I had clothes I could hardly wear them.
I am without any defence or means to resist any violence of man or beast.	But I am cast on an island, where I see no wild beasts to hurt me, as I saw on the coast of Africa; and what if I had been shipwrecked there?
I have no soul to speak to, or relieve me.	But God wonderfully sent the ship in near enough to the shore, that I have gotten out so many necessary things as will either supply my wants, or enable me to supply myself even as long as I live.

Having now brought my mind a little to relish my condition, and given over looking out to sea, to see if I could spy a ship; I say, giving over these things, I began to apply myself to accommodate my way of living, and to make things as easy to me as I could.

I have already described my habitation, which was a tent under the side of a rock, surrounded with a strong pale of posts and cables; but I might now rather call it a wall, for I raised a kind of wall up against it of turfs; about two feet thick on the outside, and after some time – I think it was a year and a half – I raised rafters from it leaning to the rock, and thatched or covered it with boughs of trees and such things as I could get to keep out the rain, which I found at some times of the year very violent.

I have already observed how I brought all my goods into this pale, and into the cave which I had made behind me. But I must observe, too, that at first this was a confused heap of goods, which as they lay in no order, so they took up all my place; I had no room to turn myself. So I set myself to enlarge my cave and works farther into the earth; for it was a loose sandy rock, which yielded easily to the labour I bestowed on it. And so, when I found I was pretty safe as to beasts of prey, I worked sideways to the right hand into the rock; and then, turning to the right again, worked quite out, and made me a door to come out on the outside of my pale or fortification. This gave me not only egress and regress, as it were a backway to my tent and to my storehouse, but gave me room to stow my goods.

And now I began to apply myself to make such necessary things as I found I most wanted, as particularly a chair and a table; for without these I was not able to enjoy the few comforts I had in the world. I could not write or eat, or do several things with so much pleasure without a table.

I had never handled a tool in my life; and yet in time, by labour, application, and contrivance, I found at last that I wanted nothing but I could have made it, especially if I had had tools. However, I made abundance of things even without tools, and some with no more tools than an adze and a hatchet, which, perhaps were never made that way before, and that with infinite labour. For example, if I wanted a board, I had no other way but to cut down a tree, set it on an edge before me, and hew it flat on either side with my axe, till I had brought it to be thin as a plank, and then dub it smooth with my adze. It is true, by this method I could make but one board out of a whole tree; but this I had no remedy for but patience, any more than I had for the prodigious deal of time and labour which it took me up to make a plank or board. But my time or labour was little worth, and so it was as well employed one way as another.

However, I made me a table and a chair, as I observed above, in the first place, and this I did out of the short pieces of boards that I brought on my raft from the ship. But when I had wrought out some boards, as above, I made large shelves of the breadth of a foot and a half one over another, all along one side of my cave, to lay all my tools, nails, and iron-work; and, in a word, to separate everything at large in their places, that I might come easily at them. I knocked pieces into the wall of the rock to hang my guns and all things that would hang up; so that had my cave been to be seen, it looked like a general magazine of all necessary things; and I had everything so ready at my hand, that it was a great pleasure to me to see all my goods in such order, and especially to find my stock of all necessaries so great.

And now it was when I began to keep a journal of every day's employment; for, indeed, at first, I was in too much hurry, and not only hurry as to labour, but in too much discomposure of mind; and my journal would have been full of many dull things.

But having gotten over these things in some measure, and having settled my household stuff and habitation, made me a table and a chair, and all as handsome about me as I could, I began to keep my journal, of which I shall here give you the copy (though in it will be told all these particulars over again) as long as it lasted; for, having no more ink, I was forced to leave it off.

EXTRACTS FROM THE JOURNAL

Nov. 4. – This morning I began to order my times of work, of going out with my gun, time of sleep, and time of diversion, viz., every morning I walked out with my gun for two or three hours, if it did not rain; then employed myself to work till about eleven o'clock; then eat what I had to live on; and from twelve to two I lay down to sleep, the weather being excessive hot; and then in the evening to work again. The working part of this day and of the next were wholly employed in making my table; for I was yet but a very sorry workman, though time and necessity made me a complete natural mechanic soon after, as I believe it would do any one else.

Nov. 5. – This day went abroad with my gun and my dog, and killed a wild cat; her skin pretty soft, but her flesh good for nothing. Every creature I killed, I took off the skins and preserved them. Coming back by the sea-shore, I saw many sorts of sea-fowls, which I did not understand; but was surprised, and almost frighted, with two or three seals, which, while I was gazing at, not well knowing what they were, got into the sea, and escaped me for that time.

Nov. 6. – After my morning walk I went to work with my table again, and finished it, though not to my liking; nor was it long before I learned to mend it.

Nov. 7. – Now it began to be settled fair weather. The 7th, 8th, 9th, 10th, and part of the 12th (for the 11th was Sunday) I took wholly up to make me a chair, and with much ado, brought it to a tolerable shape, but never to please me; and even in the making, I pulled it in pieces several times. Note I soon neglected my keeping Sundays; for, omitting my mark for them on my post, I forgot which was which.

Nov. 17. – This day I began to dig behind my tent into the rock, to make room for my farther conveniency. Note, three things I wanted exceedingly for this work, viz., a pick-axe, a shovel, and a wheelbarrow or basket; so I desisted from my work, and began to consider how to supply that want, and make me some tools. As for a pick-axe, I made use of the iron crows, which were proper enough, though heavy; but the next thing was a shovel or spade. This was so absolutely necessary, that indeed I could do nothing effectually without it; but what kind of one to make, I knew not.

Nov. 18. – The next day, in searching the woods, I found a tree of that wood, or like it, which in the Brazils they call the iron-tree, for its exceeding hardness; of this, with great labour, and almost spoiling my axe, I cut a piece, and brought it home, too, with difficulty enough, for it was exceeding heavy.

The excessive hardness of the wood, and having no other way, made me a long while upon this machine, for I worked it effectually, by little and little, into the form of a shovel or spade, the handle exactly shaped like ours in England, only that the broad part having no iron shod upon it at bottom, it would not last me so long.

I was still deficient, for I wanted a basket or a wheelbarrow. A basket I could not make by any means, having no such things as twigs that would bend to make wicker ware, at least none yet found out. And as to a wheelbarrow, I fancied I could make all but the wheel, but that I had no notion of, neither did I know how to go about it; besides, I had no possible way to make the iron gudgeons for the spindle or axis of the wheel to run in, so I gave it over; and so for carrying away the earth which I dug out of the cave, I made me a thing like a hod which the labourers carry mortar in, when they serve the bricklayers.

Nov. 23. – My other work having now stood still because of my making these tools, when they were finished I went on, and working every day, as my strength and time allowed, I spent eighteen days entirely in widening and deepening my cave, that it might hold my goods commodiously.

Note: During all this time I worked to make this room or cave spacious enough to accommodate me as a warehouse or magazine, a kitchen, a dining-room, and a cellar; as for my lodging, I kept to the tent, except that sometimes in the wet season of the year it rained so hard, that I could not keep myself dry, which caused me afterwards to cover all my place within my pale with long poles, in the form of rafters, leaning against the rock, and load them with flags and large leaves of trees, like a thatch.

December 10. – I began now to think my cave or vault finished, when on a sudden (it seems I had made it too large) a great quantity of earth fell down from the top and one side, so much, that, in short, it frighted me, and not without reason too; for if I had been under it, I had never wanted a grave-digger. Upon this disaster I had a great deal of work to do over again; for I had the loose earth to carry out; and, which was of more importance, I had the ceiling to prop up, so that I might be sure no more would come down.

Dec. 11. – This day I went to work with it accordingly, and got two shores or posts pitched upright to the top, with two pieces of boards across over each post. This I finished the next day; and setting more posts up with boards, in about a week more I had the roof secured; and the posts standing in rows, served me for partitions to part of my house.

Dec. 17. – From this day to the twentieth I placed shelves, and knocked up nails on the posts to hang everything up that could be hung up; and now I began to be in some order within doors.

Dec. 20. – Now I carried everything into the cave, and began to furnish my house, and set up some pieces of boards, like a dresser, to order my victuals upon; but boards began to be very scarce with me; also I made me another table.

Dec. 24. – Much rain all night and all day; no stirring out.

Dec. 25. – Rain all day.

Dec. 26. – No rain, and the earth much cooler than before, and pleasanter.

Dec. 27. – Killed a young goat, and lamed another, so that I catched it, and led it home in a string. When I had it home, I bound and splintered up its leg, which was broke. *N.B.* – I took such care of it, that it lived, and the leg grew well and as strong as ever; but by my nursing it so long it grew tame, and fed upon the little green at my door, and would not go away. This was the first time that I entertained a thought of breeding up some tame creatures, that I might have food when my powder and shot was all spent.

Dec. 28, 29, 30. – Great heats and no breeze, so that there was no stirring abroad, except in the evening, for food. This time I spent in putting all my things in order within doors.

January 1. – Very hot still, but I went abroad early and late with my gun, and lay still in the middle of the day. This evening, going farther into the valleys which lay towards the centre of the island, I found there was plenty of goats, though exceeding shy, and hard to come at. However, I resolved to try if I could not bring my dog to hunt them down.

Jan. 2. – Accordingly, the next day, I went out with my dog, and set him upon the goats; but I was mistaken, for they all faced about upon the dog; and he knew his danger too well, for he would not come near them.

Jan. 3. – I began my fence or wall; which, being still jealous of my being attacked by somebody, I resolved to make very thick and strong.

N.B. – This wall being described before, I purposely omit what was said in the journal. It is sufficient to observe that I was no less time than from the 3rd of January to the 14th of April working, finishing, and perfecting this wall, though it was no more than about twenty-four yards in length, being a half circle from one place in the rock to another place about eight yards from it, the door of the cave being in the centre behind it.

All this time I worked very hard, the rains hindering me many days, nay, sometimes weeks together; but I thought I should never be perfectly secure till this wall was finished. And it is scarce credible what inexpressible labour everything was done with, especially the bringing piles out of the woods, and driving them into the ground; for I made them much bigger than I need to have done.

When this wall was finished, and the outside double-fenced with a turf-wall raised up close to it, I persuaded myself that if any people were to come on shore there, they would not perceive anything like a habitation; and it was very well I did so, as may be observed hereafter upon a very remarkable occasion.

During this time, I made my rounds in the woods for game every day, when the rain admitted me, and made frequent discoveries in these walks of something or other to my advantage; particularly I found a kind of wild pigeons, who built, not as wood pigeons in a tree, but rather as house pigeons, in the holes of the rocks. And taking some young ones, I endeavoured to breed them up tame, and did so; but when they grew older they flew all away, which, perhaps, was at first for want of feeding them, for I had nothing to give them. However, I frequently found their nests, and got their young ones, which were very good meat.

And now in the managing my household affairs I found myself wanting in many things, which I thought at first it was impossible for me to make, as indeed, as to some of them, it was. For instance, I could never make a cask to be hooped; I had a small runlet or two, as I observed before, but I could never arrive to the capacity of making one by them, though I spent many weeks about it. I could neither put in the heads, or joint the staves so true to one another, as to make them hold water; so I gave that also over.

In the next place, I was at a great loss for candle; so that as soon as ever it was dark, which was generally by seven o'clock, I was obliged to go to bed. I remembered the lump of beeswax with which I made candles in my African adventure, but I had none of that now. The only remedy I had was, that when I had killed a goat I saved the tallow, and with a little dish made of clay, which I baked in the sun, to which I added a wick of some oakum, I made me a lamp; and this gave me light, though not a clear steady light like a candle.

In the middle of all my labours it happened, that rummaging my things, I found a little bag, which, as I hinted before, had been filled with corn for the feeding of poultry, not for this voyage, but before, as I suppose, when the ship came from Lisbon. What little remainder of corn had been in the bag was all devoured with the rats, and I saw nothing in the bag but husks and dust; and being willing to have the bag for some other use, I think it was to put powder in, when I divided it for fear of the lightning, or some such use, I shook the husks of corn out of it on one side of my fortification, under the rock. It was a little before the great rains, just now mentioned, that I threw this stuff away, taking no notice of anything, and not so

much as remembering that I had thrown anything there; when, about a month after, or thereabout, I saw some few stalks of something green shooting out of the ground, which I fancied might be some plant I had not seen; but I was surprised, and perfectly astonished, when, after a little longer time, I saw about ten or twelve ears come out, which were perfect green barley of the same kind as our European, nay, as our English barley.

I carefully saved the ears of this corn, you may be sure, in their season, which was about the end of June; and laying up every corn, I resolved to sow them all again, hoping in time to have some quantity sufficient to supply me with bread. But it was not till the fourth year that I could allow myself the least grain of this corn to eat, and even then but sparingly, as I shall say afterwards in its order; for I lost all that I sowed the first season, by not observing the proper time; for I sowed it just before the dry season, so that it never came up at all, at least not as it would have done; of which in its place.

Besides this barley, there was, as above, twenty or thirty stalks of rice, which I preserved with the same care, and whose use was of the same kind, or to the same purpose, viz., to make me bread, or rather food; for I found ways to cook it up without baking, though I did that also after some time. But to return to my journal.

I worked excessive hard these three or four months to get my wall done; and the

14th of April I closed it up, contriving to go into it, not by a door, but over the wall by a ladder, that there might be no sign in the outside of my habitation.

April 16. – I finished the ladder, so I went up with the ladder to the top, and then pulled it up after me, and let it down on the inside. This was a complete enclosure to me; for within I had room enough, and nothing could come at me from without, unless it could first mount my wall.

The very next day after this wall was finished, I had almost had all my labour overthrown at once, and myself killed. The case was thus: As I was busy in the inside of it, behind my tent, just in the entrance into my cave, I was terribly frighted with a most dreadful surprising thing indeed; for all on a sudden I found the earth come crumbling down from the roof of my cave, and from the edge of the hill over my head, and two of the posts I had set up in the cave cracked in a frightful manner. I was heartily scared, but thought nothing of what was really the cause, only thinking that the top of my cave was falling in, as some of it had done before; and for fear I should be buried in it, I ran forward to my ladder; and not thinking myself safe there neither, I got over my wall for fear of the pieces of the hill which I expected might roll down upon me. I was no sooner stepped down upon the firm ground, but I plainly saw it was a terrible earthquake; for the ground I stood on shook three times at about eight minutes' distance, with three such shocks, as would have overturned the strongest building that could be supposed to have stood on the earth; and a great piece of the top of a rock, which stood about half a mile from me next the sea, fell down with such a terrible noise, as I never heard in all my life. I perceived also the very sea was put into violent motion by it; and I believe the shocks were stronger under the water than on the island.

After the third shock was over, and I felt no more for some time, I began to take courage; and yet I had not heart enough to go over my wall again, for fear of being buried alive, but sat still upon the ground, greatly cast down and disconsolate, not knowing what to do. All this while I had not the least serious religious thought, nothing but the common, "Lord, have mercy upon me!" and when it was over, that went away too.

While I sat thus, I found the air overcast, and grow cloudy, as if it would rain. Soon after that the wind rose by little and little, so that in less than half-an-hour it blew a most dreadful hurricane. The sea was all on a sudden covered over with foam and froth; the shore was covered with the breach of the water; the trees were torn up by the roots; and a terrible storm it was: and this held about three hours, and then began to abate; and in two hours more it was stark calm, and began to rain very hard.

I was forced to go into my cave, though very much afraid and uneasy, for fear it should fall on my head.

This violent rain forced me to a new work, viz., to cut a hole through my new fortification, like a sink, to let the water go out, which would else have drowned my cave. After I had been in my cave some time, and found still no more shocks of the earthquake follow, I began to be more composed. And now to support my spirits, which indeed wanted it very much, I went to my little store, and took a small sup of rum, which however, I did then, and always, very sparingly, knowing I could have no more when that was gone.

It continued raining all that night and great part of the next day, so that I could not stir abroad; but my mind being more composed, I began to think of what I had best do, concluding that if the island was subject to these earthquakes, there would be no living for me in a cave; but I must consider of building me some little hut in an open place, which I might surround with a wall, as I had done here, and so make myself secure from wild beasts or men; but concluded, if I stayed where I was, I should certainly, one time or other, be buried alive.

With these thoughts I resolved to remove my tent from the place where it stood, which was just under the hanging precipice of the hill, and which, if it should be shaken again, would certainly fall upon my tent; and I spent the two next days, being the 19th and 20th of April, in contriving where and how to remove my habitation.

The fear of being swallowed up alive made me that I never slept in quiet; and yet the apprehension of lying abroad without any fence was almost equal to it. But still, when I looked about and saw how everything was put in order, how pleasantly concealed I was, and how safe from danger, it made me very loth to remove.

In the meantime it occurred to me that it would require a vast deal of time for me to do this, and that I must be contented to run the venture where I was, till I had formed a camp for myself, and had secured it so as to remove to it. So with this resolution I composed myself for a time, and resolved that I would go to work with all speed to build me a wall with piles and cables, &c., in a circle as before, and set my tent up in it when it was finished, but that I would venture to stay where I was till it was finished, and fit to remove to. This was the 21st.

April 22. – The next morning I began to consider of means to put this resolve in execution; but I was at a great loss about my tools. I had three large axes, and abundance of hatchets (for we carried the hatchets for traffic with the Indians), but with much chopping and cutting knotty hard wood, they were all full of notches and dull; and though I had a grindstone, I could not turn it and grind my tools too. This cost me as much thought as a statesman would have bestowed upon a grand point of politics, or a judge upon the life and death of a man. At length I contrived a wheel with a string, to turn it with my foot, that I might have both my hands at liberty. Note, I had never seen any such thing in England, or at least not to take notice how it was done, though since I have observed it is very common there; besides that, my grindstone was very large and heavy. This machine cost me a full week's work to bring it to perfection.

April 28, 29. – These two whole days I took up in grinding my tools, my machine for turning my grindstone performing very well.

May 1. – In the morning, looking towards the seaside, the tide being low, I saw something lie on the shore bigger than ordinary, and it looked like a cask. When I came to it, I found a small barrel, and two or three pieces of the wreck of the ship, which were driven on shore by the late hurricane; and looking towards the wreck itself, I thought it seemed to lie higher out of the water than it used to do. I examined the barrel which was driven on shore, and soon found it was a barrel of gunpowder; but it had taken water, and the powder was caked as hard as a stone. However, I rolled it farther on shore for the present, and went on upon the sands as near as I could to the wreck of the ship to look for more.

When I came down to the ship I found it strangely removed. The forecastle, which lay before buried in sand, was heaved up at least six feet; and the stern, which was broken to pieces, and parted from the rest by the force of the sea, soon after I had left rummaging her, was tossed, as it were, up, and cast on one side, and the sand was thrown so high on that side next her stern, that whereas there was a great place of water before, so that I could not come within a quarter of a mile of the wreck without swimming, I could now walk quite up to her when the tide was out. I was surprised with this at first, but soon concluded it must be done by the earthquake. And as by this violence the ship was more broken open than formerly, so many things came daily on shore, which the sea had loosened, and which the winds and water rolled by degrees to the land.

This wholly diverted my thoughts from the design of removing my habitation; and I busied myself mightily, that day especially, in searching whether I could make any way into the ship. But I found nothing was to be expected of that kind, for that all the inside of the ship was choked up with sand. However, as I had learned not to despair of anything, I resolved to pull everything to pieces that I could of the ship, concluding, that everything I could get from her would be of some use or other to me.

May 3-17. – Went every day to the wreck, and got a great deal of pieces of timber, and boards, or plank, and two or three hundredweight of iron.

May 24. – Every day to this day I worked on the wreck, and with hard labour I loosened some things so much with the crow, that the first blowing tide several casks floated out, and two of the seamen's chests. But the wind blowing from the shore, nothing came to land that day but pieces of timber, and a hogshead, which had some Brazil pork in it, but the salt water and the sand had spoiled it.

I continued this work every day to the 15th of June, except the time necessary to get food, which I always appointed, during this part of my employment, to be when the tide was up, that I might be ready when it was ebbed out. And by this time I had gotten timber, and plank, and ironwork enough to have builded a good boat, if I had known how; and also, I got at several times, and in several pieces, near one hundredweight of the sheet lead.

June 16. – Going down to the seaside, I found a large tortoise, or turtle. This was the first I had seen, which it seems was only my misfortune, not any defect of the place, or scarcity; for had I happened to be on the other side of the island, I might have had hundreds of them every day, as I found afterwards; but, perhaps, had paid dear enough for them.

June 17. – I spent in cooking the turtle. I found in her three-score eggs; and her flesh was to me, at that time, the most savoury and pleasant that ever I tasted in my life, having had no flesh, but of goats and fowls, since I landed in this horrid place.

June 18. – Rained all day, and I stayed within. I thought at this time the rain felt cold, and I was something chilly, which I knew was not usual in that latitude.

June 19. – Very ill, and shivering, as if the weather had been cold.

June 20. – No rest all night; violent pains in my head, and feverish.

June 21. – Very ill, frighted almost to death with the apprehensions of my sad condition, to be sick, and no help. Prayed to God for the first time since the storm off Hull, but scarce knew what I said, or why; my thoughts being all confused.

June 22. – A little better, but under dreadful apprehensions of sickness.

June 23. – Very bad again; cold and shivering, and then a violent headache.

June 24. – Much better.

June 25. – An ague very violent; the fit held me seven hours; cold fit, and hot, with faint sweats after it.

June 26. – Better; and having no victuals to eat, took my gun, but found myself very weak. However, I killed a she-goat, and with much difficulty got it home, and broiled some of it, and eat. I would fain have stewed it, and made some broth, but had no pot.

June 27. – The ague again so violent that I lay abed all day, and neither eat or drink. I was ready to perish for thirst; but so weak, I had not strength to stand up, or to get myself any water to drink. Prayed to God again, but was light-headed; and when I was not, I was so ignorant that I knew not what to say; only I lay and cried, "Lord, look upon me! Lord, pity me! Lord, have mercy upon me!" I suppose I did nothing else for two or three hours, till the fit wearing off, I fell asleep, and did not wake till far in the night. When I waked, I found myself much refreshed, but weak, and exceeding thirsty. However, as I had no water in my whole habitation, I was forced to lie till morning, and went to sleep again. In this second sleep I had this terrible dream.

I thought that I was sitting on the ground, on the outside of my wall, where I sat when the storm blew after the earthquake, and that I saw a man descend from a great black cloud, in a bright flame of fire, and light upon the ground. He was all over as bright as a flame, so that I could but just bear to look towards him. His countenance was most inexpressibly dreadful, impossible for words to describe. When he stepped upon the ground with his feet, I thought the earth trembled, just as it had done before in the earthquake, and all the air looked, to my apprehension, as if it had been filled with flashes of fire.

He was no sooner landed upon the earth, but he moved forward towards me, with a long spear or weapon in his hand, to kill me; and when he came to a rising ground, at some distance, he spoke to me, or I heard a voice so terrible, that it is impossible to express the terror of it. All that I can say I understood was this: "Seeing all these things have not brought thee to repentance, now thou shalt die;" at which words I thought he lifted up the spear that was in his hand to kill me.

No one that shall ever read this account, will expect that I should be able to describe the horrors of my soul at this terrible vision; I mean, that even while it was a dream, I even dreamed of those horrors; nor is it any more possible to describe the impression that remained upon my mind when I awaked, and found it was but a dream.

I had, alas! no divine knowledge; what I had received by the good instruction of my father was then worn out, by an uninterrupted series, for eight years, of seafaring wickedness, and a constant conversation with nothing but such as were, like myself, wicked and profane to the last degree. I do not remember that I had, in all that time, one thought that so much as tended either to looking upwards toward God, or inwards towards a reflection upon my ways.

It is true, when I got on shore first here, and found all my ship's crew drowned, and myself spared, I was surprised with a kind of ecstasy, and some transports of soul, which, had the grace of God assisted, might have come up to true thankfulness; but it ended where it begun, in a mere common flight of joy, or, as I may say, being glad I was alive, without the least reflection upon the distinguishing goodness of the hand which had preserved me, and had singled me out to be preserved, when all the rest were destroyed; or an inquiry why Providence had been thus merciful to me; even just the same common sort of joy which seamen generally have after they are got safe ashore from a shipwreck, which they drown all in the next bowl of punch, and forget almost as soon as it is over, and all the rest of my life was like it.

Even the earthquake, though nothing could be more terrible in its nature, or more immediately directing to the invisible Power, which alone directs such things, yet no sooner was the first fright over, but the impression it had made went off also. I had no more sense of God or His judgments, much less of the present affliction of my circumstances being from His hand, than if I had been in the most prosperous condition of life.

But now, when I began to be sick, and a leisurely view of the miseries of death came to place itself before me; when my spirits began to sink under the burthen of a strong distemper, and Nature was exhausted with the violence of the fever; conscience, that had slept so long, began to awake, and I began to reproach myself with my past life, in which I had so evidently, by uncommon wickedness, provoked the justice of God to lay me under uncommon strokes, and to deal with me in so vindictive a manner.

"Now," said I aloud, "my dear father's words are come to pass; God's justice has overtaken me, and I have none to help or hear me. I rejected the voice of Providence, which had mercifully put me in a posture or station of life wherein I might have been happy and easy; but I would neither see it myself, or learn to know the blessing of it from my parents. I refused their help and assistance, who would have lifted me into the world, and would have made everything easy to me; and now I have difficulties to struggle with, too great for even Nature itself to support, and no assistance, no help, no comfort, no advice." Then I cried out, "Lord, be my help, for I am in great distress."

This was the first prayer, if I may call it so, that I had made for many years. But I return to my journal.

June 28. – Having been somewhat refreshed with the sleep I had had, and the fit being entirely off, I got up; and though the fright and terror of my dream was very great, yet I considered that the fit of the ague would return again the next day, and now was my time to get something to refresh and support myself when I should be ill. And the first thing I did I filled a large square case-bottle with water, and set it upon my table, in reach of my bed; and to take off the chill or aguish disposition of the water, I put about a quarter of a pint of rum into it, and mixed them together. Then I got me a piece of the goat's flesh, and broiled it on the coals, but could eat very little. I walked about, but was very weak, and withal very sad and heavy-hearted in the sense of my miserable condition, dreading the return of my distemper the next day. At night I made my supper of three of the turtle's eggs, which I roasted in the ashes, and eat, as we call it, in the shell; and this was the first bit of meat I had ever asked God's blessing to, even as I could remember, in my whole life.

After I had eaten, I tried to walk, but found myself so weak, that I could hardly carry the gun (for I never went out without that); so I went but a little way, and sat down upon the ground, looking out upon the sea, which was just before me, and very calm and smooth. As I sat here, some such thoughts as these occurred to me.

That it must needs be that God had appointed all this to befall me; that I was brought to this miserable circumstance by His direction, He having the sole power, not of me only, but of everything that happened in the world. Immediately it followed, Why has God done this to me? What have I done to be thus used?

My conscience presently checked me in that inquiry, as if I had blasphemed, and methought it spoke to me like a voice:

"Wretch! dost thou ask what thou hast done? Look back upon a dreadful misspent life, and ask thyself what thou hast not done? Ask, why is it that thou wert not long ago destroyed? Why wert thou not drowned in Yarmouth Roads; killed in the fight when the ship was taken by the Sallee man-of-war; devoured by the wild beast on the coast of Africa? or drowned here, when all the crew perished but thyself? Dost thou ask, What have I done?"

I was struck dumb with these reflections, as one astonished, and had not a word to say, no, not to answer to myself, but rose up pensive and sad, walked back to my retreat, and went up over my wall, as if I had been going to bed. But my thoughts were sadly disturbed, and I had no inclination to sleep; so I sat down in my chair, and lighted my lamp, for it began to be dark. Now, as the apprehension of the return of my distemper terrified me very much, it occurred to my thought that the Brazilians take no physic but their tobacco for almost all distempers; and I had a piece of a roll of tobacco in one of the chests, which was quite cured, and some also that was green, and not quite cured.

I went, directed by Heaven no doubt; for in this chest I found a cure both for soul and body. I opened the chest, and found what I looked for, viz., the tobacco; and as the few books I had saved lay there too, I took out one of the Bibles which I mentioned before, and which to this time I had not found leisure, or so much as inclination, to look into. I say, I took it out, and brought both that and the tobacco with me to the table.

What use to make of the tobacco I knew not, as to my distemper, or whether it was good for it or no; but I tried several experiments with it, as if I was resolved it should hit one way or other. I first took a piece of a leaf, and chewed it in my mouth, which indeed at first almost stupefied my brain, the tobacco being green and strong, and that I had not been much used to it. Then I took some and steeped it an hour or two in some rum, and resolved to take a dose of it when I lay down. And lastly, I burnt some upon a pan of coals, and held my nose close over the smoke of it as long as I could bear it, as well for the heat, as almost for suffocation.

In the interval of this operation, I took up the Bible, and began to read, but my head was too much disturbed with the tobacco to bear reading, at least that time; only having opened the book casually, the first words that occurred to me were these, "Call on Me in the day of trouble, and I will deliver, and thou shalt glorify Me."

It grew now late, and the tobacco had, as I said, dozed my head so much, that I inclined to sleep; so I left my lamp burning in the cave, lest I should want anything in the night, and went to bed. But before I lay down, I did what I never had done in all my life; I kneeled down, and prayed to God to fulfil the promise to me, that if I called upon Him in the day of trouble, He would deliver me. After my broken and imperfect prayer was over, I drank the rum in which I had steeped the tobacco; which was so strong and rank of the tobacco, that indeed I could scarce get it down. Immediately upon this I went to bed. I found presently it flew up in my head violently; but I fell into a sound sleep, and waked no more till, by the sun, it must necessarily be near three o'clock in the afternoon the next day. Nay, to this hour I am partly of the opinion that I slept all the next day and night, and till almost three that day after; for otherwise I knew not how I should lose a day out of my reckoning in the days of the week, as it appeared some years after I had done. For if I had lost it by crossing and recrossing the line, I should have lost more than one day. But certainly I lost a day in my account, and never knew which way.

Be that, however, one way or the other, when I awaked I found myself exceedingly refreshed, and my spirits lively and cheerful. When I got up, I was stronger than I was the day before, and my stomach better, for I was hungry; and, in short, I had no fit the next day, but continued much altered for the better. This was the 29th.

The 30th was my well day, of course, and I went abroad with my gun, but did not care to travel too far. I killed a sea-fowl or two, something like a brand-goose, and brought them home, but was not very forward to eat them; so I eat some more of the turtle's eggs, which were very good. This evening I renewed the medicine, which I had supposed did me good the day before, viz., the tobacco steeped in rum; only I did not take so much as before, nor did I chew any of the leaf, or hold my head over the smoke. However, I was not so well the next day, which was the first of

July,as I hoped I should have been; for I had a little spice of the cold fit, but it was not much.

July 4. – In the morning I took the Bible; and beginning at the New Testament, I began seriously to read it, and imposed upon myself to read awhile every morning and every night, not tying myself to the number of chapters, but as long as my thoughts should engage me.

Now I began to construe the words mentioned above, "Call on Me, and I will deliver you," in a different sense from what I had ever done before; for then I had no notion of anything being called deliverance but my being delivered from the captivity I was in; for though I was indeed at large in the place, yet the island was certainly a prison to me, and that in the worst sense in the world. But now I learned to take it in another sense; now I looked back upon my past life with such horror, and my sins appeared so dreadful, that my soul sought nothing of God but deliverance from the load of guilt that bore down all my comfort.

My condition began now to be, though not less miserable as to my way of living, yet much easier to my mind; and my thoughts being directed, by a constant reading the Scripture, and praying to God, to things of a higher nature, I had a great deal of comfort within, which, till now, I knew nothing of. Also, as my health and strength returned, I bestirred myself to furnish myself with everything that I wanted, and make my way of living as regular as I could.

From the 4th of July to the 14th, I was chiefly employed in walking about with my gun in my hand, a little and a little at a time, as a man that was gathering up his strength after a fit of sickness; for it is hardly to be imagined how low I was, and to what weakness I was reduced. The application which I made use of was perfectly new, and perhaps what had never cured an ague before; neither can I recommend it to any one to practise, by this experiment; and though it did carry off the fit, yet it rather contributed to weakening me; for I had frequent convulsions in my nerves and limbs for some time.

I had been now in this unhappy island above ten months; all possibility of deliverance from this condition seemed to be entirely taken from me; and I firmly believed that no human shape had ever set foot upon that place. Having now secured my habitation, as I thought, fully to my mind, I had a great desire to make a more perfect discovery of the island, and to see what other productions I might find, which I yet knew nothing of.

It was the 15th of July that I began to take a more particular survey of the island itself. I went up the creek first, where, as I hinted, I brought my rafts on shore. I found, after I came about two miles up, that the tide did not flow any higher, and that it was no more than a little brook of running water, and very fresh and good; but this being the dry season, there was hardly any water in some parts of it, at least, not enough to run in any stream, so as it could be perceived.

On the bank of this brook I found many pleasant savannas or meadows, plain, smooth, and covered with grass; and on the rising parts of them, next to the higher grounds, where the water, as might be supposed, never overflowed, I found a great deal of tobacco, green, and growing to a great and very strong stalk. There were divers other plants, which I had no notion of, or understanding about, and might perhaps have virtues of their own which I could not find out.

I searched for the cassava root,which the Indians, in all that climate, make their bread of, but I could find none. I saw large plants of aloes, but did not then understand them. I saw several sugar-canes, but wild, and, for want of cultivation, imperfect. I contented myself with these discoveries for this time, and came back, musing with myself what course I might take to know the virtue and goodness of any of the fruits or plants which I should discover; but could bring it to no conclusion; for, in short, I had made so little observation while I was in the Brazils, that I knew little of the plants in the field, at least very little that might serve me to any purpose now in my distress.

The next day, the 16th, I went up the same way again; and after going something farther than I had gone the day before, I found the brook and the savannas began to cease, and the country became more woody than before. In this part I found different fruits, and particularly I found melons upon the ground in great abundance, and grapes upon the trees. The vines had spread indeed over the trees, and the clusters of grapes were just now in their prime, very ripe and rich. This was a surprising discovery, and I was exceeding glad of them; but I was warned by my experience to eat sparingly of them, remembering that when I was ashore in Barbary the eating of grapes killed several of our Englishmen, who were slaves there, by throwing them into fluxes and fevers. But I found an excellent use for these grapes; and that was, to cure or dry them in the sun, and keep them as dried grapes or raisins are kept, which I thought would be, as indeed they were, as wholesome as agreeable to eat, when no grapes might be to be had.

I spent all that evening there, and went not back to my habitation; which, by the way, was the first night, as I might say, I had lain from home. In the night, I took my first contrivance, and got up into a tree, where I slept well; and the next morning proceeded upon my discovery, travelling near four miles, as I might judge by the length of the valley, keeping still due north, with a ridge of hills on the south and north side of me.

At the end of this march I came to an opening, where the country seemed to descend to the west; and a little spring of fresh water, which issued out of the side of the hill by me, ran the other way, that is, due east; and the country appeared so fresh, so green, so flourishing, everything being in a constant verdure or flourish of spring, that it looked like a planted garden.

I descended a little on the side of that delicious vale, surveying it with a secret kind of pleasure, though mixed with my other afflicting thoughts, to think that this was all my own; that I was king and lord of all this country indefeasibly, and had a right of possession; and, if I could convey it, I might have it in inheritance as completely as any lord of a manor in England. I saw here abundance of cocoa trees,

orange, and lemon, and citron trees; but all wild, and very few bearing any fruit, at least not then. However, the green limes that I gathered were not only pleasant to eat, but very wholesome; and I mixed their juice afterwards with water, which made it very wholesome, and very cool and refreshing.

I found now I had business enough to gather and carry home; and I resolved to lay up a store, as well of grapes as limes and lemons to furnish myself for the wet season, which I knew was approaching.

In order to this, I gathered a great heap of grapes in one place, and a lesser heap in another place, and a great parcel of limes and lemons in another place; and, taking a few of each with me, I travelled homeward; and resolved to come again, and bring a bag or sack, or what I could make, to carry the rest home.

Accordingly, having spent three days in this journey, I came home (so I must now call my tent and my cave); but before I got thither, the grapes were spoiled; the richness of the fruits, and the weight of the juice, having broken them and bruised them, they were good for little or nothing: as to the limes, they were good, but I could bring but a few.

The next day, being the 19th, I went back, having made me two small bags to bring home my harvest; but I was surprised, when, coming to my heap of grapes, which were so rich and fine when I gathered them, I found them all spread about, trod to pieces, and dragged about, some here, some there, and abundance eaten and devoured. By this I concluded there were some wild creatures thereabouts, which had done this; but what they were, I knew not.

However, as I found that there was no laying them up on heaps, and no carrying them away in a sack, but that one way they would be destroyed, and the other way they would be crushed with their own weight, I took another course; for I gathered a large quantity of the grapes, and hung them up upon the out-branches of the trees, that they might cure and dry in the sun; and as for the limes and lemons, I carried as many back as I could well stand under.

When I came home from this journey, I contemplated with great pleasure the fruitfulness of that valley, and the pleasantness of the situation; the security from storms on that side the water and the wood; and concluded that I had pitched upon a place to fix my abode, which was by far the worst part of the country. Upon the whole, I began to consider of removing my habitation, and to look out for a place equally safe as where I now was situate, if possible, in that pleasant fruitful part of the island.

This thought ran long in my head, and I was exceeding fond of it for some time, the pleasantness of the place tempting me; but when I came to a nearer view of it, and to consider that I was now by the seaside, where it was at least possible that something might happen to my advantage, and, by the same ill fate that brought me hither, might bring some other unhappy wretches to the same place; and though it was scarce probable that any such thing should ever happen, yet to enclose myself among the hills and woods in the centre of the island, was to anticipate my bondage, and to render such an affair not only improbable, but impossible; and that therefore I ought not by any means to remove.

However, I was so enamoured of this place, that I spent much of my time there for the whole remaining part of the month of July; and though, upon second thoughts, I resolved, as above, not to remove, yet I built me a little kind of a bower, and surrounded it at a distance with a strong fence, being a double hedge as high as I could reach, well staked, and filled between with brushwood. And here I lay very secure, sometimes two or three nights together, always going over it with a ladder, as before; so that I fancied now I had my country house and my sea-coast house; and this work took me up to the beginning of August.

I had but newly finished my fence, and began to enjoy my labour, but the rains came on, and made me stick close to my first habitation; for though I had made me a tent like the other, with a piece of a sail, and spread it very well, yet I had not the shelter of a hill to keep me from storms, nor a cave behind me to retreat into when the rains were extraordinary.

About the beginning of August, as I said, I had finished my bower, and began to enjoy myself. The 3rd of August, I found the grapes I had hung up were perfectly dried, and indeed were excellent good raisins of the sun; so I began to take them down from the trees. And it was very happy that I did so, for the rains which followed would have spoiled them, and I had lost the best part of my winter food; for I had above two hundred large bunches of them. No sooner had I taken them all down, and carried most of them home to my cave, but it began to rain; and from hence, which was the 14th of August, it rained, more or less, every day till the middle of October, and sometimes so violently, that I could not stir out of my cave for several days.

In this season, I was much surprised with the increase of my family. I had been concerned for the loss of one of my cats, who run away from me, or, as I thought, had been dead, and I heard no more tale or tidings of her, till, to my astonishment, she came home about the end of August with three kittens. But from these three cats I afterwards came to be so pestered with cats, that I was forced to kill them like vermin, or wild beasts, and to drive them from my house as much as possible.

From the 14th of August to the 26th, incessant rain, so that I could not stir, and was now very careful not to be much wet. In this confinement, I began to be straitened for food; but venturing out twice, I one day killed a goat, and the last day, which was the 26th, found a very large tortoise, which was a treat to me, and my food was regulated thus: I eat a bunch of raisins for my breakfast, a piece of the goat's flesh, or of the turtle, for my dinner, broiled; for, to my great misfortune, I had no vessel to boil or stew anything; and two or three of the turtle's eggs for my supper.

During this confinement in my cover by the rain, I worked daily two or three hours at enlarging my cave, and by degrees worked it on towards one side, till I came to the outside of the hill, and made a door, or way out, which came beyond my fence or wall; and so I came in and out this way. But I was not perfectly easy at lying so open; for as I had managed myself before, I was in a perfect enclosure; whereas now, I thought I lay exposed, and open for anything to come in upon me; and yet I could not perceive that there was any living thing to fear, the biggest creature that I had yet seen upon the island being a goat.

Sept. 30. – I was now come to the unhappy anniversary of my landing. I cast up the notches on my post, and found I bad been on shore three hundred and sixty-five days. I kept this day as a solemn fast, setting it apart to religious exercise.

I had all this time observed no Sabbath day, for as at first I had no sense of religion upon my mind, I had, after some time omitted to distinguish the weeks, by making a longer notch than ordinary for the Sabbath day, and so did not really know what any of the days were. But now, having cast up the days, as above, I found I had been there a year, so I divided it into weeks, and set apart every seventh day for a Sabbath; though I found at the end of my account, I had lost a day or two in my reckoning.

A little after this my ink began to fail me, and so I contented myself to use it more sparingly, and to write down only the most remarkable events of my life, without continuing a daily memorandum of other things.

The rainy season and the dry season began now to appear regular to me, and I learned to divide them so as to provide for them accordingly; but I bought all my experience before I had it, and this I am going to relate was one of the most discouraging experiments that I made at all. I have mentioned that I had saved the few ears of barley and rice, which I had so surprisingly found spring up, as I thought, of themselves, and believe there were about thirty stalks of rice, and about twenty of barley; and now I thought it a proper time to sow it after the rains, the sun being in its southern position, going from me.

Accordingly I dug up a piece of ground as well as I could with my wooden spade, and dividing it into two parts, I sowed my grain; but as I was sowing, it casually occurred to my thoughts that I would not sow it all at first, because I did not know when was the proper time for it, so I sowed about two-thirds of the seed, leaving about a handful of each.

It was a great comfort to me afterwards that I did so, for not one grain of that I sowed this time came to anything, for the dry months following, the earth having had no rain after the seed was sown, it had no moisture to assist its growth, and never came up at all till the wet season had come again, and then it grew as if it had been but newly sown.

Finding my first seed did not grow, which I easily imagined was by the drought, I sought for a moister piece of ground to make another trial in, and I dug up a piece of ground near my new bower, and sowed the rest of my seed in February, a little before the vernal equinox. And this having the rainy months of March and April to water it, sprung up very pleasantly, and yielded a very good crop; but having part of the seed left only, and not daring to sow all that I had, I had but a small quantity at last, my whole crop not amounting to above half a peck of each kind. But by this experiment I was made master of my business and knew exactly when the proper season was to sow and that I might expect two seed-times and two harvests every year.

While this corn was growing, I made a little discovery, which was of use to me afterwards. As soon as the rains were over, and the weather began to settle, which was about the month of November, I made a visit up the country to my bower, where, though I had not been some months, yet I found all things just as I left them. The circle or double hedge that I had made was not only firm and entire, but the stakes which I had cut out of some trees that grew therabouts were all shot out, and grown with long branches, as much as a willow-tree usually shoots the first year after lopping its head. I could not tell what tree to call it that these stakes were cut from. I was surprised, and yet very well pleased to see the young trees grow, and I pruned them, and led them up to grow as much alike as I could. And it is scarce credible how beautiful a figure they grew into in three years; so that though the hedge made a circle of about twenty-five yards in diameter, yet the trees, for such I might now call them, soon covered it, and it was a complete shade, sufficient to lodge under all the dry season.

This made me resolve to cut some more stakes, and make me a hedge like this, in a semicircle round my wall (I mean that of my first dwelling), which I did; and placing the trees or stakes in a double row, at about eight yards' distance from my first fence, they grew presently, and were at first a fine cover to my habitation, and afterward served for a defence also, as I shall observe in its order.

I found now that the seasons of the year might generally be divided, not into summer and winter, as in Europe, but into the rainy seasons and the dry seasons. After I had found by experience the ill consequence of being abroad in the rain, I took care to furnish myself with provisions beforehand, that I might not be obliged to go out; and I sat within doors as much as possible during the wet months.

In this time I found much employment, and very suitable also to the time, for I found great occasion of many things which I had no way to furnish myself with but by hard labour and constant application; particularly, I tried many ways to make myself a basket; but all the twigs I could get for the purpose proved so brittle, that they would do nothing. It proved of excellent advantage to me now, that when I was a boy I used to take great delight in standing at a basket-maker's in the town where my father lived, to see them make their wicker-ware; and being, as boys usually are, very officious to help, and a great observer of the manner how they worked those things, and sometimes lending a hand, I had by this means full knowledge of the methods of it, that I wanted nothing but the materials; when it came into my mind that the twigs of that tree from whence I cut my stakes that grew might possibly be as tough as the sallows, and willows, and osiers in England, and I resolved to try.

Accordingly, the next day, I went to my country house, as I called it; and cutting some of the smaller twigs, I found them to my purpose as much as I could desire; whereupon I came the next time prepared with a hatchet to cut down a quantity, which I soon found, for there was great plenty of them. These I set up to dry within my circle or hedge, and when they were fit for use, I carried them to my cave; and here during the next season I employed myself in making, as well as I could, a great many baskets, both to carry earth, or to carry or lay up anything as I had occasion. And though I did not finish them very handsomely, yet I made them sufficiently serviceable for my purpose. And thus, afterwards, I took care never to be without them; and as my wicker-ware decayed, I made more, especially I made strong deep baskets to place my corn in, instead of sacks, when I should come to have any quantity of it.

Having mastered this difficulty, and employed a world of time about it, I bestirred myself to see, if possible, how to supply two wants. I had no vessels to hold anything that was liquid, except two runlets, which were almost full of rum, and some glass bottles, some of the common size, and others which were case-bottles square, for the holding of waters, spirits, &c. I had not so much as a pot to boil anything, except a great kettle, which I saved out of the ship, and which was too big for such use as I desired it, viz., to make broth, and stew a bit of meat by itself. The second thing I would fain have had was a tobacco-pipe; but it was impossible to me to make one. However, I found a contrivance for that, too, at last.

I employed myself in planting my second rows of stakes or piles and in this wicker-working all the summer or dry season, when another business took me up more time than it could be imagined I could spare.

I mentioned before that I had a great mind to see the whole island, and that I had travelled up the brook, and so on to where I built my bower, and where I had an opening quite to the sea, on the other side of the island. I now resolved to travel quite across to the seashore on that side; so taking my gun, a hatchet, and my dog, and a larger quantity of powder and shot than usual, with two biscuit-cakes and a great bunch of raisins in my pouch for my store, I began my journey. When I had passed the vale where my bower stood, as above, I came within view of the sea to the west; and it being a very clear day, I fairly descried land, whether an island or a continent I could not tell; but it lay very high, extending from the west to the W.S.W. at a very great distance; by my guess it could not be less than fifteen or twenty leagues off.

I saw abundance of parrots, and fain I would have caught one, if possible, to have kept it to be tame, and taught it to speak to me. I did, after some painstaking, catch a young parrot, for I knocked it down with a stick, and having recovered it, I brought it home; but it was some years before I could make him speak. However, at last I taught him to call me by my name very familiarly. But the accident that followed, though it be a trifle, will be very diverting in its place.

I was exceedingly diverted with this journey. I found in the low grounds hares, as I thought them to be, and foxes; but they differed greatly from all the other kinds I had met with, nor could I satisfy myself to eat them, though I killed several. But I had no need to be venturous, for I had no want of food, and of that which was very good too; especially these three sorts, viz., goats, pigeons, and turtle, or tortoise; which, added to my grapes, Leadenhall Market could not have furnished a table better than I, in proportion to the company. And though my case was deplorable enough, yet I had great cause for thankfulness, and that I was not driven to any extremities for food, but rather plenty, even to dainties.

I never travelled in this journey above two miles outright in a day, or thereabouts; but I took so many turns and returns, to see what discoveries I could make, that I came weary enough to the place where I resolved to sit down for all night; and then I either reposed myself in a tree, or surrounded myself with a row of stakes, set upright in the ground, either from one tree to another, or so as no wild creature could come at me without waking me.

As soon as I came to the seashore, I was surprised to see that I had taken up my lot on the worst side of the island, for here indeed the shore was covered with innumerable turtles; whereas, on the other side, I had found but three in a year and a half. Here was also an infinite number of fowls of many kinds, some which I had seen, and some which I had not seen of before, and many of them very good meat, but such as I knew not the names of except those called penguins.

I could have shot as many as I pleased, but was very sparing of my powder and shot, and therefore had more mind to kill a she-goat, if I could, which I could better feed on; and though there were many goats here, more than on my side the island, yet it was with much more difficulty that I could come near them, the country being flat and even, and they saw me much sooner than when I was on the hill.

I confess this side of the country was much pleasanter than mine; but yet I had not the least inclination to remove, for as I was fixed in my habitation, it became natural to me, and I seemed all the while I was here to be as it were upon a journey, and from home. However, I travelled along the shore of the sea towards the east, I suppose about twelve miles, and then setting up a great pole upon the shore for a mark, I concluded I would go home again; and that the next journey I took should be on the other side of the island, east from my dwelling, and so round till I came to my post again; of which in its place.

I took another way to come back than that I went, thinking I could easily keep all the island so much in my view, that I could not miss finding my first dwelling by viewing the country. But I found myself mistaken. I wandered about very uncomfortably, and at last was obliged to find out the seaside, look for my post, and come back the same way I went; and then by easy journeys I turned homeward, the weather being exceeding hot, and my gun, ammunition, hatchet, and other things very heavy.

In this journey my dog surprised a young kid, and seized upon it, and I running in to take hold of it, caught it, and saved it alive from the dog. I had a great mind to bring it home if I could, for I had often been musing whether it might not be possible to get a kid or two, and so raise a breed of tame goats, which might supply me when my powder and shot should be all spent.

I made a collar to this little creature, and with a string, which I made of some rope-yarn, which I always carried about me, I led him along, though with some difficulty, till I came to my bower, and there I enclosed him and left him, for I was very impatient to be at home, from whence I had been absent above a month.

I cannot express what a satisfaction it was to me to come into my old hutch, and lie down in my hammock-bed. This little wandering journey, without settled place of abode, had been so unpleasant to me, that my own house, as I called it to myself, was a perfect settlement to me compared to that; and it rendered everything about me so comfortable, that I resolved I would never go a great way from it again, while it should be my lot to stay on the island.

I reposed myself here a week, to rest and regale myself after my long journey; during which most of the time was taken up in the weighty affair of making a cage for my Poll, who began now to be a mere domestic, and to be mighty well acquainted with me. Then I began to think of the poor kid which I had penned in within my little circle, and resolved to go and fetch it home, or give it some food. Accordingly I went, and found it where I left it, for indeed it could not get out, but almost starved for want of food. I went and cut boughs of trees, and branches of such shrubs as I could find, and threw it over, and having fed it, I tied it as I did before, to lead it away; but it was so tame with being hungry, that I had no need to have tied it, for it followed me like a dog. And as I continually fed it, the creature became so loving, so gentle, and so fond, that it became from that time one of my domestics also, and would never leave me afterwards.

I was king and lord of all this country (page 281)

I victualled my ship for the voyage (page 301)

The rainy season of the autumnal equinox was now come, and I kept the 30th of September in the same solemn manner as before, being the anniversary of my landing on the island, having now been there two years, and no more prospect of being delivered than the first day I came there. I spent the whole day in humble and thankful acknowledgments of the many wonderful mercies which my solitary condition was attended with, and without which it might have been infinitely more miserable.

It was now that I began sensibly to feel how much more happy this life I now led was, with all its miserable circumstances, than the wicked, cursed, abominable life I led all the past part of my days. And now I changed both my sorrows and my joys; my very desires altered, my affections changed their gusts, and my delights were perfectly new from what they were at my first coming, or indeed for the two years past.

Thus, and in this disposition of mind, I began my third year; and though I have not given the reader the trouble of so particular account of my works this year as the first, yet in general it may be observed, that I was very seldom idle, but having regularly divided my time, according to the several daily employments that were before me, such as, first, my duty to God, and the reading the Scriptures, which I constantly set apart some time for, thrice every day; secondly, the going abroad with my gun for food, which generally took me up three hours in every morning, when it did not rain; thirdly, the ordering, curing, preserving, and cooking what I had killed or catched for my supply; these took up great part of the day; also, it is to be considered that the middle of the day, when the sun was in the zenith, the violence of the heat was too great to stir out; so that about four hours in the evening was all the time I could be supposed to work in, with this exception, that sometimes I changed my hours of hunting and working, and went to work in the morning, and abroad with my gun in the afternoon.

To this short time allowed for labour, I desire may be added the exceeding laboriousness of my work; the many hours which, for want of tools, want of help, and want of skill, everything I did took up out of my time. For example, I was full two and forty days making me a board for a long shelf, which I wanted in my cave; whereas two sawyers, with their tools and a sawpit, would have cut six of them out of the same tree in half a day.

My case was this: it was to be a large tree which was to be cut down, because my board was to be a broad one. This tree I was three days a-cutting down, and two more cutting off the boughs, and reducing it to a log, or piece of timber. With inexpressible hacking and hewing, I reduced both the sides of it into chips till it began to be light enough to move; then I turned it, and made one side of it smooth and flat as a board from end to end; then turning that side downward, cut the other side, till I brought the plank to be about three inches thick, and smooth on both sides. Any one may judge the labour of my hands in such a piece of work; but labour and patience carried me through that, and many other things. I only observe this in particular, to show the reason why so much of my time went away with so little work, viz., that what might be a little to be done with help and tools, was a vast labour, and required a prodigious time to do alone, and by hand. But notwithstanding this, with patience and labour, I went through many things, and, indeed, everything that my circumstances made necessary to me to do, as will appear by what follows.

I was now, in the months of November and December, expecting my crop of barley and rice. The ground I had manured or dug up for them was not great; for as I observed, my seed of each was not above the quantity of half a peck; for I had lost one whole crop by sowing in the dry season. But now my crop promised very well, when on a sudden I found I was in danger of losing it all again by enemies of several sorts, which it was scarce possible to keep from it; as, first the goats and wild creatures which I called hares, who, tasting the sweetness of the blade, lay in it night and day, as soon as it came up, and eat it so close, that it could get no time to shoot up into stalk.

This I saw no remedy for but by making an enclosure about it with a hedge, which I did with a great deal of toil, and the more, because it required speed. However, as my arable land was but small, suited to my crop, I got it totally well fenced in about three weeks' time, and shooting some of the creatures in the daytime, I set my dog to guard it in the night, tying him up to a stake at the gate, where he would stand and bark all night long; so in a little time the enemies forsook the place, and the corn grew very strong and well, and began to ripen apace.

But as the beasts ruined me before while my corn was in the blade, so the birds were as likely to ruin me now when it was in the ear; for going along by the place to see how it throve, I saw my little crop surrounded with fowls, of I know not how many sorts, who stood, as it were, watching till I should be gone. I immediately let fly among them, for I always had my gun with me. I had no sooner shot, but there rose up a little cloud of fowls, which I had not seen at all, from among the corn itself.

This touched me sensibly, for I foresaw that in a few days they would devour all my hopes, that I should be starved, and never be able to raise a crop at all, and what to do I could not tell. However, I resolved not to lose my corn, if possible, though I should watch it night and day. In the first place, I went among it to see what damage was already done, and found they had spoiled a good deal of it; but that as it was yet too green for them, the loss was not so great but that the remainder was like to be a good crop if it could be saved.

I stayed by it to load my gun, and then coming away, I could easily see the thieves sitting upon all the trees about me, as if they only waited till I was gone away. And the event proved it to be so; for as I walked off, as if I was gone, I was no sooner out of their sight but they dropped down, one by one, into the corn again. I was so provoked, that I could not have patience to stay till more came on, knowing that every grain that they eat now was, as it might be said, a peck-loaf to me in the consequence; but coming up to the hedge, I fired again, and killed three of them.

This was what I wished for; so I took them up, and served them as we serve notorious thieves in England, viz., hanged them in chains, for a terror to others. It is impossible to imagine almost that this should have such an effect as it had, for the fowls would not only not come at the corn, but, in short, they forsook all that part of the island, and I could never see a bird near the place as long as my scarecrows hung there.

This I was very glad of, you may be sure; and about the latter end of December, which was our second harvest of the year, I reaped my crop.

I was sadly put to it for a scythe or a sickle to cut it down, and all I could do was to make one as well as I could out of one of the broadswords, or cutlasses, which I saved among the arms out of the ship. However, as my first crop was but small, I had no great difficulty to cut it down; in short, I reaped it my way; for I cut nothing off but the ears, and carried it away in a great basket which I had made, and so rubbed it out with my hands; and at the end of all my harvesting, I found that out of my half peck of seed I had near two bushels of rice, and above two bushels and a half of barley, that is to say, by my guess, for I had no measure at that time.

However, this was a great encouragement to me, and I foresaw that, in time, it would please God to supply me with bread. And yet here I was perplexed again, for I neither knew how to grind or make meal of my corn, or indeed how to clean it and part it; nor, if made into meal, how to make bread of it, and if how to make it, yet I knew not how to bake it. These things being added to my desire of having a good quantity for store and to secure a constant supply, I resolved not to taste any of this crop, but to preserve it all for seed against the next season, and, in the meantime, to employ all my study and hours of working to accomplish this great work of providing myself with corn and bread.

Within doors, that is, when it rained, and I could not go out, I found employment on the following occasions; always observing, that all the while I was at work, I diverted myself with talking to my parrot, and teaching him to speak, and I quickly learned him to know his own name, and at last to speak it out pretty loud, "Poll," which was the first word I ever heard spoken in the island by any mouth but my own. This, therefore, was not my work, but an assistant to my work; for now, as I said, I had a great employment upon my hands, as follows, viz., I had long studied, by some means or other, to make myself some earthen vessels, which indeed I wanted sorely, but knew not where to come at them. However, considering the heat of the climate, I did not doubt but if I could find out any such clay, I might botch up some such pot as might, being dried in the sun, be hard enough and strong enough to bear handling, and to hold anything that was dry, and required to be kept so; and as this was necessary in the preparing corn, meal, &c., which was the thing I was upon, I resolved to make some as large as I could, and fit only to stand like jars, to hold what should be put into them.

It would make the reader pity me, or rather laugh at me, to tell how many awkward ways I took to raise this paste; what odd, misshapen, ugly things I made; how many of them fell in, and how many fell out, the clay not being stiff enough to bear its own weight; how many cracked by the over-violent heat of the sun, being set out too hastily; and how many fell in pieces with only removing, as well before as after they were dried; and, in a word, how, after having laboured hard to find the clay, to dig it, to temper it, to bring it home, and work it, I could not make above two large earthern ugly things (I cannot call them jars) in about two months' labour.

However, as the sun baked these two very dry and hard, I lifted them very gently up, and set them down again in two great wicker baskets, which I had made on purpose for them that they might not break; and as between the pot and the basket there was a little room to spare, I stuffed it full of the rice and barley straw, and these two pots being to stand always dry, I thought would hold my dry corn, and perhaps the meal, when the corn was bruised.

Though I miscarried so much in my design for large pots, yet I made several smaller things with better success; such as little round pots, flat dishes, pitchers, and pipkins, and any things my hand turned to; and the heat of the sun baked them strangely hard. But all this would not answer my end, which was to get an earthen pot to hold what was liquid, and bear the fire, which none of these could do. It happened after some time, making a pretty large fire for cooking my meat, when I went to put it out after I had done with it, I found a broken piece of one of my earthenware vessels in the fire, burnt as hard as a stone, and red as a tile. I was agreeably surprised to see it, and said to myself, that certainly they might be made to burn whole, if they would burn broken.

This set me to studying how to order my fire, so as to make it burn me some pots. I had no notion of a kiln, such as the potters burn in, or of glazing them with lead, though I had some lead to do it with; but I placed three large pipkins, and two or three pots in a pile, one upon another, and placed my firewood all round it, with a great heap of embers under them. I plied the fire with fresh fuel round the outside, and upon the top, till I saw the pots in the inside red-hot quite through, and observed that they did not crack at all. When I saw them clear red, I let them stand in that heat about five or six hours, till I found one of them, though it did not crack, did melt or run, for the sand which was mixed with the clay melted by the violence of the heat, and would have run into glass, if I had gone on; so I slacked my fire gradually till the pots began to abate of the red colour; and watching them all night, that I might not let the fire abate too fast, in the morning I had three very good, I will not say handsome, pipkins, and two other earthen pots, as hard burnt as could be desired, and one of them perfectly glazed with the running of the sand.

After this experiment, I need not say that I wanted no sort of earthenware for my use; but I must needs say, as to the shapes of them, they were very indifferent, as anyone may suppose, when I had no way of making them but as the children make dirt pies, or as a woman would make pies that never learned to raise paste.

No joy at a thing of so mean a nature was ever equal to mine, when I found I had made an earthen pot that would bear the fire; and I had hardly patience to stay till they were cold, before I set one upon the fire again, with some water in it, to boil me some meat, which it did admirably well; and with a piece of a kid I made some very good broth, though I wanted oatmeal and several other ingredients requisite to make it so good as I would have had it been.

My next concern was to get me a stone mortar to stamp or beat some corn in; for as to the mill, there was no thought at arriving to that perfection of art with one pair of hands. I spent many a day to find out a great stone big enough to cut hollow, and make fit for a mortar, and could find none at all, except what was in the solid rock, and which I had no way to dig or cut out; nor indeed were the rocks in the island of hardness sufficient, but were all of a sandy crumbling stone, which neither would bear the weight of a heavy pestle, or would break the corn without filling it with sand. So, after a great deal of time lost in searching for a stone, I gave it over, and resolved to look out for a great block of hard wood, which I found indeed much easier; and getting one as big as I had strength to stir, I rounded it, and formed it in the outside with my axe and hatchet, and then, with the help of fire, and infinite labour, made a hollow place in it, as the Indians in Brazil make their canoes. After this, I made a great heavy pestle, or beater, of the wood called the iron-wood; and this I prepared and laid by against I had my next crop of corn, when I proposed to myself to grind, or rather pound, my corn into meal, to make my bread.

My next difficulty was to make a sieve, or search, to dress my meal, and to part it from the bran and the husk, without which I did not see it possible I could have any bread. This was a most difficult thing, so much as but to think on, for to be sure I had nothing like the necessary thing to make it; I mean fine thin canvas or stuff; to search the meal through. And here I was at a full stop for many months, nor did I really know what to do; linen I had none left, but what was mere rags; I had goats'-hair, but neither knew I how to weave it or spin it; and had I known how, here was no tools to work it with. All the remedy that I found for this was, that at last I did remember I had, among the seamen's clothes which were saved out of the ship, some neckcloths of calico or muslin; and with some pieces of these I made three small sieves, but proper enough for the work; and thus I made shift for some years. How I did afterwards, I shall show in its place.

The baking part was the next thing to be considered, and how I should make bread when I came to have corn; for, first, I had no yeast. As to that part, as there was no supplying the want, so I did not concern myself much about it; but for an oven I was indeed in great pain. At length I found out an experiment for that also, which was this: I made some earthen vessels very broad, but not deep, that is to say, about two feet diameter, and not above nine inches deep; these I burned in the fire, as I had done the other, and laid them by; and when I wanted to bake, I made a great fire upon my hearth, which I had paved with some square tiles, of my own making and burning also; but I should not call them square.

When the firewood was burned pretty much into embers, or live coals, I drew them forward upon this hearth, so as to cover it all over, and there I let them lie till the hearth was very hot; then sweeping away all the embers, I set down my loaf, or loaves, and whelming down the earthen pot upon them, drew the embers all round the outside of the pot, to keep in and add to the heat. And thus, as well as in the best oven in the world, I baked my barley-loaves, and became, in little time, a mere pastry-cook into the bargain; for I made myself several cakes of the rice, and puddings; indeed I made no pies, neither had I anything to put into them, supposing I had, except the flesh either of fowls or goats.

It need not be wondered at, if all these things took me up most part of the third year of my abode here; for it is to be observed, that in the intervals of these things I had my new harvest and husbandry to manage; for I reaped my corn in its season, and carried it home as well as I could, and laid it up in the ear, in my large baskets, till I had time to rub it out, for I had no floor to thrash it on, or instrument to thrash it with.

And now, indeed, my stock of corn increasing, I really wanted to build my barns bigger. I wanted a place to lay it up in, for the increase of the corn now yielded me so much, that I had of the barley about twenty bushels, and of the rice as much, or more, insomuch that now I resolved to begin to use it freely; for my bread had been quite gone a great while; also, I resolved to see what quantity would be sufficient for me a whole year, and to sow but once a year.

Upon the whole, I found that the forty bushels of barley and rice was much more than I could consume in a year; so I resolved to sow just the same quantity every year that I sowed the last, in hopes that such a quantity would fully provide me with bread, &c.

All the while these things were doing, you may be sure my thoughts run many times upon the prospect of land which I had seen from the other side of the island, and I was not without secret wishes that I were on shore there, fancying the seeing the mainland, and in an inhabited country, I might find some way or other to convey myself farther, and perhaps at last find some means of escape.

But all this while I made no allowance for the dangers of such a condition, and how I might fall into the hands of savages, and perhaps such as I might have reason to think far worse than the lions and tigers of Africa; that if I once came into their power, I should run a hazard more than a thousand to one of being killed, and perhaps of being eaten; for I had heard that the people of the Caribbean coasts were cannibals, or man-eaters, and I knew by the latitude that I could not be far off from that shore. That suppose they were not cannibals, yet that they might kill me, as many Europeans who had fallen into their hands had been served, even when they had been ten or twenty together, much more I, that was but one, and could make little or no defence; all these things, I say, which I ought to have considered well of, and did cast up in my thoughts afterwards, yet took up none of my apprehensions at first, but my head ran mightily upon the thought of getting over to the shore.

Now I wished for my boy Xury, and the long-boat with the shoulder-of-mutton sail, with which I sailed above a thousand miles on the coast of Africa; but this was in vain. Then I thought I would go and look at our ship's boat, which, as I have said, was blown up upon the shore a great way, in the storm, when we were first cast away. She lay almost where she did at first, but not quite; and was turned, by the force of the waves and the winds, almost bottom upward, against a high ridge of beachy rough sand, but no water about her, as before.

If I had had hands to have refitted her, and to have launched her into the water, the boat would have done well enough, and I might have gone back into the Brazils with her easily enough; but I might have foreseen that I could no more turn her and set her upright upon her bottom, than I could remove the island. However, I went to the woods, and cut levers and rollers, and brought them to the boat, resolved to try what I could do; suggesting to myself that if I could but turn her down, I might easily repair the damage she had received, and she would be a very good boat, and I might go to sea in her very easily.

I spared no pains, indeed, in this piece of fruitless toil, and spent, I think, three or four weeks about it. At last finding it impossible to heave it up with my little strength, I fell to digging away the sand, to undermine it, and so to make it fall down, setting pieces of wood to thrust and guide it right in the fall. But when I had done this, I was unable to stir it up again, or to get under it, much less to move it forward towards the water; so I was forced to give it over. And yet, though I gave over the hopes of the boat, my desire to venture over for the main increased, rather than decreased, as the means for it seemed impossible.

This at length put me upon thinking whether it was not possible to make myself a canoe, or *periagua,* such as the natives of those climates make, even without tools, or, as I might say, without hands, viz., of the trunk of a great tree. This I not only thought possible, but easy, and pleased myself extremely with the thoughts of making it, and with my having much more convenience for it than any of the negroes or Indians; but not at all considering the particular inconveniences which I lay under more than the Indians did, viz., want of hands to move it, when it was made, into the water, a difficulty much harder for me to surmount than all the consequences of want of tools could be to them. For what was it to me, that when I had chosen a vast tree in the woods, I might with much trouble cut it down, if, after I might be able with my tools to hew and dub the outside into the proper shape of a boat, and burn or cut out the inside to make it hollow, so to make a boat of it; if; after all this, I must leave it just there where I found it, and was not able to launch it into the water?

One would have thought I could not have had the least reflection upon my mind of my circumstance while I was making this boat, but I should have immediately thought how I should get it into the sea; but my thoughts were so intent upon my voyage over the sea in it, that I never once considered how I should get it off of the land; and it was really, in its own nature, more easy for me to guide it over forty-five miles of sea, than about forty-five fathoms of land, where it lay, to set it afloat in the water.

I went to work upon this boat the most like a fool that ever man did who had any of his senses awake. I pleased myself with the design, without determining whether

I was ever able to undertake it. Not but that the difficulty of launching my boat came often into my head; but I put a stop to my own inquiries into it, by this foolish answer which I gave myself; "Let's first make it; I'll warrant I'll find some way or other to get it along when 'tis done."

This was a most preposterous method; but the eagerness of my fancy prevailed, and to work I went. I felled a cedar tree: I question much whether Solomon ever had such a one for the building of the Temple at Jerusalem. It was five feet ten inches diameter at the lower part next the stump, and four feet eleven inches diameter at the end of twenty-two feet, after which it lessened for a while, and then parted into branches. It was not without infinite labour that I felled this tree. I was twenty days hacking and hewing at it at the bottom; I was fourteen more getting the branches and limbs, and the vast spreading head of it cut off, which I hacked and hewed through with axe and hatchet, and inexpressible labour. After this, it cost me a month to shape it and dub it to a proportion, and to something like the bottom of a boat, that it might swim upright as it ought to do. It cost me near three months more to clear the inside, and work it so as to make an exact boat of it. This I did, indeed, without fire, by mere mallet and chisel, and by the dint of hard labour, till I had brought it to be a very handsome *periagua,* and big enough to have carried six and twenty men, and consequently big enough to have carried me and all my cargo.

When I had gone through this work, I was extremely delighted with it. The boat was really much bigger than I ever saw a canoe or *periagua*, that was made of one tree, in my life. Many a weary stroke it had cost, you may be sure; and there remained nothing but to get it into the water; and had I gotten it into the water, I make no question but I should have begun the maddest voyage, and the most unlikely to be performed, that ever was undertaken.

But all my devices to get it into the water failed me, though they cost me infinite labour too. It lay about one hundred yards from the water, and not more; but the first inconvenience was, it was uphill towards the creek. Well, to take away this discouragement, I resolved to dig into the surface of the earth, and so make a declivity. This I began, and it cost me a prodigious deal of pains; but who grudges pains, that have their deliverance in view? But when this was worked through, and this difficulty managed, it was still much at one, for I could no more stir the canoe than I could the other boat.

Then I measured the distance of ground, and resolved to cut a dock or canal, to bring the water up to the canoe, seeing I could not bring the canoe down to the water. Well, I began this work; and when I began to enter into it, and calculate how deep it was to be dug, how broad, how the stuff to be thrown out, I found that by the number of hands I had, being none but my own, it must have been ten or twelve years before I should have gone through with it; for the shore lay high, so that at the upper end it must have been at least twenty feet deep; so at length, though with great reluctancy, I gave this attempt over also.

This grieved me heartily; and now I saw, though too late, the folly of beginning a work before we count the cost, and before we judge rightly of our own strength to go through with it.

In the middle of this work I finished my fourth year in this place, and kept my anniversary with the same devotion, and with as much comfort as ever before; for, by a constant study and serious application of the Word of God, and by the assistance of His grace, I gained a different knowledge from what I had before. I entertained different notions of things. I looked now upon the world as a thing remote, which I had nothing to do with, no expectation from, and, indeed, no desires about. In a word, I had nothing indeed to do with it, nor was ever like to have; so I thought it looked, as we may perhaps look upon it hereafter, viz., as a place I had lived in, but was come out of it; and well might I say, as father Abraham to Dives, "Between me and thee is a great gulf fixed."

I had now brought my state of life to be much easier in itself than it was at first, and much easier to my mind, as well as to my body. I frequently sat down to my meat with thankfulness, and admired the hand of God's providence, which had thus spread my table in the wilderness. I learned to look more upon the bright side of my condition, and less upon the dark side, and to consider what I enjoyed, rather than what I wanted; and this gave me sometimes such secret comforts, that I cannot express them; and which I take notice of here, to put those discontented people in mind of it, who cannot enjoy comfortably what God has given them, because they see and covet something that He has not given them. All our discontents about what we want, appeared to me to spring from the want of thankfulness for what we have.

I spent whole hours, I may say whole days, in representing to myself, in the most lively colours, how I must have acted if I had got nothing out of the ship. How I could not have so much as got any food, except fish and turtles; and that as it was long before I found any of them, I must have perished first; that I should have lived, if I had not perished, like a mere savage; that if I had killed a goat or a fowl, by any contrivance, I had no way to flay or open them, or part the flesh from the skin and the bowels, or to cut it up; but must gnaw it with my teeth, and pull it with my claws, like a beast.

These reflections made me very sensible of the goodness of Providence to me, and very thankful for my present condition, with all its hardships and misfortunes.

In a word, as my life was a life of sorrow one way, so it was a life of mercy another; and I wanted nothing to make it a life of comfort, but to be able to make my sense of God's goodness to me, and care over me in this condition, be my daily consolation; and after I did make a just improvement of these things, I went away, and was no more sad.

I had now been here so long, that many things which I brought on shore for my help were either quite gone, or very much wasted, and near spent. My ink, as I observed, had been gone for some time, all but a very little, which I eked out with water, a little and a little, till it was so pale it scarce left any appearance of black upon the paper. As long as it lasted, I made use of it to minute down the days of the month on which any remarkable thing happened to me. And, first, by casting up times past, I remember that there was a strange concurrence of days in the various providences which befell me, and which, if I had been superstitiously inclined to observe days as fatal or fortunate, I might have had reason to have looked upon with a great deal of curiosity.

First, I had observed that the same day that I broke away from my father and my friends, and ran away to Hull, in order to go to sea, the same day afterwards I was taken by the Sallee man-of-war, and made a slave.

The same day of the year that I escaped out of the wreck of that ship in Yarmouth Roads, that same day-year afterwards I made my escape from Sallee in the boat.

The same day of the year I was born on, viz., the 30th of September, that same day I had my life so miraculously saved twenty-six years after, when I was cast on shore in this island; so that my wicked life and my solitary life began both on a day.

The next thing to my ink's being wasted, was that of my bread; I mean the biscuit, which I brought out of the ship. This I had husbanded to the last degree, allowing myself but one cake of bread a day for above a year; and yet I was quite without bread for near a year before I got any corn of my own; and great reason I had to be thankful that I had any at all, the getting it being, as has been already observed, next to miraculous.

My clothes began to decay, too, mightily. As to linen, I had none a good while, except some chequered shirts which I found in the chests of the other seamen, and which I carefully preserved, because many times I could bear no other clothes on but a shirt; and it was a very great help to me that I had, among all the men's clothes of the ship, almost three dozen of shirts. There were also several thick watch-coats of the seamen's which were left indeed, but they were too hot to wear; and though it is true that the weather was so violent hot that there was no need of clothes, yet I could not go quite naked, no, though I had been inclined to it, which I was not, though I was all alone.

The reason why I could not go quite naked was, I could not bear the heat of the sun so well when quite naked as with some clothes on; nay, the very heat frequently blistered my skin; whereas, with a shirt on, the air itself made some motion, and whistling under that shirt, was twofold cooler than without it. No more could I ever bring myself to go out in the heat of the sun without a cap or a hat. The heat of the sun beating with such violence, as it does in that place, would give me the headache presently, by darting so directly on my head, without a cap or hat on, so that I could not bear it; whereas, if I put on my hat, it would presently go away.

Upon those views, I began to consider about putting the few rags I had, which I called clothes, into some order. I had worn out all the waistcoats I had, and my business was now to try if I could not make jackets out of the great watch-coats which I had by me, and with such other materials as I had; so I set to work a-tailoring, or rather, indeed, a-botching, for I made most piteous work of it. However, I made shift to make two or three new waistcoats, which I hoped would serve me a great while. As for breeches or drawers, I made but a very sorry shift indeed till afterward.

I have mentioned that I saved the skins of all the creatures that I killed, I mean

four-footed ones, and I had hung them up stretched out with sticks in the sun, by which means some of them were so dry and hard that they were fit for little, but others it seems were very useful. The first thing I made of these was a great cap for my head, with the hair on the outside, to shoot off the rain; and this I performed so well, that after this I made me a suit of clothes wholly of these skins, that is to say, a waistcoat, and breeches open at knees, and both loose, for they were rather wanting to keep me cool than to keep me warm. I must not omit to acknowledge that they were wretchedly made; for if I was a bad carpenter, I was a worse tailor. However, they were such as I made very good shift with; and when I was abroad, if it happened to rain, the hair of my waistcoat and cap being outermost, I was kept very dry.

After this I spent a great deal of time and pains to make me an umbrella. I was indeed in great want of one, and had a great mind to make one. I had seen them made in the Brazils, where they are very useful in the great heats, which are there; and I felt the heats every jot as great here, and greater too, being nearer the equinox. Besides, as I was obliged to be much abroad, it was a most useful thing to me, as well for the rains as the heats. I took a world of pains at it, and was a great while before I could make anything likely to hold: nay, after I thought I had hit the way, I spoiled two or three before I made one to my mind; but at last I made one that answered indifferently well. The main difficulty I found was to make it to let down. I could make it to spread; but if it did not let down too, and draw in, it was not portable for me any way but just over my head, which would not do. However, at last, as I said, I made one to answer, and covered it with skins, the hair upwards, so that it cast off the rains like a penthouse, and kept off the sun so effectually, that I could walk out in the hottest of the weather with greater advantage than I could before in the coolest; and when I had no need of it, could close it, and carry it under my arm.

Thus I lived mighty comfortably, my mind being entirely composed by resigning to the will of God, and throwing myself wholly upon the disposal of His providence.

I cannot say that after this, forty-five years, any extraordinary thing happened to me; but I lived on in the same course, in the same posture and place, just as before. The chief things I was employed in, besides my yearly labour of planting my barley and rice, and curing my raisins, of both which I always kept up just enough to have sufficient stock of one year's provisions beforehand – I say, besides this yearly labour, and my daily labour of going out with my gun, I had one labour, to make me a canoe, which at last I finished; so that by digging a canal to it of six feet wide, and four feet deep, I brought it into the creek, almost half a mile. As for the first, which was so vastly big, as I made it without considering beforehand, as I ought to do, how I should be able to launch it; so, never being able to bring it to the water, or bring the water to it, I was obliged to let it lie where it was, as a memorandum to teach me to be wiser next time. Indeed, the next time, though I could not get a tree proper for it, and in a place where I could not get the water to it at any less distance than, as I have said, near half a mile, yet as I saw it was practicable at last, I never gave it over; and though I was near two years about it, yet I never grudged my labour, in hopes of having a boat to go off to sea at last.

However, though my little *periagua* was finished, yet the size of it was not at all answerable to the design which I had in view when I made the first; I mean, of venturing over to the *terra firma,* where it was above forty miles broad. Accordingly, the smallness of my boat assisted to put an end to that design, and now I thought no more of it. But as I had a boat, my next design was to make a tour round the island; for as I had been on the other side in one place, crossing, as I have already described it, over the land, so the discoveries I made in that little journey made me very eager to see other parts of the coast; and now I had a boat, I thought of nothing but sailing round the island.

For this purpose, that I might do everything with discretion and consideration, I fitted up a little mast to my boat, and made a sail to it out of some of the pieces of the ship's sail, which lay in store, and of which I had a great stock by me.

Having fitted my mast and sail, and tried the boat, I found she would sail very well. Then I made little lockers, or boxes, at either end of my boat, to put provisions, necessaries, and ammunition, &c., into, to be kept dry, either from rain or the spray of the sea; and a little long hollow place I cut in the inside of the boat, where I could lay my gun, making a flap to hang down over it to keep it dry.

I fixed my umbrella also in a step at the stern, like a mast, to stand over my head, and keep the heat of the sun off of me, like an awning; and thus I every now and then took a little voyage upon the sea, but never went far out, nor far from the little creek. But at last, being eager to view the circumference of my little kingdom, I resolved upon my tour; and accordingly I victualled my ship for the voyage, putting in two dozen of my loaves (cakes I should rather call them) of barley bread, an earthen pot full of parched rice, a food I eat a great deal of, a little bottle of rum, half a goat, and powder and shot for killing more, and two large watch-coats, of those which, as I mentioned before, I had saved out of the seamen's chests; these I took, one to lie upon, and the other to cover me in the night.

It was the 6th of November, in the sixth year of my reign, or my captivity, which you please, that I set out on this voyage, and I found it much longer than I expected; for though the island itself was not very large, yet when I came to the east side of it I found a great ledge of rocks lie out above two leagues into the sea, some above water, some under it, and beyond that a shoal of sand, lying dry half a league more; so that I was obliged to go a great way out to sea to double the point.

When first I discovered them, I was going to give over my enterprise, and come back again, not knowing how far it might oblige me to go out to sea, and, above all, doubting how I should get back again, so I came to an anchor; for I had made me a kind of an anchor with a piece of a broken grappling which I got out of the ship.

Having secured my boat, I took my gun and went on shore, climbing up upon a hill, which seemed to overlook that point, where I saw the full extent of it, and resolved to venture.

In my viewing the sea from that hill, where I stood, I perceived a strong, and indeed a most furious current, which run to the east, and even came close to the point; and I took the more notice of it, because I saw there might be some danger that when I came into it I might be carried out to sea by the strength of it, and not be able to make the island again. And indeed, had I not gotten first up upon this hill, I believe it would have been so; for there was the same current on the other side the island, only that it set off at a farther distance; and I saw there was a strong eddy under the shore; so I had nothing to do but to get in out of the first current, and I should presently be in an eddy.

I lay here, however, two days; because the wind, blowing pretty fresh at E.S.E., and that being just contrary to the said current, made a great breach of the sea upon the point; so that it was not safe for me to keep too close to the shore for the breach, nor to go too far off because of the stream.

The third day, in the morning, the wind having abated overnight, the sea was calm, and I ventured. But I am a warning piece again to all rash and ignorant pilots; for no sooner was I come to the point, when even I was not my boat's length from the shore, but I found myself in a great depth of water, and a current like the sluice of a mill. It carried my boat along with it with such violence, that all I could do could not keep her so much as on the edge of it, but I found it hurried me farther and farther out from the eddy, which was on my left hand. There was no wind stirring to help me, and all I could do with my paddlers signified nothing. And now I began to give myself over for lost; for, as the current was on both sides the island, I knew in a few leagues' distance they must join again, and then I was irrecoverably gone. Nor did I see any possibility of avoiding it; so that I had no prospect before me but of perishing; not by the sea, for that was calm enough, but of starving for hunger. I had indeed found a tortoise on the shore, as big almost as I could lift, and had tossed it into the boat; and I had a great jar of fresh water, that is to say, one of my earthen pots; but what was all this to being driven into the vast ocean, where, to be sure, there was no shore, no mainland or island, for a thousand leagues at least.

And now I saw how easy it was for the providence of God to make the most miserable condition mankind could be in worse. Now I looked back upon my desolate solitary island as the most pleasant place in the world, and all the happiness my heart could wish for was to be but there again. However, I worked hard, till indeed my strength was almost exhausted, and kept my boat as much to the northward, that is, towards the side of the current which the eddy lay on, as possibly I could; when about noon, as the sun passed the meridian, I thought I felt a little breeze of wind in my face, springing up from the S.S.E. This cheered my heart a little, and especially when, in about half-an-hour more, it blew a pretty small gentle gale. By this time I was gotten at a frightful distance from the island; and had the least cloud or hazy weather intervened, I had been undone another way too; for I had no compass on board, and should never have known how to have steered towards the island if I had but once lost sight of it. But the weather continuing clear, I applied myself to get up my mast again, and spread my sail, standing away to the north as much as possible, to get out of the current, north-west; and in about an hour came within about a mile of the shore, where, it being smooth water, I soon got to land.

When I was on shore, I fell on my knees, and gave God thanks for my deliverance, resolving to lay aside all thoughts of my deliverance by my boat; and refreshing myself with such things as I had, I brought my boat close to the shore, in a little cove that I had spied under some trees, and laid me down to sleep, being quite spent with the labour and fatigue of the voyage.

I was now at a great loss which way to get home with my boat. I had run so much hazard, and knew too much the case, to think of attempting it by the way I went out; and what might be at the other side (I mean the west side) I knew not, nor had I any mind to run any more ventures. So I only resolved in the morning to make my way westward along the shore, and to see if there was no creek where I might lay up my frigate in safety, so as to have her again if I wanted her. In about three miles, or thereabouts, coasting the shore, I came to a very good inlet or bay, about a mile over, which narrowed till it came to a very little rivulet or brook, where I found a very convenient harbour for my boat, and where she lay as if she had been in a little dock made on purpose for her. Here I put in, and having stowed my boat very safe, I went on shore to look about me, and see where I was.

I soon found I had but a little passed by the place where I had been before, when I travelled on foot to that shore; so taking nothing out of my boat but my gun and my umbrella, for it was exceedingly hot, I began my march. The way was comfortable enough after such a voyage as I had been upon, and I reached my old bower in the evening, where I found everything standing as I left it; for I always kept it in good order, being, as I said before, my country house.

I got over the fence, and laid me down in the shade to rest my limbs, for I was very weary, and fell asleep. But judge you, if you can, that read my story, what a surprise I must be in, when I was waked out of my sleep by a voice calling me by my name several times, "Robin, Robin, Robin Crusoe, poor Robin Crusoe! Where are you, Robin Crusoe? Where are you? Where have you been?"

I was so dead asleep at first, being fatigued with rowing, or paddling, as it is called, the first part of the day, and with walking the latter part, that I did not wake thoroughly; but dozing between sleeping and waking, thought I dreamed that somebody spoke to me. But as the voice continued to repeat "Robin Crusoe, Robin Crusoe," at last I began to wake more perfectly, and was at first dreadfully frighted, and started up in the utmost consternation. But no sooner were my eyes open, but I saw my Poll sitting on the top of the hedge, and immediately knew that it was he that spoke to me; for just in such bemoaning language I had used to talk to him, and teach him; and he had learned it so perfectly, that he would sit upon my finger, and lay his bill close to my face and cry, "Poor Robin Crusoe! Where are you? Where have you been? How come you here?" and such things as I had taught him.

However, even though I knew it was the parrot, and that indeed it could be nobody else, it was a good while before I could compose myself. First, I was amazed how the creature got thither, and then, how he should just keep about the place, and nowhere else. But as I was well satisfied it could be nobody but honest Poll, I got it over; and holding out my hand, and calling him by his name, Poll, the sociable creature came to me, and sat upon my thumb, as he used to do, and continued talking to me, "Poor Robin Crusoe! and how did I come here? and where had I been?" just as if he had been overjoyed to see me again; and so I carried him home along with me.

I had now had enough of rambling to sea for some time, and had enough to do for many days to sit still, and reflect upon the danger I had been in. I would have been very glad to have had my boat again on my side of the island; but I knew not how it was practicable to get it about. As to the east side of the island, which I had gone round, I knew well enough there was no venturing that way; my very heart would shrink, and my very blood run chill, but to think of it. And as to the other side of the island, I did not know how it might be there; but supposing the current ran with the same force against the shore at the east as it passed by it on the other, I might run the same risk of being driven down the stream, and carried by the island, as I had been before of being carried away from it. So, with these thoughts, I contented myself to be without any boat, though it had been the product of so many months' labour to make it, and of so many more to get it unto the sea.

In this government of my temper I remained near a year, lived a very sedate, retired life, as you may well suppose; and my thoughts being very much composed as to my condition, and fully comforted in resigning myself to the dispositions of Providence, I thought I lived really very happily in all things, except that of society.

I improved myself in this time in all the mechanic exercises which my necessities put me upon applying myself to, and I believe could, upon occasion, make a very good carpenter, especially considering how few tools I had. Besides this, I arrived at an unexpected perfection in my earthenware, and contrived well enough to make them with a wheel, which I found infinitely easier and better, because I made things round and shapable which before were filthy things indeed to look on. But I think I was never more vain of my own performance, or more joyful for anything I found out, than for my being able to make a tobacco-pipe. And though it was a very ugly clumsy thing when it was done, and only burnt red, like other earthenware, yet as it was hard and firm, and would draw the smoke, I was exceedingly comforted with it; for I had been always used to smoke, and there were pipes in the ship, but I forgot them at first, not knowing that there was tobacco in the island; and afterwards, when I searched the ship again, I could not come at any pipes at all.

In my wicker-ware also I improved much, and made abundance of necessary baskets, as well as my invention showed me; though not very handsome, yet they were such as were very handy and convenient for my laying things up in, or fetching things home in. For example, if I killed a goat abroad, I could hang it up in a tree, flay it, and dress it, and cut it in pieces, and bring it home in a basket; and the like by a turtle; I could cut it up, take out the eggs, and a piece or two of the flesh, which was enough for me, and bring them home in a basket, and leave the rest behind me. Also large deep baskets were my receivers for my corn, which I always rubbed out as soon as it was dry, and cured, and kept it in great baskets.

I began now to perceive my powder abated considerably, and this was a want which it was impossible for me to supply, and I began seriously to consider what I must do when I should have no more powder; that is to say, how I should do to kill any goats. I had, as is observed, in the third year of my being here kept a young kid, and bred her up tame. I could never find in my heart to kill her, till she died at last of mere age.

But being now in the eleventh year of my residence, and, as I have said, my ammunition growing low, I set myself to study some art to trap and snare the goats, to see whether I could not catch some of them alive.

To this purpose, I made snares to hamper them, and I do believe they were more than once taken in them; but my tackle was not good, for I had no wire, and I always found them broken, and my bait devoured. At length I resolved to try a pitfall; so I dug several large pits in the earth, in places where I had observed the goats used to feed, and over these pits I placed hurdles, of my own making too, with a great weight upon them; and several times I put ears of barley and dry rice, without setting the trap, and I could easily perceive that the goats had gone in and eaten up the corn, for I could see the mark of their feet. At length I set three traps in one night, and going the next morning, I found them all standing, and yet the bait eaten and gone; this was very discouraging. However, I altered my trap; and, not to trouble you with particulars, going one morning to see my trap, I found in one of them a large old he-goat, and in one of the other three kids.

As to the old one, I knew not what to do with him, he was so fierce I durst not go into the pit to him; that is to say, to go about to bring him away alive, which was what I wanted. So I even let him out, and he ran away, as if he had been frighted out of his wits. But I had forgot then what I learned afterwards, that hunger will tame a lion. If I had let him stay there three or four days without food, and then have carried him some water to drink, and then a little corn, he would have been as tame as one of the kids, for they are mighty sagacious, tractable creatures where they are well used.

However, for the present I let him go, knowing no better at that time. Then I went to the three kids, and taking them one by one, I tied them with strings together, and with some difficulty brought them all home.

It was a good while before they would feed, but throwing them some sweet corn, it tempted them, and they began to be tame. And now I found that if I expected to supply myself with goat-flesh when I had no powder or shot left, breeding some up tame was my only way, when perhaps I might have them about my house like a flock of sheep.

But then it presently occurred to me that I must keep the tame from the wild, or else they would always run wild when they grew up; and the only way for this was to have some enclosed piece of ground, well fenced either with hedge or pale, to keep them in so effectually, that those within might not break out, or those without break in.

This was a great undertaking for one pair of hands; yet as I saw there was an absolute necessity of doing it, my first piece of work was to find out a proper piece of ground, viz., where there was likely to be herbage for them to eat, water for them to drink, and cover to keep them from the sun.

For the first beginning, I resolved to enclose a piece of about 150 yards in length, and 100 yards in breadth; which, as it would maintain as many as I should have in any reasonable time, so, as my flock increased, I could add more ground to my enclosure.

This was acting with some prudence, and I went to work with courage. I was about three months hedging in the first piece, and, till I had done it, I tethered the three kids in the best part of it, and used them to feed as near me as possible, to make them familiar; and very often I would go and carry them some ears of barley, or a handful of rice, and feed them out of my hand; so that after my enclosure was finished, and I let them loose, they would follow me up and down, bleating after me for a handful of corn.

This answered my end, and in about a year and half I had a flock of about twelve

goats, kids, and all; and in two years more I had three and forty, besides several that I took and killed for my food. And after that I enclosed five several pieces of ground to feed them in, with little pens to drive them into, to take them as I wanted, and gates out of one piece of ground into another.

But this was not all, for now I not only had goat's flesh to feed on when I pleased, but milk too, a thing which, indeed, in my beginning, I did not so much as think of, and which, when it came into my thoughts, was really an agreeable surprise. For now I set up my dairy, and had sometimes a gallon or two of milk in a day; and as Nature, who gives supplies of food to every creature, dictates even naturally how to make use of it, so I, that had never milked a cow, much less a goat, or seen butter or cheese made, very readily and handily, though after a great many essays and miscarriages, made me both butter and cheese at last, and never wanted it afterwards.

It would have made a stoic smile, to have seen me and my little family sit down to dinner. There was my majesty, the prince and lord of the whole island; I had the lives of all my subjects at my absolute command. I could hang, draw, give liberty, and take it away; and no rebels among all my subjects.

Then to see how like a king I dined, too, all alone, attended by my servants. Poll, as if he had been my favourite, was the only person permitted to talk to me. My dog, who was now grown very old and crazy, sat always at my right hand, and two cats, one on one side the table, and one on the other, expecting now and then a bit from my hand, as a mark of special favour.

With this attendance, and in this plentiful manner, I lived; neither could I be said to want anything but society; and of that in some time after this, I was like to have too much.

I was something impatient as I have observed, to have the use of my boat, though very loth to run any more hazards; and therefore sometimes I sat contriving ways to get her about the island, and at other times I sat myself down contented enough without her. But I had a strange uneasiness in my mind to go down to the point of the island, where, as I have said, in my last ramble, I went up the hill to see how the shore lay, and how the current set, that I might see what I had to do. This inclination increased upon me every day, and at length I resolved to travel thither by land, following the edge of the shore. I did so; but had anyone in England been to meet such a man as I was, it must either have frighted them, or raised a great deal of laughter; and as I frequently stood still to look at myself, I could not but smile at the notion of my travelling through Yorkshire, with such an equipage, and in such a dress. Be pleased to take a sketch of my figure, as follows.

I had a great high shapeless cap, made of a goat's skin, with a flap hanging down behind, as well to keep the sun from me, as to shoot the rain off from running into my neck; nothing being so hurtful in these climates as the rain upon the flesh, under the clothes.

I had a short jacket of goat-skin, the skirts coming down to about the middle of my thighs; and a pair of open-kneed breeches of the same. The breeches were made of the skin of an old he-goat, whose hair hung down such a length on either side, that, like pantaloons, it reached to the middle of my legs. Stockings and shoes I had none, but had made me a pair of somethings, I scarce know what to call them, like buskins, to flap over my legs, and lace on either side like spatterdashes; but of a most barbarous shape, as indeed were all the rest of my clothes.

I had on a broad belt of goat's skin dried, which I drew together with two thongs of the same, instead of buckles; and in a kind of a frog on either side of this, instead of a sword and a dagger, hung a little saw and a hatchet, one on one side, one on the other. I had another belt, not so broad, and fastened in the same manner, which hung over my shoulder; and at the end of it, under my left arm, hung two pouches, both made of goat's skin too; in one of which hung my powder, in the other my shot. At my back I carried my basket, on my shoulder my gun, and over my head a great clumsy ugly goat-skin umbrella, but which, after all, was the most necessary thing I had about me, next to my gun. As for my face, the colour of it was really not so mulatto-like as one might expect from a man not at all careful of it, and living within nineteen degrees of the equinox. My beard I had once suffered to grow till it was about a quarter of a yard long; but as I had both scissors and razors sufficient, I had cut it pretty short, except what grew on my upper lip, which I had trimmed into a large pair of Mahometan whiskers, such as I had seen worn by some Turks whom I saw at Sallee; for the Moors did not wear such, though the Turks did. Of these mustachios or whiskers, I will not say they were long enough to hang my hat upon them, but they were of a length and shape monstrous enough, and such as, in England, would have passed for frightful.

But all this is by-the-by; for, as to my figure, I had so few to observe me, that it was of no manner of consequence; so I say no more to that part. In this kind of figure I went my new journey, and was out five or six days. I travelled first along the sea-shore, directly to the place where I first brought my boat to an anchor, to get up upon the rocks. And having no boat now to take care of, I went over the land, a nearer way, to the same height that I was upon before; when, looking forward to the point of the rocks which lay out, and which I was obliged to double with my boat, as is said above, I was surprised to see the sea all smooth and quiet, no rippling, no motion, no current, any more there than in other places.

I was at a strange loss to understand this, and resolved to spend some time in the observing it, to see if nothing from the sets of the tide had occasioned it.

My observation convinced me that I had nothing to do but to observe the ebbing and the flowing of the tide, and I might very easily bring my boat about the island again. But when I began to think of putting it in practice, I had such a terror upon my spirits at the remembrance of the danger I had been in, that I could not think of it again with any patience; but, on the contrary, I took up another resolution, which was more safe, though more laborious; and this was, that I would build, or rather make me another *periagua* or canoe; and so have one for one side of the island, and one for the other.

You are to understand that now I had, as I may call it, two plantations in the island; one, my little fortification or tent, with the wall about it, under the rock, with the cave behind me, which, by this time, I had enlarged into several apartments or caves, one within another. One of these, which was the driest and largest, and had a door out beyond my wall or fortification, that is to say, beyond where my wall joined to the rock, was all filled up with the large earthen pots, of which I have given an account, and with fourteen or fifteen great baskets, which would hold five or six bushels each, where I laid up my stores of provision, especially my corn, some in the ear, cut off short from the straw, and the other rubbed out with my hand.

As for my wall, made, as before, with long stakes or piles, those piles grew all like trees, and were by this time grown so big, and spread so very much, that there was not the least appearance, to any one's view, of any habitation behind them.

Near this dwelling of mine, but a little further within the land, and upon lower ground, lay my two pieces of corn ground, which I kept duly cultivated and sowed, and which duly yielded me their harvest in its season; and whenever I had occasion for more corn, I had more land adjoining as fit as that.

Besides this, I had my country seat, and I had now a tolerable plantation there also; for, first, I had my little bower, as I called it, which I kept in repair; that is to say, I kept the hedge which circled it in constantly fitted up to its usual height, the ladder standing always in the inside. I kept the trees, which at first were no more than my stakes, but were now grown very firm and tall, I kept them always so cut, that they might spread and grow thick and wild, and make the more agreeable shade, which they did effectually to my mind. In the middle of this, I had my tent always standing, being a piece of a sail spread over poles, set up for that purpose, and which never wanted any repair or renewing; and under this I had made me a squab or couch, with the skins of the creatures I had killed, and with other soft things, and a blanket laid on them, such as belonged to our sea-bedding, which I had saved, and a great watch-coat to cover me; and here, whenever I had occasion to be absent from my chief seat, I took up my country habitation.

Adjoining to this I had my enclosures for my cattle, that is to say, my goats. And as I had taken an inconceivable deal of pains to fence and enclose this ground, so I was so uneasy to see it kept entire, lest the goats should break through, that I never left off till, with infinite labour, I had stuck the outside of the hedge so full of small stakes, and so near to one another, that it was rather a pale than a hedge, and there was scarce room to put a hand through between them; which afterwards, when those stakes grew, as they all did in the next rainy season, made the enclosure strong like a wall, indeed, stronger than any wall.

This will testify for me that I was not idle, and that I spared no pains to bring to pass whatever appeared necessary for my comfortable support; for I considered the keeping up a breed of tame creatures thus at my hand would be a living magazine of flesh, milk, butter, and cheese for me as long as I lived in the place, if it were to be forty years; and that keeping them in my reach depended entirely upon my perfecting my enclosures to such a degree, that I might be sure of keeping them together; which, by this method, indeed, I so effectually secured, that when these little stakes began to grow, I had planted them so very thick, I was forced to pull some of them up again.

In this place also I had my grapes growing, which I principally depended on for my winter store of raisins, and which I never failed to preserve very carefully, as the best and most agreeable dainty of my whole diet. And indeed they were not agreeable only, but physical, wholesome, nourishing, and refreshing to the last degree.

As this was also about half-way between my other habitation and the place where I had laid up my boat, I generally stayed and lay here in my way thither; for I used frequently to visit my boat, and I kept all things about, or belonging to her, in very good order. Sometimes I went out in her to divert myself, but no more hazardous voyages would I go, nor scarce ever above a stone's cast or two from the shore, I was so apprehensive of being hurried out of my knowledge again by the currents or winds, or any other accident. But now I come to a new scene of my life.

It happened one day, about noon, going towards my boat, I was exceedingly surprised with the print of a man's naked foot on the shore, which was very plain to be seen in the sand. I stood like one thunderstruck, or as if I had seen an apparition.

I listened, I looked round me, I could hear nothing, nor see anything. I went up to a rising ground, to look farther. I went up the shore, and down the shore, but it was all one; I could see no other impression but that one. I went to it again to see if there were any more, and to observe if it might not be my fancy; but there was no room for that, for there was exactly the very print of a foot – toes, heel, and every part of a foot. How it came thither I knew not, nor could in the least imagine. But after innumerable fluttering thoughts, like a man perfectly confused and out of myself, I came home to my fortification, not feeling, as we say, the ground I went on, but terrified to the last degree, looking behind me at every two or three steps, mistaking every bush and tree, and fancying every stump at a distance to be a man; nor is it possible to describe how many various shapes affrighted imagination represented things to me in, how many wild ideas were found every moment in my fancy, and what strange unaccountable whimsies came into my thoughts by the way.

When I came to my castle, for so I think I called it ever after this, I fled into it like one pursued. Whether I went over by the ladder, as first contrived, or went in at the hole in the rock, which I called a door, I cannot remember; no, nor could I remember the next morning, for never frighted hare fled to cover, or fox to earth, with more terror of mind than I to this retreat.

I slept none that night. The farther I was from the occasion of my fright, the greater my apprehensions were; which is something contrary to the nature of such things, and especially to the usual practice of all creatures in fear. But I was so embarrassed with my own frightful ideas of the thing, that I formed nothing but dismal imaginations to myself, even though I was now a great way off it. Sometimes I fancied it must be the devil, and reason joined in with me upon this supposition; for how should any other thing in human shape come into the place? Where was the vessel that brought them? What marks was there of any other footsteps? And how was it possible a man should come there? But then to think that Satan should take human shape upon him in such a place, where there could be no manner of occasion for it, but to leave the print of his foot behind him, and that even for no purpose too, for he could not be sure I should see it; this was an amusement the other way. I considered that the devil might have found out abundance of other ways to have terrified me than this of the single print of a foot; that as I live quite on the other side of the island, he would never have been so simple to leave a mark in a place where it was ten thousand to one whether I should ever see it or not, and in the sand too, which the first surge of the sea, upon a high wind, would have defaced entirely. All this seemed inconsistent with the thing itself, and with all the notions we usually entertain of the subtilty of the devil.

Abundance of such things as these assisted to argue me out of all apprehensions of its being the devil; and I presently concluded then, that it must be some more dangerous creature, viz, that it must be some of the savages of the mainland over against me, who had wandered out to sea in their canoes, and, either driven by the currents or by contrary winds, had made the island, and had been on shore, but were gone away again to sea, being as loth, perhaps, to have stayed in this desolate island as I would have been to have had them.

While these reflections were rolling upon my mind, I was very thankful in my thoughts that I was so happy as not to be thereabouts at that time, or that they did not see my boat, by which they would have concluded that some inhabitants had been in the place, and perhaps have searched farther for me. Then terrible thoughts racked my imagination about their having found my boat, and that there were people here; and that if so, I should certainly have them come again in greater numbers, and devour me; that if it should happen so that they should not find me, yet they would find my enclosure, destroy all my corn, carry away all my flock of tame goats, and I should perish at last for mere want.

Thus my fear banished all my religious hope. All that former confidence in God, which was founded upon such wonderful experience as I had had of His goodness, now vanished, as if He that had fed me by miracle hitherto could not preserve, by His power, the provision which He had made for me by His goodness. I reproached myself with my easiness, that would not sow any more corn one year than would just serve me till the next season, as if no accident could intervene to prevent my enjoying the crop that was upon the ground. And. this I thought so just a reproof, that I resolved for the future to have two or three years' corn beforehand, so that, whatever might come, I might not perish for want of bread.

I then reflected that God, who was not only righteous, but omnipotent, as He had thought fit thus to punish and afflict me, so He was able to deliver me; that if He did not think fit to do it, 'twas my unquestioned duty to resign myself absolutely and entirely to His will; and, on the other hand, it was my duty also to hope in Him, pray to Him, and quietly to attend the dictates and directions of His daily providence.

These thoughts took me up many hours, days, nay, I may say, weeks and months; and one particular effect of my cogitations on this occasion I cannot omit, viz., one morning early, lying in my bed, and filled with thought about my danger from the appearance of savages, I found it discomposed me very much; upon which those words of the Scripture came into my thoughts, "Call upon Me in the day of trouble, and I will deliver, and thou shalt glorify Me."

In the middle of these cogitations, apprehensions, and reflections, it came into my thought one day, that all this might be a mere chimera of my own; and that this foot might be the print of my own foot, when I came on shore from my boat. This cheered me up a little too, and I began to persuade myself it was all a delusion, that it was nothing else but my own foot; and why might not I come that way from the boat, as well as I was going that way to the boat? Again, I considered also, that I could by no means tell, for certain, where I had trod, and where I had not; and that if at last, this was only the print of my own foot, I had played the part of those fools who strive to make stories of spectres and apparitions, and then are frighted at them more than anybody.

Now I began to take courage, and to peep abroad again, for I had not stirred out of my castle for three days and nights, so that I began to starve for provision; for I had little or nothing within doors but some barley-cakes and water. Then I knew that my goats wanted to be milked too, which usually was my evening diversion; and the poor creatures were in great pain and inconvenience for want of it; and, indeed, it almost spoiled some of them, and almost dried up their milk.

Heartening myself, therefore, with the belief that this was nothing but the print of one of my own feet, and so I might be truly said to start at my own shadow, I began to go abroad again, and went to my country house to milk my flock. But to see with what fear I went forward, how often I looked behind me, how I was ready, every now and then, to lay down my basket, and run for my life, it would have made any one have thought I was haunted with an evil conscience, or that I had been lately most terribly frighted; and so, indeed, I had.

However, as I went down thus two or three days, and having seen nothing, I began to be a little bolder, and to think there was really nothing in it but my own imagination. But I could not persuade myself fully of this till I should go down to the shore again, and see this print of a foot, and measure it by my own, and see if there was any similitude or fitness, that I might be assured it was my own foot. But when I came to the place, first, it appeared evidently to me, that when I laid up my boat, I could not possibly be on shore anywhere thereabout; secondly, when I came to measure the mark with my own foot, I found my foot not so large by a great deal. Both these things filled my head with new imaginations, and gave me the vapours again to the highest degree; so that I shook with cold, like one in an ague; and I went home again, filled with the belief that some man or men had been on shore there; or, in short, that the island was inhabited, and I might be surprised before I was aware. And what course to take for my security, I knew not.

The confusion of my thoughts kept me waking all night, but in the morning I fell asleep; and having, by the amusement of my mind, been, as it were, tired, and my spirits exhausted, I slept very soundly, and waked much better composed than I had ever been before. And now I began to think sedately; and upon the utmost debate with myself, I concluded that this island, which was so exceeding pleasant, fruitful, and no farther from the mainland than as I had seen, was not so entirely abandoned as I might imagine; that although there were no stated inhabitants who lived on the spot, yet that there might sometimes come boats off from the shore, who, either with design, or perhaps never but when they were driven by cross winds, might come to this place; that I had lived here fifteen years now, and had not met with the least shadow or figure of any people yet; and that if at any time they should be driven here, it was probable they went away again as soon as ever they could, seeing they had never thought fit to fix there upon any occasion to this time; that the most I could suggest any danger from, was from any such casual accidental landing of straggling people from the main, who, as it was likely, if they were driven hither, were here against their wills; so they made no stay here, but went off again with all possible speed, seldom staying one night on shore, lest they should not have the help of the tides and daylight back again; and that, therefore, I had nothing to do but to consider of some safe retreat, in case I should see any savages land upon the spot.

Now I began sorely to repent that I had dug my cave so large as to bring a door through again, which door, as I said, came out beyond where my fortification joined to the rock. Upon maturely considering this, therefore, I resolved to draw me a second fortification, in the same manner of a semicircle, at a distance from my wall, just where I had planted a double row of trees about twelve years before, of which I made mention. These trees having been planted so thick before, they wanted but a few piles to be driven between them, that they should be thicker and stronger, and my wall would be soon finished.

So that I had now a double wall; and my outer wall was thickened with pieces of timber, old cables, and everything I could think of to make it strong, having in it seven little holes about as big as I might put my arm out at. In the inside of this I thickened my wall to above ten feet thick, with continual bringing earth out of my cave, and laying it at the foot of the wall, and walking upon it; and through the seven holes I contrived to plant the muskets, of which I took notice that I got seven on shore out of the ship. These, I say, I planted like my cannon, and fitted them into frames, that held them like a carriage, that so I could fire all the seven guns in two minutes' time. This wall I was many a weary month a-finishing, and yet never thought myself safe till it was done.

When this was done, I stuck all the ground without my wall, for a great way every way, as full with stakes, or sticks, of the osier-like wood, which I found so apt to grow, as they could well stand; insomuch, that I believe I might set in near twenty thousand of them, leaving a pretty large space between them and my wall, that I might have room to see an enemy, and they might have no shelter from the young trees, if they attempted to approach my outer wall.

Thus in two years' time I had a thick grove; and in five or six years' time I had a wood before my dwelling, growing so monstrous thick and strong, that it was indeed perfectly impassable; and no men, of what kind soever, would ever imagine that there was anything beyond it, much less a habitation. As for the way which I proposed to myself to go in and out, for I left no avenue, it was by setting two ladders, one to a part of the rock which was low, and then broke in, and left room to place another ladder upon that; so when the two ladders were taken down, no man living could come down to me without mischieving himself; and if they had come down, they were still on the outside of my outer wall.

Thus I took all the measures human prudence could suggest for my own preservation; and it will be seen, at length, that they were not altogether without just reason; though I foresaw nothing at that time more than my mere fear suggested to me.

While this was doing, I was not altogether careless of my other affairs; for I had a great concern upon me for my little herd of goats. They were not only a present supply to me upon every occasion, and began to be sufficient to me, without the expense of powder and shot, but also without the fatigue of hunting after the wild ones; and I was loth to lose the advantage of them, and to have them all to nurse up over again.

To this purpose, after long consideration, I could think of but two ways to preserve them. One was, to find another convenient place to dig a cave under ground, and to drive them into it every night; and the other was, to enclose two or three little bits of land, remote from one another, and as much concealed as I could, where I might keep about half-a-dozen young goats in each place; so that if any disaster happened to the flock in general, I might be able to raise them again with little trouble and time. And this, though it would require a great deal of time and labour, I thought was the most rational design.

Accordingly I spent some time to find out the most retired parts of the island; and I pitched upon one which was as private indeed as my heart could wish for. It was a little damp piece of ground, in the middle of the hollow and thick woods, where, as is observed, I almost lost myself once before, endeavouring to come back that way from the eastern part of the island. Here I found a clear piece of land, near three acres, so surrounded with woods, that it was almost an enclosure by Nature; at least, it did not want near so much labour to make it so as the other pieces of ground I had worked so hard at.

I immediately went to work with this piece of ground, and in less than a month's time I had so fenced it round, that my flock, or herd, call it which you please, who were not so wild now as at first they might be supposed to be, were well enough secured in it. So, without any farther delay, I removed ten young she-goats and two he-goats to this piece. And when they were there, I continued to perfect the fence, till I had made it as secure as the other, which, however, I did at more leisure, and it took me up more time by a great deal.

All this labour I was at the expense of, purely from my apprehensions on the account of the print of a man's foot which I had seen; for, as yet, I never saw any human creature come near the island. And I had now lived two years under these uneasinesses, which, indeed, made my life much less comfortable than it was before, as may well be imagined by any who know what it is to live in the constant snare of the fear of man. And this I must observe, with grief too, that the discomposure of my mind had too great impressions also upon the religious part of my thoughts; for the dread and terror of failing into the hands of savages and cannibals lay so upon my spirits, that I seldom found myself in a due temper for application to my Maker, at least not with the sedate calmness and resignation of soul which I was wont to do.

But to go on. After I had thus secured one part of my little living stock, I went about the whole island, searching for another private place to make such another deposit; when, wandering more to the west point of the island than I had ever done yet, and looking out to sea, I thought I saw a boat upon the sea, at a great distance. I had found a prospective glass or two in one of the seamen's chests, which I saved out of our ship, but I had it not about me; and this was so remote, that I could not tell what to make of it, though I looked at it till my eyes were not able to hold to look any longer. Whether it was a boat or not, I do not know; but as I descended from the hill, I could see no more of it, so I gave it over; only I resolved to go no more out without a prospective glass in my pocket.

When I was come down the hill to the end of the island, where, indeed, I had never been before, I was presently convinced that the seeing the print of a man's foot was not such a strange thing in the island as I imagined. And, but that it was a special providence that I was cast upon the side of the island where the savages never came, I should easily have known that nothing was more frequent than for the canoes from the main, when they happened to be a little too far out at sea, to shoot over to that side of the island for harbour; likewise, as they often met and fought in their canoes, the victors having taken any prisoners would bring them over to this shore, where, according to their dreadful customs, being all cannibals, they would kill and eat them; of which hereafter.

When I was come down the hill to the shore, as I said above, being the S.W. point of the island, I was perfectly confounded and amazed; nor is it possible for me to express the horror of my mind at seeing the shore spread with skulls, hands, feet, and other bones of human bodies; and particularly, I observed a place where there had been a fire made, and a circle dug in the earth, like a cockpit, where it is supposed the savage wretches had sat down to their inhuman feastings upon the bodies of their fellow-creatures.

I was so astonished with the sight of these things, that I entertained no notion of any danger to myself from it for a long while. All my apprehensions were buried in the thoughts of such a pitch of inhuman, hellish brutality, and the horror of the degeneracy of human nature, which, though I had heard of often, yet I never had so near a view of before. In short, I turned away my face from the horrid spectacle. I got me up the hill again with all the speed I could, and walked on towards my own habitation.

When I came a little out of that part of the island, I stood still a while, as amazed; and then recovering myself, I looked up with the utmost affection of my soul, and with a flood of tears in my eyes, gave God thanks, that had cast my first lot in a part of the world where I was distinguished from such dreadful creatures as these.

In this frame of thankfulness I went home to my castle, and began to be much easier now, as to the safety of my circumstances, than ever I was before; for I observed that these wretches never came to this island in search of what they could get; perhaps not seeking, not wanting, or not expecting, anything here; and having often, no doubt, been up in the covered, woody part of it, without finding anything to their purpose. I knew I had been here now almost eighteen years, and never saw the least footsteps of human creature there before; and I might be here eighteen more as entirely concealed as I was now, if I did not discover myself to them, which I had no manner of occasion to do; it being my only business to keep myself entirely concealed where I was, unless I found a better sort of creatures than cannibals to make myself known to.

Yet I entertained such an abhorrence of the savage wretches that I have been speaking of, and of the wretched inhuman custom of their devouring and eating one another up, that I continued pensive and sad, and kept close within my own circle for almost two years after this. When I say my own circle, I mean by it my three plantations, viz., my castle, my country seat, which I called my bower, and my enclosure in the woods. Nor did I look after this for any other use than as an enclosure for my goats; for the aversion which Nature gave me to these hellish wretches was such, that I was fearful of seeing them as of seeing the devil himself.

Time, however, and the satisfaction I had that I was in no danger of being discovered by these people, began to wear off my uneasiness about them; and I began to live just in the same composed manner as before; only with this difference, that I used more caution, and kept my eyes more about me, than I did before, lest I should happen to be seen by any of them; and particularly, I was more cautious of firing my gun, lest any of them being on the island should happen to hear of it. And it was, therefore, a very good providence to me that I had furnished myself with a tame breed of goats, that I needed not hunt any more about the woods, or shoot at them. And if I did catch any of them after this, it was by traps and snares, as I had done before; so that for two years after this I believe I never fired my gun once off, though I never went out without it; and, which was more, as I had saved three pistols out of the ship, I always carried them out with me, or at least two of them, sticking them in my goat-skin belt. Also I furbished up one of the great cutlasses that I had out of the ship, and made me a belt to put it on also; so that I was now a most formidable fellow to look at when I went abroad, if you add to the former description of myself the particular of two pistols and a great broadsword hanging at my side in a belt, but without a scabbard.

Things going on thus, as I have said, for some time, I seemed, excepting these cautions, to be reduced to my former calm, sedate way of living. All these things tended to showing me, more and more, how far my condition was from being miserable, compared to some others; nay, to many other particulars of life, which it might have pleased God to have made my lot. It put me upon reflecting how little repining there would be among mankind at any condition of life, if people would rather compare their condition with those that are worse, in order to be thankful, than be always comparing them with those which are better, to assist their murmurings and complainings.

As in my present condition there were not really many things which I wanted, so indeed I thought that the frights I had been in about these savage wretches, and the concern I had been in for my own preservation, had taken off the edge of my invention for my own conveniences. And I had dropped a good design, which I had once bent my thoughts too much upon; and that was, to try if I could not make some of my barley into malt, and then try to brew myself some beer.

But my invention now run quite another way; for, night and day, I could think of nothing but how I might destroy some of these monsters in their cruel, bloody enter-

tainment, and, if possible, save the victim they should bring hither to destroy. It would take up a larger volume than this whole work is intended to be, to set down all the contrivances I hatched, or rather brooded upon, in my thought, for the destroying these creatures, or at least frighting them so as to prevent their coming hither any more. But all was abortive; nothing could be possible to take effect, unless I was to be there to do it myself. And what could one man do among them, when perhaps there might be twenty or thirty of them together, with their darts, or their bows and arrows, with which they could shoot as true to a mark as I could with my gun?

Sometimes I contrived to dig a hole under the place where they made their fire, and put in five or six pound of gunpowder, which, when they kindled their fire, would consequently take fire, and blow up all that was near it. But as, in the first place, I should be very loth to waste so much powder upon them, my store being now within the quantity of one barrel, so neither could I be sure of its going off at any certain time, when it might surprise them; and, at best, that it would do little more than just blow the fire about their ears, and fright them, but not sufficient to make them forsake the place. So I laid it aside, and then proposed that I would place myself in ambush in some convenient place, with my three guns all double-loaded, and, in the middle of their bloody ceremony, let fly at them, when I should be sure to kill or wound perhaps two or three at every shot; and then falling in upon them with my three pistols and my sword, I made no doubt but that if there was twenty I should kill them all. This fancy pleased my thoughts for some weeks; and I was so full of it, that I often dreamed of it, and sometimes that I was just going to let fly at them in my sleep.

I went so far with it in my imagination, that I employed myself several days to find out proper places to put myself in ambuscade, as I said, to watch for them; and I went frequently to the place itself, which was now grown more familiar to me; and especially while my mind was thus filled with thoughts of revenge, and of a bloody putting twenty or thirty of them to the sword, as I may call it, the horror I had at the place, and at the signals of the barbarous wretches devouring one another, abated my malice.

Well, at length I found a place in the side of the hill, where I was satisfied I might securely wait till I saw any of their boats coming; and might then, even before they would be ready to come on shore, convey myself, unseen, into thickets of trees, in one of which there was a hollow large enough to conceal me entirely; and where I might sit and observe all their bloody doings, and take my full aim at their heads, when they were so close together, as that it would be next to impossible that I should miss my shot, or that I could fail wounding three or four of them at the first shot.

In this place, then, I resolved to fix my design; and, accordingly, I prepared two muskets and my ordinary fowling-piece. The two muskets I loaded with a brace of slugs each, and four or five smaller bullets, about the size of pistol-bullets; and the fowling-piece I loaded with near a handful of swan-shot, of the largest size. I also loaded my pistols with about four bullets each; and in this posture, well provided with ammunition for a second and third charge, I prepared myself for my expedition.

After I had thus laid the scheme of my design, and in my imagination put it in practice, I continually made my tour every morning up to the top of the hill, which was from my castle, as I called it, about three miles, or more, to see if I could observe any boats upon the sea coming near the island, or standing over towards it. But I began to tire of this hard duty, after I had, for two or three months, constantly kept my watch, but came always back without any discovery; there having not, in all that time, been the least appearance, not only on or near the shore, but not on the whole ocean, so far as my eyes or glasses could reach every way.

As long as I kept up my daily tour to the hill to look out, so long also I kept up the vigour of my design, and my spirits seemed to be all the while in a suitable form for so outrageous an execution as the killing twenty or thirty naked savages for an offence which I had not at all entered into a discussion of in my thoughts, any farther than my passions were at first fired by the horror I conceived at the unnatural custom of that people of the country.

But when I had considered a little, it followed necessarily that I was certainly in the wrong in it; that these people were not murderers in the sense that I had before condemned them in my thoughts, any more than those Christians were murderers who often put to death the prisoners taken in battle; or more frequently, upon many occasions, put whole troops of men to the sword, without giving quarter, though they threw down their arms and submitted.

In the next place it occurred to me, that albeit the usage they thus gave one another was thus brutish and inhuman, yet it was really nothing to me; these people had done me no injury. That if they attempted me, or I saw it necessary for my immediate preservation to fall upon them, something might be said for it; but that as I was yet out of their power, and they had really no knowledge of me, and consequently no design upon me, and therefore it could not be just for me to fall upon them.

These considerations really put me to a pause, and to a kind of a full stop; and I began, by little and little, to be off of my design, and to conclude I had taken wrong measures in my resolutions to attack the savages; that it was not my business to meddle with them unless they first attacked me; and this it was my business, if possible, to prevent; but that if I were discovered and attacked, then I knew my duty.

On the other hand, I argued with myself that this really was the way not to deliver myself, but entirely to ruin and destroy myself; for unless I was sure to kill every one that not only should be on shore at that time, but that should ever come on shore afterwards, if but one of them escaped to tell their country people what had happened, they would come over again by thousands to revenge the death of their fellows and I should only bring upon myself a certain destruction which at present, I had no manner of occasion for.

Upon the whole, I concluded that neither in principles nor in policy I ought, one way or other, to concern myself in this affair. That my hibusiness was, by all possible means to conceal myself from them, and not to leave the least signal to them to guess by that there were any living creatures upon the island; I mean of human shape.

Religion joined in with this prudential, and I was convinced now, many ways, that I was perfectly out of my duty when I was laying all my bloody schemes for the destruction of innocent creatures; I mean innocent as to me. As to the crimes they were guilty of towards one another, I had nothing to do with them. They were national and I ought to leave them to the justice of God, who is the Governor of nations, and knows how, by national punishments, to make a just retribution for national offences, and to bring public judgments upon those who offend in a public manner by such vays as best pleases Him.

In this disposition I continued for near a year after this; and so far was I from desiring an occasion for falling upon these wretches, that in all that time I never once went up the hill to see whether there were any of them in sight, or to know whether any of them had been on shore there or not, that I might not be tempted to renew any of my contrivances against them, or be provoked, by any advantage which might present itself, to fall upon them. Only this I did, I went and removed my boat, which I had on the other side the island, and carried it down to the east end of the whole island, where I ran it into a little cove, which I found under some high rocks, and where I knew, by reason of the currents, the savages durst not, at least would not come, with their boats, upon any account whatsoever.

With my boat I carried away everything that I had left there belonging to her, though not necessary for the bare going thither, viz., a mast and sail which I had made for her, and a thing like an anchor, but indeed which could not be called either anchor or grappling; however, it was the best I could make of its kind. All these I removed, that there might not be the least shadow of any discovery, or any appearance of any boat, or of any human habitation, upon the island.

Besides this, I kept myself, as I said, more retired than ever, and seldom went from my cell, other than upon my constant employment, viz., to milk my she-goats, and manage my little flock in the wood, which, as it was quite on the other part of the island, was quite out of danger; for certain it is, that these savage people, who sometimes haunted this island, never came with any thoughts of finding anything here, and consequently never wandered off from the coast; and I doubt not but they might have been several times on shore after my apprehensions of them had made me cautious, as well as before; and indeed, I looked back with some horror upon the thoughts of what my condition would have been if I had chopped upon them and been discovered before that, when, naked and unarmed, except with one gun, and that loaded often only with small shot, I walked everywhere, peeping and peeping about the island to see what I could get. What a surprise should I have been in if, when I discovered the print of a man's foot, I had, instead of that, seen fifteen or twenty savages, and found them pursuing me, and by the swiftness of their running, no possibility of my escaping them!

I believe the reader of this will not think strange if I confess that these anxieties, these constant dangers I lived in, and the concern that was now upon me, put an end to all invention, and to all the contrivances that I had laid for my future accommodations and conveniences. I had the care of my safety more now upon my hands than that of my food. I cared not to drive a nail, or chop a stick of wood now, for fear the noise I should make should be heard; much less would I fire a gun, for the same reason; and, above all, I was intolerably uneasy at making any fire, lest the smoke, which is visible at a great distance in the day, should betray me; and for this reason I removed that part of my business which required fire, such as burning of pots and pipes, etc., into my new apartment in the woods; where, after I had been some time, I found, to my unspeakable consolation, a mere natural cave in the earth, which went in a vast way, and where, I dare say, no savage, had he been at the mouth of it, would be so hardy as to venture in; nor, indeed, would any man else, but one who, like me, wanted nothing so much as a safe retreat.

The mouth of this hollow was at the bottom of a great rock, where, by mere accident I would say (if I did not see abundant reason to ascribe all such things now to Providence), I was cutting down some thick branches of trees to make charcoal; and before I go on, I must observe the reason of my making this charcoal, which was thus.

I could plainly see the wreck of a ship (page 325)

Killed him at the first shot (page 335)

I was afraid of making a smoke about my habitation, as I said before; and yet I could not live there without baking my bread, cooking my meat, etc. So I contrived to burn some wood here, as I had seen done in England under turf; till it became chark, or dry coal; and then putting the fire out, I preserved the coal to carry home, and perform the other services which fire was wanting for at home, without danger of smoke.

But this is by-the bye. While I was cutting down some wood here, I perceived that behind a very thick branch of low brushwood, or underwood, there was a kind of hollow place. I was curious to look into it; and getting with difficulty into the mouth of it, I found it was pretty large; that is to say, sufficient for me to stand upright in it, and perhaps another with me. But I must confess to you I made more haste out than I did in when, looking farther into the place, and which was perfectly dark, I saw two broad shining eyes of some creature, whether devil or man I knew not, which twinkled like two stars, the dim light from the cave's mouth shining directly in, and making the reflection.

But plucking up my spirits as well as I could, and encouraging myself a little with considering that the power and presence of God was everywhere, and was able to protect me, upon this I stepped forward again, and by the light of a firebrand, holding it up a little over my head, I saw lying on the ground a most monstrous, frightful, old he-goat, just making his will, as we say, and gasping for life; and dying indeed, of mere old age.

I stirred him a little to see if I could get him out, and he essayed to get up, but was not able to raise himself; and I thought with myself he might even lie there; for if he had frighted me so, he would certainly fright any of the savages, if any of them should be so hardy as to come in there while he had any life in him.

I was now recovered from my surprise, and began to look round me, when I found the cave was but very small; that is to say, it might be about twelve feet over, but in no manner of shape, either round or square, no hands having ever been employed in making it but those of mere Nature. I observed also that there was a place at the farther side of it that went in farther, but was so low, that it required me to creep upon my hands and knees to go into it, and whither I went I knew not; so having no candle, I gave it over for some time, but resolved to come again the next day, provided with candles and a tinder-box, which I had made of the lock of one of the muskets, with some wild-fire in the pan.

Accordingly the next day I came provided with six large candles of my own making, for I made very good candles now of goat's tallow; and going into this low place, I was obliged to creep upon all fours, as I have said, almost ten yards; which, by the way, I thought was a venture bold enough, considering that I knew not how far it might go, nor what was beyond it. When I was got through the straight, I found the roof rose higher up, I believe near twenty feet. But never was such a glorious sight seen in the island, I dare say, as it was, to look round the sides and roof of this vault or cave; the walls reflected a hundred thousand lights to me from my two candles. What it was in the rock, whether diamonds, or any other precious stones, or gold, which I rather supposed it to be, I knew not.

The place I was in was a most delightful cavity or grotto of its kind, as could be expected, though perfectly dark. The floor was dry and level, and had a sort of small loose gravel upon it, so that there was no nauseous or venomous creature to be seen; neither was there any damp or wet on the sides or roof. The only difficulty in it was the entrance, which, however, as it was a place of security, and such a retreat as I wanted, I thought that was a convenience; so that I was really rejoiced at the discovery, and resolved, without any delay, to bring some of those things which I was most anxious about to this place; particularly, I resolved to bring hither my magazine of powder, and all my spare arms, viz., two fowling-pieces, for I had three in all, and three muskets, for of them I had eight in all. So I kept at my castle only five, which stood ready-mounted, like pieces of cannon, on my outmost fence; and were ready also to take out upon any expedition.

Upon this occasion of removing my ammunition, I took occasion to open the barrel of powder, which I took up out of the sea, and which had been wet; and I found that the water had penetrated about three or four inches into the powder on every side, which caking, and growing hard, had preserved the inside like a kernel in a shell; so that I had near sixty pounds of very good powder in the centre of the cask. And this was an agreeable discovery to me at that time; so I carried all away thither, never keeping above two or three pounds of powder with me in my castle, for fear of a surprise of any kind. I also carried thither all the lead I had left for bullets.

I fancied myself now like one of the ancient giants, which were said to live in caves and holes in the rocks, where none could come at them; for I persuaded myself, while I was here, if five hundred savages were to hunt me, they could never find me out; or, if they did, they would not venture to attack me here.

The old goat, whom I found expiring, died in the mouth of the cave the next day after I made this discovery; and I found it much easier to dig a great hole there, and throw him in and cover him with earth, than to drag him out.

I was now in my twenty-third year of residence in this island; and was so naturalised to the place, and to the manner of living, that could I have but enjoyed the certainty that no savages would come to the place to disturb me, I could have been content to have capitulated for spending the rest of my time there, even to the last moment, till I had laid me down and died, like the old goat in the cave. I had also arrived to some little diversions and amusements, which made the time pass more pleasantly with me a great deal than it did before. As, first, I had taught my Poll, as I noted before, to speak; and he did it so familiarly, and talked so articulately and plain, that it was very pleasant to me; and he lived with me no less than six and twenty years. How long he might live afterwards I know not, though I know they have a notion in the Brazils that they live a hundred years. Perhaps poor Poll may be alive there still, calling after poor Robin Crusoe to this day. I wish no Englishman the ill luck to come there and hear him; but if he did, he would certainly believe it was the devil. My dog was a very pleasant and loving companion to me for no less than sixteen years of my time, and then died of mere old age. As for my cats, they multiplied, as I have observed, to that degree, that I was obliged to shoot several of them at first to keep them from devouring me and all I had; but at length, when the two old ones I brought with me were gone, and after some time continually driving them from me, and letting them have no provision with me, they all ran wild into the woods, except two or three favourites, which I kept tame, and whose young, when they had any, I always drownied; and these were part of my family. Besides these, I always kept two or three household kids about me, whom I taught to feed out of my hand. And I had two more parrots, which talked pretty well, and would all call "Robin Crusoe," but none like my first; nor, indeed, did I take the pains with any of them that I had done with him. I had also several tame sea-fowls, whose names I know not, whom I caught upon the shore, and cut their wings; and the little stakes which I had planted before my castle wall being now grown up to a good thick grove, these fowls all lived among these low trees, and bred there, which was very agreeable to me; so that, as I said above, I began to be very well contented with the life I led, if it might but have been secure from the dread of the savages.

But it was otherwise directed; and it may not be amiss for all people who shall meet with my story, to make this just observation from it viz., how frequently, in the course of our lives, the evil which in itself we seek most to shun, and which, when we are fallen into it, is the most dreadful to us, is oftentimes the very means or door of our deliverance, by which alone we can be raised again from the affliction we are fallen into. I could give many examples of this in the course of my unaccountable life; but in nothing was it more particularly remarkable, than in the circumstances of my last years of solitary residence in this island.

It was now the month of December, as I said above, in my twenty-third year; and this, being the southern solstice (for winter I cannot call it), was the particular time of my harvest, and required my being pretty much abroad in the fields; when, going out pretty early in the morning, even before it was thorough daylight, I was surprised with seeing a light of some fire upon the shore, at a distance from me of about two miles, towards the end of the island, where I had observed some savages had been, as before. But not on the other side; but, to my great affliction, it was on my side of the island.

I was indeed terribly surprised at the sight, and stopped short within my grove, not daring to go out, lest I might be surprised; and yet I had no more peace within, from the apprehensions I had that if these savages, in rambling over the island, should find my corn standing or cut, or any of my works and improvements, they would immediately conclude that there were people in the place, and would then never give over till they had found me out. In this extremity I went back directly to my castle, pulled up the ladder after me, and made all things without look as wild and natural as I could.

Then I prepared myself within, putting myself in a posture of defence. I loaded all my cannon, as I called them, that is to say, my muskets, which were mounted upon my new fortification, and all my pistols, and resolved to defend myself to the last gasp; not forgetting seriously to commend myself to the Divine protection, and earnestly to pray to God to deliver me out of the hands of the barbarians. And in this posture I continued about two hours; but began to be mighty impatient for intelligence abroad, for I had no spies to send out.

After sitting a while longer, and musing what I should do in this case, I was not able to bear sitting in ignorance any longer, so setting up my ladder to the side of the hill where there was a flat place, as I observed before, and then pulling the ladder up after me, I set it up again, and mounted to the top of the hill; and pulling out my perspective-glass, which I had taken on purpose, I laid me down flat on my belly on the ground, and began to look for the place. I presently found there was no less than nine naked savages sitting round a small fire they had made, not to warm them, for they had no need of that, the weather being extreme hot, but, as I supposed, to dress some of their barbarous diet of human flesh which they had brought with them, whether alive or dead, I could not know.

They had two canoes with them, which they had hauled up upon the shore; and as it was then tide of ebb, they seemed to me to wait for the return of the flood to go away again. It is not easy to imagine what confusion this sight put me into, especially seeing them come on my side of the island, and so near me too. But when I observed their coming must be always with the current of the ebb, I began afterwards to be more sedate in my mind, being satisfied that I might go abroad with safety all the time of the tide of flood, if they were not on shore before; and having made this observation, I went abroad about my harvest-work with the more composure.

As I expected, so it proved; for as soon as the tide made to the westward, I saw them all take boat, and row (or paddle, as we call it) all away. I should have observed, that for an hour and more before they went off, they went to dancing; and I could easily discern their postures and gestures by my glasses.

As soon as I saw them shipped and gone, I took two guns upon my shoulders, and two pistols at my girdle, and my great sword by my side, without a scabbard, and with all the speed I was able to make I went away to the hill where I had discovered the first appearance of all. And as soon as I gat thither, which was not less than two hours (for I could not go apace, being so loden with arms as I was), I perceived there had been three canoes more of savages on that place; and looking out farther, I saw they were all at sea together, making over for the main.

This was a dreadful sight to me, especially when, going down to the shore, I could see the marks of horror which the dismal work they had been about had left behind it, viz., the blood, the bones, and part of the flesh of human bodies, eaten and devoured by those wretches with merriment and sport. I was so filled with indignation at the sight, that I began now to premeditate the destruction of the next that I saw there, let them be who or how many soever.

However, I wore out a year and three months more before I ever saw any more of the savages, and then I found them again, as I shall soon observe. It is true they might have been there once or twice, but either they made no stay or at least I did not hear them; but in the month of May as near as I could calculate, and in my four and twentieth year, I had a very strange encounter with them; of which in its place.

The perturbation of my mind during this fifteen or sixteen months' interval, was very great. I slept unquiet, dreamed always frightful dreams, and often started out of my sleep in the night. In the day great troubles overwhelmed my mind, and in the night I dreamed often of killing the savages, and of the reasons why I might justify the doing of it. But, to waive all this for a while, it was in the middle of May, on the sixteenth day, I think, as well as my poor wooden calendar would reckon, for I marked all upon the post still; I say, it was the sixteenth of May that it blew a very great storm of wind all day, with a great deal of lightning and thunder, and a very foul night it was after it. I know not what was the particular occasion of it, but as I was reading in the Bible, and taken up with very serious thoughts about my present condition, I was surprised with a noise of a gun, as I thought, fired at sea.

This was, to be sure, a surprise of a quite different nature from any I had met with before; for the notions this put into my thoughts were quite of another kind. I started up in the greatest haste imaginable, and, in a trice, clapped my ladder to the middle place of the rock, and pulled it after me; and mounting it the second time, got to the top of the hill the very moment that a flash of fire bid me listen for a second gun, which accordingly, in about half a minute, I heard; and, by the sound, knew that it was from that part of the sea where I was driven down the current in my boat.

I immediately considered that this must be some ship in distress, and that they had some comrade, or some other ship in company, and fired these guns for signals of distress, and to obtain help. I had this presence of mind, at that minute, as to think that though I could not help them, it may be they might help me; so I brought together all the dry wood I could get at hand, and, making a good handsome pile, I set it on fire upon the hill. The wood was dry, and blazed freely; and though the wind blew very hard, yet it burnt fairly out; so that I was certain, if there was any such thing as a ship, they must needs see it, and no doubt they did; for as soon as ever my fire blazed up I heard another gun, and after that several others, all from the same quarter. I plied my fire all night long till day broke; and when it was broad day, and the air cleared up, I saw something at a great distance at sea, full east of the island, whether a sail or a hull I could not distinguish, no, not with my glasses, the distance was so great, and the weather still something hazy also; at least it was so out at sea.

I looked frequently at it all that day, and soon perceived that it did not move; so I presently concluded that it was a ship at an anchor. And being eager, you may be sure, to be satisfied, I took my gun in my hand and ran toward the south side of the island, to the rocks where I had formerly been carried away with the current; and getting up there, the weather by this time being perfectly clear, I could plainly see, to my great sorrow, the wreck of a ship, cast away in the night upon those concealed rocks which I found when I was out in my boat; and which rocks, as they checked the violence of the stream, and made a kind of counter-stream or eddy, were the occasion of my recovering from the most desperate, hopeless condition that ever I had been in in all my life.

Thus, what is one man's safety is another man's destruction; for it seems these men, whoever they were, being out of their knowledge, and the rocks being wholly under water, had been driven upon them in the night, the wind blowing hard at E. and E.N.E. Had they seen the island, as I must necessarily suppose they did not, they must, as I thought, have endeavoured to have saved themselves on shore by the help of their boat; but their firing of guns for help, especially when they saw, as I imagined, my fire, filled me with many thoughts. First, I imagined that upon seeing my light, they might have put themselves into their boat, and have endeavoured to make the shore; but that the sea going very high, they might have been cast away. Other times I imagined that they might have lost their boat before, as might be the case many ways; as, particularly, by the breaking of the sea upon their ship, which many times obliges men to stave, or take in pieces their boat, and sometimes to throw it overboard with their own hands. Other times I imagined they had some other ship or ships in company, who, upon the signals of distress they had made, had taken them up and carried them off. Other whiles I fancied they were all gone off to sea in their boat, and being hurried away by the current that I had been formerly in, were carried out into the great ocean, where there was nothing but misery and perishing; and that, perhaps, they might by this time think of starving, and of being in a condition to eat one another.

As all these were but conjectures at best, so, in the condition I was in, I could do no more than look on upon the misery of the poor men, and pity them; which had still this good effect on my side, that it gave me more and more cause to give thanks to God, who had so happily and comfortably provided for me in my desolate condition; and that of two ships' companies who were now cast away upon this part of the world, not one life should be spared but mine. I learned here again to observe, that it is very rare that the providence of God casts us into any condition of life so low, or any misery so great, but we may see something or other to be thankful for, and may see others in worse circumstances than our own.

I cannot explain, by any possible energy of words, what a strange longing or hankering of desires I felt in my soul upon this sight, breaking out sometimes thus: "Oh that there had been but one or two, nay, or but one soul, saved out of this ship, to have escaped to me, that I might but have had one companion, one fellow-creature, to have spoken to me, and to have conversed with!" In all the time of my solitary life, I never felt so earnest, so strong a desire after the society of my fellow-creatures, or so deep a regret at the want of it.

But it was not to be. Either their fate or mine, or both, forbid it; for, till the last year of my being on this island, I never knew whether any were saved out of that ship or no; and had only the affliction, some days after, to see the corpse of a drowned boy come on shore at the end of the island which was next the shipwreck. He had on no clothes but a seaman's waistcoat, a pair of open-kneed linen drawers, and a blue linen shirt; but nothing to direct me so much as to guess what nation he was of. He had nothing in his pocket but two pieces of eight and a tobacco-pipe. The last was to me of ten times more value than the first.

It was now calm, and I had a great mind to venture out in my boat to this wreck, not doubting but I might find something on board that might be useful to me. But that did not altogether press me so much as the possibility that there might be yet some living creature on board, whose life I might not only save, but might, by saving that life, comfort my own to the last degree. And this thought clung so to my heart, that I could not be quiet night nor day, but I must venture out in my boat on board this wreck; and committing the rest to God's providence, I thought, the impression was so strong upon my mind that it could not be resisted, that it must come from some invisible direction, and that I should be wanting to myself if I did not go.

Under the power of this impression, I hastened back to my castle, prepared everything for my voyage, took a quantity of bread, a great pot for fresh water, a compass to steer by, a bottle of rum (for I had still a great deal of that left), a basket full of raisins. And thus, loading myself with everything necessary, I went down to my boat, got the water out of her, and got her afloat, loaded all my cargo in her, and then went home again for more. My second cargo was a great bag full of rice, the umbrella to set up over my head for shade, another large pot full of fresh water, and about two dozen of my small loaves, or barley-cakes, more than before, with a bottle of goat's milk and a cheese; all which, with great labour and sweat, I brought to my boat. And praying to God to direct my voyage, I put out; and rowing, or paddling, the canoe along the shore, I came at last to the utmost point of the island on that side, viz., N.E. And now I was to launch out into the ocean, and either to venture or not to venture. I looked on the rapid currents which ran constantly on both sides of the island at a distance, and which were very terrible to me, from the remembrance of the hazard I had been in before, and my heart began to fail me; for I foresaw that if I was driven into either of those currents, I should be carried a vast way out to sea, and perhaps out of my reach, or sight of the island again; and that then, as my boat was but small, if any little gale of wind should rise, I should be inevitably lost.

These thoughts so oppressed my mind, that I began to give over my enterprise; and having hauled my boat into a little creek on the shore, I stepped out, and sate me down upon a little rising bit of ground, very pensive and anxious, between fear and desire, about my voyage; when, as I was musing, I could perceive that the tide was turned, and the flood come on; upon which my going was for so many hours impracticable. Upon this, presently it occurred to me that I should go up to the highest piece of ground I could find and observe, if I could, how the sets of the tide, or currents, lay when the flood came in, that I might judge whether, if I was driven one way out, I might not expect to be driven another way home, with the same rapidness of the currents. This thought was no sooner in my head but I cast my eye upon a little hill, which sufficiently overlooked the sea both ways, and from whence

I had a clear view of the currents, or sets of the tide, and which way I was to guide myself in my return. Here I found, that as the current of the ebb set out close by the south point of the island, so the current of the flood set in close by the shore of the north side; and that I had nothing to do but to keep to the north of the island in my return, and I should do well enough.

Encouraged with this observation, I resolved the next morning to set out with the first of the tide, and reposing myself for the night in the canoe, under the great watch-coat I mentioned, I launched out. I made first a little out to sea, full north, till I began to feel the benefit of the current which set eastward, and which carried me at a great rate; and yet did not so hurry me as the southern side current had done before, and so as to take from me all government of the boat; but having a strong steerage with my paddle, I went at a great rate directly for the wreck, and in less than two hours I came up to it.

It was a dismal sight to look at. The ship, which, by its building, was Spanish, stuck fast, jammed in between two rocks. All the stern and quarter of her was beaten to pieces with the sea; and as her forecastle, which stuck in the rocks, had run on with great violence, her mainmast and foremast were brought by the board; that is to say, broken short off; but her bowsprit was sound, and the head and bow appeared firm.

When I came close to her a dog appeared upon her, who, seeing me coming, yelped and cried; and as soon as I called him, jumped into the sea to come to me, and I took him into the boat, but found him almost dead for hunger and thirst. I gave him a cake of my bread, and he ate it like a ravenous wolf that had been starving a fortnight in the snow. I then gave the poor creature some fresh water, with which, if I would have let him, he would have burst himself.

After this I went on board; but the first sight I met with was two men drowned in the cook-room, or forecastle of the ship, with their arms fast about one another. I concluded, as is indeed probable, that when the ship struck, it being in a storm, the sea broke so high, and so continually over her, that the men were not able to bear it, and were strangled with the constant rushing in of the water, as much as if they had been under water. Besides the dog, there was nothing left in the ship that had life; nor any goods that I could see, but what were spoiled by the water. There were some casks of liquor, whether wine or brandy I knew not, which lay lower in the hold, and which, the water being ebbed out, I could see; but they were too big to meddle with. I saw several chests, which I believed belonged to some of the seamen; and I got two of them into the boat, without examining what was in them.

Had the stern of the ship been fixed, and the forepart broken off, I am persuaded I might have made a good voyage; for by what I found in these two chests, I had room to suppose the ship had a great deal of wealth on board; and if I may guess by the course she steered, she must have been bound from the Buenos Ayres, or the Rio de la Plata, in the south part of America, beyond the Brazils, to the Havana, in the Gulf of Mexico, and so perhaps to Spain. She had, no doubt, a great treasure in her, but of no use, at that time, to anybody; and what became of the rest of her people, I then knew not.

I found, besides these chests, a little cask full of liquor, of about twenty gallons, which I got into my boat with much difficulty. There were several muskets in a cabin, and a great powder-horn, with about four pounds of powder in it. As for the muskets, I had no occasion for them; so I left them, but took the powder-horn. I took a fire-shovel and tongs, which I wanted extremely; as also two little brass kettles, a copper pot to make chocolate, and a gridiron. And with this cargo, and the dog, I came away, the tide beginning to make home again; and the same evening, about an hour within night, I reached the island again, weary and fatigued to the last degree.

I reposed that night in the boat; and in the morning I resolved to harbour what I had gotten in my new cave, not to carry it home to my castle. After refreshing myself, I got all my cargo on shore, and began to examine the particulars. The cask of liquor I found to be a kind of rum, but not such as we had at the Brazils, and, in a word, not at all good. But when I came to open the chests, I found several things of great use to me. For example, I found in one a fine case of bottles, of an extraordinary kind, and filled with cordial waters, fine, and very good; the bottles held about three pints each, and were tipped with silver. I found two pots of very good succades, or sweetmeats, so fastened also on top, that the salt water had not hurt them; and two more of the same, which the water had spoiled. I found some very good shirts, which were very welcome to me; and about a dozen and a half of linen white handkerchiefs and coloured neckcloths. The former were also very welcome, being exceeding refreshing to wipe my face in a hot day. Besides this, when I came to the till in the chest, I found there three great bags of pieces of eight, which held out about eleven hundred pieces in all; and in one of them, wrapped up in a paper, six doubloons of gold, and some small bars or wedges of gold. I suppose they might all weigh near a pound.

The other chest I found had some clothes in it, but of little value; but by the circumstances, it must have belonged to the gunner's mate; though there was no powder in it, but about two pounds of fine glazed powder, in three small flasks, kept, I suppose, for charging their fowling-pieces on occasion. Upon the whole, I got very little by this voyage that was of any use to me; for as to the money, I had no manner of occasion for it; 'twas to me as the dirt under my feet; and I would have given it all for three or four pair of English shoes and stockings, which were things I greatly wanted, but had not had on my feet now for many years. I had indeed gotten two pair of shoes now, which I took off the feet of the two drowned men whom I saw in the wreck, and I found two pair more in one of the chests, which were very welcome to me; but they were not like our English shoes, either for ease or service, being rather what we call pumps than shoes. I found in this seaman's chest about fifty pieces of eight in royals, but no gold. I suppose this belonged to a poorer man than the other, which seemed to belong to some officer.

Well, however, I lugged this money home to my cave, and laid it up, as I had done that before which I brought from our own ship; but it was great pity, as I said, that the other part of this ship had not come to my share, for I am satisfied I might have loaded my canoe several times over with money, which, if I had ever escaped to England, would have lain here safe enough till I might have come again and fetched it.

Having now brought all my things on shore, and secured them, I went back to my boat, and rowed or paddled her along the shore to her old harbour, where I laid her up, and made the best of my way to my old habitation, where I found everything safe and quiet. So I began to repose myself, live after my old fashion, and take care of my family affairs; and, for a while, I lived easy enough, only that I was more vigilant than I used to be, looked out oftener, and did not go abroad so much; and if at any time I did stir with any freedom, it was always to the east part of the island, where I was pretty well satisfied the savages never came, and where I could go without so many precautions, and such a load of arms and ammunition as I always carried with me if I went the other way.

I lived in this condition near two years more; but my unlucky head, that was always to let me know it was born to make my body miserable, was all this two years filled with projects and designs, how, if it were possible, I might get away from this island; for sometimes I was for making another voyage to the wreck, though my reason told me that there was nothing left there worth the hazard of my voyage: sometimes for a ramble one way, sometimes another; and I believe verily, if I had had the boat that I went from Sallee in, I should have ventured to sea, bound anywhere, I knew not whither.

I have been, in all my circumstances, a memento to those who are touched with the general plague of mankind, whence, for aught I know, one-half of their miseries flow; I mean, that of not being satisfied with the station wherein God and Nature has placed them.

It was one of the nights in the rainy season in March, the four and twentieth year of my first setting foot in this island of solitariness. I was lying in my bed, or hammock, awake, very well in health, had no pain, no distemper, no uneasiness of body, no, nor any uneasiness of mind, more than ordinary, but could by no means close my eyes, that is, so as to sleep; no, not a wink all night long, otherwise than as follows.

It is as impossible, as needless, to set down the innumerable crowd of thoughts that whirled through that great thoroughfare of the brain, the memory, in this night's time. I ran over the whole history of my life in miniature, or by abridgment, as I may call it, to my coming to this island, and also of the part of my life since I came to this island.

My head was for some time taken up in considering the nature of these wretched creatures, I mean the savages, and how it came to pass in the world that the wise Governor of all things should give up any of His creatures to such inhumanity; nay, to something so much below even brutality itself, as to devour its own kind. But as this ended in some (at that time fruitless) speculations, it occurred to me to inquire what part of the world these wretches lived in? how far off the coast was from whence they came? what they ventured over so far from home for? what kind of boats they had? and why I might not order myself and my business so, that I might be as able to go over thither, as they were to come to me.

I never so much as troubled myself to consider what I should do with myself when I came thither; what would become of me, if I fell into the hands of the savages; or how I should escape from them, if they attempted me; no, nor so much as how it was possible for me to reach the coast, and not be attempted by some or other of them, without any possibility of delivering myself; and if I should not fall into their hands, what I should do for provision, or whither I should bend my course. None of these thoughts, I say, so much as came in my way; but my mind was wholly bent upon the notion of my passing over in my boat to the mainland. I looked back upon my present condition as the most miserable that could possibly be; that I was not able to throw myself into anything, but death, that could be called worse; that if I reached the shore of the main, I might perhaps meet with relief, or I might coast along, as I did on the shore of Africa, till I came to some inhabited country, and where I might find some relief; and after all, perhaps I might fall in with some Christian ship that might take me in; and if the worse came to the worst, I could but die, which would put an end to all these miseries at once.

When this had agitated my thoughts for two hours, or more, with such violence that it set my very blood into a ferment, and my pulse beat as high as if I had been in a fever, merely with the extraordinary fervour of my mind about it, Nature, as if I had been fatigued and exhausted with the very thought of it, threw me into a sound sleep. One would have thought I should have dreamed of it, but I did not, nor of anything relating to it; but I dreamed that as I was going out in the morning, as usual, from my castle, I saw upon the shore two canoes and eleven savages coming to land, and that they brought with them another savage, whom they were going to kill in order to eat him; when, on a sudden, the savage that they were going to kill jumped away, and ran for his life. And I thought, in my sleep, that he came running into my little thick grove before my fortification to hide himself; and that I, seeing him alone, and not perceiving that the other sought him that way, showed myself to him, and smiling upon him, encouraged him; that he kneeled down to me, seeming to pray me to assist him; upon which I showed my ladder, made him go up, and carried him into my cave, and he became my servant; and that as soon as I had gotten this man, I said to myself, "Now I may certainly venture to the mainland; for this fellow will serve me as a pilot, and will tell me what to do, and whither to go for provisions, and whither not to go for fear of being devoured; what places to venture into, and what to escape." I waked with this thought, and was under such inexpressible impressions of joy at the prospect of my escape in my dream, that the disappointments which I felt upon coming to myself and finding it was no more than a dream were equally extravagant the other way, and threw me into a very great dejection of spirit.

Upon this, however, I made this conclusion; that my only way to go about an attempt for an escape was, if possible, to get a savage into my possession; and, if possible, it should be one of their prisoners whom they had condemned to be eaten, and should bring thither to kill. But these thoughts still were attended with this difficulty, that it was impossible to effect this without attacking a whole caravan of them, and killing them all; and this was not only a very desperate attempt, and might miscarry, but, on the other hand, I had greatly scrupled the lawfulness of it to me; and my heart trembled at the thoughts of shedding so much blood, though it was for my deliverance. I need not repeat the arguments which occurred to me against this, they being the same mentioned before. But though I had other reasons to offer now, viz., that those men were enemies to my life, and would devour me if they could; that it was self-preservation, in the highest degree, to deliver myself from this death of a life, and was acting in my own defence as much as if they were actually assaulting me, and the like; I say, though these things argued for it, yet the thoughts of shedding human blood for my deliverance were very terrible to me, and such as I could by no means reconcile myself to a great while.

However, at last, after many secret disputes with myself, and after great perplexities about it, for all these arguments, one way and another, struggled in my head a long time, the eager prevailing desire of deliverance at length mastered all the rest, and I resolved, if possible, to get one of those savages into my hands, cost what it would. My next thing then was to contrive how to do it, and this indeed was very difficult to resolve on. But as I could pitch upon no probable means for it, so I resolved to put myself upon the watch, to see them when they came on shore, and leave the rest to the event, taking such measures as the opportunity should present, let be what would be.

With these resolutions in my thoughts, I set myself upon the scout as often as possible, and indeed so often, till I was heartily tired of it; for it was above a year and half that I waited; and for great part of that time went out to the west end, and to the south-west corner of the island, almost every day, to see for canoes, but none appeared. This was very discouraging, and began to trouble me much; though I cannot say that it did in this case, as it had done some time before that, viz., wear off the edge of my desire to the thing. But the longer it seemed to be delayed, the more eager I was for it. In a word, I was not at first so careful to shun the sight of these savages, and avoid being seen by them, as I was now eager to be upon them.

Besides, I fancied myself able to manage one, nay, two or three savages, if I had them, so as to make them entirely slaves to me; to do whatever I should direct them, and to prevent their being able at any time to do me any hurt. It was a great while that I pleased myself with this affair; but nothing still presented. All my fancies and schemes came to nothing, for no savages came near me for a great while.

About a year and half after I had entertained these notions, and by long musing had, as it were, resolved them all into nothing, for want of an occasion to put them in execution, I was surprised, one morning early, with seeing no less than five canoes all on shore together on my side the island, and the people who belonged to them all landed, and out of my sight. The number of them broke all my measures; for seeing so many, and knowing that they always came four, or six, or sometimes more, in a boat, I could not tell what to think of it, or how to take my measures to attack twenty or thirty men singlehanded; so I lay still in my castle, perplexed and discomforted. However, I put myself into all the same postures for an attack that I had formerly provided, and was just ready for action if anything had presented. Having waited a good while, listening to hear if they made any noise, at length, being very impatient, I set my guns at the foot of my ladder, and clambered up to the top of the hill, by my two stages, as usual; standing so, however, that my head did not appear above the hill, so that they could not perceive me by any means. Here I observed, by the help of my perspective glass that they were no less than thirty in number, that they had a fire kindled, that they had had meat dressed. How they had cooked it, that I knew not, or what it was; but they were all dancing, in I know not how many barbarous gestures and figures, their own way, round the fire.

While I was thus looking on them, I perceived by my perspective two miserable wretches dragged from the boats, where, it seems, they were laid by, and were now brought out for the slaughter. I perceived one of them immediately fell, being knocked down, I suppose, with a club or wooden sword, for that was their way, and two or three others were at work immediately, cutting him open for their cookery, while the other victim was left standing by himself, till they should be ready for him. In that very moment this poor wretch seeing himself a little at liberty, Nature inspired him with hopes of life, and he started away from them, and ran with incredible swiftness along the sands directly towards me, I mean towards that part of the coast where my habitation was.

I was dreadfully frighted (that I must acknowledge) when I perceived him to run my way, and especially when, as I thought, I saw him pursued by the whole body; and now I expected that part of my dream was coming to pass, and that he would certainly take shelter in my grove; but I could not depend, by any means, upon my dream for the rest of it, viz., that the other savages would not pursue him thither, and find him there. However, I kept my station, and my spirits began to recover when I found that there was not above three men that followed him; and still more was I encouraged when I found that he outstripped them exceedingly in running, and gained ground of them; so that if he could but hold it for half-an-hour, I saw easily he would fairly get away from them all.

There was between them and my castle the creek, which I mentioned often at the first part of my story, when I landed my cargoes out of the ship; and this I saw plainly he must necessarily swim over, or the poor wretch would be taken there. But when the savage escaping came thither he made nothing of it, though the tide was then up; but plunging in, swam through in about thirty strokes or thereabouts, landed, and ran on with exceeding strength and swiftness. When the three persons came to the creek, I found that two of them could swim, but the third could not, and that, standing on the other side, he looked at the other, but went no further, and soon after went softly back, which, as it happened, was very well for him in the main.

I observed, that the two who swam were yet more than twice as long swimming over the creek as the fellow was that fled from them. It came now very warmly upon my thoughts, and indeed irresistibly, that now was my time to get me a servant, and perhaps a companion or assistant, and that I was called plainly by Providence to save this poor creature's life. I immediately run down the ladders with all possible expedition, fetched my two guns, for they were both but at the foot of the ladders, as I observed above, and getting up again, with the same haste, to the top of the hill, I crossed toward the sea, and having a very short cut, and all down hill, clapped myself in the way between the pursuers and the pursued, hallooing aloud to him that fled, who, looking back, was at first perhaps as much frighted at me as at them; but I beckoned with my hand to him to come back; and, in the meantime, I slowly advanced towards the two that followed; then rushing at once upon the foremost, I knocked him down with the stock of my piece. I was loth to fire, because I would not have the rest hear; though, at that distance, it would not have been easily heard, and being out of sight of the smoke too, they would not have easily known what to make of it. Having knocked this fellow down, the other who pursued with him stopped, as if he had been frighted, and I advanced apace towards him; but as I came nearer, I perceived presently he had a bow and arrow, and was fitting it to shoot at me; so I was then necessitated to shoot at him first, which I did, and killed him at the first shot.

The poor savage who fled, but had stopped, though he saw both his enemies fallen and killed, as he thought, yet was so frighted with the fire and noise of my piece, that he stood stock-still, and neither came forward or went backward, though he seemed rather inclined to fly still, than to come on. I hallooed again to him, and made signs to come forward, which he easily understood, and came a little way, then stopped again, and then a little further, and stopped again; and I could then perceive that he stood trembling, as if he had been taken prisoner, and had just been to be killed, as his two enemies were. I beckoned him again to come to me, and gave him all the signs of encouragement that I could think of; and he came nearer and nearer, kneeling down every ten or twelve steps, in token of acknowledgment for my saving his life. I smiled at him, and looked pleasantly, and beckoned to him to come still nearer. At length he came close to me, and then he kneeled down again, kissed the ground, and laid his head upon the ground; and taking me by the foot, set my foot upon his head. This, it seems, was in token of swearing to be my slave for ever. I took him up, and made much of him, and encouraged him all I could. But there was more work to do yet; for I perceived the savage whom I knocke'd down was not killed, but stunned with the blow, and began to come to himself; so I pointed to him, and showing him the savage, that he was not dead, upon this he spoke some words to me; and though I could not understand them, yet I thought they were pleasant to hear; for they were the first sound of a man's voice that I had heard, my own excepted, for above twenty-five years. But there was no time for such reflections now. The savage who was knocked down recovered himself so far as to sit up upon the ground, and I perceived that my savage began to be afraid; but when I saw that, I presented my other piece at the man, as if I would shoot him. Upon this my savage, for so I call him now, made a motion to me to lend him my sword, which hung naked in a belt by my side; so I did. He no sooner had it but he runs to his enemy, and, at one blow, cut off his head as cleverly, no executioner in Germany could have done it sooner or better; which I thought very strange for one who, I had reason to believe, never saw a sword in his life before, except their own wooden swords. However, it seems, as I learned afterwards, they make their wooden swords so sharp, so heavy, and the wood is so hard, that they will cut off heads even with them, ay, and arms, and that at one blow too. When he had done this, he comes laughing to me in sign of triumph, and brought me the sword again, and with abundance of gestures, which I did not understand, laid it down, with the head of the savage that he had killed, just before me.

But that which astonished him most, was to know how I had killed the other Indian so far off; so pointing to him, he made signs to me to let him go to him; so I bade him go, as well as I could. When he came to him, he stood like one amazed, looking at him, turned him first on one side, then on t'other, looked at the wound the bullet had made, which, it seems, was just in his breast, where it had made a hole, and no great quantity of blood had followed; but he had bled inwardly, for he was quite dead. He took up his bow and arrows, and came back; so I turned to go away, and beckoned to him to follow me, making signs to him that more might come after them.

Upon this he signed to me that he should bury them with sand, that they might not be seen by the rest if they followed; and so I made signs again to him to do so. He fell to work, and in an instant he had scraped a hole in the sand with his hands big enough to bury the first in, and then dragged him into it, and covered him, and did so also by the other. I believe he had buried them both in a quarter of an hour. Then calling him away, I carried him, not to my castle, but quite away to my cave, on the farther part of the island; so I did not let my dream come to pass in that part, viz., that he came into my grove for shelter.

Here I gave him bread and a bunch of raisins to eat, and a draught of water, which I found he was indeed in great distress for, by his running; and having refreshed him, I made signs for him to go lie down and sleep, pointing to a place where I had laid a great parcel of rice-straw, and a blanket upon it, which I used to sleep upon myself sometimes; so the poor creature laid down, and went to sleep.

He was a comely, handsome fellow, perfectly well made, with straight strong limbs, not too large, tall, and well-shaped, and, as I reckon, about twenty-six years of age. He had a very good countenance, not a fierce and surly aspect, but seemed to have something very manly in his face; and yet he had all the sweetness and softness of an European in his countenance too, especially when he smiled. His hair was long and black, not curled like wool; his forehead very high and large; and a great vivacity and sparkling sharpness in his eyes. The colour of his skin was not quite black, but very tawny; and yet not of an ugly, yellow, nauseous tawny, as the Brazilians and Virginians, and other natives of America are, but of a bright kind of a dun olive colour, that had in it something very agreeable, though not very easy to describe. His face was round and plump; his nose small, not flat like the negroes; a very good mouth, thin lips, and his fine teeth well set, and white as ivory.

After he had slumbered, rather than slept, about half-an-hour, he waked again, and comes out of the cave to me, for I had been milking my goats, which I had in the enclosure just by. When he espied me, he came running to me, laying himself down again upon the ground, with all the possible signs of an humble, thankful disposition, making a many antic gestures to show it. At last he lays his head flat upon the ground, close to my foot, and sets my other foot upon his head, as he had done before, and after this made all the signs to me of subjection, servitude, and submission imaginable, to let me know how he would serve me as long as he lived. I understood him in many things, and let him know I was very well pleased with him. In a little time I began to speak to him, and teach him to speak to me; and, first, I made him know his name should be Friday, which was the day I saved his life. I called him so for the memory of the time. I likewise taught him to say master, and then let him know that was to be my name. I likewise taught him to say Yes and No, and to know the meaning of them. I gave him some milk in an earthen pot, and let him see me drink it before him, and sop my bread in it; and I gave him a cake of bread to do the like, which he quickly complied with, and made signs that it was very good for him.

I kept there with him all that night; but as soon as it was day, I beckoned to him to come with me, and let him know I would give him some clothes; at which he seemed very glad, for he was stark naked. As we went by the place where he had buried the two men, he pointed exactly to the place, and showed me the marks that he had made to find them again, making signs to me that we should dig them up again, and eat them. At this I appeared very angry, expressed my abhorrence of it, made as if I would vomit at the thoughts of it, and beckoned with my hand to him to come away; which he did immediately, with great submission. I then led him up to the top of the hill, to see if his enemies were gone; and pulling out my glass, I looked, and saw plainly the place where they had been, but no appearance of them or of their canoes; so that it was plain that they were gone, and had left their two comrades behind them, without any search after them.

But I was not content with this discovery; but having now more courage, and consequently more curiosity, I takes my man Friday with me, giving him the sword in his hand, with the bow and arrows at his back, which I found he could use very dexterously, making him carry one gun for me, and I two for myself, and away we marched to the place where these creatures had been; for I had a mind now to get some fuller intelligence of them. When I came to the place, my very blood ran chill in my veins, and my heart sunk within me, at the horror of the spectacle. Indeed, it was a dreadful sight, at least it was so to me, though Friday made nothing of it. The place was covered with human bones, the ground dyed with their blood, great pieces of flesh left here and there, half-eaten, mangled, and scorched; and, in short, all the tokens of the triumphant feast they had been making there, after a victory over their enemies. I saw three skulls, five hands, and the bones of three or four legs and feet, and abundance of other parts of the bodies; and Friday, by his signs, made me understand that they brought over four prisoners to feast upon; that three of them were eaten up, and that he, pointing to himself, was the fourth; that there had been a great battle between them and their next king, whose subjects it seems he had been one of, and that they had taken a great number of prisoners; all which were carried to several places by those that had taken them in the fight, in order to feast upon them, as was done here by these wretches upon those they brought hither.

I caused Friday to gather all the skulls, bones, flesh, and whatever remained, and lay them together on a heap, and make a great fire upon it, and burn them all to ashes. I found Friday had still a hankering stomach after some of the flesh, and was still a cannibal in his nature; but I discovered so much abhorrence at the very thoughts of it, and at the least appearance of it, that he durst not discover it; for I had, by some means, let him know that I would kill him if he offered it.

When we had done this we came back to our castle, and there I fell to work for my man Friday; and, first of all, I gave him a pair of linen drawers, which I had out

of the poor gunner's chest I mentioned, and which I found in the wreck; and which, with a little alteration, fitted him very well. Then I made him a jerkin of goat's-skin, as well as my skill would allow, and I was now grown a tolerable good tailor; and I gave him a cap, which I had made of a hare-skin, very convenient and fashionable enough; and thus he was clothed for the present tolerably well, and was mighty well pleased to see himself almost as well clothed as his master. It is true he went awkwardly in these things at first; wearing the drawers was very awkward to him, and the sleeves of the waistcoat galled his shoulders, and the inside of his arms; but a little easing them where he complained they hurt him, and using himself to them, at length he took to them very well.

The next day after I came home to my hutch with him, I began to consider where I should lodge him. And that I might do well for him, and yet be perfectly easy myself, I made a little tent for him in the vacant place between my two fortifications, in the inside of the last and in the outside of the first; and as there was a door or entrance there into my cave, I made a formal framed door-case, and a door to it of boards, and set it up in the passage, a little within the entrance; and causing the door to open on the inside, I barred it up in the night, taking in my ladders too; so that Friday could no way come at me in the inside of my innermost wall without making so much noise in getting over, that it must needs waken me; for my first wall had now a complete roof over it of long poles, covering all my tent, and leaning up to the side of the hill, which was again laid cross with smaller sticks instead of laths, and then thatched over a great thickness with the rice-straw, which was strong, like reeds; and at the hole or place which was left to go in or out by the ladder, I had placed a kind of trap-door, which, if it had been attempted on the outside, would not have opened at all, but would have fallen down, and made a great noise; and as to weapons, I took them all into my side every night.

But I needed none of all this precaution; for never man had a more faithful, loving, sincere servant than Friday was to me; without passions, sullenness, or designs, perfectly obliged and engaged; his very affections were tied to me, like those of a child to a father; and I dare say he would have sacrificed his life for the saving mine, upon any occasion whatsoever. The many testimonies he gave me of this put it out of doubt, and soon convinced me that I needed to use no precautions as to my safety on his account.

This frequently gave me occasion to observe, and that with wonder, that however it had pleased God, in His providence, and in the government of the works of His hands, to take from so great a part of the world of His creatures the best uses to which their faculties and the powers of their souls are adapted, yet that He has bestowed upon them the same powers, the same reason, the same affections, the same sentiments of kindness and obligation, the same passions and resentments of wrongs, the same sense of gratitude, sincerity, fidelity, and all the capacities of doing good, and receiving good, that He has given to us; and that when He pleases to offer to them occasions of exerting these, they are as ready, nay, more ready, to apply them to the right uses for which they were bestowed than we are.

But to return to my new companion. I was greatly delighted with him, and made it my business to teach him everything that was proper to make him useful, handy, and helpful; but especially to make him speak, and understand me when I spake. And he was the aptest scholar that ever was; and particularly was so merry, so constantly diligent, and so pleased when he could but understand me, or make me understand him, that it was very pleasant to me to talk to him. And now my life began to be so easy, that I began to say to myself, that could I but have been safe from more savages, I cared not if I was never to remove from the place while I lived.

After I had been two or three days returned to my castle, I thought that, in order to bring Friday off from his horrid way of feeding, and from the relish of a cannibal's stomach, I ought to let him taste other flesh; so I took him out with me one morning to the woods. I went, indeed, intending to kill a kid out of my own flock, and bring him home and dress it; but as I was going, I saw a she-goat lying down in the shade, and two young kids sitting by her. I catched hold of Friday. "Hold," says I, "stand still," and made signs to him not to stir. Immediately I presented my piece, shot and killed one of the kids, The poor creature, who had, at a distance indeed, seen me kill the savage, his enemy, but did not know, or could imagine, how it was done, was sensibly surprised, trembled and shook, and looked so amazed, that I thought he would have sunk down. He did not see the kid I had shot at, or perceive I had killed it, but ripped up his waistcoat to feel if he was not wounded; and, as I found presently, thought I was resolved to kill him; for he came and kneeled down to me, and embracing my knees, said a great many things I did not understand; but I could easily see that the meaning was to pray me not to kill him.

I soon found a way to convince him that I would do him no harm; and taking him up by the hand, laughed at him, and pointing to the kid which I had killed, beckoned to him to run and fetch it, which he did; and while he was wondering, and looking to see how the creature was killed, I loaded my gun again; and by-and-by I saw a great fowl, like a hawk, sit upon a tree, within shot; so, to let Friday understand a little what I would do, I called him to me again, pointing at the fowl, which was indeed a parrot, though I thought it had been a hawk; I say, pointing to the parrot, and to my gun, and to the ground under the parrot, to let him see I would make it fall, I made him understand that I would shoot and kill that bird. Accordingly I fired, and bade him look, and immediately he saw the parrot fall. He stood like one frighted again, notwithstanding all I had said to him; and I found he was the more amazed, because he did not see me put anything into the gun, but thought that there must be some wonderful fund of death and destruction in that thing, able to kill man, beast, bird, or anything near or far off; and the astonishment this created in him was such as could not wear off for a long time; and I believe, if I would have let him, he would have worshipped me and my gun. As for the gun itself, he would not so much as touch it for several days after; but would speak to it, and talk to it, as if it had answered him, when he was by himself; which, as I afterwards learned of him, was to desire it not to kill him.

Well, after his astonishment was a little over at this, I pointed to him to run and fetch the bird I had shot, which he did, but stayed some time; for the parrot, not being quite dead, was fluttered a good way off from the place where she fell. However, he found her, took her up, and brought her to me; and as I had perceived his ignorance about the gun before, I took this advantage to charge the gun again, and not let him see me do it, that I might be ready for any other mark that might present. But nothing more offered at that time; so I brought home the kid, and the same evening I took the skin off, and cut it out as well as I could; and having a pot for that purpose, I boiled or stewed some of the flesh, and made some very good broth; and after I had begun to eat some, I gave some to my man, who seemed very glad of it, and liked it very well; but that which was strangest to him, was to see me eat salt with it. He made a sign to me that the salt was not good to eat, and putting a little into his own mouth, he seemed to nauseate it, and would spit and sputter at it, washing his mouth with fresh water after it. On the other hand, I took some meat in my mouth without salt, and I pretended to spit and sputter for want of salt, as fast as he had done at the salt. But it would not do; he would never care for salt with his meat or in his broth; at least, not a great while, and then but a very little.

Having thus fed him with boiled meat and broth, I was resolved to feast him the next day with roasting a piece of the kid. This I did by hanging it before the fire in a string, as I had seen many people do in England, setting two poles up, one on each side of the fire, and one cross on the top, and tying the string to the cross stick, letting the meat turn continually. This Friday admired very much. But when he came to taste the flesh, he took so many ways to tell me how well he liked it, that I could not but understand him; and at last he told me he would never eat man's flesh any more, which I was very glad to hear.

The next day I set him to work to beating some corn out, and sifting it in the manner I used to do, as I observed before; and he soon understood how to do it as well as I, especially after he had seen what the meaning of it was, and that it was to make bread of; for after that I let him see me make my bread, and bake it too; and in a little time Friday was able to do all the work for me, as well as I could do it myself.

I began now to consider that, having two mouths to feed instead of one, I must provide more ground for my harvest, and plant a larger quantity of corn than I used to do; so I marked out a larger piece of land, and began the fence in the same manner as before, in which Friday not only worked very willingly and very hard, but did it very cheerfully; and I told him what it was for; that it was for corn to make more bread, because he was now with me, and that I might have enough for him and myself too. He appeared very sensible of that part, and let me know that he thought I had much more labour upon me on his account, than I had for myself; and that he would work the harder for me, if I would tell him what to do.

This was the pleasantest year of all the life I led in this place. Friday began to talk pretty well, and understand the names of almost everything I had occasion to call for, and of every place I had to send him to, and talk a great deal to me; so that, in short, I began now to have some use for my tongue again, which, indeed, I had very little occasion for before, that is to say, about speech. Besides the pleasure of talking to him, I had a singular satisfaction in the fellow himself. His simple, unfeigned honesty appeared to me more and more every day, and I began really to love the creature; and, on his side, I believe he loved me more than it was possible for him ever to love anything before.

I had a mind once to try if he had any hankering inclination to his own country again; and having learned him English so well that he could answer me almost any questions, I asked him whether the nation that he belonged to never conquered in battle? At which he smiled, and said, "Yes, yes, we always fight the better;" that is, he meant, always get the better in fight; and so we began the following discourse: "You always fight the better," said I. "How came you to be taken prisoner then, Friday?"

Friday. My nation beat much for all that.

Master. How beat? If your nation beat them, how came you to be taken?

Friday. They more many than my nation in the place where me was; they take one, two, three, and me. My nation overbeat them in the yonder place, where me no was; there my nation take one, two, great thousand.

Master. But why did not your side recover you from the hands of your enemies then?

Friday. They run one, two, three, and me, and make go in the canoe; my nation have no canoe that time.

Master. Well, Friday, and what does your nation do with the men they take? Do they carry them away and eat them, as these did?

Friday. Yes, my nation eats mans too; eat all up.

Master. Where do they carry them?

Friday. Go to other place, where they think.

Master. Do they come hither?

Friday. Yes, yes, they come hither; come other else place.

Master. Have you been here with them?

Friday. Yes, I been here. *(Points to the N.W. side of the island, which, it seems, was their side.)*

By this I understood that my man Friday had formerly been among the savages who used to come on shore on the farther part of the island, on the same man-eating occasions that he was now brought for; and, some time after, when I took the courage to carry him to that side, being the same I formerly mentioned, he presently knew the place, and told me he was there once when they eat up twenty men, two women, and one child. He could not tell twenty in English, but he numbered them by laying so many stones on a row, and pointing to me to tell them over.

I have told this passage, because it introduces what follows; that after I had had this discourse with him, I asked him how far it was from our island to the shore, and whether the canoes were not often lost. He told me there was no danger, no canoes ever lost; but that, after a little way out to the sea, there was a current and a wind, always one way in the morning, the other in the afternoon.

This I understood to be no more than the sets of the tide, as going out or coming in; but I afterwards understood it was occasioned by the great draught and reflux of the mighty river Oroonoko, in the mouth of the gulf of which river, as I found afterwards, our island lay; and this land which I perceived to the W. and NW. was the great island Trinidad, on the north point of the mouth of the river. I asked Friday a thousand questions about the country, the inhabitants, the sea, the coast, and what nations were near. He told me all he knew, with the greatest openness imaginable. I asked him the names of the several nations of his sort of people, but could get no other name than Caribs; from whence I easily understood that these were the Caribbees, which our maps place on the part of America which reaches from the mouth of the river Oroonoko to Guiana, and onwards to St Martha. He told me that up a great way beyond the moon, that was, beyond the setting of the moon, which must be W. from their country, there dwelt white-bearded men, like me, and pointed to my great whiskers, which I mentioned before; and that they had killed much mans, that was his word; by all which I understood he meant the Spaniards, whose cruelties in America had been spread over the whole countries, and was remembered by all the nations from father to son.

I inquired if he could tell me how I might come from this island and get among those white men. He told me, "Yes, yes, I might go in two canoe." I could not understand what he meant, or make him describe to me what he meant by two canoe; till at last, with great difficulty, I found he meant it must be in a large great boat, as big as two canoes.

This part of Friday's discourse began to relish with me very well; and from this time I entertained some hopes that, one time or other, I might find an opportunity to make my escape from this place, and that this poor savage might be a means to help me to do it.

During the long time that Friday had now been with me, and that he began to speak to me, and understand me, I was not wanting to lay a foundation of religious knowledge in his mind; particularly I asked him one time, Who made him? The poor creature did not understand me at all, so I took it by another handle, and asked him who made the sea, the ground we walked on, and the hills and woods? He told me it was one old Benamuckee, that lived beyond all. He could describe nothing of this great person, but that he was very old, much older, he said, than the sea or the land, than the moon or the stars. I asked him then, if this old person had made all things, why did not all things worship him? He looked very grave, and with a perfect look of innocence said, "All things do say O to him." I asked him if the people who die in his country went away anywhere? He said, "Yes, they all went to Benamuckee." Then I asked him whether these they eat up went thither too? He said "Yes."

From these things I began to instruct him in the knowledge of the true God. I told him that the great Maker of all things lived up there, pointing up towards heaven; that He governs the world by the same power and providence by which He had made it; that He was omnipotent, could do everything for us, give everything to us, take everything from us; and thus, by degrees, I opened his eyes. He listened with great attention, and received with pleasure the notion of Jesus Christ being sent to redeem us, and of the manner of making our prayers to God, and His being able to hear us, even into heaven. He told me one day that if our God could hear us up beyond the sun, He must needs be a greater God than their Benamuckee, who lived but a little way off, and yet could not hear till they went up to the great mountains where he dwelt to speak to him. I asked him if he ever went thither to speak to him? He said, No; they never went that were young men; none went thither but the old men, whom he called their Oowokakee, that is, as I made him explain it to me, their religious, or clergy; and that they went to say O (so he called saying prayers), and then came back, and told them what Benamuckee said. By this I observed that there is priestcraft even amongst the most blinded, ignorant pagans in the world; and the policy of making a secret religion in order to preserve the veneration of the people to the clergy is not only to be found in the Roman, but perhaps among all religions in the world, even among the most brutish and barbarous savages.

I endeavoured to clear up this fraud to my man Friday, and told him that the pretence of their old men going up to the mountains to say O to their god Benamuckee was a cheat, and their bringing word from thence what he said was much more so; that if they met with any answer, or spoke with any one there, it must be with an evil spirit; and then I entered into a long discourse with him about the devil, the original of him, his rebellion against God, his enmity to man, the reason of it, his setting himself up in the dark parts of the world to be worshipped instead of God, and as God, and the many stratagems he made use of to delude mankind to their ruin; how he had a secret access to our passions and to our affections, to adapt his snares so to our inclinations, as to cause us even to be our own tempters, and to run upon our destruction by our own choice.

I had been telling him how the devil was God's enemy in the hearts of men, and used all his malice and skill to defeat the good designs of Providence, and to ruin the kingdom of Christ in the world, and the like. "Well," says Friday, "but you say God is so strong, so great; is He not much strong, much might as the devil?" "Yes, yes," says I, "Friday, God is stronger than the devil; God is above the devil, and therefore we pray to God to tread him down under our feet, and enable us to resist his temptations, and quench his fiery darts." "But," says he again, "if God much strong, much might as the devil, why God no kill the devil, so make him no more do wicked?"

I was strangely surprised at his question; and after all, though I was now an old man, yet I was but a young doctor, and ill enough qualified for a casuist, or a solver of difficulties; and at first I could not tell what to say; so I pretended not to hear him, and asked him what he said? But he was too earnest for an answer to forget his question, so that he repeated it in the very same broken words as above. By this time I had recovered myself a little, and I said, "God will at last punish him severely; he is reserved for the judgment, and is to be cast into the bottomless pit, to dwell with everlasting fire." This did not satisfy Friday; but he returns upon me, repeating my words, "Reserve at last! me no understand; but why not kill the devil now? not kill great ago?" "You may as well ask me," said I, "why God does not kill you and I, when we do wicked things here that offend Him; we are preserved to repent and be pardoned." He muses awhile at this. "Well, well," says he, mighty affectionately, "that well; so you, I, devil, all wicked, all preserve, repent, God pardon all."

I therefore diverted the present discourse between me and my man, rising up hastily, as upon some sudden occasion of going out; then sending him for something a good way off, I seriously prayed to God that He would enable me to instruct savingly this poor savage, and would guide me to speak so to him from the Word of God as his conscience might be convinced, his eyes opened, and his soul saved. When he came again to me, I entered into a long discourse with him upon the subject of the redemption of man by the Saviour of the world, and of the doctrine of the Gospel preached from heaven, viz., of repentance towards God, and faith in our blessed Lord Jesus. I then explained to him as well as I could why our blessed Redeemer took not on Him the nature of angels, but the seed of Abraham; and how, for that reason, the fallen angels had no share in the redemption; that He came only to the lost sheep of the house of Israel, and the like.

In this thankful frame I continued all the remainder of my time, and the conversation which employed the hours between Friday and I was such as made the three years which we lived there together perfectly and completely happy, if any such thing as complete happiness can be formed in a sublunary state. The savage was now a good Christian, a much better than I; though I have reason to hope, and bless God for it, that we were equally penitent, and comforted, restored penitents. We had here the Word of God to read, and no farther off from His Spirit to instruct than if we had been in England.

As to all the disputes, wranglings, strife, and contention which has happened in the world about religion, whether niceties in doctrines, or schemes of Church government, they were all perfectly useless to us; as, for aught I can yet see, they have been to all the rest in the world. We had the sure guide to heaven, viz., the Word of God; and we had, blessed be God, comfortable views of the Spirit of God teaching and instructing us by His Word, leading us into all truth, and making us both willing and obedient to the instruction of His Word; and I cannot see the least use that the greatest knowledge of the disputed points in religion, which have made such confusions in the world, would have been to us if we could have obtained it. But I must go on with the historical part of things, and take every part in its order.

After Friday and I became more intimately acquainted, and that he could understand almost all I said to him, and speak fluently, though in broken English, to me, I acquainted him with my own story, or at least so much of it as related to my coming into the place; how I had lived there, and how long. I let him into the mystery, for such it was to him, of gunpowder and bullet, and taught him how to shoot; I gave him a knife, which he was wonderfully delighted with, and I made him a belt, with a frog hanging to it, such as in England we wear hangers in; and in the frog, instead of a hanger, I gave him a hatchet, which was not only as good a weapon, in some cases, but much more useful upon other occasions.

I described to him the country of Europe, and particularly England, which I came from; how we lived, how we worshipped God, how we behaved to one another, and how we traded in ships to all parts of the world. I gave him an account of the wreck which I had been on board of, and showed him, as near as I could, the place where she lay; but she was all beaten in pieces before, and gone.

I showed him the ruins of our boat, which we lost when we escaped, and which I could not stir with my whole strength then, but was now fallen almost all to pieces. Upon seeing this boat, Friday stood musing a great while, and said nothing. I asked him what it was he studied upon. At last says he, "Me see such boat like come to place at my nation."

I did not understand him a good while; but at last, when I had examined further into it, I understood by him that a boat such as that had been, came on shore upon the country where he lived; that is, as he explained it, was driven thither by stress of weather. I presently imagined that some European ship must have been cast away upon their coast, and the boat might get loose and drive ashore; but was so dull, that I never once thought of men making escape from a wreck thither, much less whence they might come; so I only inquired after a description of the boat.

Friday described the boat to me well enough; but brought me better to understand him when he added with some warmth, "We save the white mans from drown." Then I presently asked him if there was any white mans, as he called them, in the boat. "Yes," he said, "the boat full of white mans." I asked him how many. He told upon his fingers seventeen. I asked him then what became of them. He told me, "They live, they dwell at my nation."

This put new thoughts into my head; for I presently imagined that these might be the men belonging to the ship that was cast away in sight of my island, as I now call it; and who, after the ship was struck on the rock, and they saw her inevitably lost, had saved themselves in their boat, and were landed upon that wild shore among the savages.

Upon this I inquired of him more critically what was become of them. He assured me they lived still there; that they had been there about four years; that the savages let them alone, and gave them victuals to live. I asked him how it came to pass they did not kill them, and eat them. He said, "No, they make brother with them"; that is, as I understood him, a truce; and then he added, "They no eat mans but when make the war fight"; that is to say, they never eat any men but such as come to fight with them and are taken in battle.

It was after this some considerable time, that being on the top of the hill, at the east side of the island (from whence, as I have said, I had in a clear day discovered the main or continent of America), Friday, the weather being very serene, looks very earnestly towards the mainland, and, in a kind of surprise, falls a-jumping and dancing, and calls out to me, for I was at some distance from him. I asked him what was the matter? "O joy!" says he, "O glad! there see my country, there my nation!"

I observed an extraordinary sense of pleasure appeared in his face, and his eyes sparkled, and his countenance discovered a strange eagerness, as if he had a mind to be in his own country again; and this observation of mine put a great many thoughts into me, which made me at first not so easy about my new man Friday as I was before; and I made no doubt but that if Friday could get back to his own nation again, he would not only forget all his religion, but all his obligation to me; and would be forward enough to give his countrymen an account of me, and come back perhaps with a hundred or two of them, and make a feast upon me, at which he might be as merry as he used to be with those of his enemies, when they were taken in war.

But I wronged the poor honest creature very much, for which I was very sorry afterwards. However, as my jealousy increased, and held me some weeks, I was a little more circumspect, and not so familiar and kind to him as before; in which I was certainly in the wrong too, the honest, grateful creature having no thought about it

but what consisted with the best principles, both as a religious Christian and as a grateful friend, as appeared afterwards to my full satisfaction.

While my jealousy of him lasted, you may be sure I was every day pumping him, to see if he would discover any of the new thoughts which I suspected were in him; but I found everything he said was so honest and so innocent, that I could find nothing to nourish my suspicion; and, in spite of all my uneasiness, he made me at last entirely his own again, nor did he in the least perceive that I was uneasy, and therefore I could not suspect him of deceit.

One day, walking up the same hill, but the weather being hazy at sea, so that we could not see the continent, I called to him, and said, "Friday, do not you wish yourself in your own country, your own nation?" "Yes," he said, "I be much O glad to be at my own nation." "What would you do there?" said I. "Would you turn wild again, eat men's flesh again, and be a savage as you were before?" He looked full of concern, and shaking his head said, "No, no; Friday tell them to live good; tell them to pray God; tell them to eat corn-bread, cattle-flesh, milk, no eat man again." "Why then," said I to him, "they will kill you." He looked grave at that, and then said, "No, they no kill me, they willing love learn." He meant by this they would be willing to learn. He added, they learned much of the bearded mans that come in the boat. Then I asked him if he would go back to them? He smiled at that, and told me he could not swim so far. I told him I would make a canoe for him. He told me he would go, if I would go with him. "I go!" says I; "why, they will eat me if I come there." "No, no," says he, "me make they no eat you; me make they much love you." He meant, he would tell them how I had killed his enemies, and saved his life, and so he would make them love me. Then he told me, as well as he could, how kind they were to seventeen white men, or bearded men, as he called them, who came on shore there in distress.

From this time I confess I had a mind to venture over, and see if I could possibly join with these bearded men, who, I made no doubt, were Spaniards or Portuguese; not doubting but, if I could, we might find some method to escape from thence, being upon the continent, and a good company together, better that I could from an island forty miles off the shore, and alone, without help. So, after some days, I took Friday to work again, by way of discourse, and told him I would give him a boat to go back to his own nation; and accordingly I carried him to my frigate, which lay on the other side of the island, and having cleared it of water, for I always kept it sunk in the water, I brought it out, showed it him, and we both went into it.

I found he was a most dexterous fellow at managing it, would make it go almost as swift and fast again as I could. So when he was in I said to him, "Well now, Friday, shall we go to your nation?" He looked very dull at my saying so, which, it seems, was because he thought the boat too small to go so far. I told him then I had a bigger; so the next day I went to the place where the first boat lay which I had made, but which I could not get into water. He said that was big enough; but then, as I had taken no care of it, and it had lain two or three and twenty years there, the sun had split and dried it, that it was in a manner rotten. Friday told me such a boat would do very well, and would carry "much enough victual, drink, bread"; that was his way of talking.

Upon the whole, I was by this time so fixed upon my design of going over with him to the continent, that I told him we would go and make one as big as that, and he should go home in it. He answered not one word, but looked very grave and sad. I asked him what was the matter with him? He asked me again thus, "Why you angry mad with Friday? what me done?" I asked him what he meant. I told him I was not angry with him at all. "No angry! no angry!" says he, repeating the words several times. "Why send Friday home away to my nation?" "Why," says I, "Friday, did you not say you wished you were there?" "Yes, yes," says he, "wish be both there, no wish Friday there, no master there." In a word, he would not think of going there without me. "I go there, Friday?" says I; "what shall I do there?" He turned very quick upon me at this: "You do great deal much good," says he; "you teach wild mans to be good, sober, tame mans; you tell them know God, pray God, and live new life." "Alas! Friday," says I, "thou knowest not what thou sayest. I am but an ignorant man myself." "Yes, yes," says he, "you teachee me good, you teachee them good." "No, no, Friday," says I:, "you shall go without me; leave me here to live by myself; as I did before." He looked confused again at that word, and running to one of the hatchets which he used to wear, he takes it up hastily, comes and gives it me. "What must I do with this?" says I to him. "You take kill Friday," said he. "What must I kill you for?" said I again. He returns very quick, "What you send Friday away for? Take kill Friday, no send Friday away." This he spoke so earnestly, that I saw tears stand in his eyes. In a word, I so plainly discovered the utmost affection in him to me, and a firm resolution in him, that I told him then, and often after, that I would never send him away from me if he was willing to stay with me.

Upon the whole, as I found by all his discourse a settled affection to me, and that nothing should part him from me, so I found all the foundation of his desire to go to his own country was laid in his ardent affection to the people, and his hopes of my doing them good; a thing which, as I had no notion of myself, so I had not the least thought or intention or desire of undertaking it. But still I found a strong inclination to my attempting an escape, as above, founded on the supposition gathered from the discourse, viz., that there were seventeen bearded men there; and, therefore, without any more delay I went to work with Friday to find out a great tree proper to fell. and make a large *periagua,* or canoe, to undertake the voyage. There were trees enough in the island to have built a little fleet, not of *periaguas* and canoes, but even of good large vessels. But the main thing I looked at was, to get one so near the water that we might launch it when it was made, to avoid the mistake I committed at first.

At last Friday pitched upon a tree, for I found he knew much better than I what kind of wood was fittest for it; nor can I tell, to this day, what wood to call the tree we cut down, except that it was very like the tree we call fustic, or between that and the Nicaragua wood, for it was much of the same colour and smell. Friday was for burning the hollow or cavity of this tree out, to make it for a boat, but I showed him how rather to cut it out with tools; which, after I had showed him how to use, he did very handily; and in about a month's hard labour we finished it, and made it very handsome; especially when, with our axes, which I showed him how to handle, we cut and hewed the outside into the true shape of a boat After this, however, it cost us near a fortnight's time to get her along, as it were inch by inch, upon great rollers into the water; but when she was in, she would have carried twenty men with great ease.

When she was in the water, and though she was so big, it amazed me to see with what dexterity, and how swift my man Friday would manage her, turn her, and paddle her along. So I asked him if he would, and if we might venture over in her. "Yes," he said, "he venture over in her very well, though great blow wind." However, I had a farther design that he knew nothing of, and that was to make a mast and sail, and to fit her with an anchor and cable. As to a mast, that was easy enough to get; so I pitched upon a straight young cedar tree, which I found near the place, and which there was great plenty of in the island; and I set Friday to work to cut it down, and gave him directions how to shape and order it. But as to the sail, that was my particular care. I knew I had old sails, or rather pieces of old sails enough; but as I had had them now twenty-six years by me, and had not been very careful to preserve them, not imagining that I should ever have this kind of use for them, I did not doubt but they were all rotten, and, indeed, most of them were so. However, I found two pieces which appeared pretty good, and with these I went to work, and with a great deal of pains, and awkward tedious stitching (you may be sure) for want of needles, I, at length, made a three-corner ugly thing, like what we call in England a shoulder-of-mutton sail, to go with a boom at bottom, and a little short sprit at the top, such as usually our ships' longboats sail with, and such as I best know how to manage; because it was such a one as I had to the boat in which I made my escape from Barbary, as related in the first part of my story.

I was near two months performing this last work, viz., rigging and fitting my mast and sails; for I finished them very complete, making a small stay, and a sail, or foresail, to it, to assist, if we should turn to windward; and, which was more than all, I fixed a rudder to the stern of her to steer with; and though I was but a bungling shipwright, yet as I knew the usefulness, and even necessity, of such a thing, I applied myself with so much pains to do it, that at last I brought it to pass; though, considering the many dull contrivances I had for it that failed, I think it cost me almost as much labour as making the boat.

After all this was done too, I had my man Friday to teach as to what belonged to the navigation of my boat; for though he knew very well how to paddle a canoe, he knew nothing what belonged to a sail and a rudder; and was the most amazed when he saw me work the boat to and again in the sea by the rudder, and how the sail jibbed, and filled this way, or that way, as the course we sailed changed; I say, when he saw this, he stood like one astonished and amazed. However, with a little use I made all these things familiar to him, and he became an expert sailor, except that as to the compass I could make him understand very little of that. On the other hand, as there was very little cloudy weather, and seldom or never any fogs in those parts, there was the less occasion for a compass, seeing the stars were always to be seen by night, and the shore by day, except in the rainy seasons, and then nobody cared to stir abroad, either by land or sea.

I was now entered on the seven and twentieth year of my captivity in this place; though the three last years that I had this creature with me ought rather to be left out of the account, my habitation being quite of another kind than in all the rest of the time. I kept the anniversity of my landing here with the same thankfulness to God for His mercies as at first; and if I had such cause of acknowledgment at first, I had much more so now, having such additional testimonies of the care of Providence over me, and the great hopes I had of being effectually and speedily delivered; for I had an invincible impression upon my thoughts that my deliverance was at hand, and that I should not be another year in this place. However, I went on with my husbandry, digging, planting, fencing, as usual. I gathered and cured my grapes, and did every necessary thing as before.

The rainy season was, in the meantime, upon me, when I kept more within doors than at other times; so I had stowed our new vessel as secure as we could, bringing her up into the creek, where, as I said in the beginning, I landed my rafts from the ship; and hauling her up to the shore at high-water mark, I made my man Friday dig a little dock, just big enough to hold her, and just deep enough to give her water enough to float in; and then, when the tide was out, we made a strong dam across the end of it, to keep the water out; and so she lay dry, as to the tide, from the sea; and to keep the rain off, we laid a great many boughs of trees, so thick, that she was as well thatched as a house; and thus we waited for the month of November and December, in which I designed to make my adventure.

When the settled season began to come in, as the thought of my design returned with the fair weather, I was preparing daily for the voyage; and the first thing I did was to lay by a certain quantity of provisions, being the stores for our voyage; and intended, in a week or a fortnight's time, to open the dock, and launch out our boat. I was busy one morning upon something of this kind, when I called to Friday, and bid him go to the sea-shore and see if he could find a turtle, or tortoise, a thing which we generally got once a week, for the sake of the eggs as well as the flesh. Friday had not been long gone when he came running back, and flew over my outer wall, or fence, like one that felt not the ground, or the steps he set his feet on; and before I had time to speak to him, he cries out to me, "O master! O master! O sorrow! O bad!" "What's the matter, Friday?" says I. "O yonder, there," says he, "one, two, three canoe! one, two, three!" By his way of speaking, I concluded there were six; but, on inquiry, I found it was but three. "Well, Friday," says I, "do not be frighted." So I heartened him up as well as I could. However, I saw the poor fellow was most terribly scared; for nothing ran in his head but that they were come to look for him, and would cut him in pieces, and eat him; and the poor fellow trembled so, that I scarce knew what to do with him. I comforted him as well as I could, and told him I was in as much danger as he, and that they would eat me as well as him. "But," says I, "Friday, we must resolve to fight them. Can you fight, Friday?" "Me shoot," says he; "but there come many great number." "No matter for that," said I again; "our guns will fright them that we do not kill." So I asked him whether, if I resolved to defend him, he would defend me, and stand by me, and do just as I bid him. He said, "Me die when you bid die, master." So I went and fetched a good dram of rum, and gave him; for I had been so good a husband of my rum, that I had a great deal left. When he had drank it, I made him take the two fowling-pieces, which we always carried, and load them with large swan-shot, as big as small pistol-bullets. Then I took four muskets, and loaded them with two slugs and five small bullets each; and my two pistols I loaded with a brace of bullets each. I hung my great sword, as usual, naked by my side, and gave Friday his hatchet.

When I had thus prepared myself, I took my perspective glass, and went up to the side of the hill to see what I could discover; and I found quickly, by my glass, that there were one and twenty savages, three prisoners, and three canoes, and that their whole business seemed to be the triumphant banquet upon these three human bodies; a barbarous feast indeed, but nothing more than, as I had observed, was usual with them.

I observed also that they were landed, not where they had done when Friday made his escape, but nearer to my creek, where the shore was low, and where a thick wood came close almost down to the sea. This, with the abhorrence of the inhuman errand these wretches came about, filled me with such indignation, that I came down again to Friday, and told him I was resolved to go down to them, and kill them all, and asked him if he would stand by me. He was now gotten over his fright, and his spirits being a little raised with the dram I had given him, he was very cheerful, and told me, as before, he would die when I bid die.

In this fit of fury, I took first and divided the arms which I had charged, as before, between us. I gave Friday one pistol to stick in his girdle, and three guns upon his shoulder; and I took one pistol, and the other three myself; and in this posture we marched out. I took a small bottle of rum in my pocket, and gave Friday a large bag with more powder and bullet; and as to orders, I charged him to keep close behind me, and not to stir, or shoot, or do anything, till I bid him, and in the meantime not to speak a word. In this posture I fetched a compass to my right hand of near a mile, as well to get over the creek as to get into the wood, so that I might come within shot of them before I should be discovered, which I had seen, by my glass, it was easy to do.

While I was making this march, my former thoughts returning, I began to abate my resolution. I do not mean that I entertained any fear of their number; for as they were naked, unarmed wretches, 'tis certain I was superior to them; nay, though I had been alone. But it occurred to my thoughts what call, what occasion, much less what necessity, I was in to go and dip my hands in blood, to attack people who had neither done or intended me any wrong; that whenever God thought fit, He would take the cause into His own hands, and by national vengeance, punish them, as a people, for national crimes; but that, in the meantime, it was none of my business; that, it was true, Friday might justify it, because he was a declared enemy, and in a state of war with those very particular people, and it was lawful for him to attack them; but I could not say the same with respect to me. These things were so warmly pressed upon my thoughts all the way as I went, that I resolved I would only go and place myself near them that I might observe their barbarous feast, and that I would act then as God should direct; but that, unless something offered that was more a call to me than yet I knew of, I would not meddle with them.

With this resolution I entered the wood, and with alt possible wariness and silence, Friday following close at my heels, I marched till I came to the skirt of the wood, on the side which was next to them; only that one corner of the wood lay between me and them. Here I called softly to Friday, and showing him a great tree, which was just at the corner of the wood, I bade him go to the tree and bring me word if he could see there plainly what they were doing. He did so, and came immediately back to me, and told me they might be plainly viewed there; that they were all about their fire, eating the flesh of one of their prisoners, and that another lay bound upon the sand, a little from them, which, he said, they would kill next;

I cut the flags that bound the poor victim (page 354)

I showed them the new captain hanging at the yard-arm
(page 381)

and, which fired all the very soul within me, he told me it was not one of their nation, but one of the bearded men, whom he had told me of, that came to their country in the boat. I was filled with horror at the very naming the white bearded man; and going to the tree, I saw plainly, by my glass, a white man, who lay upon the beach of the sea, with his hands and his feet tied with flags, or things like rushes, and that he was an European, and had clothes on.

There was another tree, and a little thicket beyond it, about fifty yards nearer to them than the place where I was, which, by going a little way about, I saw I might come at undiscovered, and that then I should be within half shot of them; so I withheld my passion, though I was indeed enraged to the highest degree; and going back about twenty paces, I got behind some bushes, which held all the way till I came to the other tree; and then I came to a little rising ground, which gave me a full view of them, at the distance of about eighty yards.

I had now not a moment to lose, for nineteen of the dreadful wretches sat upon the ground, all close huddled together, and had just sent the other two to butcher the poor Christian, and bring him, perhaps limb by limb, to their fire; and they were stooped down to untie the bands at his feet. I turned to Friday: "Now, Friday," said I, "do as I bid thee." Friday said he would. "Then, Friday," says I, "do exactly as you see me do; fail in nothing." So I set down one of the muskets and the fowling-piece upon the ground, and Friday did the like by his; and with the other musket I took my aim at the savages, bidding him do the like. Then asking him if he was ready, he said, "Yes." "Then fire at them," said I; and the same moment I fired also.

Friday took his aim so much better than I, that on the side that he shot he killed two of them, and wounded three more; and on my side I killed one, and wounded two. They were, you may be sure, in a dreadful consternation; and all of them who were not hurt jumped up upon their feet, but did not immediately know which way to run, or which way to look, for they knew not from whence their destruction came. Friday kept his eyes close upon me, that, as I had bid him, he might observe what I did; so as soon as the first shot was made I threw down the piece, and took up the fowling-piece, and Friday did the like. He sees me cock and present; he did the same again. "Are you ready, Friday?" said I. "Yes," says he. "Let fly, then," says I, "in the name of God!" and with that I fired again among the amazed wretches, and so did Friday; and as our pieces were now loaded with what I called swan-shot, or small pistol-bullets, we found only two drop, but so many were wounded, that they ran about yelling and screaming like mad creatures, all bloody, and miserably wounded most of them; whereof three more fell quickly after, though not quite dead.

"Now, Friday," says I, laying down the discharged pieces, and taking up the musket which was yet loaded, "follow me," says I, which he did with a great deal of courage; upon which I rushed out of the wood, and showed myself; and Friday close at my foot. As soon as I perceived they saw me, I shouted as loud as I could, and bade Friday do so too; and running as fast as I could, which, by the way, was not very fast, being loaden with arms as I was, I made directly towards the poor victim, who was, as I said, lying upon the beach, or shore, between the place where they sat and the sea. The two butchers, who were just going to work with him, had left him at the surprise of our first fire, and fled in a terrible fright to the seaside, and had jumped into a canoe, and three more of the rest made the same way. I turned to Friday, and bid him step forwards and fire at them. He understood me immediately, and running about forty yards, to be near them, he shot at them, and I thought he had killed them all, for I saw them all fall of a heap into the boat; though I saw two of them up again quickly. However, he killed two of them, and wounded the third, so that he lay down in the bottom of the boat as if he had been dead.

While my man Friday fired at them, I pulled out my knife and cut the flags that bound the poor victim; and loosing his hands and feet, I lifted him up, and asked him in the Portuguese tongue what he was. He answered in Latin, Christianus; but was so weak and faint, that he could scarce stand or speak. I took my bottle out of my pocket and gave it him, making signs that he should drink, which he did; and I gave him a piece of bread, which he ate. Then I asked him what countryman he was; and he said, Espagniole; and being a little recovered, let me know, by all the signs he could possibly make, how much he was in my debt for his deliverance. "Seignior," said I, with as much Spanish as I could make up, "we will talk afterwards, but we must fight now. If you have any strength left, take this pistol and sword, and lay about you." He took them very thankfully, and no sooner had he the arms in his hands but, as if they had put new vigour into him, he flew upon his murderers like a fury, and had cut two of them in pieces in an instant; for the truth is, as the whole was a surprise to them, so the poor creatures were so much frighted with the noise of our pieces, that they fell down for mere amazement and fear, and had no more power to attempt their own escape, than their flesh had to resist our shot; and that was the case of those five that Friday shot at in the boat; for as three of them fell with the hurt they received, so the other two fell with the fright.

I kept my piece in my hand still without firing, being willing to keep my charge ready, because I had given the Spaniard my pistol and sword. So I called to Friday, and bade him run up to the tree from whence we first fired, and fetch the arms which lay there that had been discharged, which he did with great swiftness; and then giving him my musket, I sat down myself to load all the rest again, and bade them come to me when they wanted. While I was loading these pieces, there happened a fierce engagement between the Spaniard and one of the savages, who made at him with one of their great wooden swords, the same weapon that was to have killed him before if I had not prevented it. The Spaniard, who was as bold and as brave as could be imagined, though weak, had fought this Indian a good while, and had cut him two great wounds on his head; but the savage being a stout, lusty fellow, closing in with him, had thrown him down, being faint, and was wringing my sword out of his hand, when the Spaniard, though undermost, wisely quitting the sword, drew the pistol from his girdle, shot the savage through the body, and killed him upon the spot before I, who was running to help him, could come near him.

Friday being now left to his liberty, pursued the flying wretches with no weapon in his hand but his hatchet; and with that he despatched those three who, as I said before, were wounded at first, and fallen, and all the rest he could come up with; and the Spaniard coming to me for a gun, I gave him one of the fowling-pieces, with which he pursued two of the savages, and wounded them both; but as he was not able. to run, they both got from him into the wood, where Friday pursued them, and killed one of them; but the other was too nimble for him, and though he was wounded, yet had plunged himself into the sea and swam with all his might off to those two who were left in the canoe; which three in the canoe, with one wounded, who we know not whether he died or no, were all that escaped our hands of one and twenty. The account of the rest is as follows:—

3 killed at our first shot from the tree.
2 killed at the next shot.
2 killed by Friday in the boat.
2 killed by ditto, of those at first wounded.
1 killed by ditto in the wood.
3 killed by the Spaniard.
4 killed, being found dropped here and there of their wounds, or killed by
   Friday in his chase of them.
4 escaped in the boat, whereof one wounded, if not dead.
—
21 in all.

Those that were in the canoe worked hard to get out of gunshot; and though Friday made two or three shots at them, I did not find that he hit any of them. Friday would fain have had me take one of their canoes, and pursued them; and, indeed, I was very anxious about their escape, lest carrying the news home to their people they should come back perhaps with two or three hundred of their canoes, and devour us by mere multitude. So I consented to pursue them by sea, and running to one of their canoes I jumped in, and bade Friday follow me. But when I was in the canoe, I was surprised to find another poor creature lie there alive, bound hand and foot, as the Spaniard was, for the slaughter, and almost dead with fear, not knowing what the matter was; for he had not been able to look up over the side of the boat, he was tied so hard, neck and heels, and had been tied so long, that he had really but little life in him.

I immediately cut the twisted flags or rushes, which they had bound him with, and would have helped him up; but he could not stand or speak, but groaned most piteously, believing, it seems, still that he was only unbound in order to be killed.

When Friday came to him, I bade him speak to him, and tell him of his deliverance; and pulling out my bottle, made him give the poor wretch a dram; which, with the news of his being delivered, revived him, and he sat up in the boat. But when Friday came to hear him speak, and look in his face, it would have moved

any one to tears to have seen how Friday kissed him, embraced him, hugged him, cried, laughed, hallooed, jumped about, danced, sung; then cried again, wrung his hands, beat his own face and head, and then sung and jumped about again, like a distracted creature. It was a good while before I could make him speak to me, or tell me what was the matter; but when he came a little to himself, he told me that it was his father.

It is not easy for me to express how it moved me to see what ecstasy and filial affection had worked in this poor savage at the sight of his father, and of his being delivered from death; nor, indeed, can I describe half the extravagancies of his affection after this; for he went into the boat, and out of the boat, a great many times. When he went in to him, he would sit down by him, open his breast, and hold his father's head close to his bosom, half-an-hour together, to nourish it; then he took his arms and ankles, which were numbed and stiff with the binding, and chafed and rubbed them with his hands; and I, perceiving what the case was, gave him some rum out of my bottle to rub them with, which did them a great deal of good.

This action put an end to our pursuit of the canoe with the other savages, who were now gotten almost out of sight; and it was happy for us that we did not, for it blew so hard within two hours after, and before they could be gotten a quarter of their way, and continued blowing so hard all night, and that from the north-west, which was against them, that I could not suppose their boat could live, or that they ever reached to their own coast.

But to return to Friday. He was so busy about his father, that I could not find in my heart to take him off for some time; but after I thought he could leave him a little, I called him to me, and he came jumping and laughing, and pleased to the highest extreme. Then I asked him if he had given his father any bread. He shook his head, and said, "None; ugly dog eat all up self." So I gave him a cake of bread out of a little pouch I carried on purpose. I also gave him a dram for himself, but he would not taste it, but carried it to his father. I had in my pocket also two or three bunches of my raisins, so I gave him a handful of them for his father. He had no sooner given his father these raisins, but I saw him come out of the boat and run away, as if he had been bewitched, he ran at such a rate; for he was the swiftest fellow of his foot that ever I saw. I say, he run at such a rate, that he was out of sight, as it were, in an instant; and though I called, and hallooed too, after him, it was all one, away he went; and in a quarter of an hour I saw him come back again, though not so fast as he went; and as he came nearer I found his pace was slacker, because he had something in his hand.

When he came up to me, I found he had been quite home for an earthen jug, or pot, to bring his father some fresh water and that he had got two more cakes or loaves of bread. The bread he gave me, but the water he carried to his father. However, as I was very thirsty too, I took a little sup of it. This water revived his father more than all the rum or spirits I had given him, for he was just fainting with thirst.

When his father had drank, I called to him to know if there was any water left. He said "Yes;" and I bade him give it to the poor Spaniard, who was in as much want of it as his father; and I sent one of the cakes, that Friday brought, to the Spaniard too, who was indeed very weak, and was reposing himself upon a green place under the shade of a tree; and whose limbs were also very stiff, and very much swelled with the rude bandage he had been tied with. When I saw that upon Friday's coming to him with the water he sat up and drank, and took the bread, and began to eat, I went to him, and gave him a handful of raisins. He looked up in my face with all the tokens of gratitude and thankfulness that could appear in any countenance; but was so weak, notwithstanding he had so exerted himself in the fight, that he could not stand up upon his feet. He tried to do it two or three times, but was really not able, his ankles were so swelled and so painful to him; so I bade him sit still, and caused Friday to rub his ankles, and bathe them with rum, as he had done his father's.

I observed the poor affectionate creature, every two minutes, or perhaps less, all the while he was here, turned his head about to see if his father was in the same place and posture as he left him sitting; and at last he found he was not to be seen; at which he started up, and without speaking a word, flew with that swiftness to him, that one could scarce perceive his feet to touch the ground as he went. But when he came, he only found he had laid himself down to ease his limbs; so Friday came back to me presently, and I then spoke to the Spaniard to let Friday help him up; if he could, and lead him to the boat, and then he should carry him to our dwelling, where I would take care of him. But Friday, a lusty strong fellow, took the Spaniard quite up upon his back, and carried him away to the boat, and set him down softly upon the side or gunnel of the canoe, with his feet in the inside of it, and then lifted him quite in, and set him close to his father; and presently stepping out again, launched the boat off, and paddled it along the shore faster than I could walk, though the wind blew pretty hard too. So he brought them both safe into our creek, and leaving them in the boat, runs away to fetch the other canoe. As he passed me, I spoke to him, and asked him whither he went. He told me, "Go fetch more boat." So away he went like the wind, for sure never man or horse ran like him; and he had the other canoe in the creek almost as soon as I got to it by land; so he wafted me over, and then went to help our new guests out of the boat, which he did; but they were neither of them able to walk, so that poor Friday knew not what to do.

To remedy this I went to work in my thought, and calling to Friday to bid them sit down on the bank while he came to me, I soon made a kind of hand-barrow to lay them on, and Friday and I carried them up both together upon it between us. But when we got them to the outside of our wall, or fortification, we were at a worse loss than before, for it was impossible to get them over, and I was resolved not to break it down. So I set to work again; and Friday and I, in about two hours' time, made a very handsome tent, covered with old sails, and above that with boughs of trees, being in the space without our outward fence, and between that and the grove of young wood which I had planted; and here we made them two beds of such things as I had, viz., of good rice-straw, with blankets laid upon it to lie on, and another to cover them, on each bed.

My island was now peopled, and I thought myself very rich in subjects; and it was a merry reflection, which I frequently made, how like a king I looked. First of all, the whole country was my own mere property, so that I had an undoubted right of dominion. Secondly, my people were perfectly subjected I was absolute lord and lawgiver; they all owed their lives to me, and were ready to lay down their lives, if there had been occasion of it, for me. It was remarkable, too, we had but three subjects, and they were of three different religions. My man Friday was a Protestant, his father was a Pagan and a cannibal, and the Spaniard was a Papist. However, I allowed liberty of conscience throughout my dominions. But this is by the way.

As soon as I had secured my two weak rescued prisoners, and given them shelter and a place to rest them upon, I began to think of making some provision for them; and the first thing I did, I ordered Friday to take a yearling goat, betwixt a kid and a goat, out of my particular flock, to be killed; when I cut off the hinder-quarter, and chopping it into small pieces, I set Friday to work to boiling and stewing, and made them a very good dish, I assure you, of flesh and broth, having put some barley and rice also into the broth; and as I cooked it without doors, for I made no fire within my inner wall, so I carried it all into the new tent, and having set a table there for them, I sat down and ate my own dinner also with them, and as well as I could cheered them, and encouraged them; Friday being my interpreter, especially to his father, and, indeed, to the Spaniard too; for the Spaniard spoke the language of the savages pretty well.

After we had dined, or rather supped, I ordered Friday to take one of the canoes and go and fetch our muskets and other firearms, which, for want of time, we had left upon the place of battle; and the next day I ordered him to go and bury the dead bodies of the savages, which lay open to the sun, and would presently be offensive; and I also ordered him to bury the horrid remains of their barbarous feast, which I knew were pretty much, and which I could not think of doing myself; nay, I could not bear to see them, if I went that way. All which he punctually performed, and defaced the very appearance of the savages being there; so that when I went again I could scarce know where it was, otherwise than by the corner of the wood pointing to the place.

I then began to enter into a little conversation with my two new subjects; and first, I set Friday to inquire of his father what he thought of the escape of the savages in that canoe, and whether we might expect a return of them, with a power too great for us to resist. His first opinion was, that the savages in the boat never could live out the storm which blew that night they went off, but must, of necessity, be drowned, or driven south to those other shores, where they were as sure to be devoured as they were to be drowned if they were cast away. But as to what they would do if they came safe on shore, he said he knew not; but it was his opinion that they were so dreadfully frighted with the manner of their being attacked, the noise, and the fire, that he believed they would tell their people they were all killed by thunder and lightning, not by the hand of man; and that the two which appeared, viz., Friday and me, were two heavenly spirits, or furies, come down to destroy them, and not men with weapons. This, he said, he knew, because he heard them all cry out so in their language to one another; for it was impossible to them to conceive that a man could dart fire, and speak thunder, and kill at a distance without lifting up the hand, as was done now. And this old savage was in the right; for, as I understood since by other hands, the savages never attempted to go over to the island afterwards. They were so terrified with the accounts given by those four men (for, it seems, they did escape the sea), that they believed whoever went to that enchanted island would be destroyed with fire from the gods.

This, however, I knew not, and therefore was under continual apprehensions for a good while, and kept always upon my guard, me and all my army; for as we were now four of us, I would have ventured upon a hundred of them, fairly in the open field, at any time.

In a little time, however, no more canoes appearing, the fear of their coming wore off, and I began to take my former thoughts of a voyage to the main into consideration; being likewise assured, by Friday's father, that I might depend upon good usage from their nation, on his account, if I would go.

But my thoughts were a little suspended when I had a serious discourse with the Spaniard, and when I understood that there were sixteen more of his countrymen and Portuguese who, having been cast away, and made their escape to that side, lived there at peace, indeed, with the savages, but were very sore put to it for necessaries, and indeed for life. I asked him all the particulars of their voyage, and found they were a Spanish ship bound from the Rio de la Plata to the Havana, being directed to leave their loading there, which was chiefly hides and silver, and to bring back what European goods they could meet with there; that they had five Portuguese seamen on board, whom they took out of another wreck; that five of their own men were drowned when the first ship was lost, and that these escaped, through infinite dangers and hazards, and arrived, almost starved, on the cannibal coast, where they expected to have been devoured every moment.

He told me they had some arms with them, but they were perfectly useless, for that they had neither powder or ball, the washing of the sea having spoiled all their powder but a little, which they used, at their first landing, to provide themselves some food.

I asked him what he thought would become of them there, and if they had formed no design of making any escape? He said they had many consultations about it; but that having neither vessel, or tools to build one, or provisions of any kind, their councils always ended in tears and despair.

I asked him how he thought they would receive a proposal from me, which might tend towards an escape; and whether, if they were all here, it might not be done? I told him with freedom, I feared mostly their treachery and ill usage of me if I put my life in their hands; for that gratitude was no inherent virtue in the nature of man, nor did men always square their dealings by the obligations they had received, so much as they did by the advantages they expected. I told him it would be very hard that I should be the instrument of their deliverance, and that they should afterwards make me their prisoner in New Spain, where an Englishman was certain to be made a sacrifice, what necessity or what accident soever brought him thither; and that I had rather be delivered up to the savages, and be devoured alive, than fall into the merciless claws of the priests, and be carried into the Inquisition. I added, that otherwise I was persuaded, if they were all here, we might, with so many hands, build a bark large enough to carry us all away, either to the Brazils, southward, or to the islands, or Spanish coast, northward; but that if, in requital, they should, when I had put weapons into their hands, carry me by force among their own people, I might be ill used for my kindness to them, and make my case worse than it was before.

He answered, with a great deal of candour and ingenuity, that their condition was so miserable, and they were so sensible of it, that he believed they would abhor the thought of using any man unkindly that should contribute to their deliverance; and that, if I pleased, he would go to them with the old man, and discourse with them about it, and return again, and bring me their answer; that he would make conditions with them upon their solemn oath that they should be absolutely under my leading, as their commander and captain; and that they should swear upon the holy sacraments and the gospel to be true to me, and to go to such Christian country as that I should agree to, and no other, and to be directed wholly and absolutely by my orders till they were landed safely in such country as I intended; and that he would bring a contract from them, under their hands, for that purpose.

Then he told me he would first swear to me himself, that he would never stir from me as long as he lived till I gave him orders; and that he would take my side to the last drop of his blood, if there should happen the least breach of faith among his countrymen.

He told me they were all of them very civil, honest men, and they were under the greatest distress imaginable, having neither weapons or clothes, or any food, but at the mercy and discretion of the savages; out of all hopes of ever returning to their own country; and that he was sure, if I would undertake their relief, they would live and die by me.

Upon these assurances, I resolved to venture to relieve them, if possible, and to send the old savage and this Spaniard over to them to treat. But when we had gotten all things in a readiness to go, the Spaniard himself started an objection, which had so much prudence in it on one hand, and so much sincerity on the other hand, that I could not but be very well satisfied in it, and by his advice put off the deliverance of his comrades for at least half a year. The case was thus.

He had been with us now about a month, during which time I had let him see in what manner I had provided, with the assistance of Providence, for my support; and he saw evidently what stock of corn and rice I had made up; which, as it was more than sufficient for myself so it was not sufficient, at least without good husbandry, for my family, now it was increased to number four; but much less would it be sufficient if his countrymen, who were, as he said, fourteen, still alive, should come over; and least of all would it be sufficient to victual our vessel, if we should build one, for a voyage to any of the Christian colonies of America. So he told me he thought it would be more advisable to let him and the two others dig and cultivate some more land, as much as I could spare seed to sow; and that we should wait another harvest, that we might have a supply of corn for his countrymen when they should come; for want might be a temptation to them to disagree, or not to think themselves delivered, otherwise than out of one difficulty into another. "You know," says he, "the children of Israel, though they rejoiced at first for their being delivered out of Egypt, yet rebelled even against God Himself, that delivered them, when they came to want bread in the wilderness."

His caution was so seasonable, and his advice so good, that I could not but be very well pleased with his proposal, as well as I was satisfied with his fidelity. So we fell to digging all four of us, as well as the wooden tools we were furnished with permitted; and in about a month's time, by the end of which it was seed-time, we had gotten as much land cured and trimmed up as we sowed twenty-two bushels of barley on, and sixteen jars of rice; which was, in short, all the seed we had to spare; nor, indeed, did we leave ourselves barley sufficient for our own food for the six months that we had to expect our crop; that is to say, reckoning from the time we set our seed aside for sowing; for it is not to be supposed it is six months in the ground in that country.

Having now society enough, and our number being sufficient to put us out of fear of the savages, if they had come, unless their number had been very great, we went freely all over the island, wherever we found occasion; and as here we had our escape or deliverance upon our thoughts, it was impossible, at least for me, to have the means of it out of mine. To this purpose I marked out several trees which I thought fit for our work, and I set Friday and his father to cutting them down; and then I caused the Spaniard, to whom I imparted my thought on that affair, to oversee and direct their work. I showed them with what indefatigable pains I had hewed a large tree into single planks, and I caused them to do the like, till they had made about a dozen large planks of good oak, near two feet broad, thirty-five feet long, and from two inches to four inches thick. What prodigious labour it took up, any one may imagine.

At the same time, I contrived to increase my little flock of tame goats as much as I could; and to this purpose I made Friday and the Spaniard go out one day, and myself with Friday the next day, for we took our turns, and by this means we got above twenty young kids to breed up with the rest; for whenever we shot the dam, we saved the kids, and added them to our flock. But above all, the season for curing the grapes coming on, I caused such a prodigious quantity to be hung up in the sun, that I believe, had we been at Alicant, where the raisins of the sun are cured, we could have filled sixty or eighty barrels; and these, with our bread, was a great part of our food, and very good living too, I assure you; for it is an exceeding nourishing food.

It was now harvest, and our crop in good order. It was not the most plentiful increase I had seen in the island, but, however, it was enough to answer our end; for from our twenty-two bushels of barley we brought in and thrashed out above two hundred and twenty bushels, and the like in proportion of the rice; which was store enough for our food to the next harvest, though all the sixteen Spaniards had been on shore with me; or if we had been ready for a voyage, it would very plentifully have victualled our ship to have carried us to any part of the world, that is to say, of America.

When we had thus housed and secured our magazine of corn, we fell to work to make more wicker-work, viz., great baskets, in which we kept it; and the Spaniard was very handy and dexterous at this part, and often blamed me that I did not make some things for defence of this kind of work; but I saw no need of it.

And now having a full supply of food for all the guests I expected, I gave the Spaniard leave to go over to the main, to see what he could do with those he had left behind him there. I gave him a strict charge in writing not to bring any man with him who would not first swear, in the presence of himself and of the old savage, that he would no way injure, fight with, or attack the person he should find in the island, who was so kind to send for them in order to their deliverance; but that they would stand by and defend him against all such attempts, and wherever they went would be entirely under and subjected to his commands; and that this should be put in writing, and signed with their hands. How we were to have this done, when I knew they had neither pen or ink, that indeed was a question which we never asked.

Under these instructions, the Spaniard and the old savage, the father of Friday, went away in one of the canoes which they might be said to come in, or rather were brought in, when they came as prisoners to be devoured by the savages.

I gave each of them a musket, with a firelock on it, and about eight charges of powder and ball, charging them to be very good husbands of both, and not to use either of them but upon urgent occasion.

This was a cheerful work, being the first measures used by me, in view of my deliverance, for now twenty-seven years and some days. I gave them provisions of bread and of dried grapes sufficient for themselves for many days, and sufficient for all their countrymen for about eight days' time; and wishing them a good voyage, I see them go, agreeing with them about a signal they should hang out at their return, by which I should know them again, when they came back, at a distance, before they came on shore.

They went away with a fair gale on the day that the moon was at full, by my account in the month of October; but as for an exact reckoning of days, after I had once lost it, I could never recover it again; nor had I kept even the number of years so punctually as to be sure that I was right, though as it proved, when I afterwards examined my account, I found I had kept a true reckoning of years.

It was no less than eight days I had waited for them, when a strange and unforeseen accident intervened, of which the like has not perhaps been heard of in history. I was fast asleep in my hutch one morning, when my man Friday came running in to me, and called aloud, "Master, master, they are come, they are come!"

I jumped up, and, regardless of danger, I went out as soon as I could get my clothes on, through my little grove, which, by the way, was by this time grown to be a very thick wood; I say, regardless of danger, I went without my arms, which was not my custom to do; but I was surprised when, turning my eyes to the sea, I presently saw a boat at about a league and half's distance standing in for the shore, with a shoulder-of mutton sail, as they call it, and the wind blowing pretty fair to bring them in; also I observed presently that they did not come from that side which the shore lay on, but from the southernmost end of the island. Upon this I called Friday in, and bid him lie close, for these were not the people we looked for, and that we might not know yet whether they were friends or enemies.

In the next place, I went in to fetch my perspective glass, to see what I could make of them; and having taken the ladder out, I climbed up to the top of the hill, as I used to do when I was apprehensive of anything, and to take my view the plainer, without being discovered.

I had scarce set my foot on the hill, when my eye plainly discovered a ship lying at an anchor at about two leagues and an half's distance from me, south-south-east, but not above a league and an half from the shore. By my observation, it appeared plainly to be an English ship, and the boat appeared to be an English longboat.

I cannot express the confusion I was in; though the joy of seeing a ship, and one who I had reason to believe was manned by my own countrymen, and consequently friends, was such as I cannot describe. But yet I had some secret doubts hung about me, I cannot tell from whence they came, bidding me keep upon my guard. In the first place, it occurred to me to consider what business an English ship could have in that part of the world, since it was not the way to or from any part of the world where the English had any traffic; and I knew there had been no storms to drive them in there as in distress; and that if they were English really, it was most probable that they were here upon no good design; and that I had better continue as I was, than fall into the hands of thieves and murderers.

I had not kept myself long in this posture, but I saw the boat draw near the shore, as if they looked for a creek to thrust in at, for the convenience of landing. However, as they did not come quite far enough, they did not see the little inlet where I formerly landed my rafts; but run their boat on shore upon the beach, at about half a mile from me, which was very happy for me; for otherwise they would have landed just, as I may say, at my door, and would soon have beaten me out of my castle, and perhaps have plundered me of all I had.

When they were on shore, I was fully satisfied that they were Englishmen, at least most of them; one or two I thought were Dutch, but it did not prove so. There were in all eleven men, whereof three of them I found were unarmed and, as I thought, bound; and when the first four or five of them were jumped on shore, they took those three out of the boat, as prisoners. One of the three I could perceive using the most passionate gestures of entreaty, affliction, and despair, even to a kind of extravagance; the other two, I could perceive, lifted up their hands sometimes, and appeared concerned indeed, but not to such a degree as the first.

I was perfectly confounded at the sight, and knew not what the meaning of it should be. Friday called out to me in English as well as he could, "O master! you see English mans eat prisoner as well as savage mans." "Why," says I, "Friday, do you think they are a-going to eat them then?" "Yes," says Friday, "they will eat them." "No, no," says I, "Friday, I am afraid they will murder them indeed, but you may be sure they will not eat them.

All this while I had no thought of what the matter really was, but stood trembling with the horror of the sight, expecting every moment when the three prisoners should be killed; nay, once I saw one of the villains lift up his arm with a great cutlass, as the seamen call it, or sword, to strike one of the poor men; and I expected to see him fall every moment, at which all the blood in my body seemed to run chill in my veins.

I wished heartily now for my Spaniard, and the savage that was gone with him; or that I had any way to have come undiscovered within shot of them, that I might have rescued the three men, for I saw no firearms they had among them; but it fell out to my mind another way.

After I had observed the outrageous usage of the three men by the insolent seamen, I observed the fellows run scattering about the land, as if they wanted to see the country. I observed that the three other men had liberty to go also where they pleased; but they sat down all three upon the ground, very pensive, and looked like men in despair.

This put me in mind of the first time when I came on shore, and began to look about me; how I gave myself over for lost; how wildly I looked round me; what dreadful apprehensions I had; and how I lodged in the tree all night, for fear of being devoured by wild beasts.

As I knew nothing that night of the supply I was to receive by the providential driving of the ship nearer the land by the storms and tide, by which I have since been so long nourished and supported; so these three poor desolate men knew nothing how certain of deliverance and supply they were, how near it was to them, and how effectually and really they were in a condition of safety, at the same time that they thought themselves lost, and their case desperate.

It was just at the top of high-water when these people came on shore; and while partly they stood parleying with the prisoners they brought, and partly while they rambled about to see what kind of a place they were in, they had carelessly stayed till the tide was spent, and the water was ebbed considerably away, leaving their boat aground.

They had left two men in the boat, who, as I found afterwards, having drank a little too much brandy, fell asleep. However, one of them waking sooner than the other, and finding the boat too fast aground for him to stir it, hallooed for the rest, who were straggling about, upon which they all soon came to the boat; but it was past all their strength to launch her, the boat being very heavy, and the shore on that side being a soft oozy sand, almost like a quicksand.

In this condition, like true seamen, who are perhaps the least of all mankind given to forethought, they gave it over, and away they strolled about the country again; and I heard one of them say aloud to another, calling them off from the boat, "Why, let her alone, Jack, can't ye? she will float next tide;" by which I was fully confirmed in the main inquiry of what countrymen they were.

All this while I kept myself very close, not once daring to stir out of my castle, any farther than to my place of observation near the top of the hill; and very glad I was to think how well it was fortified. I knew it was no less than ten hours before the boat could be on float again, and by that time it would be dark, and I might be at more liberty to see their motions, and to hear their discourse, if they had any.

In the meantime, I fitted myself up for a battle, as before, though with more caution, knowing I had to do with another kind of enemy than I had at first. I ordered Friday also, whom I had made an excellent marksman with his gun, to load himself with arms. I took myself two fowling-pieces, and I gave him three muskets. My

figure, indeed, was very fierce. I had my formidable goat-skin coat on, with the great cap I have mentioned, a naked sword by my side, two pistols in my belt, and a gun upon each shoulder.

It was my design, as I said above, not to have made any attempt till it was dark; but about two o'clock, being the heat of the day, I found that, in short, they were all gone straggling into the woods, and, as I thought, were laid down to sleep. The three poor distressed men, too anxious for their condition to get any sleep, were, however, set down under the shelter of a great tree, at about a quarter of a mile from me, and, as I thought, out of sight of any of the rest.

Upon this I resolved to discover myself to them, and learn something of their condition. Immediately I marched in the figure as above, my man Friday at a good distance behind me, as formidable for his arms as I, but not making quite so staring a spectre-like figure as I did.

I came as near them undiscovered as I could, and then, before any of them saw me, I called aloud to them in Spanish, "What are ye, gentlemen?"

They started up at the noise, but were ten times more confounded when they saw me, and the uncouth figure that I made. They made no answer at all, but I thought I perceived them just going to fly from me, when I spoke to them in English.

"Gentlemen," said I, "do not be surprised at me; perhaps you may have a friend near you, when you did not expect it." "He must be sent directly from heaven then," said one of them very gravely to me, and pulling off his hat at the same time to me, "for our condition is past the help of man." "All help is from heaven, sir," said I. "But can you put a stranger in the way how to help you, for you seem to me to be in some great distress? I saw you when you landed; and when you seemed to make applications to the brutes that came with you, I saw one of them lift up his sword to kill you."

The poor man, with tears running down his face, and trembling, looking like one astonished, returned, "Am I talking to God, or man? Is it a real man, or an angel?" "Be in no fear about that, sir," said I. "If God had sent an angel to relieve you, he would have come better clothed, and armed after another manner than you see me in. Pray lay aside your fears; I am a man, an Englishman, and disposed to assist you, you see. I have one servant only; we have arms and ammunition; tell us freely, can we serve you? What is your case?"

"Our case," said he, "sir, is too long to tell you while our murderers are so near; but in short, sir, I was commander of that ship; my men have mutinied against me, they have been hardly prevailed on not to murder me; and at last have set me on shore in this desolate place, with these two men with me, one my mate, the other a passenger, where we expected to perish, believing the place to be uninhabited, and know not yet what to think of it."

"Where are those brutes, your enemies?" said I. "Do you know where they are gone?" "There they lie, sir," said he, pointing to a thicket of trees. "My heart trembles for fear they have seen us, and heard you speak. If they have, they will certainly murder us all."

"Have they any firearms?" said I. He answered, they had only two pieces, and one which they left in the boat. "Well then," said I, "leave the rest to me, I see they are all asleep; it is an easy thing to kill them all; but shall we rather take them prisoners?" He told me there were two desperate villains among them that it was scarce safe to show any mercy to; but if they were secured, he believed all the rest would return to their duty. I asked him which they were. He told me he could not at that distance describe them, but he would obey my orders in anything I would direct. "Well," says I, "let us retreat out of their view or hearing, lest they awake, and we will resolve further." So they willingly went back with me, till the woods covered us from them.

"Look you, sir," said I, "if I venture upon your deliverance, are you willing to make two conditions with me?" He anticipated my proposals, by telling me that both he and the ship, if recovered, should be wholly directed and commanded by me in everything; and if the ship was not recovered, he would live and die with me in what part of the world soever I would send him; and the two other men said the same.

"Well," says I, "my conditions are but two. 1. That while you stay on this island with me, you will not pretend to any authority here; and if I put arms into your hands, you will, upon all occasions, give them up to me, and do no prejudice to me or mine upon this island; and in the meantime, be governed by my orders. 2. That if the ship is, or may be, recovered, you will carry me and my men to England, passage free."

He gave me all the assurances that the invention and faith of man could devise that he would comply with these most reasonable demands; and, besides, would owe his life to me, and acknowledge it upon all occasions, as long as he lived.

"Well then," said I, "here are three muskets for you, with powder and ball; tell me next what you think is proper to be done." He showed all the testimony of his gratitude that he was able, but offered to be wholly guided by me. I told him I thought it was hard venturing anything; but the best method I could think of was to fire upon them at once, as they lay; and if any was not killed at the first volley, and offered to submit, we might save them, and so put it wholly upon God's providence to direct the shot.

He said very modestly that he was loth to kill them, if he could help it; but that those two were incorrigible villains, and had been the authors of all the mutiny in the ship, and if they escaped, we should be undone still; for they would go on board and bring the whole ship's company, and destroy us all. "Well then," says I, "necessity legitimates my advice, for it is the only way to save our lives." However, seeing him still cautious of shedding blood, I told him they should go themselves, and manage as they found convenient.

In the middle of this discourse we heard some of them awake, and soon after we saw two of them on their feet. I asked him if either of them were of the men who he had said were the heads of the mutiny. He said, "No." "Well then," said I, "you may let them escape; and Providence seems to have wakened them on purpose to save themselves. Now," says I, "if the rest escape you, it is your fault."

Animated with this, he took the musket I had given him in his hand, and a pistol in his belt, and his two comrades with him, with each man a piece in his hand. The two men who were with him going first made some noise, at which one of the seamen who was awake turned about, and seeing them coming cried out to the rest; but it was too late then, for the moment he cried out they fired; I mean the two men, the captain wisely reserving his own piece. They had so well aimed their shot at the men they knew, that one of them was killed on the spot, and the other very much wounded; but not being dead, he started up upon his feet, and called eagerly for help to the other. But the captain stepping to him, told him 'twas too late to cry for help, he should call upon God to forgive his villainy; and with that word knocked him down with the stock of his musket, so that he never spoke more. There were three more in the company, and one of them was also slightly wounded. By this time I was come; and when they saw their danger, and that it was in vain to resist, they begged for mercy. The captain told them he would spare their lives if they would give him any assurance of their abhorrence of the treachery they had been guilty of, and would swear to be faithful to him in recovering the ship, and afterwards in carrying her back to Jamaica, from whence they came. They gave him all the protestations of their sincerity that could be desired, and he was willing to believe them, and spare their lives, which I was not against, only I obliged him to keep them bound hand and foot while they were upon the island.

While this was doing, I sent Friday with the captain's mate to the boat, with orders to secure her, and bring away the oars and sail, which they did; and by-and-by three straggling men, that were (happily for them) parted from the rest, came back upon hearing the guns fired; and seeing their captain, who before was their prisoner, now their conqueror, they submitted to be bound also, and so our victory was complete.

It now remained that the captain and I should inquire into one another's circumstances. I began first, and told him my whole history, which he heard with an attention even to amazement; and particularly at the wonderful manner of my being furnished with provisions and ammunition; and, indeed, as my story is a whole collection of wonders, it affected him deeply. But when he reflected from thence upon himself, and how I seemed to have been preserved there on purpose to save his life, the tears ran down his face, and he could not speak a word more.

After this communication was at an end, I carried him and his two men into my apartment, leading them in just where I came out, viz., at the top of the house, where I refreshed them with such provisions as I had, and showed them all the contrivances I had made during my long, long inhabiting that place.

All I showed them, all I said to them, was perfectly amazing; but above all, the captain admired my fortification, and how perfectly I had concealed my retreat with a grove of trees, which, having been now planted near twenty years, and the trees growing much faster than in England, was become a little wood, and so thick, that it was unpassable in any part of it but at that one side where I had reserved my little winding passage into it. I told him this was my castle and my residence, but that I had a seat in the country, as most princes have, whither I could retreat upon occasion, and I would show him that too another time; but at present, our business was to consider how to recover the ship. He agreed with me as to that, but told me he was perfectly at a loss what measures to take, for that there were still six and twenty hands on board, who having entered into a cursed conspiracy, by which they had all forfeited their lives to the law, would be hardened in it now by desperation, and would carry it on, knowing that if they were reduced, they should be brought to the gallows as soon as they came to England, or to any of the English colonies; and that therefore there would be no attacking them with so small a number as we were.

I mused for some time upon what he said, and found it was a very rational conclusion, and that therefore something was to be resolved on very speedily, as well to draw the men on board into some snare for their surprise, as to prevent their landing upon us, and destroying us. Upon this it presently occurred to me that in a little while the ship's crew, wondering what was become of their comrades, and of the boat, would certainly come on shore in their other boat to see for them; and that then, perhaps, they might come armed, and be too strong for us. This he allowed was rational.

Upon this, I told him the first thing we had to do was to stave the boat, which lay upon the beach, so that they might not carry her off; and taking everything out of her, leave her so far useless as not to be fit to swim. Accordingly we went on board, took the arms which were left on board out of her, and whatever else we found there, which was a bottle of brandy, and another of rum, a few biscuit-cakes, a horn of powder, and a great lump of sugar in a piece of canvas – the sugar was five or six pounds; all which was very welcome to me, especially the brandy and sugar, of which I had had none left for many years.

When we had carried all these things on shore (the oars, mast, sail, and rudder of the boat were carried away before, as above), we knocked a great hole in her bottom, that if they had come strong enough to master us, yet they could not carry off the boat.

Indeed, it was not much in my thoughts that we could be able to recover the ship; but my view was, that if they went away without the boat, I did not much question to make her fit again to carry us away to the Leeward Islands, and call upon our friends the Spaniards in my way; for I had them still in my thoughts.

While we were thus preparing our designs, and had first, by main strength, heaved the boat up upon the beach so high that the tide would not fleet her off at high-water mark; and besides, had broke a hole in her bottom too big to be quickly stopped, and were sat down musing what we should do, we heard the ship fire a gun, and saw her make a waft with her ancient as a signal for the boat to come on board. But no boat stirred; and they fired several times, making other signals for the boat.

At last, when all their signals and firings proved fruitless, and they found the boat did not stir, we saw them, by the help of my glasses, hoist another boat out, and row towards the shore; and we found, as they approached, that there was no less than ten men in her, and that they had firearms with them.

As the ship lay almost two leagues from the shore, we had a full view of them as they came, and a plain sight of the men, even of their faces; because the tide having set them a little to the east of the other boat, they rowed up under shore, to come to the same place where the other had landed, and where the boat lay.

By this means, I say, we had a full view of them, and the captain knew the persons and characters of all the men in the boat, of whom he said that there were three very honest fellows, who, he was sure, were led into this conspiracy by the rest, being overpowered and frighted; but that as for the boatswain, who, it seems, was the chief officer among them, and all the rest, they were as outrageous as any of the ship's crew, and were no doubt made desperate in their new enterprise; and terribly apprehensive he was that they would be too powerful for us.

I smiled at him, and told him that men in our circumstances were past the operation of fear; that seeing almost every condition that could be was better than that which we were supposed to be in, we ought to expect that the consequence, whether death or life, would be sure to be a deliverance. I asked him what he thought of the circumstances of my life, and whether a deliverance were not worth venturing for? "And where, sir," said I, "is your belief of my being preserved here on purpose to save your life, which elevated you a little while ago? For my part," said I, "there seems to be but one thing amiss in all the prospect of it." "What's that?" says he. "Why," said I, "'tis that, as you say, there are three or four honest fellows among them, which should be spared; had they been all of the wicked part of the crew I should have thought God's providence had singled them out to deliver them into your hands; for depend upon it, every man of them that comes ashore are our own, and shall die or live as they behave to us."

As I spoke this with a raised voice and cheerful countenance, I found it greatly encouraged him; so we set vigorously to our business. We had, upon the first appearance of the boat's coming from the ship, considered of separating our prisoners, and had, indeed, secured them effectually.

Two of them, of whom the captain was less assured than ordinary, I sent with Friday and one of the three delivered men to my cave, where they were remote enough, and out of danger of being heard or discovered, or of finding their way out of the woods if they could have delivered themselves. Here they left them bound, but gave them provisions, and promised them, if they continued there quietly, to give them their liberty in a day or two; but that if they attempted their escape, they should be put to death without mercy. They promised faithfully to bear their confinement with patience, and were very thankful that they had such good usage as to have provisions and a light left them; for Friday gave them candles (such as we made ourselves) for their comfort; and they did not know but that he stood sentinel over them at the entrance.

The other prisoners had better usage. Two of them were kept pinioned, indeed, because the captain was not free to trust them; but the other two were taken into my service, upon their captain's recommendation, and upon their solemnly engaging to live and die with us; so with them and the three honest men we were seven men well armed; and I made no doubt we should be able to deal well enough with the ten that were a-coming, considering that the captain had said there were three or four honest men among them also.

As soon as they got to the place where their other boat lay, they ran their boat into the beach, and came all on shore, hauling the boat up after them, which I was glad to see; for I was afraid they would rather have left the boat at an anchor some distance from the shore, with some hands in her to guard her, and so we should not be able to seize the boat.

Being on shore, the first thing they did they ran all to their other boat; and it was easy to see that they were under a great surprise to find her stripped, as above, of all that was in her, and a great hole in her bottom.

After they had mused a while upon this, they set up two or three great shouts, hallooed with all their might, to try if they could make their companions hear; but all was to no purpose. Then they came all close in a ring, and fired a volley of their small arms, which, indeed, we heard, and the echoes made the woods ring. But it was all one; those in the cave we were sure could not hear, and those in our keeping, though they heard it well enough, yet durst give no answer to them.

They were so astonished at the surprise of this, that, as they told us afterwards, they resolved to go all on board again, to their ship, and let them know there that the men were all murdered, and the longboat staved. Accordingly, they immediately launched their boat again, and gat all of them on board.

The captain was terribly amazed, and even confounded at this, believing they would go on board the ship again, and set sail, giving their comrades for lost, and so he should still lose the ship, which he was in hopes we should have recovered; but he was quickly as much frighted the other way.

They had not been long put off with the boat but we perceived them all coming on shore again; but with this new measure in their conduct, which it seems they consulted together upon, viz., to leave three men in the boat, and the rest to go on shore, and go up into the country to look for their fellows.

This was a great disappointment to us, for now we were at a loss what to do; for our seizing those seven men on shore would be no advantage to us if we let the boat escape, because they would then row away to the ship, and then the rest of them would be sure to weigh and set sail, and so our recovering the ship would be lost. However, we had no remedy but to wait and see what the issue of things might present. The seven men came on shore, and the three who remained in the boat put her off to a good distance from the shore, and came to an anchor to wait for them; so that it was impossible for us to come at them in the boat.

Those that came on shore kept close together, marching towards the top of the little hill under which my habitation lay; and we could see them plainly, though they could not perceive us. We could have been very glad they would have come nearer to us, so that we might have fired at them, or that they would have gone farther off, that we might have come abroad.

But when they were come to the brow of the hill, where they could see a great way into the valleys and woods which lay towards the north-east part, and where the island lay lowest, they shouted and hallooed till they were weary; and not caring, it seems, to venture far from the shore, nor far from one another, they sat down together under a tree, to consider of it. Had they thought fit to have gone to sleep there, as the other party of them had done, they had done the job for us; but they were too full of apprehensions of danger to venture to go to sleep, though they could not tell what the danger was they had to fear neither.

The captain made a very just proposal to me upon this consultation of theirs, viz., that perhaps they would all fire a volley again, to endeavour to make their fellows hear, and that we should all sally upon them, just at the juncture when their pieces were all discharged, and they would certainly yield, and we should have them without bloodshed. I liked the proposal, provided it was done while we were near enough to come up to them before they could load their pieces again.

But this event did not happen, and we lay still a long time, very irresolute what course to take. At length I told them there would be nothing to be done, in my opinion, till night; and then, if they did not return to the boat, perhaps we might find a way to get between them and the shore, and so might use some stratagem with them in the boat to get them on shore.

We waited a great while, though very impatient for their removing; and were very uneasy when, after long consultations, we saw them start all up, and march down toward the sea. It seems they had such dreadful apprehensions upon them of the danger of the place, that they resolved to go on board the ship again, give their companions over for lost, and so go on with their intended voyage with the ship.

As soon as I perceived them go towards the shore, I imagined it to be, as it really was, that they had given over their search, and were for going back again; and the captain, as soon as I told him my thoughts, was ready to sink at the apprehensions of it; but I presently thought of a stratagem to fetch them back again, and which answered my end to a tittle.

I ordered Friday and the captain's mate to go over the little creek westward, towards the place where the savages came on shore when Friday was rescued, and as soon as they came to a little rising ground, at about half a mile distance, I bade them halloo as loud as they could, and wait till they found the seamen heard them; that as soon as ever they heard the seamen answer them, they should return it again; and then keeping out of sight, take a round, always answering when the other hallooed, to draw them as far into the island, and among the woods, as possible, and then wheel about again to me by such ways as I directed them.

They were just going into the boat when Friday and the mate hallooed; and they presently heard them, and answering, run along the shore westward, towards the voice they heard, when they were presently stopped by the creek, where the water being up, they could not get over, and called for the boat to come up and set them over, as, indeed, I expected.

When they had set themselves over, I observed that the boat being gone up a good way into the creek, and, as it were, in a harbour within the land, they took one of the three men out of her to go along with them, and left only two in the boat, having fastened her to the stump of a little tree on the shore.

That was what I wished for; and immediately leaving Friday and the captain's mate to their business, I took the rest with me, and crossing the creek out of their sight, we surprised the two men before they were aware; one of them lying on shore, and the other being in the boat. The fellow on shore was between sleeping and waking, and going to start up. The captain, who was foremost, ran in upon him, and knocked him down, and then called out to him in the boat to yield, or he was a dead man.

There needed very few arguments to persuade a single man to yield when he saw five men upon him, and his comrade knocked down; besides, this was, it seems, one of the three who were not so hearty in the mutiny as the rest of the crew, and therefore was easily persuaded not only to yield, but afterwards to join very sincerely with us.

In the meantime, Friday and the captain's mate so well managed their business with the rest, that they drew them, by hallooing and answering, from one hill to another, and from one wood to another, till they not only heartily tired them, but left them where they were very sure they could not reach back to the boat before it was dark; and, indeed, they were heartily tired themselves also by the time they came back to us.

We had nothing now to do but to watch for them in the dark, and to fall upon them, so as to make sure work with them.

It was several hours after Friday came back to me before they came back to their boat; and we could hear the foremost of them, long before they came quite up, calling to those behind to come along, and could also hear them answer and complain how lame and tired they were, and not able to come any faster; which was very welcome news to us.

At length they came up to the boat; but 'tis impossible to express their confusion when they found the boat fast aground in the creek, the tide ebbed out, and their two men gone. We could hear them call to one another in a most lamentable manner, telling one another they were gotten into an enchanted island; that either there were inhabitants in it, and they should all be murdered, or else there were devils and spirits in it, and they should all be carried away and devoured.

They hallooed again, and called their two comrades by their names a great many times; but no answer. After some time we could see them, by the little light there was, run about, wringing their hands like men in despair, and that sometimes they would go and sit down in the boat to rest themselves, then come ashore again, and walk about again, and so the same thing over again.

My men would fain have me give them leave to fall upon them at once in the dark; but I was willing to take them at some advantage, so to spare them, and kill as few of them as I could; and especially I was unwilling to hazard the killing any of our own men, knowing the other were very well armed. I resolved to wait, to see if they did not separate; and, therefore, to make sure of them, I drew my ambuscade nearer, and ordered Friday and the captain to creep upon their hands and feet, as close to the ground as they could, that they might not be discovered, and get as near them as they could possibly, before they offered to fire.

They had not been long in that posture but that the boatswain, who was the principal ringleader of the mutiny, and had now shown himself the most dejected and dispirited of all the rest, came walking towards them, with two more of their crew. The captain was so eager, as having this principal rogue so much in his power, that he could hardly have patience to let him come so near as to be sure of him, for they only heard his tongue before; but when they came nearer, the captain and Friday, starting up on their feet, let fly at them.

The boatswain was killed upon the spot; the next man was shot into the body, and fell just by him, though he did not die till an hour or two after; and the third ran for it.

At the noise of the fire I immediately advanced with my whole army, which was now eight men, viz., myself, generalissimo; Friday, my lieutenant-general; the captain and his two men, and the three prisoners of war, whom we had trusted with arms.

We came upon them, indeed, in the dark, so that they could not see our number; and I made the man we had left in the boat, who was now one of us, call to them by name, to try if I could bring them to a parley, and so might perhaps reduce them to terms, which fell out just as we desired; for indeed it was easy to think, as their condition then was, they would be very willing to capitulate. So he calls out as loud as he could to one of them, "Tom Smith! Tom Smith!" Tom Smith answered immediately, "Who's that? Robinson?" For it seems he knew his voice. The other answered, "Ay, ay; for God's sake, Tom Smith, throw down your arms and yield, or you are all dead men this moment."

"Who must we yield to? Where are they?" says Smith again. "Here they are," says he; "here's our captain, and fifty men with him, have been hunting you this two hours; the boatswain is killed, Will Frye is wounded, and I am a prisoner; and if you do not yield, you are all lost."

"Will they give us quarter then," says Tom Smith, "and we will yield?" "I'll go and ask, if you promise to yield," says Robinson. So he asked the captain, and the captain then calls himself out, "You, Smith, you know my voice, if you lay down your arms immediately, and submit, you shall have your lives, all but Will Atkins."

Upon this Will Atkins cried out, "For God's sake, captain, give me quarter; what have I done? They have been all as bad as I"; which, by the way, was not true neither; for, it seems, this Will Atkins was the first man that laid hold of the captain when they first mutinied, and used him barbarously, in tying his hands, and giving him injurious language. However, the captain told him he must lay down his arms at discretion, and trust to the governor's mercy; by which he meant me, for they all called me governor.

In a word, they all laid down their arms, and begged their lives; and I sent the man that had parleyed with them and two more, who bound them all; and then my great army of fifty men, which, particularly with those three, were all but eight, came up and seized upon them all, and upon their boat; only that I kept myself and one more out of sight for reasons of state.

Our next work was to repair the boat, and think of seizing the ship; and as for the captain, now he had leisure to parley with them, he expostulated with them upon the villainy of their practices with him, and at length upon the farther wickedness of their design, and how certainly it must bring them to misery and distress in the end, and perhaps to the gallows.

They all appeared very penitent, and begged hard for their lives. As for that, he told them they were none of his prisoners, but the commander of the island; that they though they had set him on shore in a barren, uninhabited island; but it had pleased God so to direct them that the island was inhabited, and that the governor was an Englishman; that he might hang them all there, if he pleased; but as he had given them all quarter, he supposed he would send them to England, to be dealt with there as justice required, except Atkins, whom he was commanded by the governor to advise to prepare for death, for that he would be hanged in the morning.

Though this was all a fiction of his own, yet it had its desired effect. Atkins fell upon his knees, to beg the captain to intercede with the governor for his life; and all the rest begged of him, for God's sake, that they might not be sent to England.

It now occurred to me that the time of our deliverance was come, and that it would be a most easy thing to bring these fellows in to be hearty in getting possession of the ship; so I retired in the dark from them, that they might not see what kind of a governor they had, and called the captain to me. When I called, as at a good distance, one of the men was ordered to speak again, and say to the captain, "Captain, the commander calls for you." And presently the captain replied, "Tell his excellency I am just a-coming." This more perfectly amused them, and they all believed that the commander was just by with his fifty men,

Upon the captain's coming to me, I told him my project for seizing the ship, which he liked of wonderfully well, and resolved to put it in execution the next morning. But in order to execute it with more art, and secure of success, I told him we must divide the prisoners, and that he should go and take Atkins and two more of the worst of them, and send them pinioned to the cave where the others lay. This was committed to Friday and the two men who came on shore with the captain.

They conveyed them to the cave, as to a prison. And it was, indeed, a dismal place, especially to men in their condition. The others I ordered to my bower, as I called it, of which I have given a full description; and as it was fenced in, and they pinioned, the place was secure enough, considering they were upon their behaviour.

To these in the morning I sent the captain, who was to enter into a parley with them; in a word, to try them, and tell me whether he thought they might be trusted or no to go on board and surprise the ship. He talked to them of the injury done him, of the condition they were brought to; and that though the governor had given them quarter for their lives as to the present action, yet that if they were sent to England they would all be hanged in chains, to be sure; but that if they would join in so just an attempt as to recover the ship, he would have the governor's engagement for their pardon.

Any one may guess how readily such a proposal would be accepted by men in their condition. They fell down on their knees to the captain, and promised, with the deepest imprecations, that they would be faithful to him to the last drop, and that they should owe their lives to him, and would go with him all over the world; that they would own him for a father to them as long as they lived.

"Well," says the captain, "I must go and tell the governor what you say, and see what I can do to bring him to consent to it." So he brought me an account of the temper he found them in, and that he verily believed they would be faithful.

However, that we might be very secure, I told him he should go back again and choose out five of them, and tell them they might see that he did not want men, that he would take out those five to be his assistants, and that the governor would keep the other two and the three that were sent prisoners to the castle, my cave, as hostages for the fidelity of those five; and that if they proved unfaithful in the execution, the five hostages should be hanged in chains alive upon the shore.

This looked severe, and convinced them that the governor was in earnest. However, they had no way left them but to accept it; and it was now the business of the prisoners, as much as of the captain, to persuade the other five to do their duty.

Our strength was now thus ordered for the expedition. 1. The captain, his mate, and passenger. 2. Then the two prisoners of the first gang, to whom, having their characters from the captain, I had given their liberty, and trusted them with arms. 3. The other two whom I had kept till now in my bower, pinioned, but upon the captain's motion had now released. 4. These five released at last; so that they were twelve in all, besides five we kept prisoners in the cave for hostages.

I asked the captain if he was willing to venture with these hands on board the ship; for as for me and my man Friday, I did not think it was proper for us to stir, having seven men left behind, and it was employment enough for us to keep them asunder and supply them with victuals. As to the five in the cave, I resolved to keep them fast; but Friday went in twice a day to them, to supply them with necessaries, and I made the other two carry provisions to a certain distance, where Friday was to take it.

When I showed myself to the two hostages, it was with the captain, who told them I was the person the governor had ordered to look after them, and that it was the governor's pleasure they should not stir anywhere but by my direction; that if they did, they should be fetched into the castle, and be laid in irons; so that as we never suffered them to see me as governor, so I now appeared as another person, and spoke of the governor, the garrison, the castle, and the like, upon all occasions.

The captain now had no difficulty before him but to furnish his two boats, stop the breach of one, and man them. He made his passenger captain of one, with four other men; and himself, and his mate, and five more went in the other; and they contrived their business very well, for they came up to the ship about midnight. As soon as they came within call of the ship, he made Robinson hail them, and tell them they brought off the men and the boat, but that it was a long time before they had found them, and the like, holding them in a chat till they came to the ship's side; when the captain and the mate entering first, with their arms, immediately knocked down the second mate and carpenter with the butt-end of their muskets, being very faithfully seconded by their men. They secured all the rest that were upon the main and quarter decks, and began to fasten the hatches to keep them down who were below; when the other boat and their men entering at the fore-chains, secured the forecastle of the ship, and the scuttle which went down into the cook-room, making three men they found there prisoners.

When this was done, and all safe upon deck, the captain ordered the mate, with three men, to break into the roundhouse, where the new rebel captain lay, and having taken the alarm was gotten up, and with two men and a boy had gotten firearms in their hands; and when the mate with a crow split open the door, the new captain and his men fired boldly among them, and wounded the mate with a musket-ball, which broke his arm, and wounded two more of the men, but killed nobody.

The mate calling for help, rushed however into the roundhouse wounded as he was, and with his pistol shot the new captain through the head, the bullet entering at his mouth and came out again behind one of his ears, so that he never spoke a word; upon which the rest yielded, and the ship was taken effectually, without any more lives lost.

As soon as the ship was thus secured, the captain ordered seven guns to be fired, which was the signal agreed upon with me to give me notice of his success, which you may be sure I was very glad to hear, having sat watching upon the shore for it till near two of the clock in the morning.

Having thus heard the signal plainly, I laid me down; and it having been a day of great fatigue to me, I slept very sound, till I was something surprised with the noise of a gun; and presently starting up, I heard a man call me by the name of "Governor," "Governor," and presently I knew the captain's voice; when climbing up to the top of the hill, there he stood, and pointing to the ship, he embraced me in his arms. "My dear friend and deliverer," says he, "there's your ship, for she is all yours, and so are we, and all that belong to her." I cast my eyes to the ship, and there she rode within little more than half a mile of the shore; for they had weighed her anchor as soon as they were masters of her, and the weather being fair, had brought her to an anchor just against the mouth of the little creek, and the tide being up, the captain had brought the pinnace in near the place where I at first landed my rafts, and so landed just at my door.

I was at first ready to sink down with the surprise; for I saw my deliverance, indeed, visibly put into my hands, all things easy, and a large ship just ready to carry me away whither I pleased to go. At first, for some time, I was not able to answer him one word; but as he had taken me in his arms, I held fast by him, or I should have fallen to the ground.

He perceived the surprise, and immediately pulls a bottle out of his pocket, and gave me a dram of cordial, which he had brought on purpose for me. After I had drank it, I sat down upon the ground; and though it brought me to myself, yet it was a good while before I could speak a word to him.

All this while the poor man was in as great an ecstasy as I, only not under any surprise, as I was; and he said a thousand kind tender things to me, to compose me and bring me to myself. But such was the flood of joy in my breast, that it put all my spirits into confusion. At last it broke out into tears, and in a little while after I recovered my speech.

Then I took my turn, and embraced him as my deliverer, and we rejoiced together. I told him I looked upon him as a man sent from heaven to deliver me, and that the whole transaction seemed to be a chain of wonders; that such things as these were the testimonies we had of a secret hand of Providence governing the world, and an evidence that the eyes of an infinite Power could search into the remotest corner of the world, and send help to the miserable whenever He pleased.

I forgot not to lift up my heart in thankfulness to heaven; and what heart could forbear to bless Him, who had not only in a miraculous manner provided for one in such a wilderness, and in such a desolate condition, but from whom every deliverance must always be acknowledged to proceed?

When we had talked a while, the captain told me he had brought me some little refreshment, such as the ship afforded, and such as the wretches that had been so long his masters had not plundered him of. Upon this he called aloud to the boat, and bid his men bring the things ashore that were for the governor; and, indeed, it was a present as if I had been one, not that was to be carried away along with them, but as if I had been to dwell upon the island still, and they were to go without me.

First, he had brought me a case of bottles full of excellent cordial waters, six large bottles of Madeira wine (the bottles held two quarts apiece), two pounds of excellent good tobacco, twelve good pieces of the ship's beef, and six pieces of pork, with a bag of peas, and about a hundredweight of biscuit.

He brought me also a box of sugar, a box of flour, a bag full of lemons, and two bottles of lime-juice, and abundance of other things; but besides these, and what was a thousand times more useful to me, he brought me six clean new shirts, six very good neck-cloths, two pair of gloves, one pair of shoes, a hat, and one pair of stockings, and a very good suit of clothes of his own, which had been worn but very little; in a word, he clothed me from head to foot.

It was a very kind and agreeable present, as any one may imagine, to one in my circumstances; but never was anything in the world of that kind so unpleasant, awkward, and uneasy, as it was to me to wear such clothes at their first putting on.

After these ceremonies passed, and after all his good things were brought into my little apartment, we began to consult what was to be done with the prisoners we had; for it was worth considering whether we might venture to take them away with us or no, especially two of them, whom we knew to be incorrigible and refractory to the last degree; and the captain said he knew they were such rogues, that there was no obliging them; and if he did carry them away, it must be in irons, as malefactors, to be delivered over to justice at the first English colony he could come at; and I found that the captain himself was very anxious about it.

Upon this I told him that, if he desired it, I durst undertake to bring the two men he spoke of to make it their own request that he should leave them upon the island. "I should be very glad of that," says the captain, "with all my heart."

"Well," says I, "I will send for them up, and talk with them for you." So I caused Friday and the two hostages, for they were now discharged, their comrades having performed their promise; I say, I caused them to go to the cave and bring up the five men, pinioned as they were, to the bower, and keep them there till I came.

After some time I came thither, dressed in my new habit; and now I was called governor again. Being all met, and the captain with me, I caused the men to be brought before me, and I told them I had had a full account of their villainous behaviour to the captain, and how they had run away with the ship, and were preparing to commit farther robberies, but that Providence had ensnared them in their own ways, and that they were fallen into the pit which they had digged for others.

I let them know that by my direction the ship had been seized, that she lay now in the road, and they might see, by and by, that their new captain had received the reward of his villainy, for that they might see him hanging at the yard-arm; that as to them, I wanted to know what they had to say why I should not execute them as pirates, taken in the fact, as by my commission they could not doubt I had authority to do.

One of them answered in the name of the rest that they had nothing to say but this, that when they were taken the captain promised them their lives, and they humbly implored my mercy. But I told them I knew not what mercy to show them; for as for myself, I had resolved to quit the island with all my men, and had taken passage with the captain to go for England. And as for the captain, he could not carry them to England other than as prisoners in irons, to be tried for mutiny, and running away with the ship; the consequence of which, they must needs know, would be the gallows; so that I could not tell which was best for them, unless they had a mind to take their fate in the island. If they desired that, I did not care, as I had liberty to leave it. I had some inclination to give them their lives, if they thought they could shift on shore.

They seemed very thankful for it, said they would much rather venture to stay there than to be carried to England to be hanged; so I left it on that issue.

However, the captain seemed to make some difficulty of it, as if he durst not leave them there. Upon this I seemed a little angry with the captain, and told him that they were my prisoners, not his; and that seeing I had offered them so much favour, I would be as good as my word; and that if he did not think fit to consent to it, I would set them at liberty, as I found them; and if he did not like it, he might take them again if he could catch them.

Upon this they appeared very thankful, and I accordingly set them at liberty, and bade them retire into the woods to the place whence they came, and I would leave them some firearms, some ammunition, and some directions how they should live very well, if they thought fit.

Upon this I prepared to go on board the ship, but told the captain that I would stay that night to prepare my things, and desired him to go on board in the meantime, and keep all right in the ship, and send the boat on shore the next day for me; ordering him, in the meantime, to cause the new captain, who was killed, to be hanged at the yard-arm, that these men might see him.

When the captain was gone, I sent for the men up to me to my apartment, and entered seriously into discourse with them of their circumstances. I told them I thought they had made a right choice; that if the captain carried them away, they would certainly be hanged. I showed them the new captain hanging at the yard-arm of the ship, and told them they had nothing less to expect.

When they had all declared their willingness to stay, I then told them I would let them into the story of my living there, and put them into the way of making it easy to them. Accordingly I gave them the whole history of the place, and of my coming to it, showed them my fortifications, the way I made my bread, planted my corn, cured my grapes; and in a word, all that was necessary to make them easy. I told them the story also of the sixteen Spaniards that were to be expected, for whom I left a letter, and made them promise to treat them in common with themselves.

I left them my firearms, viz., five muskets, three fowling-pieces, and three swords. I had above a barrel and half of powder left; for after the first year or two I used but little, and wasted none. I gave them a description of the way I managed the goats, and directions to milk and fatten them, and to make both butter and cheese.

In a word, I gave them every part of my own story, and I told them I would prevail with the captain to leave them two barrels of gunpowder more, and some garden seeds, which I told them I would have been very glad of. Also I gave them the bag of peas which the captain had brought me to eat, and bade them be sure to sow and increase them.

Having done all this, I left them the next day, and went on board the ship. We prepared immediately to sail, but did not weigh that night. The next morning early two of the five men came swimming to the ship's side, and making a most lamentable complaint of the other three, begged to be taken into the ship for God's sake, for they should be murdered, and begged the captain to take them on board, though he hanged them immediately.

Upon this the captain pretended to have no power without me; but after some difficulty, and after their solemn promises of amendment, they were taken on board, and were some time after soundly whipped and pickled, after which they proved very honest and quiet fellows.

Some time after this the boat was ordered on shore, the tide being up, with the things promised to the men, to which the captain, at my intercession, caused their chests and clothes to be added, which they took, and were very thankful for. I also encouraged them by telling them that if it lay in my way to send any vessel to take them in, I would not forget them.

When I took leave of this island, I carried on board, for relics, the great goatskin cap I had made, my umbrella, and my parrot; also I forgot not to take the money I formerly mentioned, which had lain by me so long useless that it was grown rusty or tarnished, and could hardly pass for silver till it had been a little rubbed and handled; as also the money I found in the wreck of the Spanish ship.

And thus I left the island, the 19th of December, as I found by the ship's account, in the year 1686, after I had been upon it eight and twenty years, two months, and nineteen days, being delivered from this second captivity the same day of the month that I first made my escape in the *barco-longo*, from among the Moors of Sallee.

In this vessel, after a long voyage, I arrived in England, the 11th of June, in the year 1687, having been thirty and five years absent.

When I came to England, I was as perfect a stranger to all the world as if I had never been known there. My benefactor and faithful steward, whom I had left in trust with my money, was alive, but had had great misfortunes in the world, was become a widow the second time, and very low in the world. I made her easy as to what she owed me, assuring her I would give her no trouble; but on the contrary, in gratitude to her former care and faithfulness to me, I relieved her as my little stock would afford; which, at that time, would indeed allow me to do but little for her; but I assured her I would never forget her former kindness to me, nor did I forget her when I had sufficient to help her, as shall be observed in its place.

I went down afterwards into Yorkshire; but my father was dead, and my mother and all the family extinct, except that I found two sisters, and two of the children of one of my brothers; and as I had been long ago given over for dead, there had been no provision made for me; so that, in a word, I found nothing to relieve or assist me; and that little money I had would not do much for me as to settling in the world.

I met with one piece of gratitude, indeed, which I did not expect; and this was, that the master of the ship whom I had so happily delivered, and by the same means saved the ship and cargo, having given a very handsome account to the owners of the manner how I had saved the lives of the men, and the ship, they invited me to meet them, and some other merchants concerned, and all together made me a very handsome compliment upon the subject, and a present of almost £200 sterling.

But after making several reflections upon the circumstances of my life, and how little way this would go towards settling me in the world, I resolved to go to Lisbon, and see if I might not come by some information of the state of my plantation in the Brazils, and of what was become of my partner, who I had reason to suppose had some years now given me over for dead.

With this view I took shipping for Lisbon, where I arrived in April following; my man Friday accompanying me very honestly in all these ramblings, and proving a most faithful servant upon all occasions.

When I came to Lisbon, I found out, by inquiry, and to my particular satisfaction, my old friend the captain of the ship who first took me up at sea off of the shore of Africa. He was now grown old, and had left off the sea, having put his son, who was far from a young man, into his ship, and who still used the Brazil trade. The old man did not know me; and, indeed, I hardly knew him; but soon brought him to my remembrance, and as soon brought myself to his remembrance, when I told him who I was.

After some passionate expressions of the old acquaintance, I inquired, you may be sure, after my plantation and my partner. The old man told me he had not been in the Brazils for about nine years; but that he could assure me that, when he came away, my partner was living; but the trustees, whom I had joined with him to take cognisance of my part, were both dead. That, however, he believed that I would have a very good account of the improvement of the plantation; for that upon the general belief of my being cast away and drowned, my trustees had given in the account of the produce of my part of the plantation to the procurator-fiscal, who had appropriated it, in case I never came to claim it, one-third to the king, and two-thirds to the monastery of St Augustine, to be expended for the benefit of the poor, and for the conversion of the Indians to the Catholic faith; but that if I appeared, or anyone for me to claim the inheritance, it should be restored; only that the improvement, or annual production, being distributed to charitable uses, could not be restored. But he assured me that the steward of the king's revenue from lands, and the *provedidore*, or steward of the monastery, had taken great care all along that the incumbent, that is to say, my partner, gave every year a faithful account of the produce, of which they received duly my moiety.

I asked him if he knew to what height of improvement he had brought the plantation, and whether he thought it might be worth looking after; or whether, on my going thither, I should meet with no obstruction to my possessing my just right in the moiety.

He told me he could not tell exactly to what degree the plantation was improved; but this he knew, that my partner was growing exceeding rich upon the enjoying but one-half of it; and that, to the best of his remembrance, he had heard that the king's third of my part, which was, it seems, granted away to some other monastery or religious house, amounted to above two hundred moidores a year. That as to my being restored to a quiet possession of it, there was no question to be made of that, my partner being alive to witness my title, and my name being also enrolled in the register of the country. Also he told me that the survivors of my two trustees were very fair, honest people, and very wealthy; and he believed I would not only have their assistance for putting me in possession, but would find a very considerable sum of money in their hands for my account, being the produce of the farm while their fathers held the trust, and before it was given up, as above; which, as he remembered, was for about twelve years.

I showed myself a little concerned and uneasy at this account, and inquired of the old captain how it came to pass that the trustees should thus dispose my effects, when he knew that I had made my will, and had made him, the Portuguese captain, my universal heir, etc.

He told me, that was true; but that as there was no proof of my being dead, he could not act as executor until some certain account should come of my death; and that besides, he was not willing to intermeddle with a thing so remote; that it was true he had registered my will, and put in his claim; and could he have given any account of my being dead or alive, he would have acted by procuration, and taken possession of the *ingenio*, so they called the sugar-house, and had given his son, who was now at the Brazils, order to do it.

"But," says the old man, "I have one piece of news to tell you, which perhaps may not be so acceptable to you as the rest; and that is, that believing you were lost, and all the world believing so also, your partner and trustees did offer to account to me, in your name, for six or eight of the first years of profits, which I received; but there being at that time," says he "great disbursements for increasing the works, building an *ingenio*, and buying slaves, it did not amount to near so much as afterwards it produced. However," says the old man, "I shall give you a true account of what I have received in all, and how I have disposed of it."

After a few days' farther conference with this ancient friend, he brought me an account of the six first years' income of my plantation, signed by my partner and the merchant-trustees, being always delivered in goods, viz., tobacco in roll, and sugar in chests, besides rum, molasses, etc., which is the consequence of a sugar-work; and I found, by this account, that every year the income considerably increased; but, as above, the disbursement being large, the sum at first was small. However, the old man let me see that he was debtor to me 470 moidores of gold, besides 60 chests of sugar, and 15 double rolls of tobacco, which were lost in his ship, he having been shipwrecked coming home to Lisbon, about eleven years after my leaving the place.

The good man then began to complain of his misfortunes, and how he had been obliged to make use of my money to recover his losses, and buy him a share in a new ship. However, my old friend," says he, "you shall not want a supply in your necessity; and as soon as my son returns, you shall be fully satisfied."

Upon this he pulls out an old pouch, and gives me 160 Portugal moidores in gold; and giving me the writing of his title to the ship, which his son was gone to the Brazils in, of which he was a quarter-part owner, and his son another, he puts them both into my hands for security of the rest.

I was too much moved with the honesty and kindness of the poor man to be able to bear this; and remembering what he had done for me, how he had taken me up at sea, and how generously he had used me on all occasions, and particularly how sincere a friend he was now to me, I could hardly refrain weeping at what he said to me; therefore first I asked him if his circumstances admitted him to spare so much money at that time, and if it would not straiten him? He told me he could not say but it might straiten him a little; but, however, it was my money, and I might want it more than he.

Everything the good man said was full of affection, and I could hardly refrain from tears while he spoke; in short, I took 100 of the moidores, and called for a pen and ink to give him a receipt for them. Then I returned him the rest, and told him if ever I had possession of the plantation, I would return the other to him also, as, indeed, I afterwards did; and that as to the bill of sale of his part in his son's ship, I would not take it by any means; but that if I wanted the money, I found he was honest enough to pay me; and if I did not, but came to receive what he gave me reason to expect, I would never have a penny more from him.

When this was passed, the old man began to ask me if he should put me into a method to make my claim to my plantation? I told him I thought to go over to it myself. He said I might do so if I pleased; but that if I did not, there were ways enough to secure my right, and immediately to appropriate the profits to my use; and as there were ships in the river of Lisbon just ready to go away to Brazil, he made me enter my name in a public register, with his affidavit, affirming, upon oath, that I was alive, and that I was the same person who took up the land for the planting the said plantation at first.

This being regularly attested by a notary, and a procuration affixed, he directed me to send it, with a letter of his writing, to a merchant of his acquaintance at the place, and then proposed my staying with him till an account came of the return.

Never anything was more honourable than the proceedings upon this procuration; for in less than seven months I received a large packet from the survivors of my trustees, the merchants, for whose account I went to sea, in which were the following particular letters and papers enclosed.

First, there was the account-current of the produce of my farm or plantation from the year when their fathers had balanced with my old Portugal captain, being for six years; the balance appeared to be 1174 moidores in my favour.

Secondly, there was the account of four years more, while they kept the effects in their hands, before the government claimed the administration, as being the effects of a person not to be found, which they called civil death; and the balance of this, the value of the plantation increasing, amounted to 38,892 crusadoes, which made 3241 moidores.

Thirdly, there was the prior of the Augustines' account, who had received the profits for above fourteen years; but not being to account for what was disposed to the hospital, very honestly declared he had 872 moidores not distributed, which he acknowledged to my account; as to the king's part, that refunded nothing.

There was a letter of my partner's, congratulating me very affectionately upon my being alive, giving me an account how the estate was improved, and what it produced a year, with a particular of the number of squares or acres that it contained; how planted, how many slaves there were upon it, and making two and twenty crosses for blessings, told me he had said so many *Ave Marias* to thank the blessed Virgin that I was alive; inviting me very passionately to come over and take possession of my own; and in the meantime, to give him orders to whom he should deliver my effects, if I did not come myself; concluding with a hearty tender of his friendship, and that of his family; and sent me as a present seven fine leopards' skins, which he had, it seems, received from Africa by some other ship which he had sent thither, and who, it seems, had made a better voyage than I. He sent me also five chests of excellent sweetmeats, and a hundred pieces of gold uncoined, not quite so large as moidores. By the same fleet, my two merchant trustees shipped me 1200 chests of sugar, 800 rolls of tobacco, and the rest of the whole account in gold.

I might well say now, indeed, that the latter end of Job was better than the beginning. It is impossible to express the flutterings of my very heart when I looked over these letters, and especially when I found all my wealth about me; for as the Brazil ships come all in fleets, the same ships which brought my letters brought my goods, and the effects were safe in the river before the letters came to my hand. In a word, I turned pale, and grew sick; and had not the old man run and fetched me a cordial, I believe the sudden surprise of joy had overset Nature, and I had died upon the spot.

Nay, after that I continued very ill, and was so some hours, till a physician being sent for, and something of the real cause of my illness being known, he ordered me to be let blood, after which I had relief, and grew well; but I verily believe, if it had not been eased by a vent given in that manner to the spirits, I should have died.

I was now master, all on a sudden, of above £5000 sterling in money, and had an estate, as I might well call it, in the Brazils of above a thousand pounds a year, as sure as an estate of lands in England; and in a word, I was in a condition which I scarce knew how to understand, or how to compose myself for the enjoyment of it.

The first thing I did was to recompense my original benefactor, my good old captain, who had been first charitable to me in my distress, kind to me in my beginning, and honest to me at the end. I showed him all that was sent me. I told him that, next to the providence of Heaven, which disposes all things, it was owing to him; and that it now lay on me to reward him, which I would do a hundredfold. So I first returned to him the hundred moidores I had received of him; then I sent for a notary, and caused him to draw up a general release or discharge for the 470 moidores which he had acknowledged he owed me in the fullest and firmest manner possible; after which I caused a procuration to be drawn, empowering him to be my receiver of the annual profits of my plantation, and appointing my partner to account to him, and make the returns by the usual fleets to him in my name; and a clause in the end, being a grant of 100 moidores a year to him, during his life, out of the effects, and 50 moidores a year to his son after him, for his life; and thus I requited my old man.

I was now to consider which way to steer my course next, and what to do with the estate that Providence had thus put into my hands; and, indeed, I had more care upon my head now than I had in my silent state of life in the island, where I wanted nothing but what I had, and had nothing but what I wanted; whereas I had now a great charge upon me, and my business was how to secure it. I had ne'er a cave now to hide my money in, or a place where it might lie without lock or key till it grew mouldy and tarnished before anybody would meddle with it. On the contrary, I knew not where to put it, or whom to trust with it. My old patron, the captain, indeed, was honest, and that was the only refuge I had.

In the next place, my interest in the Brazils seemed to summon me thither; but now I could not tell how to think of going thither till I had settled my affairs, and left my effects in some safe hands behind me. At first I thought of my old friend the widow, who I knew was honest, and would be just to me; but then she was in years, and but poor, and for aught I knew might be in debt; so that, in a word, I had no way but to go back to England myself, and take my effects with me.

It was some months, however, before I resolved upon this; and therefore, as I had rewarded the old captain fully, and to his satisfaction, who had been my former benefactor, so I began to think of my poor widow, whose husband had been my first benefactor, and she, while it was in her power, my faithful steward and instructor. So the first thing I did, I got a merchant in Lisbon to write to his correspondent in London, not only to pay a bill, but to go find her out, and carry her in money an hundred pounds from me, and to talk with her, and comfort her in her poverty, by telling her she should, if I lived, have a further supply. At the same time I sent my two sisters in the country each of them an hundred pounds, they being, though not in want, yet not in very good circumstances; one having been married, and left a widow; and the other having a husband not so kind to her as he should be.

But among all my relations or acquaintances, I could not yet pitch upon one to whom I durst commit the gross of my stock, that I might go away to the Brazils, and leave things safe behind me; and this greatly perplexed me.

I had once a mind to have gone to the Brazils and have settled myself there, for I was, as it were, naturalised to the place. But I had some little scruple in my mind about religion, which insensibly drew me back, of which I shall say more presently. However, it was not religion that kept me from going there for the present; and as I had made no scruple of being openly of the religion of the country all the while I was among them, so neither did I yet; only that, now and then, having of late thought more of it than formerly, when I began to think of living and dying among them, I began to regret my having professed myself a papist, and thought it might not be the best religion to die with.

But, as I have said, this was not the main thing that kept me from going to the Brazils, but that really I did not know with whom to leave my effects behind me; so I resolved, at last, to go to England with it, where, if I arrived, I concluded I should make some acquaintance, or find some relations, that would be faithful to me; and accordingly I prepared to go for England with all my wealth.

In order to prepare things for my going home, I first, the Brazil fleet being just going away, resolved to give answers suitable to the just and faithful account of things I had from thence. And first, to the prior of St Augustine I wrote a letter full of thanks for their just dealings, and the offer of the 872 moidores which was undisposed of, which I desired might be given, 500 to the monastery, and 372 to the poor, as the prior should direct, desiring the good padre's prayers for me, and the like.

I wrote next a letter of thanks to my two trustees, with all the acknowledgment that so much justice and honesty called for. As for sending them any present, they were far above having any occasion of it.

Lastly, I wrote to my partner, acknowledging his industry in the improving the plantation, and his integrity in increasing the stock of the works, giving him instructions for his future government of my part, according to the powers I had left with my old patron, to whom I desired him to send whatever became due to me till he should hear from me more particularly; assuring him that it was my intention not only to come to him, but to settle myself there for the remainder of my life. To this I added a very handsome present of some Italian silks for his wife and two daughters.

Having thus settled my affairs, sold my cargo, and turned all my effects into good bills of exchange, my next difficulty was which way to go to England. I had been accustomed enough to the sea, and yet I had a strange aversion to going to England by sea at that time; and though I could give no reason for it, yet the difficulty increased upon me so much, that though I had once shipped my baggage in order to go, yet I altered my mind, and that not once, but two or three times.

It is true I had been very unfortunate by sea, and this might be some of the reason; but let no man slight the strong impulses of his own thoughts in cases of such moment. Two of the ships which I had singled out to go in, I mean more particularly singled out than any other, that is to say, so as in one of them to put my things on board, and in the other to have agreed with the captain; I say, two of these ships miscarried, viz., one was taken by the Algerines, and the other was cast away on the Start, near Torbay, and all the people drowned except three; so that in either of those vessels I had been made miserable; and in which most, it was hard to say.

Having been thus harassed in my thoughts, my old pilot, to whom I communicated everything, pressed me earnestly not to go by sea, but either to go by land to the Groyne, and cross over the Bay of Biscay to Rochelle, from whence it was but an easy and safe journey by land to Paris, and so to Calais and Dover; or to go up to Madrid, and so all the way by land through France.

In a word, I was so prepossessed against my going by sea at all, except from Calais to Dover, that I resolved to travel all the way by land; which, as I was not in haste, and did not value the charge, was by much the pleasanter way. And to make it more so, my old captain brought an English gentleman, the son of a merchant in Lisbon, who was willing to travel with me; after which we picked up two more English merchants also, and two young Portuguese gentlemen, the last going to Paris only; so that we were in all six of us, and five servants; the two merchants and the two Portuguese contenting themselves with one servant between two, to save the charge; and as for me, I got an English sailor to travel with me as a servant, besides my man Friday, who was too much a stranger to be capable of supplying the place of a servant on the road.

In this manner I set out from Lisbon; and our company, being all very well mounted and armed, we made a little troop, whereof they did me the honour to call me captain, as well because I was the oldest man as because I had two servants, and indeed was the original of the whole journey.

As I have troubled you with none of my sea journals, so I shall trouble you now with none of my land journal; but some adventures that happened to us in this tedious and difficult journey I must not omit.

When we came to Madrid, we being all of us strangers to Spain, were willing to stay some time to see the court of Spain, and to see what was worth observing; but it being the latter part of the summer we hastened away, and set out from Madrid about the middle of October; but when we came to the edge of Navarre, we were alarmed at several towns on the way with an account that so much snow was fallen on the French side of the mountains, that several travellers were obliged to come back to Pampeluna, after have attempted, at an extreme hazard, to pass on.

When we came to Pampeluna itself, we found it so indeed; and to me, that had been always used to a hot climate, and indeed to countries where we could scarce bear any clothes on, the cold was insufferable; nor indeed was it more painful than it was surprising to come but ten days before out of the Old Castile, where the weather was not only warm, but very hot, and immediately to feel a wind from the Pyrenean mountains so very keen, so severely cold, as to be intolerable, and to endanger benumbing and perishing of our fingers and toes.

Poor Friday was really frighted when he saw the mountains all covered with snow, and felt cold weather, which he had never seen or felt before in his life.

To mend the matter, when we came to Pampeluna it continued snowing with so much violence, and so long, that the people said winter was come before its time; and the roads, which were difficult before, were now quite impassable; for, in a word, the snow lay in some places too thick for us to travel, and being not hard frozen, as is the case in northern countries, there was no going without being in danger of being buried alive every step. We stayed no less than twenty days at Pampeluna; when seeing the winter coming on, and no likelihood of its being better, for it was the severest winter all over Europe that had been known in the memory of man, I proposed that we should all go away to Fontarabia, and there take shipping for Bordeaux, which was a very little voyage.

But while we were considering this, there came in four French gentlemen, who having been stopped on the French side of the passes, as we were on the Spanish, had found out a guide, who, traversing the country near the head of Languedoc, had brought them over the mountains by such ways, that they were not much incommoded with the snow; and where they met with snow in any quantity, they said it was frozen hard enough to bear them and their horses.

We sent for this guide, who told us he would undertake to carry us the same way with no hazard from the snow, provided we were armed sufficiently to protect us from wild beasts; for he said, upon these great snows it was frequent for some wolves to show themselves at the foot of the mountains, being made ravenous for want of food, the ground being covered with snow. We told him we were well enough prepared for such creatures as they were, if he would ensure us from a kind of two-legged wolves, which, we were told, we were in most danger from, especially on the French side of the mountains.

He satisfied us there was no danger of that kind in the way that we were to go; so we readily agreed to follow him, as did also twelve other gentlemen, with their servants, some French, some Spanish, who, as I said, had attempted to go, and were obliged to come back again.

Accordingly we all set out from Pampeluna, with our guide, on the 15th of November; and, indeed, I was surprised when, instead of going forward, he came directly back with us on the same road that we came from Madrid, above twenty miles; when being passed two rivers, and come into the plain country, we found ourselves in a warm climate again, where the country was pleasant, and no snow to be seen; but on a sudden, turning to his left, he approached the mountains another way; and though it is true the hills and precipices looked dreadful, yet he made so many tours, such meanders, and led us by such winding ways, that we were insensibly passed the height of the mountains without being much encumbered with the snow; and all on a sudden he showed us the pleasant fruitful provinces of Languedoc and Gascoign, all green and flourishing, though, indeed, it was at a great distance, and we had some rough way to pass yet.

We were a little uneasy, however, when we found it snowed one whole day and a night so fast, that we could not travel; but he bid us be easy, we should soon be past it all. We found, indeed, that we began to descend every day, and to come more north than before; and so, depending upon our guide, we went on.

It was about two hours before night when, our guide being something before us, and not just in sight, out rushed three monstrous wolves, and after them a bear, out of a hollow way adjoining to a thick wood. Two of the wolves flew upon the guide, and had he been half a mile before us he had been devoured indeed before we could have helped him. One of them fastened upon his horse, and the other attacked the man with that violence, that he had not time, or not presence of mind enough, to draw his pistol, but hallooed and cried out to us most lustily. My man Friday being next to me, I bid him ride up, and see what was the matter. As soon as Friday came in sight of the man, he hallooed as loud as t'other, "O master! O master!" but, like a bold fellow, rode directly up to the poor man, and with his pistol shot the wolf that attacked him into the head.

It was happy for the poor man that it was my man Friday, for he having been used to that kind of creature in his country, had no fear upon him, but went close up to him and shot him, as above; whereas any of us would have fired at a farther distance, and have perhaps either missed the wolf, or endangered shooting the man.

But it was enough to have terrified a bolder man than I; and, indeed, it alarmed all our company, when, with the noise of Friday's pistol, we heard on both sides the dismallest howling of wolves; and the noise, redoubled by the echo of the mountains, that it was to us as if there had been a prodigious multitude of them; and perhaps indeed there was not such a few as that we had no cause of apprehensions.

However, as Friday had killed this wolf, the other that had fastened upon the horse left him immediately and fled, having happily fastened upon his head, where the bosses of the bridle had stuck in his teeth, so that he had not done him much hurt. The man indeed was most hurt; for the raging creature had bit him twice, once on the arm, and the other time a little above his knee; and he was just as it were tumbling down by the disorder of his horse, when Friday came up and shot the wolf.

It is easy to suppose that at the noise of Friday's pistol we all mended our pace, and rid up as fast as the way, which was very difficult, would give us leave, to see what was the matter. As soon as we came clear of the trees, which blinded us before, we saw clearly what had been the case, and how Friday had disengaged the poor guide, though we did not presently discern what kind of creature it was he had killed.

But never was a fight managed so hardily, and in such a surprising manner, as that which followed between Friday and the bear, which gave us all, though at first we were surprised and afraid for him, the greatest diversion imaginable. As the bear is a heavy, clumsy creature, and does not gallop as the wolf does, who is swift and light, so he has two particular qualities, which generally are the rule of his actions: first, as to men, who are not his proper prey; I say, not his proper prey, because, though I cannot say what excessive hunger might do, which was now their case, the ground being all covered with snow; but as to men, he does not usually attempt them, unless they first attack him. On the contrary, if you meet him in the woods, if you don't meddle with him, he won't meddle with you; but then you must take care to be very civil to him, and give him the road, for he is a very nice gentleman. He won't go a step out of his way for a prince; nay, if you are really afraid, your best way is to look another way, and keep going on; for sometimes if you stop, and stand still, and look steadily at him, he takes it for an affront; but if you throw or toss anything at him, and it hits him, though it were but a bit of a stick as big as your finger, he takes it for an affront, and sets all his other business aside to pursue his revenge; for he will have satisfaction in point of honour. That is his first quality; the next is, that if he be once affronted, he will never leave you, night or day, till he has his revenge, but follows, at a good round rate, till he overtakes you.

My man Friday had delivered our guide, and when we came up to him he was helping him off from his horse; for the man was both hurt and frighted, and indeed the last more than the first; when, on the sudden, we spied the bear come out of the wood, and a vast monstrous one it was, the biggest by far that ever I saw. We were all a little surprised when we saw him; but when Friday saw him, it was easy to see joy and courage in the fellow's countenance. "O! O! O!" says Friday, three times pointing to him. "O master! you give me te leave; me shakee te hand with him; me make you good laugh."

I was surprised to see the fellow so pleased. "You fool you," says I, "he will eat you up." "Eatee me up ! eatee me up!" says Friday, twice over again; "me eatee him up; me make you good laugh; you all stay here, me show you good laugh." So down he sits, and gets his boots off in a moment, and put on a pair of pumps, as we call the flat shoes they wear, and which he had in his pocket, gives my other servant his horse, and with his gun away he flew, swift like the wind.

The bear was walking softly on, and offered to meddle with nobody till Friday, coming pretty near, calls to him, as if the bear could understand him, "Hark ye, hark ye," says Friday, "me speakee wit you." We followed at a distance; for now being come down on the Gascoign side of the mountains, we were entered a vast great forest, where the country was plain and pretty open, though many trees in it scattered here and there.

Friday, who had, as we say, the heels of the bear, came up with him quickly, and takes up a great stone and throws at him, and hit him just on the head, but did him no more harm than if he had thrown it against a wall. But it answered Friday's end, for the rogue was so void of fear, that he did it purely to make the bear follow him, and show us some laugh, as he called it.

As soon as the bear felt the stone, and saw him, he turns about, and comes after him, taking devilish long strides, and shuffling along at a strange rate, so as would have put a horse to a middling gallop. Away runs Friday, and takes his course as if he run towards us for help; so we all resolved to fire at once upon the bear, and deliver my man; though I was angry at him heartily for bringing the bear back upon us, when he was going about his own business another way; and especially I was angry that he had turned the bear upon us, and then run away; and I called out, "You dog," said I, "is this your making us laugh? Come away, and take your horse, that we may shoot the creature." He hears me, and cries out, "No shoot, no shoot; stand still, you get much laugh." And as the nimble creature run two feet for the beast's one, he turned on a sudden, on one side of us, and seeing a great oak tree fit for his purpose, he beckoned to us to follow; and doubling his pace, he gets nimbly up the tree, laying his gun down upon the ground, at about five or six yards from the bottom of the tree.

The bear soon came to the tree, and we followed at a distance. The first thing he did, he stopped at the gun, smelt to it, but let it lie, and up he scrambles into the tree, climbing like a cat, though so monstrously heavy. I was amazed at the folly, as I thought it, of my man, and could not for my life see anything to laugh at yet, till seeing the bear get up the tree, we all rode nearer to him.

When we came to the tree, there was Friday got out to the small end of a large limb of the tree, and the bear got about half way to him. As soon as the bear got out to that part where the limb of the tree was weaker, "Ha!" says he to us, "now you see me teachee the bear dance." So he falls a-jumping and shaking the bough, at which the bear began to totter, but stood still, and began to look behind him, to see how he should get back. Then, indeed, we did laugh heartily. But Friday had not done with him by a great deal. When he sees him stand still, he calls out to him again, as if he had supposed the bear could speak English, "What, you no come farther? pray you come farther"; so he left jumping and shaking the tree; and the bear, just as if he had understood what he said, did come a little farther: then he fell a-jumping again, and the bear stopped again.

We thought now was a good time to knock him on the head, and I called to Friday to stand still, and we would shoot the bear; but he cried out earnestly, "O pray! O pray! no shoot, me shoot by and then"; he would have said by-and-by. However, to shorten the story, Friday danced so much, and the bear stood so ticklish, that we had laughing enough indeed, but still could not imagine what the fellow would do: for first we thought he depended upon shaking the bear off and we found the bear was too cunning for that too; for he would not go out far enough to be thrown down, but clings fast with his great broad claws and feet, so that we could not imagine what would be the end of it, and where the jest would be at last.

But Friday put us out of doubt quickly; for seeing the bear cling fast to the bough, and that he would not be persuaded to come any farther, "Well, well," says Friday, "you no come farther, me go, me go; you no come to me, me go come to you"; and upon this he goes out to the smallest end of the bough, where it would bend with his weight, and gently lets himself down by it, sliding down the bough till he came near enough to jump down on his feet, and away he ran to his gun, takes it up, and stands still.

"Well," said I to him, "Friday, what will you do now? Why don't you shoot him?" "No shoot," says Friday, "no yet; me shoot now, me no kill; me stay, give you one more laugh." And, indeed, so he did, as you will see presently; for when the bear sees his enemy gone, he comes back from the bough where he stood, but did it mighty leisurely, looking behind him every step, and coming backward till he got into the body of the tree; then with the same hinder end foremost he comes down the tree, grasping it with his claws, and moving one foot at a time, very leisurely. At this juncture, and just before he could set his hind feet upon the ground, Friday stepped up close to him, clapped the muzzle of his piece into his ear, and shot him dead as a stone.

Then the rogue turned about to see if we did not laugh; and when he saw we were pleased by our looks, he falls a-laughing himself very loud. "So we kill bear in my country," says Friday. "So you kill them?" says I; "why, you have no guns." "No," says he, "no gun, but shoot great much long arrow."

This was indeed a good diversion to us; but we were still in a wild place, and our guide very much hurt, and what to do we hardly knew. The howling of wolves ran much in my head; and indeed, except the noise I once heard on the shore of Africa, of which I have said something already, I never heard anything that filled me with so much horror.

These things, and the approach of night, called us off, or else, as Friday would have had us, we should certainly have taken the skin of this monstrous creature off, which was worth saving; but we had three leagues to go, and our guide hastened us; so we left him, and went forward on our journey.

The ground was still covered with snow, though not so deep and dangerous as on the mountains; and the ravenous creatures, as we heard afterwards, were come down into the forest and plain country, pressed by hunger, to seek for food, and had done a great deal of mischief in the villages, where they surprised the country people, killed a great many of their sheep and horses, and some people too.

We had one dangerous place to pass, which our guide told us if there were any more wolves in the country we should find them there; and this was in a small plain, surrounded with woods on every side, and a long narrow defile, or lane, which we were to pass to get through the wood, and then we should come to the village where we were to lodge. We had but little more than loaded our fusees, and put ourselves into a readiness, when we heard a terrible noise in the same wood, on our left, only that it was further onward, the same way we were to go.

The night was coming on, and the light began to be dusky, which made it worse on our side; but the noise increasing, we could easily perceive that it was the howling and yelling of those hellish creatures; and on a sudden, we perceived two or three troops of wolves, one on our left, one behind us, and one on our front, so that we seemed to be surrounded with them, However, as they did not fall upon us, we kept our way forward as fast as we could make our horses go, which, the way being very rough, was only a good large trot, and in this manner we came in view of the entrance of a wood, through which we were to pass, at the farther side of the plain; but we were greatly surprised when, coming nearer the lane, or pass, we saw a confused number of wolves standing just at the entrance.

On a sudden, at another opening of the wood, we heard the noise of a gun, and looking that way, out rushed a horse, with a saddle and a bridle on him, flying like the wind, and sixteen or seventeen wolves after him, full speed; indeed, the horse had the heels of them; but as we supposed that he could not hold it at that rate, we doubted not but they would get up with him at last, and no question but they did.

But here we had a most horrible sight; for riding up to the entrance where the horse came out, we found the carcass of another horse and of two men, devoured by the ravenous creatures; and one of the men was no doubt the same whom we heard fire the gun, for there lay a gun just by him fired off; but as to the man, his head and the upper part of his body was eaten up.

This filled us with horror, and we knew not what course to take; but the creatures resolved us soon, for they gathered about us presently in hopes of prey, and I verily believe there were three hundred of them. It happened very much to our advantage that, at the entrance into the wood, but a little way from it, there lay some large timber-trees, which had been cut down the summer before, and I suppose lay there for carriage. I drew my little troop in among those trees, and placing ourselves in a line behind one long tree, I advised them all to light, and keeping that tree before us for a breastwork, to stand in a triangle, or three fronts, enclosing our horses in the centre,

We did so, and it was well we did; for never was a more furious charge than the creatures made upon us in the place. They came on us with a growling kind of a noise, and mounted the piece of timber, which, as I said, was our breastwork, as if they were only rushing upon their prey; and this fury of theirs, it seems, was principally occasioned by their seeing our horses behind us, which was the prey they aimed at. I ordered our men to fire as before, every other man; and they took their aim so sure, that indeed they killed several of the wolves at the first volley; but there was a necessity to keep a continual firing, for they came on like devils, those behind pushing on those before.

When we had fired our second volley of our fusees, we thought they stopped a little, and I hoped they would have gone off; but it was but a moment, for others came forward again; so we fired two volleys of our pistols; and I believe in these four firings we had killed seventeen or eighteen of them, and lamed twice as many, yet they came on again.

I was loth to spend our last shot too hastily; so I called my servant, not my man Friday, for he was better employed, for with the greatest dexterity imaginable he had charged my fusee and his own while we were engaged; but as I said, I called my other man, and giving him a horn of powder, I bade him lay a train all along the piece of timber, and let it be a large train. He did so, and had but just time to get away when the wolves came up to it, and some were got up upon it, when I, snapping an uncharged pistol close to the powder, set it on fire. Those that were upon the timber were scorched with it, and six or seven of them fell, or rather jumped, in among us with the force and fright of the fire. We despatched these in an instant, and the rest were so frighted with the light, which the night, for it was now very near dark, made more terrible, that they drew back a little; upon which I ordered our last pistol to be fired off in one volley, and after that we gave a shout. Upon this the wolves turned tail, and we sallied immediately upon near twenty lame ones, whom we found struggling on the ground, and fell a-cutting them with our swords, which answered our expectation; for the crying and howling they made was better understood by their fellows, so that they all fled and left us.

We had, first and last, killed about threescore of them, and had it been daylight, we had killed many more. The field of battle being thus cleared, we made forward again, for we had still near a league to go. We heard the ravenous creatures howl and yell in the woods as we went several times, and sometimes we fancied we saw some of them, but the snow dazzling our eyes, we were not certain. So in about an hour more we came to the town where we were to lodge, which we found in a terrible fright, and all in arms; for it seems that the night before the wolves and some bears had broke into the village in the night, and put them in a terrible fright; and they were obliged to keep guard night and day, but especially in the night, to preserve their cattle, and, indeed, their people.

The next morning our guide was so ill, and his limbs swelled with the rankling of his two wounds, that he could go no farther; so we were obliged to take a new guide there, and go to Toulouse, where we found a warm climate, a fruitful, pleasant country, and no snow, no wolves, or anything like them. But when we told our story at Toulouse, they told us it was nothing but what was ordinary in the great forest at the foot of the mountains, especially when the snow lay on the ground; but they inquired much what kind of a guide we had gotten that would venture to bring us that way in such a severe season, and told us it was very much we were not all devoured. When we told them how we placed ourselves, and the horses in the middle they blamed us exceedingly, and told us it was fifty to one but we had been all destroyed; for it was the sight of the horses which made the wolves so furious, seeing their prey; and that, at other times, they are really afraid of a gun; but the being excessive hungry, and raging on that account, the eagerness to come at the horses had made them senseless of danger; and that if we had not, by the continued fire, and at last by the stratagem of the train of powder, mastered them, it had been great odds but that we had been torn to pieces; whereas had we been content to have sat still on horseback, and fired as horsemen, they would not have taken the horses for so much their own, when men were on their backs, as otherwise; and withal they told us, that at last, if we had stood all together, and left our horses, they would have been so eager to have devoured them, that we might have come off safe, especially having our firearms in our hands, and being so many in number.

For my part, I was never so sensible of danger in my life; for seeing above three hundred devils come roaring and open-mouthed to devour us, and having nothing to shelter us or retreat to, I gave myself over for lost; and as it was, I believe I shall never care to cross those mountains again. I think I would much rather go a thousand leagues by sea, though I were sure to meet with a storm once a week.

I have nothing uncommon to take notice of in my passage through France; nothing but what other travellers have given an account of with much more advantage than I can. I travelled from Toulouse to Paris, and without any considerable stay came to Calais, and landed safe at Dover, the 14th of January, after having had a severe cold season to travel in.

I was now come to the centre of my travels, and had in a little time all my new-discovered estate safe about me, the bills of exchange which I brought with me having been very currently paid.

My principal guide and privy councillor was my good ancient widow; who, in gratitude for the money I had sent her, thought no pains too much, or care too great, to employ for me; and I trusted her so entirely with everything, that I was perfectly easy as to the security of my effects; and indeed I was very happy from my beginning, and now to the end, in the unspotted integrity of this good gentlewoman.

And now I began to think of leaving my effects with this woman and setting out for Lisbon, and so to the Brazils. But now another scruple came in my way, and that was religion; for as I had entertained some doubts about the Roman religion even while I was abroad, especially in my state of solitude, so I knew there was no going to the Brazils for me, much less going to settle there, unless I resolved to embrace the Roman Catholic religion without any reserve; unless on the other hand I resolved to be a sacrifice to my principles, be a martyr for religion, and die in the Inquisition. So I resolved to stay at home, and if I could find means for it, to dispose of my plantation.

To this purpose I wrote to my old friend at Lisbon, who in return gave me notice that he could easily dispose of it there; but that if I thought fit to give him leave to offer it in my name to the two merchants, the survivors of my trustees, who lived in the Brazils, who must fully understand the value of it, who lived just upon the spot, and whom I knew were very rich, so that he believed they would be fond of buying it, he did not doubt but I should make 4000 or 5000 pieces of eight the more of it.

Accordingly I agreed, gave him order to offer it to them and he did so; and in about eight months more, the ship being then returned, he sent me an account that they had accepted the offer, and had remitted 33,000 pieces of eight to a correspondent of theirs at Lisbon to pay for it.

In return, I signed the instrument of sale in the form which they sent from Lisbon, and sent it to my old man, who sent me bills of exchange for 32,800 pieces of eight to me, for the estate; reserving the payment of 100 moidores a year to him, the old man, during his life, and 50 moidores afterwards to his son for his life, which I had promised them, which the plantation was to make good as a rent-charge. And thus I have given the first part of a life of fortune and adventure, a life of Providence's chequer-work, and of a variety which the world will seldom be able to show the like of; beginning foolishly, but closing much more happily than any part of it ever gave me leave so much as to hope for.

Any one would think that in this state of complicated good fortune I was past running any more hazards; and so indeed I had been, if other circumstances had concurred. But I was inured to a wandering life, had no family, not many relations, nor, however rich, had I contracted much acquaintance; and though I had sold my estate in the Brazils, yet I could not keep the country out of my head, and had a great mind to be upon the wing again; especially I could not resist the strong inclination I had to see my island, and to know if the poor Spaniards were in being there, and how the rogues I left there had used them.

My true friend, the widow, earnestly dissuaded me from it, and so far prevailed with me, that for almost seven years she prevented my running abroad, during which time I took my two nephews, the children of one of my brothers, into my care. The eldest having something of his own, I bred up as a gentleman, and gave him a settlement of some addition to his estate after my decease. The other I put out to a captain of a ship, and after five years, finding him a sensible, bold, enterprising young fellow, I put him into a good ship, and sent him to sea; and this young fellow afterwards drew me in, as old as I was, to farther adventures myself.

In the meantime, I in part settled myself here; for, first of all, I married, and that not either to my disadvantage or dissatisfaction, and had three children, two sons and one daughter; but my wife dying, and my nephew coming home with good success from a voyage to Spain, my inclination to go abroad, and his importunity, prevailed, and engaged me to go in his ship as a private trader to the East Indies. This was in the year 1694.

In this voyage I visited my new colony in the island, saw my successors the Spaniards, had the whole story of their lives, and of the villains I left there; how at first they insulted the poor Spaniards, how they afterwards agreed, disagreed, united, separated, and how at last the Spaniards were obliged to use violence with them; how they were subjected to the Spaniards; how honestly the Spaniards used them; a history, if it were entered into, as full of variety and wonderful accidents as my own part; particularly also as to their battles with the Caribbeans, who landed several times upon the island, and as to the improvement they made upon the island itself; and how five of them made an attempt upon the mainland, and brought away eleven men and five women prisoners, by which, at my coming, I found about twenty young children on the island.

Here I stayed about twenty days, left them supplies of all necessary things, and particularly of arms, powder, shot, clothes, tools, and two workmen, which I brought from England with me, viz., a carpenter and a smith.

Besides this, I shared the island into parts with them, reserved to myself the property of the whole, but gave them such parts respectively as they agreed on; and having settled all things with them, and engaged them not to leave the place, I left them there.

From thence I touched at the Brazils, from whence I sent a bark, which I bought there, with more people, to the island; and in it, besides other supplies, I sent seven women, being such as I found proper for service, or for wives to such as would take them. As to the Englishmen, I promised them to send them some women from England, with a good cargo of necessaries, if they would apply themselves to planting; which I afterwards performed; and the fellows proved very honest and diligent after they were mastered, and had their properties set apart for them. I sent them also from the Brazils five cows, three of them being big with calf, some sheep, and some hogs, which, when I came again, were considerably increased.

But all these things, with an account how three hundred Caribbees came and invaded them, and ruined their plantations, and how they fought with that whole number twice, and were at first defeated and three of them killed; but at last a storm destroying their enemies' canoes, they famished or destroyed almost all the rest, and renewed and recovered the possession of their plantation, and still lived upon the island; – all these things, with some very surprising incidents in some new adventures of my own, for ten years more, I may perhaps give a farther account of hereafter.

Classic Library Titles

Jane Eyre
by Charlotte Brontë
Illustrated by Monro S. Orr and Edmund H. Garrett
Wuthering Heights
by Emily Brontë
Illustrated by Percy Tarrant

Treasure Island
Kidnapped
by R. L. Stevenson
Illustrated by Eleanor Plaisted Abbott, Wal Paget and David Price

Anne of Green Gables
Anne of Avonlea
by L. M. Montgomery
Illustrated by Kim Palmer

The Call of the Wild
White Fang
by Jack London
Illustrated by Philip R. Goodwin and Charles Livingstone Bull

Robinson Crusoe
by Daniel Defoe
Illustrated by J. Ayton Symington
Swiss Family Robinson
by M. Wiss
Illustrated by Bob Ellis

Pride and Prejudice
Sense and Sensibility
by Jane Austen
Illustrated

The Story of King Arthur and his Knights
The Merry Adventures of Robin Hood
by Howard Pyle
Illustrated by Roland Wheelwright and Howard Pyle

Norse Myths
by Dorothy Belgrave and Hilda Hart
Illustrated by Harry G. Theaker
Classical Myths
by Nathaniel Hawthorne
Illustrated by Milo Winter